Lost Kings MC #5

WHITE HEAT

AUTUMN JONES LAKE

COPYRIGHT

THE QUEEN ALWAYS PROTECTS HER KING.

For straight-laced attorney, Hope Kendall, loving an outlaw has never been easy. New challenges test her loyalty as she discovers how far she's willing to go to protect her man.

IF YOU HAVE HOPE, YOU HAVE EVERYTHING.

MC President, Rochlan "Rock" North finally has everything he's ever wanted. Hope as his ol' lady and his MC earning money while staying out of trouble. The only thing left is to make Hope his wife. But as their wedding day nears, an old adversary threatens Rock's freedom, the wedding, and throws the Lost Kings MC into chaos.

LOVE MAKES THE RIDE WORTHWHILE.

While the club waits for Rock's fate to be decided, Wrath has to balance solidifying his new relationship with Trinity and fulfilling his president's orders.

LOYALTY GIVES AN OUTLAW STRENGTH.

Threats from unexpected places will challenge every member, but in the Lost Kings MC, brotherhood isn't about the blood you share. It's about those who are willing to bleed for you.

White Heat is the 5th full-length novel of the Lost Kings MC series and is not intended to be read as a standalone.

When you finish White Heat, make sure you check out Between Embers (Lost Kings MC #5.5) to find out what the Teller, Murphy, and Z were doing during the wedding!

THE LOST KINGS MC® SERIES

Slow Burn (Lost Kings MC #1)
Corrupting Cinderella (Lost Kings MC #2)
Three Kings, One Night (Lost Kings MC #2.5)
Strength from Loyalty (Lost Kings MC #3)
Tattered on my Sleeve (Lost Kings MC #4)
White Heat (Lost Kings MC #5)
Between Embers (Lost Kings MC #5.5)
More Than Miles (Lost Kings MC #6)
White Knuckles (Lost Kings MC #7)
Beyond Reckless (Lost Kings MC #8)
Beyond Reason (Lost Kings MC #9)
One Empire Night (Lost Kings MC #9.5)
After Burn (Lost Kings MC #10)
After Glow (Lost Kings MC #11)
Zero Hour (Lost Kings MC #11.5)
Zero Tolerance (Lost Kings MC #12)
Zero Regret (Lost Kings MC #13)
Zero Apologies (Lost Kings MC #14)
White Lies (Lost Kings MC #15)

ACKNOWLEDGMENTS

Without the following people, White Heat would not be in your hands right now.

My husband who encourages me and listens to me talk about writing stuff and my imaginary friends every day—for *hours* sometimes and never complains.

My critique partners. I am so proud and happy that I get to work with you every week. Cara Connelly, Kari W. Cole, and Virginia Frost, thank you for checking to make sure I'm alive every Tuesday night. I don't know what I'd do without you.

K.A. Mitchell, you're an inspiration to me and help me remember what's important.

Jeanette Grey, Jenna Kendrick and Marie Lark, who are always so supportive.

Angi J., Amanda, Brandy, Chris, Clarisse, Elizabeth, Iveta, Tamra, and Shelly. Thank you for hanging in there for another book. Tanya, thank you for taking a last look and letting me bug you with a bunch of extra questions. Sue, thank you for last-minute catches!

Vanessa, thank you for going above and beyond.

Amanda R. Thank you so much for everything!

Elizabeth, Tanya, Terra, Johnnie-Marie, Natalie, and Iza thank you for the time you spend promoting my books.

My Lost Kings MC Ladies Facebook group. Each one of you means so much to me. I love our little group. Thank you for hanging out with me. I think shit's about to get real in the Murphy/Axel debate.

Jeanie V. and Sunny H., thank you for your thoughtfulness.

Sometimes I'm asked what I'll do when this "MC Fad" dies out. I don't think MC Romances are going anywhere, and that's because of its loyal, generous, and enthusiastic readers—you!

GLOSSARY

I first used a glossary in the *Road to Royalty* Limited-Edition box set and again in *Tattered on My Sleeve*. I've made a few small updates and changes here.

The Lost Kings MC Organizational Structure

President: *Rochlan "Rock" North.* Leader of the Upstate NY charter of the Lost Kings MC. The word of the President is law within the club. He takes advice from senior club members. He is the public "face" of the MC.

Sergeant-at-Arms: *Wyatt "Wrath" Ramsey.* Responsible for the security of the club. Keeps order at club events. Responsible for the safety and protection of the president, the club, its members and its women. Disciplines club members who violate the rules. Keeps track of club by-laws. Will challenge Rock when he deems it necessary.

Vice President: *Zero or "Z."* In most clubs, I think the VP would be considered the second-in-command. In mine, I see the VP and SAA on equal footing within the club. Carries out the orders of the President. Communicates with other chapters of the club. Assumes the responsibilities of the President in his absence. Keeps records of club patches and colors issued.

Treasurer: *Marcel "Teller" Whelan.* Keeps records of income, expenses and investments.

Road Captain: *Blake "Murphy" O'Callaghan.* Responsible for researching, planning and organizing club runs. Responsible for obtaining and maintaining club vehicles.

The Lost Kings MC Ladies

Hope Kendall, Esq.: The object of Rock's love and obsession. Their epic love story spans four books; *Slow Burn, Corrupting Cinderella, Strength From Loyalty,* and now *White Heat.*

Trinity Hurst: Caretaker of the Lost Kings MC clubhouse and the brothers. She and Wrath have a long, tattered love story full of lust, fury, and forgiveness in *Tattered on My Sleeve (Lost Kings MC #4)*

Heidi Whelan: Teller's little sister. Has nurtured a crush on her brother's best friend, Murphy, since she was a little girl. You've briefly met Heidi throughout the series *Corrupting Cinderella, Three Kings, One Night (Lost Kings MC #2.5), Strength From Loyalty, Tattered on My Sleeve, and White Heat.* She is a major character in *More Than Miles (Lost Kings MC #6).*

Lilly: One of Hope's best friends and frequent "booty call" of Z. You've met her in *Slow Burn, Corrupting Cinderella, Strength From Loyalty, Tattered on My Sleeve, White Heat* and two short stories, "Z and Lilly" in *Three Kings, One Night* and "Infatuated" from the *Pink: Hot 'n Sexy for a Cure anthology.* She will be featured in *Zero Tolerance (Lost Kings MC #12).*

Mara Oak: Friend of Hope. Also an attorney. She's appeared in *Slow Burn, Corrupting Cinderella, Strength From Loyalty, Tattered on My Sleeve, and White Heat.* She's married to Empire city court judge, Damon Oak.

Sophie: Friend of Hope. Also an attorney. Helped orchestrate Hope and Rock's get together in *Slow Burn.* She's appeared in *Corrupting Cinderella, Strength From Loyalty, Tattered on My Sleeve, and White Heat.*

She's in an on-again-off-again relationship with heavy metal singer, Jonny Cage.

Lost Kings MC Terminology

Crystal Ball – The strip club owned by the Lost Kings MC and one of their legitimate businesses. They often refer to it as "CB."

"Conference Center" – The clubhouse of the Lost Kings MC. It was previously used as a conference center and is sometimes jokingly referred to this way.

Empire – The fictional city in Upstate NY, run by the Lost Kings.

Green Street Crew – Street gang the Lost Kings do business with. Often referred to as "GSC." "Loco" is their leader and frequent nuisance to Rock.

LOKI – Short for Lost Kings.

Vipers MC – Rival and frequent enemy MC. Runs Ironworks which borders the Lost Kings' territory. Their president, Ransom and his SAA, Killa appeared in *Tattered on My Sleeve*.

Wolf Knights MC – Rival and sometimes ally of the Lost Kings. Their president, Ulfric appeared in *Slow Burn*. Their SAA, Whisper is a partner in Wrath's gym and appeared in *Tattered on My Sleeve* as well as *Slow Burn*.

DEDICATION

Dedicated to those who've found love in the most unexpected places.

CHAPTER ONE

ROCK

"Ever seen a green wedding dress?"

Hope glances up at me with one of her adorable, baffled expressions I love so much.

"You said you didn't want to wear white," I explain.

"Oh." She pauses and I can see the excitement building.

Tracing a finger down her arm, I remind her. "You were wearing green the day we met."

Another confused face and I don't even know what to think about the fact that I remember what she was wearing the day we met better than she does.

"My jewel green suit."

"That's my favorite color on you," I tell her while brushing her hair off her shoulder and planting a kiss on her neck.

"Guys, seriously, chunks rising." Wrath gags from across the table.

Hope chuckles, then looks at him more seriously. "I assume Rock is going to ask you to be his best man?" Wrath's gaze skips to me and he shrugs.

"Do you think Trinity…"

Curling my hand over her shoulder, I give her a squeeze. "What about Sophie?" I can't say I'd be super comfortable with Sophie standing up at our wedding, but I don't want Hope to feel pressured to only include club family either.

She sighs and drags her gaze to her lap, where her hands are nervously twisting. "She did it for my first wedding…and I don't know. It feels weird? Plus—" she flicks her gaze at Wrath, waiting to see if he's going to make fun of her I guess. "I feel closer to Trinity, than, So—"

"I can't believe you'd want Sophie as your maid of whatever after she pulled that stunt with Rock," Wrath says.

Motherfucker.

Hope turns her head very slowly in my direction. "What's he talking about?"

Wrath's eyes widen. At least he didn't let that slip on purpose. Still gonna kick his fuckin' ass.

"She doesn't know?" Wrath asks, making it worse.

"No. So, thanks for *that.*"

"Know what?" Hope insists.

"Your girl Sophie tried to climb him like a jungle gym."

Hope's gaze shoots to me. "What? When?"

"Uh, at that fundraiser thing we went to. She was drunk."

"Yeah, I remember. What happened?"

"Hope—"

"Rock." She turns and faces me, Wrath apparently forgotten. "You told me there were no more secrets. Why did you keep this from me?"

"I didn't want you to get hurt," I answer honestly. Taking her hands in mine, I give it to her straight. "She was drunk. She tried to kiss me. I left her and sent Ross to take care of her. I didn't know if she would even remember it, so I didn't want to ruin your friendship for no reason. I know she's been a good friend to you otherwise."

She swipes a tear off her cheek and I shoot a glare at Wrath.

"Damn. Is that why she didn't stick around the hospital for long? Why she's been acting so weird lately?"

2

I shrug. I'd been too fucked up when Hope was in the hospital to give Sophie much thought. "I don't know, sweetheart."

"You're not mad at *him*, are you?" Wrath asks.

"Why are you still here?" I snap back.

He ignores me and focuses on Hope, waiting for her answer.

"No. Well, I'm mad he didn't tell me about it. Not mad at him that it happened. Is that what you're asking me?"

"Yeah."

"When did he tell *you*?"

"I dunno. The night it happened? You believe him though, right?"

Hope cocks her head and narrows her eyes. "Of course I do. You're like his excited utterance witness," she says with a soft chuckle.

Wrath and I share a look.

"Lawyer thing," she explains with a head shake. "Of course I believe him. Why would you ask me that?"

I let out a breath I didn't realize I'd been holding. That's why Wrath asked her. He knows me well.

He nods. "That's good."

Suddenly her face falls and her eyes go shiny. "Wait. That's not why after—"

She means why after the party, I needed to have her so bad, we pulled over and frantically fucked in the front seat of my car.

Slipping my arms around her waist, I pull her—chair and all—closer to me. "No, baby. All you," I whisper in her ear.

She grins against my face and tucks in closer to me.

"What happened after?" Wrath asks.

"None of your business," I growl.

Hope lets out a soft giggle. "At least you don't tell him *everything*."

"Never mind," Wrath says with a knowing smirk.

"Shut up."

"What'd you do now, Wyatt?" Trinity asks from behind us.

His face breaks into a genuine grin and he holds out his hand. I'm happy to see them finally together and not trying to torture each other every chance they get.

She shuffles over to us and Wrath wraps her in a hug, making her wince.

"Shit. Sorry, babe."

That gets Hope's attention and she smiles at Trinity. "You okay?"

Trin pulls out of Wrath's embrace and turns her left side toward Hope. She's got a shiny piece of plastic taped over fresh ink.

I raise an eyebrow. "When'd you get that, hon?"

"Tuesday," she answers softly with a look at Wrath.

"Can we see?" Hope asks.

"Yeah, I can take it off today." Trin curls her body and starts picking at the tape, but Wrath brushes her hands away and starts undoing it for her.

"Oh! That's Wrath's star," Hope exclaims with a big smile. "Let me see." Trinity moves closer. "Wrath's girl," she reads out. "Aw, that's so sweet. I love it."

Trinity looks surprised at Hope's enthusiasm.

A playful grin curves Hope's lips. "So, you branded Trinity. Where's her name on you?"

My brother surprises me. Instead of getting pissy with Hope, he breaks into a huge grin and lifts his shirt.

"Christ, brother, I just ate," I grumble.

"Don't be jealous, bro. You keep up with your workouts maybe someday you'll look this good."

Hope snickers. Hell, I do too. Cocky, fuckin' asshole.

Wrath taps his finger at the Celtic symbol over his heart. "What is it?" Hope asks.

"A Triquetra. For Trinity."

Hope leans over. "Trinity's man. Oh. My. God. You two are the cutest ever," she says with a laugh. Wrath drops his shirt and pulls Trin into his lap.

Hope's gaze darts to me. "I feel left out now."

"It's okay, babe. I know it's not your thing."

"You get her name on you, Rock?" Trin asks.

I nod and tap my hip.

"Wow. Never thought you'd do that."

"Never had a good enough reason to before."

Trinity points to the wedding magazine Hope has on the chair next to her. "Making any progress?"

"Yeah. I think so. Rock gave me a good idea for a dress."

Trinity bursts out laughing and Wrath—dick that he is—joins her. "Really?" Trinity gasps.

Hope has this cute indignant expression on her face. "Anyway. I guess I'd like to be laid back and simple this time."

"Sounds good to me. His first wedding was a fucking circus," Wrath says.

"Seriously, asshole?" I mutter.

"What?"

Trinity glares at him too. "It's not nice."

"What? Hope knows he was married before. It's not a fucking secret. She fuckin' met Carla. Man, I was busy protesting that shit right up until the end, too."

Hope bursts out laughing. "Really?"

"Fuck, yeah."

Hope turns to me for confirmation. "I guess." I shrug.

A hurt look spreads across Hope's face. "You're not going to—"

Wrath cuts her off. "No, sweetheart."

HOPE

My supposed best friend hit on my fiancé.

I know Sophie's been acting strange for a few months now, but I never expected *that* was the reason. I thought it was me. That she was tired of me being a whiny pain in the ass.

"Hope?"

Rock left for his office down the hall and Trinity followed to ask about a few things she wants to do around here. I'd been so caught up I forgot it was just Wrath and me in the kitchen.

"Can I ask you something?"

The tone of his voice is what finally pulls me out of my kicking-Sophie's-ass fantasies.

Focusing on him, I note that it's the first time I've ever seen Wrath not one hundred percent cocky and sure of himself.

"What's wrong?"

"Nothing." He rubs his hand over his head in a move that's very similar to what Rock does when he's uncertain and it tugs the corners of my mouth up. By blood or not, they're truly brothers. "Would you mind if I patched Trin at your engagement party?"

"What? Ohmygosh, that's awesome! Of course not. Why would I mind?"

My enthusiasm seems to have shocked him because he stares at me for a few seconds before answering. "I don't know. I figure some chicks would get pissed that their thunder's being stolen or something."

I guess that's true and I stop to think about whether it bothers me. It doesn't. "I'm not just any chick."

He finally laughs. "No kidding."

"How are you going to do it?"

His massive shoulders lift. "On my knees?"

That's too much. A few snort-giggles escape me.

"It's a thing—never mind." He waves it off. "It's just everyone—the whole family—and people from other chapters, will be in one place at the same time and Trinity will be so busy, she won't expect it."

"Makes perfect sense to me."

"You know Kings will close that party down. I'll wait until your friends leave, so I don't embarrass you or anything."

That knocks the breath out of me. Never in a million years would I expect Wrath to be so sensitive or thoughtful to something like that. Especially about a club ritual. While I love Rock enough to accept their strange custom of giving their women the property patch, it's true people in my world might not as easily understand or accept something that on the surface seems demeaning.

"I'd never be embarrassed. Yes, it seemed odd and confused me at first." Oh, hell, let's be honest it still does. "I understand what it means to you guys."

"Thanks."

"But you're also right, and it's an important moment for you two. I wouldn't want anyone—even without meaning to—to ruin it for Trinity, so yes, that's probably best."

He stares at me for so long, I end up looking away. "I'm sorry," I mumble.

One of his big, warm hands closes over mine. "Nothing to be sorry about." He stands and stretches, rolling his shoulders. "Think those two are done discussing whatever it was?"

I snicker at that. "Probably. I think she just wants to put lockers in the girls' bathroom or something."

He laughs too.

"Hey, Wrath?" I stand and before I can change my mind, wrap my arms around him and squeeze. "I'm so happy for you two."

A second or two later, his arms envelope me. "Thanks."

My chin barely clears his chest and I tip my head up. "Gosh you're big. You and Trinity will have very tall children."

He laughs so hard I get jostled back a few steps. "I don't know what we ever did without you, Hope."

WRATH

"Hey, angel. What was so important you took off before?" I ask Trinity when I spot her in the hallway.

She tips her head back and smiles. "Missed me that bad?"

"You know it," I say, sweeping her up and planting a kiss on her forehead.

Love the way she easily wraps her arms and legs around me. Even better when she runs her hand over my cheek. "I needed to ask Rock about getting some lockers in the girls' bathroom."

"Ah. That's what Hope thought."

"I've been meaning to do it for a while."

7

I can't answer, because she leans in close, brushing her lips against mine for just a second. Then she unwinds herself and slides down my body. "All the trouble makers are gone, now. But it's still a good idea I think."

"What is?"

She laughs at my question. "The lockers."

"Oh. Sorry. All my blood rushed down to my dick when you kissed me."

"You're nuts."

I am. About her. She makes me fuckin' nuts.

Z worked his magic and Trinity's patch showed up this morning. Hope doesn't mind me doing it at the party, and I'm stupidly excited thinking about Trinity wearing my property patch and nothing else.

CHAPTER TWO

HOPE

MY BEST FRIEND hit on my fiancé.

The thought is still on my mind the next morning.

Sophie. Who was there for me when Clay died. Who helped Rock and I hook up.

Betrayed me?

The last few months play over in my head. She was drunk at the fundraiser. But I'd partied pretty hard with Sophie when we were in law school. Or rather watched *her* party hard. Clay and I picked her up and poured her into the back seat of our car many times. I don't think she ever tried anything with Clay. Maybe she did. And maybe Clay wanted to spare my feelings the same way Rock did, so he never told me. I guess I'll never know.

All of this sort of runs through my semi-conscious brain before I'm fully awake.

Rock. My anchor.

Turning over, I find his side of the bed empty.

Well, that's disappointing.

Rolling back the other way, I check my phone and find a reminder waiting on the screen. Dinner with Mara. Tonight.

Crap.

I can't back out. It's the dinner to celebrate Mara's birthday. She'd spent the actual day with her family, and I know how much she's looking forward to going out with her friends. But I don't think I can look at Sophie without puking. Or punching her.

I'm not angry. I'm *hurt*. Sophie and I have been friends for a long time. Drunk or not, I can't comprehend her actions. It's so out of character for her.

Maybe I don't know her as well as I thought.

I don't doubt for one second Rock's version of the story. And the reason he didn't tell me rings true. As always he was trying to protect me from getting hurt.

Normally I'd talk to, well Sophie, about something like this. I could call Lilly, but she and Sophie have been friends since childhood. It's not fair to stick her in the middle. I can't ruin Mara's birthday celebration with this either.

Honestly, I wish Wrath hadn't opened his big mouth.

"What's wrong, Baby Doll?" Rock calls from the doorway.

He enters and shuts the door behind him before I answer. "Nothing…I'm supposed to go out to dinner with Mara tonight. I really hope Sophie doesn't show up. I don't know what the hell to say to her."

"I'm so sorry," he says as he rounds the bed, sitting next to me. He brushes my hair off my cheek. "I didn't want to—"

"I blame Wrath and his big mouth."

The corners of his mouth lift. "Yeah."

"How come you're up so early?"

"Contractor's coming. Need to let him in the gate and show him out to the house."

"Oh. You need my help?"

"Nah, you look nice and cozy."

My hand settles on his leg, idly stroking. "I don't like waking up without you." My lips purse into a pout to emphasize just how much I dislike it.

He chuckles and covers my hand with his own. "Don't be bad. They'll be here any minute."

A bunch of unhappy grumbles tumble out of my mouth. Rock chuckles and moves so I can get up.

When I emerge from the bathroom, he's gone

The morning's barely started and already this day is pretty sucky.

My mood improves once I arrive downstairs a few hours later. Wrath and Trinity are wrapped up together on one of the couches and happiness at the sight of them kicks my mouth up into a smile.

"Morning, lovebirds."

"Nice of you to join us. It's almost noon," Wrath teases.

"It's Saturday."

Trinity unravels herself from Wrath and sits up. "You want anything?"

"No. Well, I just wanted to talk to you for a second." My gaze lands on Wrath, hoping he'll take the hint and get lost. No such luck.

Trinity glances at the envelope in my hands. "What's that?"

My voice falters, it's really too hard to explain. And Wrath's *still* here. "Shouldn't you be helping Rock?" I ask.

The bastard smirks at me. "No, why?"

A disgusted snort spills out of me, and I plop down next to Trinity. "This is for you." She frowns as I hand over the envelope.

What I thought was funny-cute, now seems embarrassing with Wrath staring over her shoulder.

Nervous laughter escapes Trinity as she reads the front of the card. "I might pee on you? What is this, Hope?"

"Open it." When she unfolds the card, the full message reads. *I might make you hold my dress as I pee, make you go on silly errands and annoy the crap out of you...*

"Turn it over," I tell her.

But I've grown to cherish your loyal friendship and would be thrilled to have you stand next to me on my wedding day.

"Hope?"

My throat's so tight I can barely get out my question. "Will you be my maid of honor, Trinity?"

Her jaw drops for a second before she shouts, "Oh my God! Yes, of course!" She throws her arms around me and knocks me into the back of the couch. We're both laughing—well, one of us might have a few tears in her eyes.

"Are you sure?" she asks.

"Yes. You know what a pain in the ass I'll be, so I won't be offended if you say no."

"Oh, stop. I'm thrilled. I've never done it before. Thank you."

Wrath seems a bit queasy from all the girly emotions suddenly taking over his morning. I pin him with an amused stare. "Hey, it's not my fault you wouldn't take a hint."

"What's up? Bro, you're supposed to alert me when there's girl on girl happening," Z's voice intrudes on our moment. Trinity and I both scramble to sit up.

"Stop being a perv." Trinity waves her card at him. "Hope asked me to be her maid of honor."

"Oh, cool." He smirks and lifts his chin. "Is Wrath gonna be a bridesmaid?"

Wrath rolls his eyes. "Shut up, dick."

It's probably left over nerves, but once I start laughing I can't stop. The three of them eye me with concern.

"Sorry. I was just picturing Wrath in a dress," I explain, then fall into another fit of giggles.

"I think I liked it better when you were scared of me," Wrath grouses as he stands.

Ignoring the guys, I tap Trinity on the arm. "Hey, I'm meeting Mara for her birthday dinner. You want to come with?"

She hesitates before answering, so I try to convince her. "She asked me to bring you—"

"No, it's not that. I have a class tonight."

"On a Saturday?"

"Yeah—"

Wrath's shaking his head before Trinity can get another word out.

"Oh, no. No fucking way are you going to Ironworks after what happened—"

"I'm not. This is a different center, up in Saratoga."

He eyes her suspiciously. "Why are you just telling me this now?"

"I only found out about it this morning and called them to see if I could get in. That's what I came out here to tell you."

It looked more like they were about to boink on the couch when I got here, but that's probably not a helpful observation at the moment.

Wrath's still eyeing her, but it's Z who opens his mouth. "You need a ride, Trin?"

"I got her," Wrath growls.

Z's mouth twists into a smirk and he turns his attention on me. "Where's your man?"

"Out at the house. He said there were contractors coming today."

"Okay. I'll go see if he needs help."

Not for the first time, I'm overcome with how much of a family the brothers are. Z thinks nothing of giving up his Saturday afternoon to help Rock build our house. It's a lot to take in.

"What's wrong, Hope?" Z asks.

"Nothing. That's nice. Thank you."

He cocks his head like he doesn't understand my words. "Of course." Then he's out the door.

"You okay, Hope?" Trinity asks.

How can I explain how much it means to be part of this family? "Yup, I'm good."

ROCK

House is looking good. I think we're on schedule to be done by our wedding. Love the club. Love my brothers. But fuck am I looking forward to Hope and I having our own space.

Z rides up on one of the ATVs and waves as he shuts the machine down.

"Everything okay?"

"Yeah, checking to see if you need any help."

"Sure."

We end up working side-by-side with the contractor. I don't think this guy is used to his customers being so hands on, but I don't really give a fuck. The sooner I can get him and his crew off club property, the better.

"Girls were having a moment," Z informs me.

"Oh yeah?"

"Hope asked Trinity to be in the wedding?"

"Good. I know she was nervous about it."

"Why?"

"How the fuck should I know."

"You gonna want a bachelor party and shit?"

I nail him with an *are you kidding* stare. "What do you think?"

"We have to do something for you."

"No strippers. Seen enough of that shit."

Z doesn't know what to do with that information. "We can go skydiving, there's that place over in—"

"Didn't someone die there last year?"

"Good point."

Wrath joins us maybe an hour later.

"Shouldn't you be picking out a bridesmaid dress?" Z calls out to him and gets a middle finger in return.

"Everyone's almost here, and the girls kicked me out of my room."

I snort and finish up what I'm working on. "Church now?"

"Oh, yeah. Dex has a great CB story for you," Z says.

"Jesus Christ, what now?"

After setting up a time for the contractor to arrive on Monday, the three of us head back to the clubhouse. "I gotta leave by three thirty," Wrath informs us before we go inside.

"What the fuck for?"

His mouth twists, and I know whatever it is, he doesn't want to share. Tough shit.

"Need to run Trinity somewhere."

Z snickers and heads inside after thumping Wrath on the back. And you know, I'd love to make a joke about Wrath being whipped. To pay him back for all the shit he's given me, but I'm too fuckin' happy the two of them have worked out their issues and settled into whatever domestic bliss they've found to poke at him today.

"Good. Let's get your business out of the way first, just in case we run long."

He raises an eyebrow, clearly expecting me to hassle him. It's good to be unpredictable. We've known each other so long, it's not often I surprise him.

"Prospects invited?" Murphy asks from inside the doorway.

I spot Hoot and Birch out in the garage, but there's no reason to bring them in today. "Nah."

Inside, brothers are scattered around the living room catching up. "Did you say Hope's down in your room?" I ask Wrath.

"She was when I left."

"Okay. I'll be right back. Start moving everyone inside."

"You got it."

Wrath's also full of surprises today. Not even a sarcastic smirk.

I'm not sure what the hell I stumble into once I get to Trinity's room. Door's open, so I push it wide. My girl's perched on the edge of the bed, while Trinity's poking at her with a bunch of different tools.

"Stop squirming. I don't want to stab you in the eye," Trinity grumbles.

"I'm trying, but it tickles."

Sure, it's goofy, but I sort of enjoy watching them together for a second. "You leaving soon, Baby Doll?"

They both turn my way.

"Yes. Our reservation's for four o'clock like a bunch of old biddies."

"Just means you'll be home earlier for me."

That gets a smile from her. "You sure you don't want to come?" she asks as she turns back to Trinity.

I'm pretty sure the fancy-ass place they're headed has a dress code. No fucking way. "I'm good, thanks."

"That's okay. Damon's not going either."

Good, then I don't feel so bad. "You need me to drive you?"

"No. I'm not planning to drink."

"Well, if you—"

"If I do, I'll call you. Promise."

"Good. We're heading into church. Come give me a kiss in case I don't see you before you leave."

Trinity snickers, gathers up her supplies and heads into the bathroom. "Don't smudge my hard work, Rock," she calls over her shoulder.

Hope approaches slow and I take my time appreciating the wispy, bright blue dress she's wearing. "Fuck, you're fucking beautiful."

She tips her head down, and I love the way she still shyly takes a compliment. It's sweet and something else I love about her. When she's within grabbing distance she stops. "That dress looks delicate and I don't want to snag it." I hold up my hands, rough from working all day. Her shy smile turns into a sly one as she presses her hands against my chest and rubs herself against me, taking the longest route possible to lay a kiss on my cheek. I turn and catch her for a deeper kiss. My hands thread into her hair, holding her still.

"Mmm, suddenly I feel like staying home," she murmurs as she pulls away.

"Don't tempt me." My hand reaches out to finger the silver metal beading dotting the shoulders of her dress. "This is interesting."

Her shoulders lift and she glances away. "I bought it a while ago but haven't had anywhere to wear it yet."

All right, I feel a little shitty about that. Don't take my girl out as often as I should. She never complains about it either. And I know how much she likes getting dolled up. "I should take you out more."

"Sorry. That's not why I said it," she says in a rush, making me feel worse.

"I know. Just an observation. Next time we go out, will you wear this for me?"

"Sure."

She says it quick, as if she'll never have to worry about honoring my request because I'm not going to take her anywhere.

Guess that means I need to prove her wrong.

"Rock! We're ready!" Wrath shouts down the hall.

"Give me another kiss."

This time she's quick about it.

"Text me when you get downtown."

"Okay."

Guys are all waiting for me and I don't feel a lick of guilt. I've certainly waited on their asses plenty of times.

"Let's do this."

Wrath shuts the war room doors behind us and we get down to business.

Sparky's finishing up drying time on a new crop which we'll be delivering to Green Street Crew tomorrow night. "We're all set for that?" I eye the guys who'll be joining me for that adventure and get a round of yeses.

I point at Wrath first, which raises a few eyebrows.

"Gym's good. Got Twitch working there, cleaning after hours."

"You trust him?"

"Yeah. He's a good kid. Got a fucked-up home life. No different than any of us had."

"Okay. Anything else?"

He shakes his head.

Bricks lifts his chin. "No fights?"

"Nah, I think I'm done."

Z and I are the only ones who don't react as if he said he planned to take up stripping in his spare time.

"Dex, you're up."

He sits forward and grins. "The two Viper chicks you okay'd? Mariella didn't work out. Chick had no I.D. and looked about fifteen."

"Christ," I mutter. Fucking president of the Vipers talking me into that shit still pisses me off. "What'd you do?"

Z pipes up. "Sent her home. We were nice about it, but I ain't risking our legit business on that nonsense."

"Good. Ransom has a problem with it, I'll handle it. What about the other one?"

Z and Dex share a look I don't care for before Dex answers. "She's quiet. Hot, good dancer, but keeps to herself."

"Good. Keep your dicks out of her," I warn.

Z has the nerve to act offended. Dex just rolls his eyes.

"Anything else from there?"

"Money took a dip. End of the semester slow down. I think it will pick back up during wedding season," Z reports with a smirk.

"I'm sure."

Teller relays his usual thorough money report. Everyone's interested in the bottom line, which he knows, so of course he takes his time getting to the good part.

Murphy's agitated about the run he's trying to organize to Virginia Beach. "Can't find a large enough block of rooms."

"Should have started looking earlier, dick," Wrath snarks.

"No shit, brother. With everything happening, I wasn't sure we'd be able to go or not."

"Can't guys just double-up?" Dex asks.

Z punches Dex in the arm. "What do you want to do, put a sock on the doorknob?"

"Prospects sure as shit don't need their own room," Murphy grumbles.

"Why you guys bein' such pussies? Fucking get a sleeping bag and drop it on the ground," Ravage offers. He's usually quiet during church, so I'm amused at his suggestion.

"No offense, but I don't picture Hope roughing it," Z says. He's right, so I don't bother disputing it.

Wrath chuckles. "I doubt Trin cares, but I'm getting too old to sleep on the fucking ground. If that makes me a pussy so be it."

Ravage waves his hand through the air. "Can't find a sleeping bag to fit your big ass anyway."

Sparky signals me. "Boss, I can't leave the plants, so you gotta count me out."

That's not exactly a surprise. I turn to Stash, because I assume he'll also want to stay put. He just shrugs.

Wrath points at Murphy and Teller. "You two share everything else, can't you share a room?"

I roll my eyes to the ceiling.

Teller shakes his head. "If Heidi comes, she's staying with me."

"Since when do prospects bring chicks?" Murphy asks.

"Since the chick in question is *my* sister, and she wants to go. She'll ride with her boyfriend and stay with me." The tone of his voice makes the *mind your business* message in Teller's words clear.

Z reaches over and punches Teller. "Gonna make it tough to get laid, bro."

Murphy's mouth curves into a sly smile. "She can always stay with me."

Teller glares, but I cut in before their bullshit snowballs. "We're looking at five or six rooms, if we double up. Can you make that work?"

"Yeah."

Wrath's brow wrinkles and he slides his gaze to me. "Who're you staying with, prez?"

"You."

Instead of mouthing off, he nods.

HOPE

Mara sent me a text earlier to say dinner would only be the four of us. Ross, Lilly, Mara and me. Adam's out of town and Sophie's sick. *Shucks.*

I hate confrontation, which is silly. As a lawyer, you'd think I love it. But I don't. Especially since I still don't know what the hell to say to her. When I finally confront her slutty butt, if she makes some sort of "he must have misunderstood" excuse, I'll scratch her damn eyes out.

Mara wanted to meet at 518 Prime, a fancier restaurant than we usually end up at.

"Jeez, some of these steaks are more than my first car payment," she mutters as she looks over the menu.

It's true, but, "It's not every day you turn thirty-five."

She lifts her head from her vigorous study of the menu and glares at me. "Shut up. Thirty-five sucks. It's that much closer to forty."

"If it makes you feel better, you still look twenty-five," Ross says while patting her arm.

"True," I add.

"Look who's talking. Hope looks like a fresh-faced college girl."

"Why are we talking about me? It's *your* birthday we're celebrating."

"Sorry we're late!"

Sophie's voice jars me out of our conversation. *You've got to be kidding.*

Mara stands to greet Lilly and Sophie. The flustered hostess rushes over to slide in an extra chair. This isn't the sort of establishment that takes change in stride. Sophie ends up seated across from me.

Wonderful.

"So sorry we're late. I've been sick all week. Didn't think I'd make it."

"That sucks." What am I supposed to say? Serves your whoring ass right?

Sophie glances at me. "Hi, Hope."

"Hey."

Her wide-eyed, scared expression gives me a measure of satisfaction. She knows something's up.

"So, how's wedding planning land?" Lilly asks after we place our orders.

"Uneventful so far." Shoot. This is awkward. I hadn't discussed my decision to have Trinity as my maid of honor with anyone, and I don't want hurt feelings. I'd still like Mara to be a bridesmaid. Lilly too. But I'll be dammed if I even want Sophie *at* my wedding let alone *in* it.

Sophie's been chugging wine since she got here and signals the waiter for more before turning my way. "Are you going to be a deadbeat bride again?" Sophie asks.

Ross snickers. "Do I even want to know?"

"She wasn't—"

"I'm not into all that girly, wedding crap," I explain to Ross's shock and disgust.

"But...but, you're like the girliest girl I know," he says with mock surprise.

"I am not. That would be Mara."

At the sound of her name, she tips her head up. "What now?"

"Are you on your phone at the dinner table?" Ross asks.

Mara's cheeks turn pink. "I was checking on the baby."

"Yeah, right. Damon's probably texting her all the filthy stuff he plans to do to her when she gets home," Lilly fake-whispers.

The pink on Mara's face deepens. "Shut up."

"Oh my God! He is!" Lilly snickers and points at Mara's now crimson face.

"Why didn't he come?" Ross asks. Lilly giggles at the word "come" like a fifteen-year-old boy. Dear God, are we really a group of thirty-something professionals, because you'd never know it by listening to us. Which is why I love my friends so much.

Well some of them.

My gaze flicks to Sophie and she gives me a weak smile. I can't help but notice how uncomfortable she seems around me. I realize she and I haven't been alone together since the night of the fundraiser. Somewhere down deep, her conscience must have some shame.

"Where's Rock?" she asks.

Nope. Any softness I was feeling toward her poofs away when his name rolls off her tongue.

"Home."

"With the muffler bunnies?" she jokes.

I glare at her. The table falls silent and I hate that I made everyone uncomfortable. "No," is my clipped response. "They're gone."

"Yeah, but more always find their way there, don't they?" Lilly asks.

"Sure. But I *trust* Rock. He's not interested in scheming, backstabbing tramps."

Sophie opens her mouth to say God-only-knows-what, but we're interrupted by the waitress bringing our salads and baskets of Brazilian cheese breads. Sophie plucks a slice out before the waitress even places it on the table. Ross wrinkles his brow. "What?" She shrugs. "I haven't eaten all week."

Thankfully everyone turns the discussion on Mara and whether Damon's going to run for the vacant family court seat that just opened up.

"Hope, would you end up in front of him, then?" Sophie asks.

It's not the brightest question, and I'm a little surprised.

"Nah, something like that he'd have to recuse himself," Mara says, shaking her head.

The rest of dinner is uneventful. Everything's fantastic and I wonder if I can cajole Rock into throwing on his suit and having dinner here one night. Then I remember the last time I got him in a suit was when Sophie hit on him and I'm right back to my foul mood.

We end dinner with coffee and coconut cream pie. As I'm thinking about whipping out my Visa, our waitress informs us that the bill's already been paid. "Happy birthday, from Damon," she explains.

"Jeez, Mara, that was awfully sweet of him," I say.

Ross chuckles. "Yeah, if I'd known that, I would have ordered the Hennessy X.O."

While we're walking out, the girls bring up my wedding again.

"Did you set an actual date yet?" Sophie asks.

"Not really."

We did. But I don't feel like telling Sophie.

"Will Rock wear his cut to your wedding or do you think you can get him in a suit?" she asks and I don't care for the snide tone I detect in her voice.

"Why? Are you planning to try and fuck him again?" I snap. *Whoops.* Almost made it through the evening without losing my temper.

I said it low enough that we're not causing a scene. Yet. But everyone in our party heard my question. No one seems to know what to say or do.

"Uncomfortable," Ross mutters, looking around for the valet.

"What are you talking about, Hope?"

"Are you really going to go the innocent route, Sophie?"

Lilly slips an arm between us. "Girls—"

"I'm fine, Lilly." I'm not though. I'm seething. I want Sophie to fucking admit what she did and apologize or show remorse. Something besides standing there staring at me like I'm the one who did something wrong. I want reassurance that the last ten years of our friendship weren't a massive waste of time. "Don't you have anything to say, Sophie?"

Mara also gets between us. "Girls, why don't we discuss this somewhere else?" She lowers her voice. "You know where half of the Empire County bar association *isn't* having dinner. We can go back to—"

"There's nothing to discuss."

"I wondered when he'd get around to telling you," Sophie finally says.

Lilly gasps. So, at least she didn't know. Mara rocks back on her heels. I raise an eyebrow, waiting for Sophie to continue.

"What do you want me to say, Hope? I'm so fucking sorry. I've tried a million times to come clean with you, but I didn't know what to say. You saw me that night. I barely remember what happened."

"You're going with the drunk defense?"

"She *was* in rough shape that night." Ross wanders back from the valet and into our conversation.

I whirl on him. "Did you know?"

"Know what? Rock told me to go get her. That she was acting like a fool. She was babbling a lot of nonsense when I found her."

"I'd like to blame it on the alcohol," Sophie says. Then she dares to look me in the eye. "But I've always kind of liked Rock."

Lilly and Mara both gasp and stare Sophie down.

Whoa. Okay. For some reason, that's the *last* thing I expected her to say. Noting the glares from our friends, she rushes to explain. "I'd normally never, ever do anything about it. You deserve the best, Hope, and it's been so hard…and Johnny and I had this fight. I don't know. It was stupid."

Well, that was a lot to absorb.

"If it makes you feel any better, he never hesitated. He couldn't push me off him fast enough. We were all alone. He could have…and no one would—"

"Enough!" My stomach rolls as I envision what must have happened. Wrath's description of Sophie climbing Rock must have been pretty accurate. The ugly thought that's been bothering me all day tumbles out of my mouth. "Did you ever come onto Clay?"

The flash of distaste across her face punches me in the gut. "No, Hope. Never. Clay wasn't my type."

"Jesus Christ, shut up, Sophie," Ross mumbles.

Both of us ignore him. A deadly sort of calm washes over me. "But Rock *is* your type?"

"Yes." My face must betray the violence welling up inside, because she takes a step back and stutters. "No. I don't mean it that way."

"Why'd you even bother setting us up?"

"I just thought he'd pull you out of your funk. I never thought you'd consider marrying him."

"Wait, what?"

"Hope. Be serious. I figured with the type of girls he's used to… being around all those strippers… he'd go back to that eventually."

I can't suck in enough oxygen to deal with her mountain of crap. "You don't know a fucking thing about him. Or us."

"Hope." She reaches out to take my hand, but I snatch it away, shoving her back a few steps in the process.

"Don't you dare touch me. I can't even. I don't even know what to say to you right now."

Out of the corner of my eye I notice the valet pulling up with my car.

"Hope, please. I'm so sorry. I couldn't face you after what I did. I realized how wrong I was when you were in the hospital. He was so… broken at the thought of losing you and I felt even worse about what I'd done. The guilt's been making me crazy."

"Coming clean with me might have helped," I snap. "Not being a backstabbing bitch would have also worked." I take a few steps away from our group. Everyone's uncomfortable and we're definitely making a scene now. I'll have to add "embarrassing me to death" to Sophie's list of crimes after this.

"Please, Hope. I'd undo it if I could. What do you want me to do?"

I glance back at my friend. Former friend? All I feel is one more loss.

She's right about one thing. What's done can't be undone.

"Don't come to our wedding."

And then I go home.

CHAPTER THREE

HOPE

I'M SO FLUSTERED after that scene with Sophie, I have to pull over when I get on the highway. My hands are shaking so bad. I ball them into fists and a little part of me wishes I'd popped Sophie in her slutty face.

God, that was awkward.

I don't know how to fix it.

And honestly I shouldn't have to be the one to fix it.

I'm stopped on the shoulder for so long, that a state trooper pulls up behind me.

"Fantastic."

"Miss, do you need help?" he calls out.

"No, sir." I roll my window down all the way and wait for him to approach with my hands on the steering wheel.

"Everything all right, young lady?"

"Yes, officer. I, uh, just had a fight with my friend and I needed to pull over to cool off before driving home." Seriously? Don't I always warn my clients not to volunteer too much information to the police? What's wrong with me?

"Have you been drinking?"

"No, sir. I never drink when I'm driving." *Shut up, Hope!*

He chuckles and leans in, I assume to try to smell any alcohol on me. "Are you okay to drive now?"

"Yes. I'm just going to call my fiancé so he can meet me."

"Sounds like a good idea. I'll wait behind you until you take off. This is a dangerous place to be stopped."

"Sorry, officer."

I don't end up calling Rock after all. I just want to get home to see him. I'm afraid if I call him, I'll end up bursting into tears and it will take me even longer to get into his arms.

He meets me at the front door of the clubhouse anyway.

"How'd you know it was me?" I tease, but my voice comes out strained.

"Got radar when it comes to you, Baby Doll."

I fling myself against him. As soon as he wraps his arms around me my mind settles. "What's the matter?" he murmurs against my ear.

I pull away so I can see his face. "Sophie showed up."

"Shit. How'd that go?"

"Bad. It was so awkward. I held it together during dinner, but then we caused a huge scene downstairs outside the restaurant. Half the lawyers and politicians in Empire probably overheard us. She admitted it. Apologized. Asked how she could fix it. But I didn't have an answer." I leave out the uglier bits of our fight, especially the part about how she always liked Rock, because on my way home, some of her words hit their target.

"I'm so sorry, baby. I—"

"Rock, it's fine. I understand why you didn't want to tell me."

He nods once, but I can tell it's still weighing on him. "Don't turn this into a bigger deal than it is. You and I are fine. Sophie and me, not so much."

One corner of his mouth turns up and I can see the comforting reply forming on his tongue when Trinity's voice interrupts.

"I'm glad you're back, Hope. I have a few things I want to go over with you." She doesn't pick her head up once as she rounds the corner and nestles into the sofa while flipping through a huge white binder. Seems she was busy while I was away. I raise an eyebrow at Rock, making him laugh.

"I'm afraid to ask," I whisper.

"I heard you asked her this morning? She's been waiting for you since she got home."

"Oh boy."

Curling my hand around Rock's I pull him over to the couch and sit him down. If I have to suffer through this wedding planning stuff, so does he. "Hey, Trin, let me go change. I'll be right back."

She pats Rock's arm like she knows exactly why I sat him there.

If we end up in the bedroom together, we won't come back downstairs anytime soon.

"I'm not sure I like you two conspiring together," Rock grumbles.

When I return, Trinity's chattering away and Rock looks like he wants to run away. I stifle my laughter and squeeze in between them. She's not seeking any opinions from me though. It's more like she wants to run things by me, which is fine. Honestly, if I didn't think she'd kill me, I'd drag Rock down to City Hall, marry him tomorrow and skip all this.

Z joins us by propping half his butt on the arm of the couch. He's tense, as if he's ready to run the second Trinity turns her maid-of-honor-zilla eyes on him.

My phone stirs, and I yank it out of my pocket.

"Think it's Sophie?" Rock asks.

"Maybe." My face *squinches* into a frown as the unfamiliar alert of a video text blinks back at me. "Weird," I mumble. There's no chance to figure out how to play it, before it starts.

And I just stare.

The angle is terrible. The screen is fuzzy. But I'd recognize those rippling muscles and the inked forearms no matter what. I also recognize Rock's office at Crystal Ball.

What I *don't* recognize is the backside of the girl my fiancé is nailing over his desk. The image of the hands I've held and kissed hundreds of times, curled around some strange girl's waist, holding her down while he fucks her, burns my eyes. Their pornographic moans and grunts fill the air.

I can't breathe.

Hot and cold prickles over my skin.

My stomach lurches.

"Hope?"

I'm going to be sick.

The phone clatters to the floor as I jump up and run to the bathroom. Pity the drop didn't break my phone.

The sounds of my fiancé fucking someone else follow me all the way down the hall.

ROCK

"What the ever-loving fuck?" I'm not shouting, but I'm damn fucking close. Z snatches the phone out of my hand just as Wrath and Murphy walk in the front door.

Wrath lifts his chin at me. "What's wrong, brother?"

I can't even put it into words.

Trinity unfolds herself from the couch and gently taps my arm. "I'll go make sure she's okay." She practically runs out of the room.

I need to go check on Hope myself, but I'm frozen. Two questions won't stop pounding through my head.

One. How do I have a sex tape floating around and didn't even know it?

Two. Who the fuck would send it to Hope?

Z gives the guys a rundown. As if more people need to know about this.

"Bro, you're safe. It ain't recent." He taps the phone. "No anchor tat."

Wrath glares at him. "It's disturbing how well you know his body."

I wrestle the phone out of his hands. "I know it's not recent, you dick."

"Shit. That's cold. She okay?" Murphy asks.

"I don't know."

"She *saw* it?" Wrath asks. "Jesus Christ, where is she?"

I'm shaking with so much rage, I can't even answer. As I stalk down the hallway, I take a number of deep breaths to calm myself so I can take care of my girl.

My hand presses against the bathroom door, swinging it open just enough to hear the girls' muffled voices.

"It's never going to end, is it?" Hope asks.

Trinity mumbles something back, then someone runs water. "Here wash your face."

"Ugh. I need to brush my teeth. I feel disgusting."

"Barfing will do that to ya," Trinity teases. Hope actually laughs and I'm able to relax a notch.

"I don't think I've ever had such a visceral reaction to something."

"Honey, that's fucking horrible. I know…I understand, believe me."

"I have to get out of here." The panic in Hope's voice is clear. *Fuck me*. Things have been so good lately. Something bothers her, we talk it out. No running. Not that she has anywhere to run *to* now that she sold her house. But my girl's resourceful; if she wanted to hide out, she would.

"Hope," I call out.

"Just a sec."

Trinity brushes past me first and squeezes my arm.

Hope's pale and water still clings to the ends of her hair from where she must have splashed it on her face.

"You okay, Baby Doll?"

She gives me a weak smile. "Yeah." She edges out of the bathroom door, careful not to touch me. I want to reach out and hug her to me, but I feel like an utterly disgusting jackass who shouldn't be anywhere near her.

"Hope, I'm—"

"It's okay. I'm okay. I uh, just need a few minutes to myself."

She walks to the front door and I follow. At the last second, I grab her hand and spin her around to face me. "Please don't go."

Her big green eyes stare up and I see it. It's still there. The love she has for me. "I'm not going anywhere, Rock. Well, I do want to take a walk. Can you give me that? Please?"

Christ, I'd give this woman anything in the entire world. "Yeah, baby, I can do that." My fucking throat's so tight, I barely get the words out.

"Thank you." She reaches up and rubs her cheek against mine. "I'm not mad at you, okay? I love you."

She pulls away and before I answer, she darts out the door, jogging across the parking lot to the trail that will take her to the house we're building on the property.

She's not leaving.

I turn to find Z, Wrath and Murphy watching me. "Please tell me one of you fucks recognizes who it is?"

"You don't even know who it is?" Murphy asks. Wrath slaps him upside the head, saving me the trouble.

"No. Fucking video has to be more than two years old."

Murphy shakes his head. "What kind of sick bitch keeps that shit for so long?"

"Never mind that, what kind of sick bitch sends it to his ol' lady? And why?" Z asks.

I got nothin'.

"I'll make sure Z works on it. Go check on your girl," Wrath says while slapping Z's back.

"Knock it off, asshole," he says while shrugging Wrath off. He pins me with an irritated look. "I love ya, brother, but I don't know how many more times I feel like watching this."

Murphy snickers and takes the phone out of Z's hands. "Gotta be one of the dancers? Unless you were taking randoms back to your office."

The look on my face has to be murderous. The smile slides off Murphy's face and he hurries into the war room to get away from me.

Wrath lifts his chin. "Go. We got this."

The crisp evening air emphasizes how hot I am. Furious hot. I take my time walking through the woods until my head's clearer. As I approach the house, my heart kicks up for different reasons. Hope's sitting on one of the steps to the unfinished front porch. Her head's turned away, so I have a minute to observe her before she realizes I'm here. She's not crying, thank fuck.

The snap of a twig under my boot turns her attention on me. A soft smile lights up her face. "Hey. How'd you know I'd be here?"

"A guess."

She pats the stone beside her and I take a seat. "You okay?"

"I'll be fine."

"Hope, I'm—"

She curls her hand over mine and squeezes. "Don't. It's not your fault."

"Yeah it is. Why do I even know people who do shit like that?"

"Was it a girl from CB?"

Admitting to her that I have no clue who's on the video is the last thing I want to do. "Don't do this, Hope."

We sit there silently holding hands. Both of us staring into the woods.

"I'm sorry I acted like a baby," she says after a while. I glance over and her cheeks are bright pink. "I'm so embarrassed."

"Don't be." Christ, I'd be worried if it *didn't* upset her. "I don't—I don't even want to work there anymore."

"You don't really."

"I mean, I shouldn't be around naked chicks who aren't my wife."

She laughs so hard she snorts, which makes her laugh even harder. "I love you, Rock."

"I'm serious."

She turns and settles her hand on my cheek. "I knew from day one you owned a strip club. Don't think because we're getting married, I expect you to never set foot in there again. I'm not that woman."

"Yeah, I know you wouldn't ask that." I wrap my arms around her shoulders. "Maybe I'll just make you come with me."

She snorts again, then turns serious. "Are there any more homemade pornos floating around I should know about?"

"There better not be. I didn't know about that one."

She shakes her head, but there's a smile twitching at the corners of her mouth. She stands and holds her hands out to me. "I'm a lucky girl. My man's got ladies hanging on to old videos, but the real deal is all mine."

Should I feel like a pussy because she's trying to cheer me up? Probably. Do I? No. I'm too fuckin' happy this fucked-up mess hasn't made her change her mind.

HOPE

The guys are all watching me when we return. Waiting to see if I'll fall apart probably. I'm sure they're thinking Cinderella's too soft to take some stupid prank. I stiffen my spine and hold my head up. It's bad enough they know I ran and threw up after seeing the video. My stomach tilts even thinking about the image of Rock and—

No. Don't go there.

Wrath's the first one to ask if I'm okay.

"I'm fine."

I can tell he's not convinced but he nods anyway.

Z is much more proactive in defending his president's reputation. "Hope, you know it wasn't recent. The tat with your name's missing."

My mouth twists down. Is that why they're worried? "I knew it had to be old."

Z raises an eyebrow, but doesn't voice what's on his mind.

Behind me, Rock slips his arms around my waist and pulls me against him. "Thank you, baby," he whispers against my ear.

I raise my hand and ruffle his hair, then turn my head to whisper back. "I didn't think for one second it was recent, Rochlan. I know you. I trust you."

"I've been obsessed with you from the day we met. Couldn't get hard for another woman if I tried."

He's completely serious and instead of laughing, I turn and kiss his cheek. "Good. You want to make our own movie?"

He raises his eyebrows and I love the power I have to still surprise him. He flicks his gaze to something behind me and shakes his head. "No. Because if one of them ever saw it, I'd kill them."

"Why're you making murder faces at us, prez?" Z asks and I burst out laughing.

Rock shakes his head, then lifts his chin at Z, I assume, since he's the one to answer Rock's unspoken question. "Nah, Murphy's still looking at it. Might be Lexi."

I glance up at Rock, but he won't meet my eyes. He's too busy staring daggers at Z.

Turning, I catch the look on Z's face.

Rock, takes my hand, and pulls me toward the war room. "Wait a second, you don't know who it is?"

"Thanks, dick," Rock snarls at Z.

It's sort of disgusting, but also tragically funny. My lips struggle not to smirk. "The trials and tribulations of a reformed manwhore. You could be your own reality television show."

The guys laugh. Rock's eyes widen for a second, then he shakes his head. "What have I done to you?"

"Would you rather I laugh or cry?"

He slings his arm over my shoulder. "Neither, if you're gonna laugh at my expense."

There's humor underneath his words, so I didn't offend him. "Well, who took your off-the-market status the hardest?" Rock rolls his eyes at my question. "That's probably the best place to start."

"We'll figure it out. It won't happen again," Z assures me, his expression dark and unreadable.

Understanding whaps me upside the head. "You're not going to hurt her, are you?"

"No, Hope. I was thinking about asking her to join me for a spa day."

"Watch it, asshole," Rock says low enough for Z to sense the danger and back off.

"At the very least she's fired. Girls know better than to film shit like that. Then to send it to an old lady—no." Wrath says.

"Yeah, but what if another girl there sent it? Or a jealous boyfriend?"

Wrath places both hands on his hips and narrows his eyes at me.

"Are you really defending some bitch who sent you a porno featuring your man, Hope?" he asks.

It *is* pretty ridiculous, so I laugh. "Honestly, can we just forget about the whole thing? If that's the worst thing someone can throw at me, I'll be fine." My voice betrays my brave words, but the guys nod at me. "Where's Trinity? We weren't done with our party stuff."

Wrath seems to notice Trinity's absence for the first time. "Shit, I'll get her," he grumbles and stalks down the hallway.

WRATH

Trinity's coming out of the bathroom when I walk into our room. Rubbing a towel over her face, so she doesn't see me at first.

"Trin, Hope's back. She's looking for you."

"Is she okay?"

"She's fine." Better than I expected honestly. I assumed we were all in for those two taking another "break" after something like *that*. "Are *you* okay?" For some reason my girl seems more rattled than anyone.

"Yeah, I just feel bad for her, that's all." She hesitates like there's more on her mind but she doesn't want to upset me.

"You worried you're going to get a video next?"

"Am I?"

"No." Well, at least I don't think so. It seems Rock wasn't aware of his. "Babe, I love Rock like a brother, but he's got blinders when it comes to women. Thinks they're all sweet, innocent darlings, when in reality most of those bitches would stab their own mother to make an extra buck."

"Your point?"

My point is, any of the dancers I nailed at CB, I paid close attention to. And there weren't that many anyway. I preferred club girls who understood the consequences of pulling that kind of stunt. I don't think any of that is helpful at the moment.

When I don't answer, Trinity cocks her head. "Is that how you feel about me?"

"No. Fuck no."

36

"I'm—"

"One of the sweetest, most generous people I know." She opens her mouth to protest, I'm sure. "Don't. Whether you accept it or not, you've always been more than just a club girl. And now you're a maid of honor who has a bride out there waiting for all your great ideas."

That finally gets a smile out of her. "I think I left my binder out there."

"Yeah. Better go get it before Hope starts flipping through it and messing up your stuff."

Now I've got her. I hold out my hand and she takes it, staring up at me. "I love you, Wyatt. I want all that stuff to be in our past."

"It is."

I wish I felt as convinced as I sound.

ROCK

"Rock, can I ask you something?" Hope whispers just as I'm on the edge of sleep.

"What, baby?" I mumble.

"I need you to answer honestly. No sparing my feelings or self-esteem boosts."

Now, I'm fully awake. "What's wrong, Hope?"

"Can you do that?"

"Yes," I answer slowly. This feels like a trap and I wonder why she waited until I was half-asleep to ask.

"Am I enough for you?"

"What?"

"Am I enough for you? Do I satisfy you? Make you happy?" Her voice barely rises above a whisper, and I roll over to snap the light on. I need to see her face.

"What's this about?" I might as well just say it. "The video?"

"No. Yes. I don't know."

"How can you ask me that?"

"I don't know."

"Hope, look at me."

37

It takes her a second but she turns and meets my eyes. "Aren't we past this?"

Her teeth sink into her bottom lip, rolling half into her mouth and she nods.

"You're all I've ever wanted."

"But do I—"

"Yes, whatever you're about to ask, the answer is yes."

"Okay," she answers, still not sounding convinced.

"Can't you tell from the way I can't keep my hands off you or my dick out of you?"

Finally, I get a smile out of her. "Will you promise to tell me if that changes?"

"Yes, Baby Doll. That will absolutely be a conversation I want to have with my wife."

I get a thump on my chest for the sarcasm. "I'm serious. I want you tell me if I don't make you happy so we can fix it before—"

I finally understand what she's saying. "Okay. Promise me the same thing, though. I know I'm a prick sometimes. And I know I get wrapped up in club stuff. You need to knock some sense into me, do it."

"Yum. Sounds like foreplay."

That's it. She's tested me enough tonight. My hand shoots out and clicks the lamp off. I roll to the side and scoop her up, settling her on top of me so we're nose to nose. "If you wanted some dick all you had to do was ask."

She chuckles as she kisses the side of my face. "So full of yourself."

"I'm about to fill you with *myself*." My thumbs hook into her underwear, dragging them over her ass and down her legs. While she wriggles out of them, I strip off her shirt. "The first rule in our new house, is you're sleeping naked. Always."

"Excuse me?"

Before answering I flip us so she's pinned under me. My mouth takes time exploring the skin of her neck down to her breasts, licking and sucking until she's squirming under me. "You. Naked. Every. Night."

"Hmm…it was the *rule* part I was questioning."

I kiss and nuzzle my way to her ear. "Rule number two: never stop being a sass-mouth." She gasps as I slide the head of my cock along her slick pussy. Enough to tease her but nothing more.

"Rock?"

"Yes, sass-mouth?"

"You're everything I've ever wanted too," she whispers.

CHAPTER FOUR

HOPE

I'M NOT happy about the way my clothes have been fitting lately. Especially when I know I need to squeeze myself into some sort of dress soon.

Rock seems to think sex is the only exercise I need.

Attempting yoga around him is only asking to have my ass groped.

With that in mind, I slide out of bed early the next morning. I plan to run downstairs, ease in a short work-out, then slip back into bed for a different type of workout.

"Where're you going?" Rock's sleepy-rough voice calls out as my hand closes over the door knob.

So close. "Gym. I have a wedding dress I need to fit into."

"You haven't even picked out a dress yet."

"Well, I won't be able to if I can't fit into anything."

He tosses back the covers, scrubbing his hands over his face. "Give me a second. I'll go with you."

My mouth twitches in irritation. Working out next to Mr. Rock-hard everything is the last thing I want to do. But I don't want to say no and hurt his feelings, when I know he just wants to spend time with me.

While I'm waiting for him, I gather my hair into a high pony tail. Rock eyes me like the big, bad wolf he is when he joins me.

"You look too pretty for the gym."

"Thank you," I answer and throw open the door before we get sidetracked. Behind me, Rock's sigh makes me chuckle.

"It's so quiet," I mutter as we walk downstairs.

"Yeah, most of these degenerate fucks probably just went to bed."

"Don't talk about your brothers like that," I tease.

"Babe. Please. You know it's true."

Rock senses my unease as we get started. "What's wrong?"

"Nothing. I'm just used to working out alone or with Trinity."

He doesn't get it.

"You," I point to this well-defined arms. "Are all chiseled and perfect."

"And?"

"Working out next to you kind of sucks."

Instead of laughing, he shakes his head. "I see you naked every day." He flashes a dirty smirk. "Or at least I try to."

"That's different."

"You're exasperating."

"I know."

"Do your thing and quit leering at me. You're making me uncomfortable," he says with a girly, shivery gesture you wouldn't expect from Rock.

"Jerk," I laugh-grumble. But I know he did it to make me laugh.

Eventually I get over myself and fall into a rhythm. I can't help glancing at Rock every few minutes—okay seconds. My girly bits do a little tap-dance watching him concentrate on each movement and repetition. Even the thin sheen of sweat rolling over his skin looks sexy on him. From time to time he catches me watching him, but never says anything.

He's too busy doing his own thing to pay much attention to me. Or so I think.

As I walk over to the wall to grab a towel, there's an unexpected tug on my ponytail. His hot, heavy body press, press, presses against my back, until I'm flat against the wall.

Ohmygod. A rush of a desire sizzles through me. His spicy scent spins my thoughts until the need for him to strip me down and fuck me raw right here, right now, becomes impossible to ignore.

His warm lips taste the back of my neck. A sharp, pleasurable prick as he nips my earlobe. "Wearing this ponytail around me was a bad idea, Baby Doll," Rock whispers into my ear.

ROCK

"Why?" Hope's soft, nervous laughter floats back to me.

I wrap her hair around my fist a little tighter and give her a gentle tug. "Because all I've been able to think about the entire time we've been down here is how perfect it is for grabbing while I'm fucking you from behind."

She gasps as I pull again. "Am I hurting you?"

"No," she breathes out.

My other hand slides right down the front of her stretchy pants. "Fucking tight little work out pants have been messing with me all morning."

No answer, just a sharp intake of breath as my fingers find her soft, wet flesh. "Hit the lights."

"What? Here? Rock, no."

"I didn't *ask*, Baby Doll."

She reaches out and snaps off the light switch. "Rock, Wrath and Trin are right across the hall."

"Then we better be quick and quiet." My lips trail down her neck, while my hand yanks her pants down.

"Rock." She's bending over and offering her ass at the same time she pretends to protest. I *never* tire of this unspoken game we play.

I said quick, but I can't help taking my time to bare her ass with one hand, while keeping hold of her hair in the other. "Put your hands on the wall."

She moans as she complies. I think it has more to do with my hand sneaking under the tight material of her sports bra, pulling it down to free her breasts.

"Love every inch of you, baby," I whisper as my fingers roll her nipple. "Don't like it when you're so hard on yourself."

She raises her ass up.

"You want it?" I ask.

She tries to shake her head, but I've still got a tight hold on her hair.

"I'm going to give it to you." Freeing myself with one hand takes an extra second, but as I push inside, all her warmth wraps around me. I want to rip off her clothes, so there's nothing between us. "Admit you're a little turned on, Hope."

She shakes her head as I keep thrusting gently. "Don't lie, Baby Doll. You're fucking soaked. Your pussy's gripping me so tight when I pull out. Like it doesn't want to let go."

Moans fall from her lips and she pushes back against me. "Admit how much you love when I fuck you. Anywhere. Any time. Any place. Any way I want."

Even in the shadowy room, the pink spreading across her face and chest stands out. "Love the way you blush when I whisper filthy things to you."

Her mouth twitches as she fights the urge to smile. Still teasing me. Fuck, if I don't love that the most. In the short time she's been mine, I've mastered how her body responds to all the ways I enjoy pleasuring her.

Each thrust knocks her forward. I'm dying to see her lips part in pleasure, but my girl's stubborn this morning.

One of her hands reaches back, wrapping around my neck, fingers brushing through my hair. My lips kiss her exposed skin. Now, each time I jam myself inside her, a soft *ah* sound falls from her lips.

"Fuck, please don't stop, Rochlan."

There it is. "That's my girl. Say it again."

"Please don't stop fucking me."

Jesus, as much as her shyness turns me on, it fires me up even more when I get her to talk dirty. My hips snap into her so hard, she can't hold herself up and we end up with her cheek pressed up against the wall. My hand untangles from her hair, so I can hold her, while the force of my thrusts lifts her up.

"You'll let me do what I want, won't you, Baby Doll?" I tease her in a harsh whisper.

"Oh, God, yes," she whimpers.

My hand slides down, rubbing her clit. Her lips part and at the last second, I remind her not to scream.

"Rock," she whispers like a plea.

Her fear of getting caught must be messing with her. Her muscles tense, but she's not quite where she needs to be to go off. And I need her to go off. Need to see her face and what I do to her. Need to *feel* it. "Don't fight it, baby. Come for me." She's almost there. A little more pressure on her clit and she jerks against me. I cover her mouth with mine to muffle her moans. Her pussy pulses against me setting me off. A few more frantic thrusts and I push as far as I can, groaning through my release.

My forehead rests against her shoulder for a few seconds until the sex fog clears my brain. I brush a few stray pieces of hair off her face. "You good, Baby Doll?"

She mumbles and laughter bubbles out of her at the same time I slide out of her. When I release her, she slumps against the wall, giggling again.

I pop her on the ass once. "You okay?"

"I can't stand up. My legs are like jelly."

I let out my own breathless laughter. "Same here."

"Pull my pants up," she demands, sounding very indignant for someone with underwear around her knees.

I chuckle as I hook my fingers in the material, dragging it into place. "Better?"

"No," she mumbles, looking down her T-shirt and adjusting her bra. She glances up, laughter on her lips. "You and your magic dick always get your way, don't you?"

"Magic dick. I like that, sass-mouth."

"You would." She throws her arms around my neck and I lift her up for a kiss.

"Mad at me?"

She grins and scrunches up her nose. "Furious."

"Liar."

She opens her mouth, but someone clearing their throat outside the gym stops her.

As I slowly turn us, Hope slides down my body 'til her feet touch the floor, then she buries her face against me. "I'm so mad at you," she whispers against my shirt.

We find Wrath and Trin standing across the hallway. Trin's expression lies somewhere between shocked and amused, while Wrath has a predictably devious smile on his face. He nudges Trinity. "Hey, can you grab some Clorox from the laundry room? I need to bleach my eyes."

Hope glares at me.

Trin chuckles and shakes her head as I usher Hope out of the gym.

Wrath's not done being a jackass. "Next time can you at least face the other way, so I don't have to stare at your ass, brother?"

Trin reaches up and clamps her hand over his big mouth. "Ignore him, Hope. He's just jealous, he's not spontaneous any more."

Hope giggles, but Wrath's eyes widen and he turns his head. "What did you say? Game fucking on, angel."

Five seconds later, their door slams shut and laughing that turns to moaning is all we hear.

I grab a handful of Hope's ass and nudge her down the hall.

"Let's go be *spontaneous* again."

"You're not done?"

"Never."

WRATH

As if having my eyesight assaulted first thing this morning wasn't bad enough, now my manhood's been questioned by my girl. I need to fix that.

Trinity backs away from me as I shut the door.

"You should be more careful, Angel Face. I'll fuck you in every corner of this clubhouse if you don't watch your mouth."

Her nervous giggles stir me up. "I was just trying to make Hope feel better. You embarrassed the shit out of her."

"Price you pay for fucking in public. She'll live." That's it. We're done talking. I gather her in my arms and cut off any more noise by covering her mouth with mine.

"Oh, fuck," she whispers when I back off.

"Exactly."

I give her a quick spin, the slight friction of her skin against mine excites me and I take a breath to calm down. I want to have fun with her and I want it to last.

Once her back's nice and tight against my front, my arm bands around her waist to keep her there. The noise from across the hall woke us up, so she's still in her sleep clothes—a soft, loose tanktop that provides a nice teasing view of her tits and a tiny pair of cotton shorts. My hand skims down her body going straight for her sleek legs. With firm fingers, I trace her inner thigh, sneaking right up under her shorts.

"Spread your legs." She makes a soft moaning whimper at the harsh sound of my voice against her ear. "Now."

Her feet inch apart. Just enough for me to shove my big hand against her pussy and stroke the soft, slick skin. "Hmm, turned on, angel?"

"Yes," she whispers.

My hand that's wrapped around her waist moves up to cup her tit, squeezing gently, brushing my thumb over her nipple. Under the flimsy fabric her nipples harden. I bury my nose against her neck to inhale more of her sweet-sleepy scent. My fingers keep working and rubbing in a way to build her up quick—because what I'm doing is torture for me. She squirms, her breathing harsh and uncontrolled.

Right there.

My fingers rub, increasing in speed. She shudders and lets out another moan. Just about to go off.

47

Abruptly, I jerk my hand away, kiss her cheek and head for the bathroom. "I'm off to take a spontaneous shower."

"What?"

Spontaneous shower my ass. I need to jerk myself off. Now. I flip the water on, assuming she'll follow me in to bitch me out. I plan to grab her, fuck her senseless against the shower wall...my crazed eyes dart around the bathroom...or maybe bend her over the sink? I haven't decided.

The soft click of the bathroom door finally reaches me. I'm waiting in the shower, dick in hand for her to join me.

"Wrath?"

"Yeah, babe?" I answer before I really take notice of the tone of her voice.

"Are you mad at me?"

Aw fuck.

I whip open the shower door. "Get in here, you nut." I grab her hand and yank her into the shower—clothes and all—with me. She yelps, drenched in seconds, thin, wet fabric clinging to every curve. Scared honey eyes blink up at me. Cradling her head with my hand, I brush my thumb over her cheek while backing her up against the wall.

"I'm sorry," she whispers.

I'm not sure where our little game went wrong, but I hate that she feels she has to apologize to me. "Nothing to be sorry for, angel. I was just messing around with you."

Her eyes widen and her mouth forms a small O of surprise. She glances down at her wet clothes. "I'm all wet now."

"Sounds good to me," I growl and rip her shirt off, hulk-style. Grab it and tear it in two, right down the center. She gasps as I pick her up, shove her shorts out of my way and press my dick inside.

"Nothing that comes out of that angel mouth of yours could ever make me mad." I grunt the words to her as I keep thrusting, moving my hands up to keep something between her delicate back and the unforgiving tile. Her legs tighten around me, and she rests her forehead against mine, staring into my eyes.

"I'm sure that's not true."

I ignore that. "Grab the bar."

Last week, I installed a safety bar in here just for this purpose. It's not strong enough for us to hang from or some crazy shit, but it's prefect for her to hold onto so she can arch her back and put her tits in my face. Eagerly I latch on to one nipple, sucking and licking. Then the other. She's moaning louder, wiggling her hips against me. "I can't," she gasps.

Fuck. Teasing her like that had not been one of my smarter ideas.

"Yes you can, baby. Relax." I claim every bit of skin I can reach with kisses and angle my thrusts up.

"There," she whimpers. "There."

I keep one hand on her ass, supporting her, while the other one strokes down her stomach. My thumb brushes against her clit and she jerks, pushing herself into me. "You're so beautiful, Trinity. Come for me."

I rub firmer circles around her clit. She shivers and moans. I answer her with my own guttural groan. Around my hips, her legs tremble. "Ah," she moans again and again, body shuddering. She opens her eyes and stares at me in wonderment and it triggers my own orgasm. I'm spilling into her, while she keeps whispering, "I love you. I love you. I love you." Over and over.

"Love you, too."

My mouth seals over hers, silencing what started to sound more like a plea.

CHAPTER FIVE

ROCK

HOPE WAS relentless in her determination to get me down to the restaurant that's catering our engagement party. I don't have strong opinions about any of it. As long as I'm not required to wear a suit, and she's happy, it's all good.

On the way home, she's very animated, practically bouncing out of her seat. "I know the boneless will be less messy, but they don't feel like real wings—"

"I think having both was a great idea."

"Okay. Trinity was going to make these cute little ice cream sandwich things—oh! That reminds me, did Wrath tell you he plans to patch Trinity at the party? Well, after the party." She's talking so fast, my head spins. Her hands are a blur of movement out of the corner of my eye.

"You okay with that?"

"Of course. It's great. I won't be the only old lady in the house. And they've finally…whatever their issues."

My hand reaches over and captures one of hers, bringing it to my mouth, so I can kiss her knuckles. "Thank you."

We're interrupted by my phone ringing. I press the button on the steering wheel that answers and puts the call over Bluetooth.

"Can you come down to CB?" Z asks.

"Not right now."

"Come on, we caught your porn star." I grind my teeth, while next to me Hope breaks into giggles.

"Where are you?" Z asks.

"In the car. With Hope, so thanks, asshole."

Hope laughs even harder.

The line's silent, as I guess Z must be trying to figure out how to dig himself out of the hole he created.

"Go ahead, Z," Hope says with another chuckle.

"Uh, well. Wrath's here. He wants to fire Lexi, but I thought you might want to question her first. She's saying—well, it will be easier to tell you in person."

I'd rather ram my forehead into the steering wheel a couple dozen times than go to Crystal Ball right now. Hope makes a gesture that I interpret either as "go ahead" or "drop me off at the nearest bus station, so I can get away from your degenerate ass." Before I can clarify, she answers Z.

"We're leaving downtown Empire, now, Z. He'll be there in twenty minutes."

"Thanks." Z hangs up.

"What'd you tell him that for?"

"Just go get it over with. Otherwise they'll end up calling you fifty more times throughout the day."

She has a point.

"I'm sorry, Baby Doll."

"Rock, it's fine. I can wait in the car."

Like fuck. "It's a safe area, but I'd feel better if you were inside." Where I can keep an eye on her.

She huffs. "Seriously?" I'm about to answer when she chuckles. "Is this part of your not-wanting-to-see-naked-chicks-without-me crisis?" The way she characterizes my words makes me laugh.

"Probably. You can wait in the—" I was about to say office. *Yes, jackass. Why don't you invite her to sit at the same desk she watched you nail some chick on. Brilliant plan.*

"The room where some girl you were nailing before we were together videotaped you? Is that what you were going to say?"

"It's scary how well you know me."

She snorts and puts her hand on my leg. "To me it will always be the room where we had our first kiss."

Jesus Christ. Every time I think I can't possibly love this woman more than I already do, she says something like that. "Thank you."

"For?"

"For not making me feel like shit over the whole thing."

The warmth of her hand on my leg disappears, and she sighs. "I think we've already conquered worse things, Rock." I don't know how to answer. Before I come up with anything reasonably intelligent, she speaks again. "I just want you to be sure my...lack of worldliness in that department won't bore you eventually?"

We're almost at the club, so I wait to answer her. I need to be looking at her when I figure out the right words.

"Sorry. You shouldn't have to keep reassuring me over and over. I trust you."

I shut the truck down and think about how to say what I want. I turn and take her hands, so she'll face me. "I love everything about you. You're the only woman I've ever felt truly comfortable with and that's way more interesting than a woman who fucks anyone she meets for reasons that have nothing to do with love."

"Wow."

"Yeah, wow. And, you're too classy to film someone without permission."

"That's true."

"And I'll mold you just the way I like."

"Oh my. Sounds kinky."

"You have no idea, Baby Doll."

She waits for me to open her door, and takes my hand so she can jump down from the truck. "I'm sorry. I should put running boards or something on it."

The naughty smile that spreads across her face surprises me— given our location and all. "But I like having your hands on me to get in and out," she says.

"And I like having my hands on you."

Two of the nomads we brought in for security are on the door. So far Iron Jim and Butcher are working out well. If that continues, I'll ask the club if we want to offer them a more permanent place.

I nod to both of them. "Butch, Jim, this is my ol' lady, Hope."

After the introductions, Jim cracks up. "You're a lucky man. I couldn't get my ex near a strip club."

The corner of Hope's mouth twists up.

I don't bother explaining why we're actually here. Inside, the music throbs right through us and I feel like I'm walking into my past.

Hope braces herself on my shoulder and leans up. "Did you do that a lot?" she yells in my ear.

"Do what?"

She gestures at the back hallway, where my office used to be. I understand what she's asking—if I took a lot of women over the desk in my office. I almost say "it got a lot busier after I met you" but don't. She doesn't need to hear that in the year before her husband died, I used a lot of women in an attempt to fuck Hope out of my stubborn mind. Now she's mine and that's a time in my life I'd rather forget.

"Don't," I warn her.

She raises an eyebrow and the question she's asking is written all over her mischievous face. "No. Absolutely not," I say before she even asks. Grabbing her hand, I tug her over to the bar. "Come on, troublemaker."

Willow's at the bar. She's worked here long enough without causing trouble that I trust her with Hope.

"Where are Wrath and Z at?"

She lifts her chin toward the back. "Office."

I make the introductions and ask Willow to keep an eye on my woman.

"You'll behave, Baby Doll?"

"I'll do my best," she sasses back. Fucking *love* her.

A bit of unease follows me down the hall. Before I enter the office, I take one last look at Hope. She's busy chatting with Willow.

Wrath and Z are two grumpy bookends leaning on the edges of my old desk. Lexi's sniffling on the couch. Her head snaps up, eyes wide with relief when she spots me. "Rock! Please don't fire me. I didn't—"

"Sit back down." I point at the couch.

I pull one of the chairs in front of her—keeping a safe distance—and pin her with a hard stare. "Why?"

"Why what?"

I turn to Wrath and Z. "Did you show it to her?"

Before either of them answer, Lexi sobs out a miserable. "Yes."

"Did you like seeing yourself on video, Lexi?"

Her scared doe eyes peek up at me, full of confusion. "What? N-No," she finally stammers out.

"Well, someone sent that to my fiancée. How do you think she felt watching it?"

She bursts into tears. "I'm so sorry. I didn't send it though. I've met her. She's nice. I wouldn't do something like that, I swear."

"Why did you even have it?"

"I don't know," she wails. Behind me Wrath sighs, long and loud to let me know how annoyed he is to be here. Just for that I'm gonna make him stay until closing.

"It was stupid. I must have hit record by accident, later when I realized what it was I just kept it, then I forgot about it."

Unbelievable how something so stupid could cause so much trouble.

Suddenly, Lexi's tears vanish and she points an accusatory finger in Z's direction. "I told him!"

I turn and raise an eyebrow at Z. "Told him what?" I ask.

Z shrugs. "She told me her phone got stolen a couple days before Hope received the video."

"Yeah, settin' up her alibi," Wrath grumbles.

Lexi shoots him a vicious glare. "I've always been nice to you. Why are you being such a dick?"

I hold up a hand, so Wrath keeps his mouth shut. "Simmer down. Tell me what happened."

"After that *new girl*," she spits the word out like venom, "got here, Gabriella, shit started going missing. You know we've never had problems like that here, Rock. All the girls get along for the most part. Shit, we hardly ever use our lockers. We all trust each other. Then Gabriella shows up and iPods go missing, money, cell phones. We tried telling Z but—"

"I just figured they were upset about the new competition," Z finishes.

Lexi's always been a bit…hysterical and dramatic. But never a liar or troublemaker. If she'd come to me with her complaint, I would have taken it seriously. Although, given the awkward way Gabriella ended up working for us, I don't know that the outcome would have been any different.

"Okay, Lexi. Say I believe your story. Why would Gabriella send the video to Hope? How does she even know who my ol' lady is?"

She chews on her lip and redirects her gaze to her feet. "Well… when she first got here, she kept asking about you. Where you were, why you didn't work here anymore. Stuff like that. And, um, I might have told her it was because you were getting married. But I never told her your girl's name. I don't even *know* her last name and I certainly don't have her number."

Easy enough to figure out once you start asking questions. Especially if it was Vipers doing the asking.

"You get a new phone?"

"Yeah, and you guys really should reimburse me for it since it's your fault my old one got stolen."

Ignoring that, I ask. "Where is it?"

"In my locker."

"Good. Keep it there and tell the rest of the girls the same thing. Anyone gets caught with their phone out of the dressing room, they're fired." I turn to make sure Z's absorbing this information.

"Got it," he says.

I give Lexi a critical eye. What she did was stupid, but I believe her story. The fact that Gabriella was so concerned about me from day one is unnerving. Fucking Vipers, always up to something.

"All right. Go on," I stand and motion for Lexi to do the same.

"Are you still firing me?" she squeals.

"No." Behind me Wrath curses and Lexi sticks her tongue out at him. "Hey!" I snap my fingers in front of her face to draw her attention away from Wrath. "Razor thin ice you're standing on, Lexi. Behave. Act like a professional."

She straightens up and marches to the door. "I'll be professional. And I *won't* be fucking anyone I work for ever again," she snaps as she opens the door.

"Good plan," I call out.

"What the fuck, Rock?" Wrath shouts as soon as the door shuts.

"You want to be involved here even less than I do, so why are you sticking your nose in this anyway?" I'm not yelling. But somewhere in the neighborhood of it.

"Uh, excuse me, but that's the little bitch responsible for making Hope throw the fuck up the other day, or did you forget?"

I actually look around for a hidden camera or some shit, because I can't believe what I'm hearing.

"Are you trying to say you're more worried about my girl than I am?" I ask in a controlled tone. I'm furious enough to consider planting my fist in his face but also sort of amused.

To my astonishment, he closes his mouth and sits back against the desk. "No."

Z's still ping-ponging between the two of us. "Can we focus on the bigger problem here?" Z puts his hands up. "I'm upset about Hope seeing that shit too, but she handled it fine. Our bigger problem is the Vipers. Why the fuck did they plant Gabby here? Why's she so concerned about you? And how'd she know who to send the video to?"

Christ, Z's acting more presidential than I am.

"You're right, brother," I answer.

"We can't fire Gabriella. We should keep closer tabs on her," Wrath suggests.

Z shakes his head. "Don't look at me."

"No, you dick." Wrath nods at me. "The kid I told you about from the gym, Twitch? He's a stealthy little fucker. Be a good way to see if he's prospect material."

"All right. Have Hoot check in with him though. I don't want him going into Viper territory alone."

"Got it."

"Are we done here? Because I'd rather not leave Hope out there any longer."

The two asses laugh. "She's here? Fuck, I hope she's not up on stage," Wrath jokes.

"I hope she is," Z answers but drops his smirk when he sees my face. "Still not in a joking mood, prez?"

"Not about Hope. Never about her."

HOPE

My first fifteen minutes hanging out with Willow aren't too bad. She presents herself as a bit of an airhead to any of the men who come up to the bar. But when we're alone she's got a fantastic, biting wit, cracking jokes about everything and anyone in sight.

The only way to describe my next ten minutes is awkward. While Willow's busy washing glasses, I swivel my stool around to watch the girls on stage. Somehow it's not as vulgar as I expected. These girls shed their clothes in a graceful, almost artistic way, that's hard not to appreciate.

It also makes me never, ever want to get naked in front of Rock again. But we'll save the *Diary of Hope's Body Image Issues* for another time.

Between songs, I spot a short brunette stalking toward the bar. She's dressed in street clothes, but seems so at ease, I assume she works here.

"Everything okay?" Willow asks, when the girl sits next to me.

"Yeah, I guess." Now that her back's to the rest of the club, her face loses some of the cheekiness she strutted out here with. She looks familiar and by her expression, she might cry any minute.

Willow sets another water in front of me and takes my empty away. "Lex, have you met Rock's woman? This is Hope."

For a second I can't draw in any air. Blood rushes through my ears drowning out everything around us.

Luckily for me, Lexi seems to have a similar reaction. Her cheeks redden, mouth opens, but no words come out.

"Hi," I finally manage. What am I supposed to say? Thanks for the engagement present, and by the way, if you so much as look at my man, I'll kill you? Because that's rattling around in my head somewhere.

"I'm sorry!" she blurts out.

So I guess she knows I know who she is. Awesome.

"All three of them just reamed me out—and not in the fun way," she moans. "I'm so sorry. I swear to God, I didn't send it to you."

I'm still not sure what to say to her.

Wait a second, all three of them, *what?*

As I'm about to ask she jerks her head to the side. "Oh, fuck that. I'm not in the mood to get yelled at again." She scoots off the stool and throws me another apologetic look. "Congratulations on your engagement," she says before running away.

I don't have to tip my head up to know it's my favorite trio of scary bikers encircling me.

"Are you okay? What'd she say to you?" Wrath asks, earning a scowl from Rock.

"Nothing," I answer. All three of their faces are screwed into slightly different forms of unhappiness. Z's—indifference, Wrath's—irritation, Rock's—exasperation.

"How can three of the horniest men I've ever met be so miserable in a strip club?" I blurt out. The tension drains from Wrath and Z as they burst out laughing. Rock just looks more strained even though he flashes a tight smile my way.

"You okay, Baby Doll? I'm done here. We can go."

"I'm fine." I wag my finger at all three of them. "Did you three really gang up on that poor girl and question her?"

Guilty faces all around.

"Do you guys have any idea how intimidating the three of you are?"

"That's the point," Z says.

I shake my head at them. "You guys are begging for a sexual harassment law suit. You should hire a female manager."

When they finish laughing at me, Z turns his impish eyes my way. "You applying for the job, Hope?"

"Uh, no."

Wrath pats my shoulder. "Don't worry, Cinderella, no one's suing us."

WRATH

I'm still laughing after Hope and Rock take off.

Z smirks at me. "Can you believe that girl? Worried about us harassing the chick who made a sex tape with her man?"

"She's so square it hurts sometimes."

Z cracks up at that. "Man, I love the girl. But if I were Rock, I might've choked her by now."

"Apparently he enjoys the challenge."

Eventually we stop laughing at Rock's predicament. Z lifts his chin. "You can go. With Butch and Jim here and Dex coming in, I got more than enough coverage. Murphy's supposed to stop in later too."

"To work or fuck around?"

"Probably both." He snickers. "Nah, he's clearing some stuff out of the basement and bringing it up to the property."

"You want me to help?"

"It's not what you think. Just old bike parts and shit."

"Okay. Then, yeah, I need to stop by Furious and talk to Twitch."

"Sounds good."

He gives me a fist bump and I'm free from stripper hell.

Don't get me wrong, the money the MC rakes in from Crystal Ball pays a lot of bills, but I've paid my dues and spent enough time there over the years.

My gym's a short ride from Crystal Ball and I find a nice surprise waiting for me in the parking lot. Trinity's Jeep. She mentioned stopping by to take some photos of Jake. At the time, I said sure, because I figured there was no way in hell Jake would say yes to something like that.

Well aren't I in for a surprise. Trinity and Jake are in one of the training rings. He's shirtless making all sorts of goofy poses for my girl.

"Hey, angel." I plant a kiss on the back of Trinity's neck, startling her. The smile that lights up her face when she turns around guts me.

She throws her arms around my neck, whacking me with her camera in the process, but any twinge of jealousy that was creepin' up disappears. "Are you surprised to see me?" she asks.

"A little. Happy though." I lift my chin at Jake. "Trin do your hair and makeup?"

He throws up two middle fingers. "Don't be jealous 'cause your girl thinks I'm cover material and you're not."

My gaze drops to Trinity, and I let out a snicker. "Kept my secret, huh?"

"Yup."

"Seen Twitch?"

"Not yet. It's early for him, isn't it?" she asks as she's bending over to put her camera away. I should be professional, but I own the fucking gym, so I help myself to a squeeze of Trinity's ass. She jumps and squeals.

"Jesus Christ, get a room," Jake bitches as he approaches us. "You done with me Trinity?"

"I think so. We got a lot of good stuff."

"Cool. Let me know how it turns out." He taps my arm on his way to the locker room. Before I have a chance to talk to Trinity, I get interrupted. Then I'm dealing with members until my kids show up for class. I set Twitch up to talk with Z about following Gabriella. Kid just needed to hear the word "stripper" to sign on to that gig.

Trin sticks around the whole time. I get glimpses of her hanging out in my office every now and then. Might be sappy as fuck, but I love having her here.

CHAPTER SIX

ROCK

Now that the fuckery with Lexi's over with, I'm hoping we can put the whole sex video to rest. Permanently. Go on with our lives like it never happened.

Other than giving us grief over harassing Lexi—and hell, I'm pretty fucking sure Hope's the only woman in the world who would worry about *that* under the circumstances—she's been quiet. Thinking about her indignant face back at the club twists my mouth up.

"What are you laughing about?" Hope asks.

"You."

"Me? Why?"

Out of the corner of my eye I catch her pouting and I reach over to take her hand. "Nothing bad. You're fucking sweet. Love you." It was on the tip of my tongue to say exactly what I'd been picturing, but I catch myself at the last minute. Better to drop it.

"I love you too." She squeezes my hand.

After a few stops on the way home, we're not even back at the clubhouse for fifteen minutes when Z calls. Enough time for me to hustle Hope upstairs. My greedy hands are about to strip her down when my phone goes off. She chuckles when she sees who's calling and passes my phone over. "Fucker has the worst timing," I grumble.

"What?" No pleasant greeting for Z this afternoon.

"We got a situation."

"What now?"

"I sat Gabby down when she came in for her shift, just a general discussion about stuff going missing, keeping phones in lockers, shit like that. Oh, and I took Hope's advice and had Willow sit in on it."

A short chuckle eases out of me and I flick my gaze at Hope. "I'll let her know. So, what's the situation?"

"She flipped the fuck out. Started cursing me out and saying I was accusing her of something—which I didn't."

"What the fuck?"

"Yeah, I know. So, I sent her home for the night. Told her to calm down and come back with a better attitude."

"What does any of this have to do with me?"

"Ransom called. He's all pissed we're not giving his girls a fair shake. He wants to talk to you."

"*Motherfuckingsonofabitch*. I'm done dealing with this fuck."

"I hear you. He wanted to meet over the border. I said no. So, he's coming here."

"Are you fucking serious?"

"I told him he can bring one guy. Killa probably. And that's it."

I glance at Hope again. My end of the conversation has her watching me with an intent expression.

"Fine. When?"

"Seven."

"Fuck me. Did you call—"

"Wrath's over at Furious. He'll be here in a few. Murphy's here. I'll call Dex, Bricks, and ask the nomads to stick around."

"Good. I want everyone laid back and chill, but enough to make an impression. I'll track down Ravage and have him ride with me."

"Dirty side down, brother."

"Someone's pessimistic."

Z laughs, short and clipped. "Just get your ass down here in one piece, prez. I don't want to deal with this fuck on my own. Otherwise I'm gonna end up burying him in our basement."

"I'm okay with that."

"Everything okay?" Hope asks after I'm done with the call.

"Sorry, Baby Doll. I need to run back to Crystal Ball."

"Okay."

The atmosphere at Crystal Ball when I arrive can only be described as tense. All the girls seem anxious, even though they shouldn't have any idea what's going on.

Butcher frisks Ransom and Killa at the door. Since Butch isn't one of our local guys, I can pretend I didn't know he was going to do such a thing to my "guests."

I don't invite them into the back office. We sit at a table in the back corner. They're seated with their backs to the stage.

Ransom gets right to the point. "I did you a solid. Took care of the guy who tried to jack your girl." He jabs a finger in the air in Wrath's direction. Wrath keeps a blank face, but I know it's probably killing him. "You said you'd give my girls a fair shot. First one you toss out and now Gabby comes home cryin'."

"Bullshit," Z mutters.

Ransom cocks his head to the side.

"Listen. Your girl, Mariella, had no identification. How can we have her dancing here if we can't verify her age?"

"What the fuck you talkin' bout? She's got ID."

Z shakes his head. "Well, she refused to give it to me. Said she had none. What'd you want me to do, beat it out of her?"

Killa sneers at Z, because yes, that's how he'd handle that sort of personnel issue.

"Fine. We'll deal with Mariella. But Gabby said you fired her."

"Jesus Christ," Z says. "I didn't fucking fire her. I should have. She's been causing trouble here since day one. Bitch cursed me out. I told her to go home and cool off. Told her to come back tomorrow."

Ransom and Killa share another look.

My irritation's rising to epic proportions the longer I sit here and deal with this bullshit. "Did you two really drag me down here because of some lies one of your girls told you?"

"Gabby don't lie."

"The fuck she doesn't," Z snaps. "She's been lying and stirring up shit since the day she showed up."

Killa leans in close to Z's face. "Watch your mouth, she's my cousin."

Z isn't intimidated by anyone, not even this loony fuck. "Well, your cousin's a trouble-makin' liar."

I put my hand on Z's arm and he sits back.

"Okay. Obviously this isn't going to work out. We gave it a shot. But it's not a good fit." I could mention we suspect she's been stealing shit and is responsible for sending a porno to my girl, but I'm not about to let him know something so trivial had any effect on my life.

Ransom glares and I keep my bored expression in place.

"If Mariella has the ID, she can come back. But we're done with Gabby." Shit, I've never even *met* Gabby and I'm sick to death of her.

Next to me, Wrath shifts and Ransom focuses on him. "Maybe Gabby can work over at Furious Fitness?"

"We're not hiring," Wrath answers smoothly without hesitation.

"You got Wolf Knights workin' there."

"One. I got one Wolf Knight there. And he's been there since the beginning. It ain't a club business." I'm surprised Wrath explained at all. I fully expected him to knock Ransom out.

"Everything's club business." When none of us respond, Ransom gets up from the table slowly. "You hear about our brother that got pulled out of the river?" he asks me.

I stand and meet his stare head-on. "Heard about it. Didn't know the body was connected to you."

"Yeah. Went missing back when our clubs were having some issues. His brother disappeared too."

The tension around the table rises. "That's unfortunate."

"Yeah. It is." He keeps giving me that evil-blank stare.

"You got something you want me to say, Ransom?"

"No. Just wondering how long this truce between the clubs will last."

"That a threat?"

"Not at all." He motions for Killa to follow him. "Later, Rock."

After I'm certain they're gone, I sit back down at the table.

"What the fuck was that all about?" Z asks.

"I think he sent the girls here to get info on his missing guys."

"How did he think that would ever work?" Wrath asks.

"Probably figured we'd fuck 'em and pillow talk?" Z offers.

Wrath's mouth twists down. "Christ, if we were that stupid we would have been dead a long time ago."

"Shit, if I was that big a whore, my dick would have fallen off a long time ago," Z jokes.

We all stare at him.

"Hey, I could be a lot worse."

This whole night's giving me a headache. "No one rides alone. No one near Ironworks for any reason. That goes for the girls too."

No one argues.

CHAPTER SEVEN

HOPE

IT SEEMS like years ago that Trinity sat down and planned this party. I've been looking forward to it and it's finally here.

The location has changed to Rock's house. The house Bricks and his girlfriend, Winter are now renting. I feel awful imposing on them, but neither of them seem to mind. Winter throws herself into decorating and follows Trinity's precise orders for, well, everything.

I haven't heard from Sophie since our showdown, and I'm not sure what to think. My heart hurts for the years of friendship we shared which apparently mean nothing to her.

Wing Fling, the caterer Trinity found to provide the chicken wings, arrives early and sets up outside on the stone patio out back.

"I love this patio. Can we do something like this at our house?"

Rock's mouth turns up and his arms slip around my waist, pulling my back to his chest. "I love hearing you say 'our house'." He leans down and whispers in my ear. "We can do anything you want."

It's simple, but I love him for it.

"We can clear more trees so there's a better view of the mountains if you want."

"Okay."

"Anything my girl wants, she gets."

"Thank you, Rock." My hands rub over his forearms, finally settling on his hands clasped over my middle. His chin rests on my head.

"Should we call the fire department?" Z asks as he walks up.

"Why, what's wrong?"

"Nothing. Worried you two were fused together."

"Very funny, asshat."

Rock and Z both laugh at my comeback. Sometimes I think they egg me on just so I'll insult them.

Z drops into one of the chairs, and Rock pulls one over next to him. Rock hooks an arm around my waist and tugs me into his lap. We watch while Z puts on a show of inhaling about fifty chicken wings.

"Aren't you going to eat anything, Hope?" Trinity asks as she joins us. "You know, before Z eats everything in sight."

"I'm a growing boy," he mumbles.

"Yeah, outward not upward," Wrath jokes.

"I'm too nervous," I explain. Answering Trinity's earlier question.

Rock gently squeezes my hip. "What are you nervous about, Baby Doll?"

Flustered because now I have four sets of eyes on me, I try to kid around. "Oh the usual, someone choking on a chicken bone."

"You worried Sophie's gonna show up?" Wrath asks. Perceptive bastard.

"A little."

"Lilly wouldn't do that to you," Z says. It makes me wonder just how often Z and Lilly see each other. Trinity hands him a napkin as he's about to wipe his hands on his jeans.

"Great idea, but messy."

"Maybe you can find someone to lick your fingers, bro," Wrath says, nodding at Lilly who just arrived.

I push myself out of Rock's lap before he has a chance to grab me. "Excuse me, guys." Rock's approach to parties has always been to let

70

everyone come to him. As MC president, I guess that makes sense. I've always been a mingler, and I feel bad about neglecting our guests.

"Lilly," I call out before she wanders inside.

She turns and breaks into a smile. "Hey, bride-to-be! You look beautiful."

"Thank you." I was nervous the pomegranate-red dress was too short. Rock assured me it was the perfect length. For what, he didn't specify.

She hands me a card and I shake my head. "We meant it when we said we didn't want anything."

"It's not from me. It's from Sophie."

"Oh. Sorry you're in the middle."

"I'm not. What she did was shitty. I know she feels awful. Not only about Rock, but about not telling you and then causing the scene at Mara's birthday. All of it."

"Well, her fingers aren't broken, are they? She could call me."

"She's afraid you won't talk to her and she didn't want to stress you out."

Sounds more cowardly to me. But I don't want to argue with Lilly today. Turning, I take in the scene of our big, extended Lost Kings family and I'm struck by how happy I am to be a part of it.

"Z's over with Rock if you want to say hello. Or lick his fingers. Up to you."

She gives me the strangest look, then grins. "Rock's good for you, Hope."

"Hey, don't be mad, but I'm going to stick this in my purse and read it later. I just don't—"

She settles her hand on my arm to stop my rambling. "You don't have to explain yourself to me. I understand."

She bites her lip and stares at me before finally, asking, "Is Z here with anyone?"

"Nope."

She nods, but still doesn't make a move. Rock joins us, by slipping an arm around my waist. "Thanks for coming, Lilly."

"I wouldn't miss this for anything."

"Z's over there." Rock tips his head in the direction of the patio. "Was bugging me all morning about whether or not you'd be here."

"Oh, really?" She looks to me for confirmation, but I just shrug.

"I was here early with Trinity setting up."

"Oh, where's Trinity? I want to say hi to her."

"Somewhere. Just find the big blond guy, she won't be far." Rock jokes.

"Okay."

Lilly sways into the crowd, definitely turning a lot of heads. She's a brave one. In a backyard full of bikers, she ignores everyone until she finds Trinity.

"They seem to get along," Rock says.

"Yes." I tap him with the card I'm still holding. "This is from Sophie, but I don't want to deal with it right now."

"So don't. I don't want you upset today."

Rocking up on my tiptoes I brush a kiss on his cheek. "You're the sweetest."

His arm tightens around my waist. "I want to make you happy from now on."

"You do." I turn so I can entwine my arms around him and press my cheek to his chest.

"You okay?" he asks after a few minutes.

"More than okay. I'm very content. Thank you for giving me a family." Just as that thought comes out of my mouth, the guys start whistling and making all sorts of obnoxious noises at us.

"A family full of degenerate fuckwits," he says. But it's said with affection. "Are you happy?"

"I'm always happy when I'm with you."

His faces relaxes and he presses a kiss to my forehead. "You mean that?"

"With everything in me."

"Good. I'm happiest when I'm with you too."

High-pitched squeals are the only warning I have before someone slams into me from behind, wrapping her arms around Rock and me.

"Uncle Rock! I'm so excited." She squeezes even tighter. "I can't wait to call you Aunt Hope," Heidi babbles out breathlessly against my ear.

Extracting myself from Rock's hold isn't easy. But I do and face Heidi for a proper greeting. Axel's patiently waiting behind her and flashes a quick smile.

"Thanks, honey."

I feel incredibly old while she rattles off a bunch of things she has planned before the end of school.

"Got your college application in yet, Heidi?" Rock asks.

She dips her head. "No. With everything that happened with Grams and moving into Marcel's place, I—"

My heart aches for Heidi. "I can help you, if you need it, Heidi."

"Thanks, Hope. I might. There were a few forms I wasn't sure what to do with."

"How're your classes, Axel?" Rock asks. I guess he gets a day off from being just "prospect."

"Okay."

"He's being modest, Uncle Rock. He was offered an apprenticeship over the summer."

"That's great."

Axel seems unsure. As if maybe the club won't give him time for the job or something.

Teller joins us and tries to give his sister a hug, but she shies away from him. Because I'm nosy, I ask what everyone else is thinking. "What's wrong, Heidi?"

"Oh, she's pissed at me because I told her she doesn't need to get a job," Teller explains. "She won't even go get her permit, but she wants to get a job."

"I can walk there. It's right down the street!" she fumes.

I tap her shoulder to draw her attention from her brother before she attacks him. "Where?"

"At Stewart's. I can ring up ice cream and sell coffee. I'm not dumb."

"I didn't say you were dumb," Teller grumbles.

"Honey, I think you have to be twenty-one to work there. Or at least eighteen, since they sell cigarettes, alcohol and lottery tickets."

"Oh. Really?"

"Pretty sure. I know it looks like an easy job, but a friend of mine worked there one summer and said they were strict."

"Oh."

"See," Teller says with a raised-eyebrow-big-brother face.

"Whatever," Heidi snaps.

"Where you been, bug?" Murphy shouts as he ambles over.

Heidi backs up a few steps and takes Axel's hand. "We just got here."

Murphy raises an eyebrow at the "we" and behind me Rock sighs.

"Hey, Axel," Murphy actually greets the kid. *Huh.* He bumps me with his elbow next. "I'm heading inside. Need anything, First Lady?"

"I'm good. Thank you, though."

"Is Bricks here?" Heidi asks, as he walks away.

"Yup. I think Winter and the kids are inside—"

"Oh, goodie." She grabs Axel's hand and drags him away, leaving Rock and me with Teller.

Rock's shaking his head when I turn around. "She's gonna give you gray hairs," he says to Teller.

Teller rolls his eyes skyward. "You're not kidding."

"You know, Teller, she's a really smart girl. It might be easier on you if you just explain things to her like an adult instead of a blanket *no*," I say as gently as possible.

"You're probably right. She's my baby sister, Hope. I can't deal with her being an adult. Freaks me the fuck out."

I cover up my laugh with a cough and Rock pinches my ass. "I know, but it's happening whether you're ready for it or not."

"Don't I know it." He lowers his voice. "Jesus Christ, she asked me if Axel could stay over the other night. I sure as fuck don't feel like dealing with that."

Okay, this time I can't cover up my laughter. Neither can Rock. Teller glares at both of us. "It's not funny."

"I know. I'm sorry."

"Goddammit. *I* can't have women over and she's asking me if her boyfriend can spend the night. Fucking hell."

I'm dying trying keep my laughter to a minimum. "At least she asked," I offer with a shrug.

"Yeah, I guess. I don't even think the poor kid knew what she was up to. He was ready to piss himself when I kicked his ass out."

"You didn't."

"Damn fucking right I did. As if that's not bad enough, I've got my best friend's pervy ass sniffing all over her. I swear to fuck, I'm going to send her away to boarding school or some shit for the rest of the school year."

That's it. I'm done. I turn and bury my head against Rock's chest, and laugh until tears wet my lashes. Underneath me, his chest rumbles and shakes with laughter.

"Laugh it up you two. You ever decide to have kids, I hope you end up with one just like her."

"What crawled up your ass, welterweight?" Wrath asks. Even before I turn around, I hear him slap Teller on the back in his standard greeting.

"Knock it off, fucker. I ain't in the mood today."

That sets me off laughing again.

"What's up with her?" Wrath asks Rock.

"She's laughing because Heidi's driving me nuts," Teller answers.

"Where is the little brat? I haven't seen her yet."

Teller nods at the house, not even bothering to get upset that Wrath just called his sister a brat. "Inside."

ROCK

For some reason, I'm feeling extra sappy today. The party's perfect. The family's all together. My woman is beautiful.

And I wish the wedding was a lot closer than four months away.

I also wish I hadn't rented my house out to Bricks, because the dress Hope chose is the perfect length for me to bend her over, flip it up and—

"Rock?" Wrath snaps his fingers in front of my face and I smack his hand away.

"What?"

"Did you warn Hope about Virginia Beach?" By his tone, I don't think this is the first time he's asked the question.

What the fuck's he talking about? Trinity's staring up at him with a confused expression. Hope raises an eyebrow. "Is it falling into the ocean?" she asks.

That snaps me out of it. "Sass-mouth." I press a kiss to her cheek and grab her ass. There are some bushes and crap planted by the house, so no one can probably see where my hand is. Doesn't mean they can't tell, by the expression on her face.

"If you can stop grabbing her ass for a minute," Wrath interrupts. Guess not.

"What about it?"

"That we're sharing a room."

"Wait, who's we?" Hope asks.

"Don't get too excited," Wrath says. "The four of us."

Hope wriggles out of my hold and grabs Trinity, pulling her away from us. "Maybe Trinity and I will share a room, and you two can sleep on the beach."

"Oh, I think that works way better," Trinity agrees, while trying not to laugh. Lilly joins them.

"Who's sleeping on the beach?" she asks and Hope nods at us. "They are."

Wrath's face settles into a frown. "How'd this get away from us?"

"You started it."

"Well, knowing you, you'd just spring it on her at the last minute."

"That's true," Hope says.

"Hey. I don't like you two conspiring together," I joke, while pointing my finger at her and Wrath. "It's worse than when you two get together." This time I point at Hope and Trinity.

I don't think Lilly knows what to make of any of this nonsense. I'm sure she expected some scary bikers today. Instead all she's finding are a bunch of whipped men whose women lead them around by their dicks.

Oh well.

"Mara's here!" Hope bounces up and down, and drags Trinity down the driveway to meet Mara and Damon.

"Murph really couldn't find any extra rooms?" I ask Wrath.

"Don't know if he looked. Still should warn her."

"Why? Can't you behave for one long weekend?"

Like the dick he loves being, he scratches his chin and pretends to think about it. "I can try."

"You ready for tonight?"

"Fuck yeah."

"Does she know?"

"Not if your woman kept her mouth shut. Trin's been so fixated on all this stuff, she hasn't been paying attention to much else."

"Sorry about that."

"No, it's fine. It makes her happy. That's all I care about."

We're interrupted by Damon before I can respond. "Hey, Rock. Congratulations."

We shake hands like old friends, and then I introduce him to Wrath.

"I think we met once before," Damon says.

"Probably. You're not nearly as scary as Hope makes you out to be."

I shake my head. But Damon, not one bit insulted, bursts out laughing.

"From when she used to lawyer in front of you," Wrath explains.

"I figured. Mara has made similar remarks."

I chuckle at that. "I bet she has."

"Hope's not lawyering much these days is she?" Damon asks.

My shoulders lift. I'm not quite comfortable discussing my girl's career path with someone I barely know. "She's never seemed happy doing it."

"That's too bad. She's a good attorney. Smart, obviously. But she's possesses a lot of empathy, something most attorneys—even the female ones—don't usually have."

"I know. I try not to stick my nose in her career stuff. Only gets me in trouble."

Next to me Wrath snorts. "No joke."

"I feel your pain," Damon agrees.

Wrath's socialized about as much as he can tolerate today. "Good to see you again, Damon."

He nods at Wrath and turns back my way. "Looking forward to the wedding?"

"Yeah. I really am. Wish it wasn't so far away."

"Get a license and come down to City Hall. I'll do it for you this week. You can still have the celebration whenever she wants it."

"Yeah?"

"Sure. I have couples do that all the time. If one needs to get on the other's health insurance or whatever. It's just a formality."

"I think she was going to ask you to do the ceremony up at our property. Can you do it outside city limits?"

"Anywhere in the state. I'd be honored if that's what you guys want."

"Thanks. I'll talk to her about doing it sooner."

HOPE

"You could have brought Cora," I say to Mara as she checks her phone for the fifth time since she got here.

"Well, Hope. Let me tell you." Sometimes I swear, Mara should have been a teacher. "Damon's mother's visiting us. So my options were to leave the baby with her or bring the baby *and* Mrs. Oak here. Trust me, you did *not* want her here."

"You should probably see what they're up to, Hope." Lilly points to Rock and Damon on the other side of the yard.

"Hmm, no good can come of this. Come on, Hope," Mara says as she grabs my hand and drags me over to our men.

"Can't you stand to be away from him for five seconds," I grumble at her.

"You want him giving your man ideas? No. You don't. Trust me."

78

Remembering what Rock told me he plans to put in our basement, I snicker. "Too late."

"Sucks for you. Your ass doesn't have as much padding as mine does," she says while dropping my hand to run hers over her ass for emphasis.

"Oh, good grief."

"What on earth were you two discussing that my wife felt compelled to rub her ass in public?" Damon asks when we reach the guys.

"Wouldn't you like to know," Mara snips back. She's too slow to evade Damon's grasp and ends up tucked tight to his side.

"I asked Damon about performing the ceremony at the property," Rock says.

"Oh. Can you?"

"Yeah, absolutely. Any time you want." He and Rock share a look and now I *am* wondering what they were talking about before we interrupted.

"Is that it?"

"We'll talk about it later, babe," Rock says, pulling me closer.

Trinity comes over and rests her forehead on my shoulder. "Heidi's exhausting," she whispers and I try not to laugh too loud.

She shakes her head and grins.

After I introduce her to Damon, he asks what she does. Trinity blinks a few times before Wrath, comes up behind us and answers for her. "She designs book covers. She's very talented."

"Oh. Interesting." Damon peppers her with more questions, which Trinity nervously answers. I feel bad because I know how much she hates having the spotlight on her, but she *is* good at what she does. I glance at Wrath and smile, happy he seems to appreciate her and brags about her skill.

"She's a fantastic photographer too," I mention with a straight face.

Wrath glares at me.

"I dabble. Hope's exaggerating."

The rest of the afternoon goes pretty much the same. I'm happier than I remember being in a long time.

"What are you thinking about, Baby Doll?" Rock asks the next time we're alone.

"How happy I am." I wave my hand at the scene around us. "See everyone's mixing nicely."

"Yup. I take back anything I said otherwise."

After everyone gorges themselves on Trinity's amazing ice cream sandwiches, people start leaving. As Wrath predicted it's just Lost Kings left. Well Lilly's still here. Sitting in Z's lap. Even the sight of them together fills me with joy.

As the sun sets, the guys get a small fire going in the patio fire pit.

I raise an eyebrow at Wrath and the corner of his mouth lifts, so I know he's almost ready to present Trinity with her patch.

I'm so happy I could burst.

ROCK

Trinity left to go inside and clean up a while ago. "You ready?" I ask Wrath.

"Yeah. Just need to grab it. Can you two lure her out here?"

"Yup." Hope whips out her cell phone and taps out a text to Trinity. Wrath and I both stare at her. "What? I don't want to miss anything."

Wrath grins and stalks off.

"As soon as that's done. We need to go home," I explain, as I gather Hope in my arms.

"What's wrong?"

I press her tighter against me, so she can *feel* what's wrong. "I'm so fucking hard for you it hurts."

"Aw." She snuggles and nuzzles against me, presses her lips against my neck and kisses her way to my ear. "Why don't I take care of you before we leave, Mr. President?"

Fuck yes.

I don't know what's gotten into her, but she nips my earlobe, licks and kisses my neck. It's almost dark, but there are still people all around us. Not that I plan to stop her.

"I can't wait to be your wife. I love you so much," she whispers in

my ear, right before sliding her hand down over my dick. Rubbing
back and forth, just enough to drive me nuts.

"Fuck," I breathe out. My fingers inch toward the hem of her dress,
touching her bare thighs. "Love you too, Hope."

"I've got very tiny panties on, and they are very damp right now,
Rochlan," she murmurs against my lips.

What the fuck's happening here?

Hope's not usually this forward, so the fact that I'm already eager
to fuck her and the way she's rubbing herself against me, has me ready
to blow in my jeans like a fuckin' teenager.

"Rock!" Wrath breaks into our sex-crazed bubble. Hope laughs as
she pulls away.

"What?" I snap.

"Cops pulled up out front."

"What?"

All playfulness vanishes from Hope's face. The fear in her eyes
infuriates me the most.

"What's wrong, Rock?" she asks.

"Nothing, babe. Neighbors probably complained about the noise
or fire or something."

I have to wait a few seconds before I can walk straight. "Stay here,
Baby Doll."

"Like hell."

"At least until we know what's going on."

Thankfully, she listens. I stride down the driveway with Wrath and
Bricks at my back. "What the fuck is it with cops crashing our
parties?" I toss out as we walk down.

Then I stop. There are two state troopers along with a local
Empire PD car blocking the driveway. This is much more than a
simple noise complaint.

"Can I help you?" I call out.

"Rochlan North?"

Cold fear slices through me, but I answer with complete calm
"Yeah."

The fucker actually touches his weapon.

This is bad. Whatever this is, it's *bad*.

"Hands where we can see them."

"Why?"

"We've got a warrant for your arrest."

Jesus Christ.

"For what?" Wrath snaps. His low deadly voice only triggers the cop to reach for his weapon again. "Don't," I mutter at Wrath. "Whatever it is. I'll be fine."

"Can I see it?" I keep my hands stretched out in as non-threatening a gesture as I can come up with, still hoping this is a mistake.

"You two need to step back," the taller trooper says to Wrath and Bricks.

"Like fuck," Bricks snaps. "You're trespassing."

"We have a warrant, asshole. Now shut the fuck up and step back."

"Guys, it's fine. Back up." My heart's hammering like crazy, but I don't want to show any fear in front of the cops or my brothers. We've been through whatever this is before, we'll get through it again. It's New York State Troopers, not ATF or FBI, so our grow operation is probably fine.

I go over the list of crimes I've committed in the last few years, and it's a surprisingly long one for an outlaw who keeps trying to live as close to the right side of the law as my world allows.

"Walk down a little farther, hands up, sir."

Everything in me wants to tell them to fuck off. Thank fuck, the rational part of me is in control. Fighting this will only make it worse in the end. I'm maybe three feet away from them when the youngest-looking trooper lunges at me, tackling me to the ground. "I was doing what you asked," I grunt out.

Most men, I suppose would be scared shitless. And I won't lie, I'm unnerved. But above all else I'm *pissed* and I'm worried about Hope.

As if she heard me, she comes running down the driveway. "Rock!? Oh my God. What's going on?"

Shit.

"Are you at least going to let me see the warrant?" I ask with a civility I'm not really feeling at the moment.

The little fuck lifts himself off my back, only to slap cuffs on me. That's when I panic. I can't leave Hope unprotected. This is starting to feel like a set-up. Although we've had peace with the other clubs in the area, that last meeting I had with Ransom isn't sitting well right now. They've never used police to do their dirty work before, but there's a first time for everything. Even for that worthless crew. If I'm locked up, they might decide it's a good time to come after her.

The officer cinches the cuffs tight around my wrists and I wince as he lifts me off the ground. There's no hiding the pain of my skin mercilessly scraping against the unforgiving metal or the way my teeth rattle when he slams me up against the car.

"Go inside, Hope," I gasp out. This is the last image I ever wanted in her head.

Of course she ignores me. "Officer, you're mistaken. You can't—"

"Miss, we have a warrant." At least the tone they use with her is respectful.

"Let me see it."

"What are you his lawyer?"

Even with my face mashed up against the cold metal of the trooper's car, Hope's in my line of sight. I should've known better. She won't leave. No, instead my girl straightens up and nails the cops with her tough-girl, lawyer face. "I'm a lawyer, yes. I'm also his fiancée, and you're interrupting our engagement party."

The pig can't meet her stare. "It's all in here." He hands over the warrant and Hope immediately flips through the pages. Right away I know it's bad. "Jesus Christ," she whispers. She sways backwards. Her eyes meet mine, wide and scared. The raw grief on her face cuts worse than the metal digging into my wrists.

"Don't say anything, Rock," she warns me as one of the cops starts reading me my rights. Some form of a smile pulls my mouth up. "I know."

Christ, her big green eyes shining with terror are all I can see. "I can't do this," she says.

The way she's struggling to stay calm even though horror is clearly written over her face, shreds my insides. "I know, Baby Doll. It's okay. Call Glassman," I reassure her as smoothly as possible.

Wrath moves in behind her, settling his hands on her shoulders. My brother nods as if he already knows the thought forming on my tongue. "Keep her safe," I order anyway.

One of the officers pats me down. "Weapons?"

"No."

He yanks my keys and cell phone out of my pocket and turns to Hope. "Miss, you want to take these?" One of the other officers steps between us, stopping her from getting too close, and hands over my stuff.

"Where are you taking him, officer?"

Piece of shit hesitates before answering. It's not a complicated question. "You can't ride with us, Miss."

"No kidding," Hope snaps. "He needs counsel present, and right now, that's me."

Absolutely fucking not.

Faced with the thought of her following me to the police station, I manage to find my presidential voice. "Take her home, Wrath."

The cop at my back presses his hand against my shoulder blades. "Shut up."

Hope, whips open my cell phone and takes a picture. "I know exactly what condition he left in, officers. He better arrive at the station the same way," she warns before slipping my phone into her pocket. I both love and want to strangle her at the same time. Wrath wraps his hand around her arm. "Come on, Hope."

She attempts to shake him off. "No. Where are you taking him?"

One of the other troopers rounds the car. "Barracks. You can meet us there."

"Could you be more specific?" my courageous little spitfire snaps. Under any other circumstance, I might laugh at the way she's so brazen with six armed officers.

They ignore her. Someone grips my arm and shoves me into the back seat.

As if I'd been watching this scene unfold from above, my body jolts and panic grips me. This is it. I struggle to draw in a breath. This is really happening.

"Take care of her. Do *not* let her out of your sight," I choke out with a lot more calm than I'm feeling inside. Wrath nods and pulls my girl back. Those are the last words I'm able to get out before the door slams in my face. No chance to reassure Hope. Tell her how fucking much I love her. Beg her to go home and do what Wrath asks her to do so I know she's safe.

I have to twist to see out the window. Catch sight of her as she falls back against Wrath and he holds her up. "It's gonna be okay, baby. You'll be okay," I whisper to myself.

Trinity and Z form a circle around her. I'm absolutely gutted leaving her this way. The pain in my arms and shoulders is nothing compared to the wrenching in my chest.

My eyes close and I struggle to take deep breaths. She'll be taken care of. The brotherhood we've worked so hard to create is solid. She won't be alone. I have to assure myself she's taken care of before I can even deal with the bullshit I'm about to drown in.

Fuck. Even though I trust every one of my brothers, cold sweat and fear crawl over my skin. Whatever this nightmare I've walked into turns out to be, it means I'm leaving my girl alone.

In an instant my life's been ripped out of my control. Hope's become the most precious thing in my life and now I have to trust her safety to others.

CHAPTER EIGHT

WRATH

I CAN'T BELIEVE this is actually happening. A few seconds ago I was about to finally put my property patch on my girl. Instead I'm watching my best friend get shoved into the back of a police car and driven away.

In my hands Hope's shaking so hard, her teeth click.

"Take care of her. Do not let her out of your sight."

I have my orders from my president and I plan to follow them. Getting Rock out of jail and keeping everyone safe are my only two objectives from now on.

The papers in Hope's hands flutter as she starts to break down.

She turns and buries her face against my chest.

I don't know what to do to comfort her, so I rub my hand over her back. "It's gonna be okay, Hope. Good girl, keeping it together. It'd drive him crazy if the last thing he saw was you crying."

My words must flip some internal switch for her. She pulls away, staring up at me. "We have to go." Her voice comes out clear and determined. She may be falling apart on the inside, but outside, she's icy calm.

"Call Glassman," she orders Z.

"Already on it," he answers as he walks up toward the house, Trinity following behind.

My hands squeeze her shoulders. "Hope, I need to get you home."

"Like fuck," she snaps. Pulling out of my grasp, she marches over to the Empire PD car still blocking the driveway.

"Where are they taking him?" she demands.

The cops feed her a line of bullshit and she argues with them for a minute before turning her attention toward Rock's car.

Fuck no.

Her intention's obvious. She places her hand over her pocket and storms up the driveway. I race over the grass to catch up. I must sound like a bull bearing down on her because she breaks into a run. She's in the driver's seat of Rock's SUV, adjusting the seat, before I reach her. I narrowly miss getting my fingers caught in the door when I jerk it out of her hand.

"Out."

Son of a bitch, if she doesn't jab the key in the ignition and turn it over.

"That's a fucking *murder indictment* they handed me. He needs a lawyer, and until you find Glassman and get his ass down there, it's *me*. So either get in or get out of my way, Wrath."

Fuck! "Move over. I'll drive."

"I'm not falling for that." She slams the car into gear. "In or out, Wrath?"

"Godfuckingdammit! Z get over here!"

I don't even have to explain myself. He's at my side, throwing open the back door and sliding in. "Murphy, get the girls home. Get everyone to the clubhouse," I shout while I round the front of the vehicle and jump in on the other side. My door's not even closed before Hope takes off.

"Uh, Hope, are you planning to ram the cop car?" Z asks.

By the expressions on their useless, donut-munching faces, the cops're wondering the same thing.

"Nope," she says and jerks the steering wheel to the left, driving over the lawn.

"Sorry, Bricks," she mutters as she plows through the ornamental bushes Bricks recently planted around the mailbox.

"They said barracks, but there are three fucking trooper barracks between here and Slater County Jail," she says.

If she wasn't frustrating the fuck out of me by not listening, I'd be proud as hell at her determination to get to her man. "Why Slater?"

She tosses the indictment at me. "That's what the caption says. The warrant's out of Slater County."

Z curses.

"Slow down, Hope," I caution. She doesn't answer, but she eases off the gas.

"I'll start with Scotland Ave. It's closest."

Rock's not there. Of course the cops are completely useless and pretend to have no idea what we're talking about.

Hope slams out through the front door, back into the parking lot. "Shit!" She turns to us. "I don't know if we should wait here or try another one."

Shaking my head, I grab her hand to keep her still. "Hope, I have to get you home."

Z's phone stops us from arguing. "It's Glassman."

He answers the phone, while Hope motions for him to hand it over. Her gaze darts between me and the car before finally landing on me. She motions for me to get in the driver's seat, but still won't give me the God damned keys.

Any minute Hope will collapse into tears or something, right?

Nope. She's all business as she takes the phone out of Z's hand.

"Mr. Glassman, this is Hope Kendall. We met at a CLE a few years back. I'm Rock's fiancée." She pauses while I guess Glassman is absorbing the fact that one of his best clients is marrying a lawyer. If the situation weren't so dire, I'd laugh.

After the introductions, she fires off a bunch of details at the club's lawyer. "It's a two-count indictment. Slater County, but troopers and Empire PD showed up."

Slater County. Wolf Knights territory.

"Murder two...I don't know. Grand Jury. Sealed. No, there's a witness. No, the name is sealed...Yes, but not until closer to trial."

Witness. No fucking way.

"An Isaac 'Cabo' Cruz...No, I have no idea. They give a time frame, so I don't know...No...I'm not...Mr. Glassman, I'm not a criminal attorney...Not something of this magnitude...Okay. Whatever you need. I'll bring you a retainer right now if you...Good. Will you go find him? Arraign...forty-eight...no... Bail? Murder two. Unlikely, no?"

She's silent listening to whatever Glassman has to say.

"We already tried the Scotland Ave. barracks. He wasn't there and no one would tell us anything." I can't hear the exact words, but from the tone of his voice, Glassman's pretty pissed. While she's distracted, I ease the keys out of her hands.

"That's fine. Rock wanted us to go home. So if you're going to track him down now, that's what I'll do. But call us as soon as you hear something."

Thank fucking fuck.

"And, Mr. Glassman, I want you to understand something, Rock and I *will* be getting married in a few months. I *won't* be doing it inside a jail. No falling through the cracks on this. If your calendar's full, pull in other associates to help you. No matter how scary you think Rock and his brothers are, I'll be your worst nightmare. Do we understand each other?"

I don't think I've ever been prouder.

ROCK

Guilt worms through my stomach as I keep picturing Hope's anxious face over and over. We're driving who-the-fuck-knows-where. The officers won't say a fucking word.

Over their radio a call comes in. "The girlfriend's throwing a fit—"

One of the officers turns the volume down and murmurs into the radio low enough that I can't make out every word. The few words I can decipher sound like Hope took off after me.

Any other time, I'd shake my head, imagining Wrath's agitation. Now, the apprehension in my gut intensifies. I want her at the clubhouse where she's safe, not running around Empire searching for me.

We end up driving for much longer than seems necessary. Eventually, they take me to a trooper barracks for questioning.

A bunch of photographs of the same dead, bloated body are thrown in front of me.

Jesus Christ. It's a battle to keep my face neutral.

"I'd like to call my lawyer now."

"Yeah, we'll get you a call in a minute." The officer keeps lining up photos. "Isaac 'Cabo' Cruz? Ring a bell?"

Actually, no it doesn't.

And then it does. I lean over and take another look at one of the photos. *There.* The body's decomposed but I can make out the edge of a Vipers tat.

Motherfucking Ulfric.

"No," I answer in the most bored tone I can come up with. This is going to shit real fucking fast. While I know Hope has always said not to say a word to the cops, it's harder than it sounds and "no" seems pretty harmless.

"You sure? He's one of your Viper buddies. Oh, wait. You're not buddies at all. Your gangs are at war all the time."

"You watch too much television."

"Yeah. Yeah. I know. You're just president of a *club*. A club full of honest, misunderstood, guys who happen to love motorcycles."

I fake an *aw, shucks* smile and shrug.

"Well, sorry, prez. We've got an eye witness who saw you with the victim right around the time the ME guesses he went in the water."

Now I'm pissed. "You got me down here on a motherfuckin' guess?"

See, this is a problem if they can't give me a narrower time frame. I know *exactly* when Ulfric murdered Cabo and carelessly dumped his body in the Hudson River. The first night Hope spent with me. She—and my entire club—are my alibi. But how the fuck do I know when he died, unless I was involved with his death?

Which technically I wasn't.

I found out about the murder a day later. Didn't give a single fuck about it. Still don't. Except that my freedom's at stake over it. Not that I'd rat Ulfric out. That's just not what we do. I could choke the life out of the sloppy fuck right now, but I won't speak his name to the cops.

Even though I'm sitting here for a murder I didn't commit.

Cabo's brother on the other hand. No one's ever finding *that* body. I'd laugh at the irony of the whole fucking mess if I could.

This supposed eyewitness is a problem though. I never even met Cabo. Ulfric and I look nothing alike. So either someone's confused or someone's lying and setting me up.

That's a big fucking problem.

"Members of his club say Cabo made the trip up here specifically to see you about the disappearance of his brother. You wouldn't know anything about that, would you?"

Inside, fear rattles me down to my bones. A murder conviction. A long stretch of prison time. On the outside, I execute another careless shrug

"Keep shrugging at me, asshole."

"Can I call my lawyer now?"

CHAPTER NINE

WRATH

HOPE'S COURAGE IS SHORT-LIVED. When we get to the clubhouse, she's as limp as a wet noodle. Z and I have to help her upstairs.

"Call me if you hear something, no matter what," she whispers before closing the door.

"This is so fucked," Z says as we head to the war room.

Within the next hour, everyone's assembled in the war room. Not sure what we're dealing with, Bricks brought Winter and their kids to the clubhouse. Teller brought Heidi. Dex brought up Swan and a few other girls who are known to associate with us.

It's a full house and it's somber as fuck with everyone worried about Rock.

Trinity takes care of finding rooms for our extra guests. She also explains to the girls to keep tits and ass covered at all times in all common areas, since there're kids here.

"Swan won't be a problem. The other two should be fine too," she assures me as I place a kiss on her forehead.

"You okay?"

"No. Not at all. Should I go check on Hope?"

Fuck. I don't fuckin' know. Part of me doesn't like leaving her alone at a time like this, part of me thinks that's probably what she wants right now.

"Go up and knock. See if she's okay. We're gonna be at the table for a few."

Z's phone goes off as soon as we all sit at the table. "Glassman."

"Answer it."

Murphy offers to go grab Hope.

Z sets the phone in the middle of the table and puts it on speaker. "Who am I talking to?" Glassman asks.

I'm the one who answers. "The whole club."

Glassman mutters and curses and I know he's pissed about confidentiality bullshit. But I don't fuckin' care right now.

"Look, I just wanted to update you. I can't find him. They haven't brought him in to Slater County for processing yet. Best guess is he's at one of the trooper barracks."

"Motherfucks!" Z slams his fist into the table.

"There are at least three stations they could have taken him to between his house and Slater County jail. I'll try Scotland Ave. again."

"What the fuck?" I grumble. This is a nightmare.

"He's probably being questioned. But he knows better than to talk without me there. My guess is they're dragging their heels in letting him have his phone call."

Murphy leads Hope in and I point for her to sit in Rock's chair.

"Can they do that?" I ask.

"It's the cops. They'll do whatever the fuck they want," Glassman answers.

I risk a glance at Hope. Her eyes are dry, but her jaw's tight, cheeks red and she's the one who looks ready to commit murder.

"It's Hope, Mr. Glassman. Will you continue looking for him?"

"Yes. I've got myself and one of my associates trying to track him down. Rock knows my cell number. Honestly, Hope, there's nothing you can do right now. Try to get some rest. I might need you to come down and post bail first thing in the morning."

"You think they'll give him bail?"

"I don't know. But I'll fight for it."

"Make sure you do."

HOPE

Get some rest my ass. How the hell am I supposed to sleep or even breathe without Rock next to me? Without knowing where he is? If he's okay? Harsh sobs tear out of my chest as soon as I'm in our room alone. This time there's no one there to keep me upright, and I slide down until my ass hits the floor and bawl.

What am I going to do? Is Rock okay? I should be out trying to find him, but Wrath made it clear leaving the clubhouse isn't an option. Wrath took control, barking out orders to everyone left and right. Z handled everything else. All this time, I never thought to ask Rock who'd be left in charge if he—

More tears flow down my cheeks. The thought of sleeping in our bed alone rips me to shreds. My heart splinters at the memory of his wrists bound behind his back as he's shoved into the police car.

In the hallway I hear some of the guys. I concentrate on breathing deep and drying my face. Crying won't get Rock out of jail. From now until he's home with me, that's all I plan to focus on.

While I was downstairs, I scanned in a copy of the indictment and sent it to Glassman's office. I left a copy with the guys and stuffed my copy in my pocket. Now, I slide it out, unfold it and study the words until they make sense.

Some guy—Cabo. Pulled out of the Hudson River weeks ago. A witness came forward, swears they saw Rock with the victim around the time the medical examiner estimates the body was dumped in the river.

What kind of crap is this?

A sketchy eyewitness and a medical examiner's *guess*. Are they kidding?

Part of the reason I'm disillusioned with the law is that it's not always applied fairly or correctly. Yes, in theory I think we have one of the best criminal justice systems in the world. But mistakes happen and innocent people go to prison all the time. I'll be dammed if Rock's one of those statistics.

If he's innocent.

Oh, yes. That thought's been bothering me the most. Rock's outright admitted to me that he's killed rival club members to keep me safe. I don't know if this Cabo guy is one of them.

Surprisingly, it doesn't matter to me. From what I've gathered from Rock and the things I've learned from Trinity, the Vipers are not bikers I would have wanted knocking on my door. Rock is *not* some monster. He wouldn't have taken such an extreme measure if he didn't legitimately believe I was in danger.

I know that deep in my soul.

That's why I'll do everything I can to get him out and clear of these charges. Maybe he's done bad things, but he's a good man. He brought me back to life after Clay died. He's been so patient and understanding with me. Accepted all of me—flaws and everything. He fought his brothers' doubts to give me a place within his family—the club. He's given me love unlike anything I've ever known.

He once put his life and liberty at risk for my safety.

Now it's my turn.

I pull myself off the floor and stagger over to the bed.

Getting my man home and back in my arms is all that matters.

CHAPTER TEN

HOPE

IT TOOK TWO DAYS.

Two days before we located Rock. At Slater County Jail.

At his arraignment, the judge refused to grant bail. Not even some ridiculously high number.

We're requesting a new bail hearing. But it will take time.

More time with Rock being locked up.

And if the next hearing is in front of the same judge, no matter how hard we argue, he'll probably be denied again.

I'm absolutely hollow inside without Rock.

The club's in chaos. Not knowing what to expect, we're all keeping tight to the clubhouse. That means we're all starting to wear on each other's nerves. Rock truly is the anchor that keeps everyone grounded. The glue that holds us all together.

Today's the first day Wrath let me leave the property. Even *on* the property he and Z are so far up my butt, I taste leather on my tongue.

I can finally see Rock today. Wrath and I may have clashed a few times over the last couple days, but he knew better than to mess with me on this one.

I'm ready to bite his head off when he takes me aside before we walk inside the county jail. Only the concerned look on his face stops me.

"Listen to me, Hope. You ever visited a loved one in lock up before?"

"No."

"It ain't pretty. But you need to keep it together."

My eyes widen while I wait for him to continue. He shakes his head. "I know how much you fuckin' love him and I swear we are doing everything we can to beat this bullshit and get him out. But you want him to stay whole inside, you need to keep it together while we're visiting him. He sees you cry or get upset, it'll fuck with his head."

Suddenly I'm terrified. I don't want to do anything to make Rock worry. "Okay."

He nods once. "You can do it. Pretend you're seeing a client. Show him that pretty smile he loves so much, okay?"

"Yes."

"Good girl. Let's go see your man."

I'm actually grateful for Wrath's warning.

"Thank you," I say when he opens the door for me. I stop inside and tap his chest. "For everything. Thank you."

He flashes a tight smile, but the hard glint in his eyes softens.

Slater County Jail is a little more intense than the one in Empire I visited a couple years ago to see a client. The twenty-foot high chain-link fence sports rows of barbed wire at the top.

We're allowed in the front door and immediately ushered to the visitor's check-in window. We decided to play this like I was part of Rock's legal team, so I'm dressed in a suit and carrying my briefcase. Wrath's dressed plainly, but given his size, and angry indifference, he still looks pretty suspicious. The guards go through everything in my briefcase and give me a skeptical look when I say Wrath is my assistant. It's not really a lie. I don't know what I'd do without his assistance today.

We're finally led into a small room with a table and four chairs.

The guards bring Rock in but leave him cuffed. He nods at us. I sink my teeth into my bottom lip to stop myself from crying. The guard tells me to tap on the door when we're through and closes it behind him.

"Hey, baby," Rock says softly.

"Hey, handsome. You're pretty sexy in orange. You know that's the color you were wearing the day we met?"

Rock snorts and one corner of his mouth lifts up in wry sort of smile.

"You okay?" he asks.

I bob my head once, because I can't open my mouth and lie to him. I'm not okay at all. I won't be okay until he's home.

"You all right, brother?" Wrath asks.

"Yeah. County ain't nothin'. Like a fuckin' boring vacation, really. Almost got a whole wing to myself."

Inside I sigh in relief. My biggest fear had been him getting hurt by an enemy of the Lost Kings.

"Good," Wrath says, echoing my thoughts.

Leaning closer, Rock gets down to business. "Glassman is working on shit. He can't get a read on the DA though. Hope, I need you to give Tony Cain a courtesy call. Lawyer to lawyer. Are you okay with that?"

My fingertips brush the back of his hand. "I'll do anything for you, Rock," I whisper. "Just like chess, the queen always protects her king."

His throat works for a few seconds before the corners of his mouth twitch up. "Thank you, Baby Doll. Make sure you tell him you're my fiancée."

"Okay. Is there anything else I can do?"

"No. I'm sure he already knows but reach out to him for me, okay?"

"Of course."

He lifts his chin at Wrath. "Talk to U?"

Wrath shoots a look at me and Rock shakes his head. "Doesn't really matter at this point, brother."

"Yeah," Wrath says, "he's fuckin' livid. Got no fuckin' idea how this happened."

"You buyin' it?"

Wrath seems to think it over before answering Rock's question. "Yeah. I do. We've known him a long time. He's got no reason to fuck us like this."

Rock nods. "Gotta be Viper."

"Fuckin' bitch move."

"Amen." Rock glances at me again and smiles. "Miss you, Baby Doll."

My breath catches in my throat, my chest tightens, but I force my mouth to smile. "Miss you too," I whisper.

"We're working on putting CB up for bail, so if the judge sets an amount we can get you out right away," Wrath says, surprising me. I didn't know they were doing that.

Rock shakes his head. "Don't. It's too big an income stream. Besides, they ain't gonna give me anything less than a couple mil."

We talk a little longer. The whole visit is killing me.

"I'll be home soon, Baby Doll. In time for our wedding."

I almost lose it at that point. I'm trying so hard to follow Wrath's orders and be strong. But those words are almost my undoing.

"You sticking close to the clubhouse?"

Wrath answers before I even open my mouth. "Don't worry, Rock. She ain't going anywhere alone. Either me or Z are with her at all times."

"Good. Thank you."

I risk giving Rock a quick hug before we leave, even knowing that the room is being monitored. I don't care. I need to touch him and reassure myself that he's okay.

When we finally get outside, the sunlight stabs me in the eyes and the thin veneer of calm I'd been hanging on to vanishes. Deep, ragged sobs tear out of me and my knees go weak. Wrath catches me with an arm around my waist and pulls me to him. Wrapping me in his big arms, he rubs my back and makes *shhhh* noises at me.

"It's okay, sweetheart. You did real good."

Still keeping me close, he walks us to his truck and helps me inside. Hugging my knees, I press my face into my lap and sob so hard it hurts.

I don't even hear Wrath get in, but suddenly he's right next to me, rubbing my back and reassuring me.

"Let it out. You did good, Hope. You did good. That's what he needed. I know it was hard."

"I hate seeing him like that."

"I know. Me too."

"It's not fair."

He snorts. "No, it's really not."

Something about his words make my head snap up and I pin him with a hard stare. "Tell me the truth. Don't hide behind club business, now. Did he do it?"

Wrath doesn't hesitate. "No. I'm not going to lie and say we ain't done plenty of bad shit. But this, he had no part of."

"You know who did do it though, don't you?"

"I can take a guess."

"Someone outside of LOKI?"

He seems to sense where I'm going with this. "Yes. But we don't snitch. We'll figure out another way, I promise."

"Wrath, it could be years until he goes to trial."

"Babe, it's not going to go that far, I promise. We're gonna figure it out. You need to do your part and call Tony when we get back to the house, okay?"

"Of course I will. I just don't understand. Rock's always saying because of his club role, he has connections and—"

"Honey, it's one thing to look away when we're moving a truckload of weed through Empire county. An entirely different thing to look the other way on murder when they've been offered manufactured evidence up on a silver platter."

I can't argue with that logic. "Let's go."

WRATH

I'm torn. Struggling to stay fuckin' sane. Seeing my best friend behind bars has me ready to fuckin' murder.

Poor Hope. Knowing I need to keep her from falling apart is oddly the only thing keeping me together.

Never woulda thought she could survive this shit when I first met her. And that's why I think we've been rubbing each other raw the last few days.

But she's stayed strong. She's stayed focused. Heard what I said to her before we went in and took it to heart.

I'm not dumb enough to think Rock was fooled for a second. But the fact that she kept it together for his sake means something.

"You gonna be able to call Tony?" I ask her once we're on the road. She's stopped crying and put herself together.

"Yeah."

I glance over at her, but she's busy staring out the window.

This is awkward, because I'm not touchy-feely. Hope knows that. I don't think she expects different from me.

Even so, I reach out and pat her leg. "It's gonna be okay, sugar. I promise."

She sniffles. "I know."

Good.

She's quiet the rest of the drive, but there're no more tears. When we get to the clubhouse, she's slow to get out of the truck. I help her down and she shuffles into the house.

Z greets us at the door. "How'd it go?" He directs his question to me, but holds out his hand to stop Hope.

"Fine. He looks good."

Z puts his hand on Hope's shoulder. "You okay, sweetheart?"

"Yeah."

"She did good," I tell Z.

He grins and pulls Hope in for a hug. "Of course she did." Over her shoulder he quirks an eyebrow at me and I shrug. Yeah, she did better than I expected.

Drawing back from Z, she glances at me. "I better make that call."

Z looks at me for an explanation.

"Rock wants her to reach out to Tony Cain." Since Tony has held a number of important government jobs, he and Rock keep their connection quiet. None of us have ever spoken to the guy.

With a hand on her back, Z ushers Hope into the office we share with Rock. "Take Rock's desk."

I shoot him a dirty look and he shrugs.

Hope doesn't seem to mind. She drops into his chair and her demeanor completely changes.

"Do you want us to leave?" I ask.

She seems startled by the question. "No. Of course not. But you can both stop hovering over me."

Z and I both burst out laughing. Some of the tension eases for all of us. She flashes a quick smile and fires up Rock's computer. It's doubtful there's anything top secret on it and as Rock said, it doesn't really matter at this point.

She looks up a few things, jots down a bunch of notes and stares at the phone for a few seconds before picking it up.

Z and I end up staring at each other, so we're not making her nervous while she's on the phone. I've got to give the girl credit, she's brisk, business-like and unemotional the entire time she's speaking to Tony. Lawyer-like. Seeing her so soft around Rock all the time has made me forget she can be a hard-ass in her own world when she needs to be.

"Yes, I can arrange that. How do you want me to get you the number?" She pauses. "No. That's not a problem. Is tomorrow afternoon okay?" She jots down more notes and taps the pen against desk.

When she hangs up, she spins the chair around to face us. Her eyes narrow as she seems to be thinking how to word what she has to tell us. "Can you guys obtain a burner phone for me?"

Z's quick to answer. "Yeah, no problem."

"Good. He wants me to email him the number tomorrow." She rolls her eyes and shrugs. "Is that weird? I have no idea, so I just said it was fine."

"No. He's cagey. It makes sense," Z says. "Anything else?"

She shakes her head. "He's upset. Said he'll do whatever he can to help Rock. He says he has some connections in Slater County." Cocking her head to the side, her gaze slides between the two of us. "What exactly *is* their connection? Rock told me once they grew up near each other."

Z takes her question. "As far as I know, they lived in the same neighborhood and were real tight. When Rock had to get out of his dad's house, I think he lived with Tony for a while. Then they sort of went in opposite directions."

Hope snorts. Opposite directions is an understatement. She raises an eyebrow for Z to finish.

"That's about all I know. They stay in touch. Tony feels like he owes Rock, but Rock doesn't ever impose on him unless he really needs to."

She seems to think that over, but before she gets out any follow-up questions, Trinity stops by. "Hey," she says from the doorway. "How'd it go?"

I motion for her to come in and she wraps her arm around Hope's shoulders. "Is Rock okay?"

Hope squeezes Trinity back and nods. "I think so."

Trinity meets my eyes. I give her a subtle signal and she turns back to Hope. "Want to come help me with a project?"

"Sure." Hope looks to us. "Do you guys need me?"

"Nah, go ahead."

Hope shuts the door behind them and Z throws himself back against his chair, stretching his legs out, crossing them at the ankles. "Tell me straight."

"It was fine. She was chin-up while we were visiting him. Broke down afterward in the parking lot." I shrug.

"She gonna be able to make it through this?"

I give it some serious thought before answering. "After today? Yeah, I think so. She's tougher than we give her credit for."

"Yeah, okay. Long term though? Think she'll stick it out?"

"Why're you going worst-case-scenario?"

"You were there, brother. That shit Carla pulled was hard for him

104

to swallow. I don't think he felt a tenth of what he's got for Hope, for that bitch. Hope leaves, I think it would break him."

"Rock doesn't break. He would be a miserable bastard though."

Z snorts and sits up. "Yeah."

"Let's stay positive, bro."

Z smirks. "You dishing out feel-good advice is fucking unnatural."

"Fuck off."

"That's more like it."

Despite the joking around, now I've got another thing to worry about.

ROCK

The guard who leads me back to my cell is a decent guy. I don't think he's been a guard for very long. He follows all the protocols to the letter, but he doesn't improvise or get creative. He's not a sadistic fuck, like the guard who comes in on the next shift.

Izzard. Hank Izzard. In my head he's *Lizard* 'cause he looks and acts like one. I haven't exactly decided on the right course of payback for this fuck yet.

If you think sitting in jail would have me re-examining my life choices and deciding to take the high road, you'd be wrong.

I'm on my back staring up at the ceiling. Picturing Hope. Felt so fucking good to see her.

Felt unbelievably fucking awful to watch her go.

At least I know Wrath and the rest of my brothers are taking good care of her. My girl didn't fool me one bit. Her glossy eyes and trembling bottom lip gave her away. But she held it together and I know she did that for me. I'm fuckin' proud of her.

I hate myself for puttin' her through this shit. We've talked about what my lifestyle means. I know she's come to understand and accept the club. Doesn't make it any easier to know she's suffering over this bullshit.

There're a lot of people who are owed some payback over this bit of fuckery.

Ulfric. Known that fuck a long time. But he's gotten damn sloppy lately. Don't give a fuck when it affects his MC. When it interferes with my life. Takes my freedom away?

No. Something needs to be done about him too.

Maybe I'm rehashing all the people I need to get even with over this because there's one thought I keep pushing away. After seeing Hope, I can't help dwelling on it. As whatever *this* is drags on, can she hang in there? Is it even fair for me to expect her to?

Inside, I'm jittery as fuck. I work hard to control my breathing. In my head I'm pacing back and forth. I'm ripping the bars off the windows. And escaping. Outside, I'm calm. If it wasn't for my eyes staring up at the ceiling, you'd think I was asleep.

Izzard strolls up and taps his baton against the bars of my cell. Such a bad-guard cliché. I'm offended by his lack of originality.

"Heard you had some hot piece-of-ass lawyer visit you today, North."

I don't respond or react in any way. Not too long ago, I would have attempted to choke him through the bars for talking 'bout my woman like that. But I like to think I've grown older and wiser over the years.

"Funny, I think I ran into her when she was leaving. Had some big, blond dude all over her. Swear it looked like one of the guys in your crew, but that can't be right. She signed him in as her assistant."

He knows.

Fuck. The last thing Hope needs is to get in trouble. Because of our "gang association" Wrath probably wouldn't be allowed in to visit with me. To avoid that possibility, we decided he should come in with Hope as her assistant. They wouldn't dig as deep if he came in with a lawyer. Especially one who appeared as innocent as Hope. We've worked that angle with Glassman in the past. Now I'm rethinking the whole thing as far as Hope is concerned. Except, I can't let her run around unprotected. And I know it will hurt her if I tell her not to come visit me.

"Guy looked more like her boyfriend the way he had his hands all over her."

That finally gets my attention and I flick my gaze in Lizard's direction. Not for the reasons he's thinking though.

I trust Wrath with my life.

I trust Hope more than I trust anyone.

No fucking way is anything going on between them. It's not even a question in my mind.

The more likely scenario is that after seeing me in here—in my spiffy orange jumpsuit, and isn't that just some sort of full-circle irony bullshit—and putting on such a brave face for my benefit, she fucking lost her shit the minute they stepped outside.

I fuckin' hate that I did that to her.

"They finally moved their make-out session to his truck. Tinted windows—couldn't see much."

I contemplate the wisdom of asking Lizard if his son should grow up without a father. See, I've done my research on the asshole.

But I'm really not in the mood to take a beating right now. My ribs are still sore from the "conversation" I had with this asshole yesterday. Inside these walls, my options are limited. I fight back, I'll get time added or worse.

And I have a wedding I plan to be at in a few short months.

CHAPTER ELEVEN

HOPE

ANOTHER NIGHT AND NO SLEEP. Every time I close my eyes, shiny metal wrapped around Rock's wrists is all I see.

Wrath told me the guys are taking shifts patrolling the property. Keeping an eye on things.

I don't plan to go far when I open our door and step into the hallway. My bare feet make no sound as I creep down the hallway. At the top of the stairs, I catch the glow from the war room. Worried, something's wrong, I hurry down the stairs.

Wrath's in the war room by himself. In his chair. Staring at a stack of photographs. Nursing what looks like the bottle of scotch I bought Rock for his birthday.

"You can come in, Hope," he says without turning around.

"How'd you know it was me?"

"My job."

He still hasn't turned around, so I walk around the table until I'm facing him. He points to Rock's chair. "Sit."

"What's wrong?" he asks after I settle in to the big, leather "throne."

"I can't sleep."

"Yeah. Rough day."

"You?" I ask.

"Same."

I point to the bottle. "Are you drinking Rock's scotch?"

"*Yeahhhp.* Whiskey wasn't cuttin' it." He half-smiles and taps the bottle, making a muted clinking sound. "Last time we drank this together was the night he told me he was gonna marry you."

"Really?"

"Mmmhhmmm."

I nod at the photos. "What's that?"

He picks up the one on top of the stack and tosses in my direction. "Ancient history."

"Oh my gosh, is that—"

"Yup."

The photo's of a much-younger Rock, Wrath, Z and a guy I don't recognize.

"You're all so baby-faced and un-inked."

He snorts at my observation.

"Who's the fourth guy?"

"Lucky."

"Who—"

"Unluckiest bastard ever. That's how he got his road name." He tips his head down and meets my eyes. "Rock's never mentioned him?"

"No," I whisper. The air pulses around me heavy with whatever's on Wrath's mind tonight.

"They were friends when I met Rock. Hell, Lucky's probably the one who brought Rock to one of my fights."

I keep quiet because, except for bits and pieces this is the most I've heard about their shared past in a long time.

"When Rock found out I had nowhere to live, he invited me to stay with him. Granted, he wanted me to teach him how to fight. Didn't mean he had to give me a place to stay."

"Were he and Lucky roommates?"

"Nah. Rock doesn't share space well." He snorts. "Found that out *after* I moved in." He snickers at some private memory and I try to picture what they must have been like back then.

His face darkens and he takes another sip of scotch. "Rock got blamed for Lucky's death too," he says after a few minutes.

"Landon Michaels," I whisper.

Wrath sits up straighter. "How—"

"I had Rock's rap sheet when I represented him. Manslaughter. I always thought he must have been a rival, or it was an accident…I never asked for details…"

"It was no accident. And he was no rival. Our greedy fuck ex-president was responsible. Rock and Grinder went to prison for it."

"Who's Grinder?"

"Rock's mentor. He was the SAA."

"Where's he?"

"Prison."

"Oh. Rock never mentions him."

"It's…awkward. He went to see him not long ago." He waves his hand in the air. "When you two were on a break."

"Oh." I've got so many more questions. But Wrath seems to be getting agitated, so I wait to see if he'll speak again.

"Club's supposed to be a brotherhood. All seen each other at our worst. Doing our worst. Need to know they can keep their mouths shut. Have to be able to trust your brothers with your life. Literally."

"And you couldn't do that before?"

"No. This brotherhood's supposed to be about giving your brother half of what you have if he needs it. Ruger—that was the old prez—cared way more about lining his own fucking pockets."

Wow. The way he explains it makes me understand the guys' attitudes—the way they're always eager to help each other out, no matter what—so much better.

"Grinder wanted to change that. That's what attracted guys like him to this in the first place."

"Rock too, obviously."

"Yup. Brothers should always have each other's backs. Doesn't matter why. Doesn't matter if he's wrong, you defend him anyway."

"I'm surprised Ruger let Rock back in the club when he got out?"

"He didn't have a choice. Rock never lost his place here. It's the risk we all take. Club members suck it up and do their time. No bitching. No snitching. That's how it is. Everyone knew he didn't have shit to do with Lucky's death."

"What did you and Z do while he was away?"

"Bided our time and gathered information. Well, Teller and Murphy gathered information. Ruger just assumed they were dumb kids and he could mold them the way he wanted. But those two have never been stupid. They knew what their futures looked like if Ruger stayed in."

He glances down and flips through a bunch of photos, then flings one to me.

"Oh my. Oh my God! Is that Murphy?"

"Yup. Chubby little bastard, wasn't he?"

"Aw, he's so cute. He's so baby-faced." Dear God, Murphy's been part of the club in one way or another since he was a kid.

The next one he tosses to me has to be of Murphy and Teller.

"Where were these?"

"In Rock's cabinet." Wrath pulls out a set of keys from his pocket and dangles them in front of me. Rock's keys. I raise an eyebrow at him.

He lifts his shoulder. "He can kick my ass when he gets out if he wants."

The sound of the front door opening has me jumping out of my chair, but Wrath motions at me to sit back down. As I do, we hear someone punching the alarm code into the keypad.

Z pokes his head in the door and lifts his chin at me. "Everything okay?"

Correction, shirtless Z is in the doorway. He saunters in, rounds the table, patting me on the shoulder as he passes and drops into his seat.

"Christ, brother, put your fuckin' shirt on," Wrath mutters.

"Fucking hot out, dick."

"Everything okay?" I ask.

"Yup. Didn't see a single bear."

"What are you talking about? There's no bears up here."

"Uh, yeah there are, Hope."

"Jeez."

The two of them laugh at me. Jerks.

"Anyway, Murphy's finishing up his round. What are you two up to?"

I hand over one of the photos Wrath gave me earlier. Z cracks up. "Jesus. Where did you find these?"

"Rock's locker," Wrath answers.

Z nods as if that doesn't surprise him.

"So, Wrath must be in the mellow reminiscing stage of drunkenness. Don't let him drink much more, he's a nasty drunk, Hope."

"Fuck you."

"See?" Z snickers. He pushes out of the chair and jogs out into the common area.

Wrath holds the scotch out to me. "Want?"

"No, thanks."

He leans back in his chair, stretching his impossibly long body, to reach for a small refrigerator against the wall, and pulls out a bottle of water to hand me.

"Thanks," I say as I uncap it.

Z returns—completely dressed—carrying a small box.

"Wrath says you're a pro at this," Z teases as he rolls a joint and lights it.

"At rolling it or smoking it? Both are lies."

Wrath and Z both laugh at that.

Z rolls a second joint and hands it over. "I think you've earned your own."

"No kidding," I say through a mouthful of giggles.

We're quiet until I choke on a lungful of smoke.

Once I can breathe again, Z leans forward. "Can I ask you something, Hope?"

"Of course."

"That video you were sent. How come you were so positive it was old? It wasn't even a question in your mind."

A glance at Wrath shows he's interested in the answer too and my cheeks heat up under their scrutiny.

"I know him. Even before we were together I understood fidelity meant something to him." I inhale longer than necessary so I can think over how to explain it in a way that might make sense. When my lungs are screaming, I blow the smoke out and answer his question. "He told me what he did after my husband passed away. I don't know what the point of that would have been if he planned to cheat on me."

Wrath nods, but Z bursts with laughter. "He told you about his year of monkhood? Holy shit. We all thought he lost his fuckin' mind."

"He was gone over you from the day you met," Wrath says.

"I know," I answer quietly.

"Do you understand how rare that is in our world, Hope?" Z asks.

"What? A year without sex?"

He snorts. "Yeah, that too. No, committing to one woman. That's sort of the appeal of all of this." He throws his arms up in the air, indicating the whole clubhouse. "The free and easy sex."

"So I've gathered," I answer while rolling my eyes.

Wrath's watching Z closely and I'm not sure if he knows where his brother's going with this conversation. If he figures it out, I hope he clues me in.

"A lot of guys in the life will have a citizen wife, outside the MC. Never has anything to do with the club. Then he'll have an old lady or whatever muffler bunnies at the club."

Yuck. "So? Lots of men have mistresses on the side."

Z shakes his head. "It's different."

"What's your point?"

"Do I need to have one?"

"I think the deviant's point is that Rock really loves you," Trinity says from the doorway.

Z picks his head up and grins. "Exactly. Thank you, Trinity."

She steps in the room, shaking her head. "What are you guys all doing up so late?"

Wrath holds his hand out to her. As she comes closer, she takes it and he yanks her into his lap. "Why you up, angel?"

"I woke up, and you weren't there," she says softly.

He skims the back of his hand over her cheek. "Sorry."

They're so sweet together, my chest aches.

"Anyway, our old prez was one of the wife and mistress types. I think it always disgusted Rock," Z says.

"He doesn't really seem like he would interfere if that's what the guys want to do," I say.

Wrath shakes his head. "No. He wouldn't. It's not his place."

"You said you grew up in a club, Trinity. Was it like that?" I ask.

"Worse," is all she says.

Wrath tightens his hold on her.

"Carla cut him deep when she split while he was doing time," Z says.

"I know. When I met her down at Sway's place, she told me it was because she was scared."

Z and Wrath share a look. "Club was in a different place back then. As much as I hate to defend that skank, the club wouldn't have protected her," Wrath elaborates.

"Because she was already running around on him, or because of something else?" I ask.

"Because our old prez wouldn't have given two shits about someone's bitch. She would have had to earn her keep some other way," Wrath clarifies.

"Huh."

"I'm glad I met you guys after," Trinity says softly.

Wrath scowls at the table but doesn't answer.

Trinity turns to me. "The three of them were something else. I must have met you guys right after you got voted in."

Z and Wrath stare at each other briefly. "Yeah, right after," Z says slowly.

"First thing I did was tease them about how clean their patches were."

"Yes, she did," Z agrees affectionately.

"Then she blew me off," Wrath says with a smile.

"No, I didn't."

"Oh, *that's* right. She tricked me into giving her a ride," Wrath says with the first genuine smile I've seen all night.

Trinity laughs. "I hadn't been on a bike since I left home. I just wanted a ride." She glances at Wrath. "I got one."

Wrath squeezes her hip and kisses her cheek. "Yeah you did," he whispers in her ear.

I'm curious because it's not until recently that they seem to have made up. "Rock said it was partially his fault you guys didn't stay together…" I prod.

"Oh, that's not fair," Trinity says.

Wrath rolls his eyes. "He should have told me," he murmurs just loud enough for me to hear.

"That's not fair," Trinity protests again. "I begged him not to. Especially you."

Wrath growls and finishes his scotch. "Ancient history, babe. Forward not backward, right?"

She presses a kiss to his cheek. "Right."

Z glances over at me with a mixture of guilt and curiosity. "They both should have said something to someone," he says. Trinity and Wrath both stare at him and I decide it's a good time to keep my mouth shut.

"Anyway," Trinity says. "Rock was nice. Didn't talk to me like I was a T-bone steak."

Z throws his hand over his heart. "*I* was nice to you."

"True." She turns my way. "Then, I had some trouble and Wrath was out of town, so I called Rock—"

"Still wish you'd called me," Wrath growls.

Trinity's hand brushes his cheek. "I know. But you were gone. Anyway. I called Rock. I don't know what he was doing—"

"Probably getting head," Z interrupts.

All three of us scowl at him.

"Sorry," he says to me.

"Anyway, he didn't hesitate. He brought Dex and Teller and they got me the hell out of there. He gave me protection and shelter. Not many guys in this world, if any, would do that for some chick they barely knew. He could have... you know, said, sure we'll protect you if you blow me, but he *never* did. Instead, he told me to stay here. He didn't know me from—"

"Rock's always been able to read people well," Z says.

"Why you smoking up without me, bro?" Murphy calls out, then enters the war room. "Oh, hey. You're all up."

He takes the seat next to Z and grabs the joint from him. I hand Z mine. "I'm done."

Z flips one of the photographs to Murphy, who snorts. "Jesus Christ, why'd you show her this?"

"So she could see what a chubby little fuck you were until we got our hands on you," Wrath says.

"Dude, that sounds so gay," Murphy snaps back. "I was *husky*," Murphy says with false-indignation. "Not chubby." Murphy looks me in the eye. "I had to be resourceful. My mom was a fuckin' crackwhore, so I used to get all the neighborhood ladies to feed me."

"Obviously you made out well," Z says with a snicker.

"Fuck yeah, I did. Even Teller's grandmother would have me over for dinner, until we got in deeper with the club."

"What were you, bro, like twelve when you started comin' around the old clubhouse?" Wrath asks.

"I dunno. Probably."

"He used to follow Teller down on his little huffy," Z explains, while miming riding a bike.

Instead of being insulted, Murphy seems to enjoy when the guys pick on him.

"Rock saw his potential right away." Wrath points at Murphy. "Little fucker's always been talented with a wrench. He could fix anything you put in front of him."

Murphy sits up a little straighter and grins. "Remember that piece of shit Jeep I fixed up for Trin?"

Trinity snorts. "It was better than the beater I had. I loved that thing."

"Oh man, it was rough though. Rock used to give me projects like that all the time."

"Had to keep you out of trouble somehow," Wrath says

"True, I was a little asshole."

"What do you mean, *was*?" Z asks and punches Murphy's arm.

Murphy just laughs harder. "We'd never get away with that shit now. Rock doesn't let guys prospect 'til they're eighteen. Closest thing we've got are the kids at Wrath's gym."

That's news to me.

Wrath smirks at my raised eyebrow. "Didn't know I was kid-friendly, did ya?"

"Grinder would get a kick out of that," Z says.

"Aw fuck, I gotta go pay him a visit and let him know what's going on before he hears it from someone else," Murphy says. "Poor old guy was thrilled Rock came out to visit him a while back. This will crush him."

"When we were on a break?" I ask before they change subject. I can't help wondering why Rock's never mentioned his mentor and why he doesn't visit him more often.

"Which one?" Z snickers.

Wrath shoots him a dirty look. "Phone."

Pulling my legs up to my chest, I wrap my arms around them and prop my chin on my knees. The soft flannel of my pants feels good, and I must be high, because I end up rubbing my face over the material. "You guys must think I'm a real bitch, huh? Here's Rock's giving up all this free pussy and I'm giving him a hard time over a phone?"

Wrath laughs so hard he jostles Trinity around. "His own fucking fault."

Z bobs his head up and down. "We told him women like you—"

"What do you mean women like me?"

Trinity sits up watching Z intently and he falters. I think he realizes whatever he's about to say will insult one of us.

"What he means is, women who aren't familiar with MCs," Wrath explains.

Trinity pats him on the chest. "Oh, good save, Wrecking Ball."

"Thank you. Anyway, what was the conversation he had with you about the phone, Hope?"

"He didn't."

"Right." Wrath points at Z.

"Here's Hope's phone, install a tracking app for me," Z repeats.

Wrath nods. "You're a reasonable girl. All he had to do was explain—"

"Yes!" I say a little louder than I meant to. "Thank you."

Wrath turns to Trinity. "What did I say to you, babe?"

She grins. "Give Z your phone so he can stick a tracker in it, just in case, babe," she says in a lousy imitation of Wrath's deep rumbly voice.

"Exactly. Rock's conversation with you would have needed to be about five minutes longer." He holds up his hand, wiggling his fingers in the air to emphasize his point.

"Rock does what Rock thinks is best," Z says.

"And it gets his ass in trouble," Wrath snickers.

Trinity shakes her head. "You guys are mean."

Suddenly the conversation weighs on me. "Seems insignificant now. I'd let him stick a tracking collar around my *neck* this minute, if it meant he'd be home."

The guys stop and stare at me.

"For fuck's sake, Hope, don't give these cavemen any ideas," Trinity snaps.

WRATH

"Somehow, I missed all of that," Murphy says after we all stop laughing at the girls.

I have a sneaking suspicion I know the answer to my next

question, but curiosity forces me to ask anyway. "Hope, I gotta ask. How did you two end up resolving that?"

Z opens his mouth and I can see the "pussy whipped" comment forming so I cut him off. "I want to know if my guess is right."

Her cheeks turn pink and she glances away before answering. "Rock gave me the same thing."

I raise an eyebrow for her to add some detail.

"He gave me the same tracking app, but made me promise to never, ever come looking for him. If I was worried to let you guys know." Her big green eyes seem to plead with me not to be upset with her man. And I'm not. I understand why Rock would do something like that and trust his judgment.

Trinity sits up a little straighter. "Hey. Where's mine?"

"On your phone, angel. You should pay better attention."

She smacks her hand against my chest and settles back down, rubbing her forehead against my cheek.

Z's dying to bust on someone and since I ruined his fun, he turns his mischief-making face on Murphy. "Weren't we busting your balls?"

"Bust away, asshole."

Teller wanders in while we're still chuckling at Murphy's expense. He scrubs his hands over his face and looks us all over. "What the fuck you all doing up?"

"Pull up a chair." Z's laughing so hard he can barely get any words out. "We're filling first lady in on what a chubby little fucker Murphy was."

Teller snorts and pulls out the chair across from Murphy. His eyes go to me and Trin briefly, then Hope. "They're exaggerating, Hope. He was husky not chubby."

Everyone at the table bursts out laughing.

Hope giggles like a little girl and I'm glad we cheered her up, even if it's only for a few minutes. "Gosh, you two *are* brothers."

Teller and Murphy grin at each other. "Fuck yeah," Teller says. "I kept bitching at my mother to give me a little brother for years. When she got pregnant with Heidi, I was like what the fuck is this shit? I asked for a brother."

Murphy snorts and shakes his head. "What'd you want her to do, put an order in?"

"Dude, I was ten. What the fuck did I know? Anyway, there's this chubby little ginger getting the shit kicked out of him one day, so I wander over, beat the snot out of the two punks harassing him and found my own little brother."

"He told his mom that too," Murphy says.

"I did. I was like I got this. You can give Heidi back."

Hope's laughing so hard she almost falls out of Rock's chair. "Very proactive, Teller, I like that."

"Of course that's not what happened. And my mother was such a space cadet that I ended up taking care of Heidi more often than not, which meant Murphy did too."

Murphy nods. "Yeah, she was like the size of a loaf of bread the first time I ever saw her." Dumbass uses his hands to demonstrate something between the size of a football and bale of hay.

"Awww," Hope coos and I roll my eyes. She's such a softy.

"Christ, if I'd known she was gonna be such a holy terror, I would have insisted she give her back," Teller says affectionately.

I snort. "Please, you love that little brat."

"Of course I do."

"You've had a lot of responsibility since you were little." Hope looks at each of us. "You all have."

"That's how I started doing jobs for the club. Rock would pay me to run stupid errands and stuff. I needed money for shit for Heidi or whatever, and he'd always have something for me to do."

"And you were always trying to talk him into letting you take his—"

Teller cuts Z off with an excited head shake. "Hope, he had this classic kickstart '76 Super Glide. Rock's rule was—"

Murphy groans, but the two of them say it together. "If you can't kickstart your bike, you're not allowed to ride it."

I doubt Hope knows what to make of any of it, but she's smiling as she listens to the two of them reminisce. "What happened to it?" she finally asks.

Teller flicks his gaze at me, unsure of how to answer. "Carla sold it behind his back when he went inside," I end up explaining.

"Oh. He told me she sold it. I didn't realize it had been a classic—"

"Wasn't worth shit," Z interrupts. "Mid-AMF years. It was more sentimental value. Rebuilt that Shovelhead himself and worked on every inch of that ride."

Teller groans. "I spent a lot of afternoons fetching him all the shit for that rebuild."

Z snorts. "Teller wouldn't take charity, even when he actually needed it. Preferred to earn every penny."

"Nothing wrong with that," I add.

"It's an attractive quality in a man," Hope says and we all turn our heads her way. "What? It is."

Trinity yawns and pushes herself upright. "Not if they work so much they have no time for you."

"Trying to tell me something, Angel Face?"

She settles back down, laying her cheek against my shoulder and squeezes her arms around me. "Nope."

Z shrugs. "None of us are slouches. Fuck, I was working for my dad's landscaping company when I was shorter than the fucking mowers he had me pushing."

"Jeez, really?" Hope asks with wide eyes. I know Rock's told me she had it tough growing up too, but sometimes she really does give off a pampered princess vibe.

"Fuck, yeah," Z answers. He opens his mouth to say something else, then shakes his head.

Hope hums an affirmative sound and by the way her eyelids keep drooping, it seems all the wrench talk is about to put her to sleep.

"Wanna go upstairs, Hope?" I ask.

"No, I like listening to you guys. Keep talking."

Across the table, Z's watching her doze off with a smile on his face. In my lap, Trinity's half-asleep herself.

When it looks like the girls are out, I lift my chin at Murphy. "Everything okay on your rounds?"

"Yeah. All good. Z changed the code for the front gate too, so we gotta let the others know."

"Okay."

Teller glances at Hope, then me. "How'd it go today?"

"It fucking sucked. Why do you think I'm down here at three a.m. downing a bottle of scotch and she's high as a fuckin' kite?"

"Sorry," Teller mutters.

Jesus, I actually feel bad for snapping at Teller. "No. It's just—he said everything's fine. But I know Rock. He wouldn't say if there was a problem in front of Hope. I hate him being unprotected in there. He can handle himself. But guards fuck with him, there ain't a lot he can do but take it right now."

Hope sort of moans in her sleep, and Z puts his finger to his lips. "Watch what you say, brother," he warns me.

Normally, I'd flip him off, but he's right. Like the girl doesn't have enough awful shit in her head right now.

Teller stands and stretches. "I fuckin' hate this. I want to do something for him, but I don't know what."

"You are, just by helping out," Z says. He tips his head toward Hope. "We all know keeping her safe's his biggest concern, so when she starts giving us shit for escorting her everywhere, use your Teller charm on her, okay?"

Teller grins. "That only works on chicks I wanna fuck. *She's* like a big sister." He fake-shivers "Gross."

Z shakes his head at him. "You're an ass."

"I'm gonna start my rounds, unless you guys need me here?"

"Nah, go ahead," I say.

Murphy lifts his chin. "I won't be able to sleep for a while, I'll go with you, T."

"Yeah, okay."

"Wake Ravage when you get back. His lazy ass needs to do a few rounds too," I remind them on their way to the front door.

"You got it," Murphy calls out.

Glancing down, I brush a few strands of hair off Trin's face. She's so still, I almost want to shake her. Only her soft warm breath drifting over my skin stops me.

"She okay?" Z asks.

"Yeah. She wanted to see Rock too, but I didn't know how to pull it off, ya know?"

"Maybe Hope can take her down one day. One of us will wait outside."

"Yeah, maybe." Honestly, I'm not sure it's a good idea. Don't want Trinity visiting Rock in jail to stir up bad memories about her dad's time inside. Last thing my girl needs.

Taking another look at Hope, she looks awfully uncomfortable with her head thrown back against the chair at a weird angle. "Maybe we should lay her out on the couch?"

Z shrugs. "I'll take her upstairs."

"Okay," I answer.

Now, if Rock were here, he'd whap Z upside the head with his caveman club. But he ain't here and we're all just trying to take care of each other best we can.

HOPE

I'm surprised to be in my own bed the next morning. It takes me a few minutes to orient myself since I don't remember coming upstairs last night. For the first time in a couple days, a small smile tugs at the corners of my mouth. Listening to the guys' stories last night somehow made me feel closer to Rock. Even if today I'm forced to wake up alone. I enjoyed hearing all the good things he's done for the people he considers his family.

Once we figured out which jail Rock was being held at—and oh my God, I still can *not* believe Rock's in jail—I memorized the visitor's schedule. Even attorneys are only allowed to go in at certain times. I know if I go too often the guards will be suspicious. And of course, Glassman does actually need to meet with Rock. So today, I'm not allowed to go.

And I hate it.

I can't stand not being able to send him texts to see what he's up to. Every time I try to picture him or wonder what he's doing, all I see is that horrid orange jumpsuit and handcuffs. All I think about is how much he hates being caged up and how awful it must be for him to have no say over anything.

Good grief. If I don't get up and get dressed, I'll end up crawling under the covers and crying myself into a coma. Nope. I need to be strong. I told Glassman I'd do some research on bail hearings and research whether we need to appeal the decision to a higher court. I plan to head to Adam's office after breakfast and wonder which lucky brother will tag along.

As I'm leaving our room, I bump into Z. "How you feeling today, sugar?" he asks as he walks down the hall with me.

"Okay. Are you responsible for putting me to bed?"

I swear Z seems flustered by my question. "Yeah. I didn't want to leave you downstairs."

"Thanks. I'm sorry, I conked out like that."

"You had a rough day."

"It's been a rough *week*."

"I hear that."

At the top of the stairs Z stops me with a hand on my arm. "Do you remember our conversation last night?"

"Which one? We had a lot of them."

"About club life and stuff."

I thought *all* we discussed was club life, but Z must see it a little different. "Yeah," I answer slowly.

He glances away but still manages to maintain his signature cockiness. "Don't laugh. Do you think Lilly would accept this stuff the way you have?"

My hand flies to my chest and I stop the "awwww" coming out of my mouth just in time. I sense Z asking me this took some courage and I don't want to squelch it. "I don't know, honestly. If you'd asked her if I could accept this life a few years ago, I'm sure she would have told you *hell no*."

The corners of his mouth curl into a smirk. "Good point."

"Wait a second. Are you talking about the whole *having a wife and still banging other chicks* thing?"

Z laughs so hard, he clutches his stomach. When he finally settles down he shakes his head. "No. I think I could commit to just her, if she'd take me seriously."

Okay, this time I can't stop the *awwww*. "Z, that's so sweet that you'd stop sticking your dick in every chick you meet for my friend."

He chuckles again. "That sounds like something Rock would say."

"He *has* been a good influence on me."

"Seriously, you've known her a long time, right?"

"Yes. I'm, or I was, closer to Sophie, but I've spent a lot of time with Lilly."

"Well, what does she want?"

"Honestly? I've only ever seen her seriously date older men with money. Which is weird because she always makes a big fuss to her family about supporting herself."

"Yeah, I've gotten that impression," he says dryly.

"You know she comes from a strict Russian-Italian family, right?"

"Yeah, I'm familiar with the type."

This is news to me. Except for the tiny bit he revealed last night, I don't know a whole heck of a lot about Z's background. I don't know why I feel guilty about that, since none of the guys are really forthcoming about their pasts. Unless they're drunk or high. "Don't take this the wrong way, but her parents might not be happy about her bringing a tattooed, badass biker home for Sunday dinners."

Not at all insulted, Z grins. "Yeah, I met her brother once. He wasn't a fan."

Alex has never been anything but nice to me. Then again, I don't want to bang his sister.

We finally make it downstairs and it's killing me, so I have to ask. "What is it about Lilly? You don't seem like you'd have a lot in common."

Once again, thankfully, he's not insulted. "Besides the obvious?"

"Her boobs, yeah I know," I mutter, glancing down at my own rack.

"Don't worry, yours are two thumbs up too, Hope."

"Gee, thanks."

He stops me with a hand on my shoulder before we enter the dining room. "I just like her. She's smart and fun to talk to. We come from similar families. Although, I don't think she'd ever be a traditional wife."

"Is that what you want?"

"Kind of."

I'm so confused, because Z could have his pick of any club girl here who would probably be thrilled to stay home and tend to his every whim—which is what he seems to be implying. Why on earth he thinks a career driven woman like Lilly is a good match, I have no idea.

"I'd let her keep working if that's what she wanted," he adds.

"How nice of you," I mutter.

Instead of smirking, he frowns. "I can actually have a conversation with her."

Murphy chooses that moment join our conversation. "Since when do you talk to chicks?"

"Please. Look who's talking, blow and go."

Murphy glances at me and he's a little red in the face. I shrug. "Z fills me in on everyone's exploits."

"Asshole," Murphy says, along with a fist to Z's upper arm.

Z snickers and bounces on his toes away from Murphy. My hand settles on Z's arm, so he doesn't leave before we finish. "Have you ever tried having a conversation with any of your other, uh, friends?"

"Who? Club girls? No."

"Why?"

"That's not what they're here for, Hope."

See, it's this attitude that pisses me off the most about the guys. "So, they're good enough to fuck, but not talk to?"

"I talk to Serena," Murphy says with a smug look at Z.

"Telling her how you like your dick sucked isn't a conversation," Z snaps back.

These two are giving me a headache. I rub my fingers into my temples. Both of them notice and quit their bickering.

"Sorry, Hope," Murphy says and Z echoes him.

Z glances at Murphy as if he's willing him away. "I've always been able to talk to Trinity, but that's about it. She's probably the only girl I'd consider a friend." He must think my feelings are hurt, because he rushes to add, "You too."

"Lucky me."

Murphy chuckles at my sarcasm.

"Anyway, you want to know the difference, Hope? Club girls don't care. One di—brother's as good as the next."

"Yeah, but you see them the same way."

"It's a mutually beneficial arrangement. The ones who want a patch? It could be any one of ours. Mine, Murphy's, don't matter. Preferably an officer so they have some power over the other girls, but that's about it."

"That's sad."

His shoulders lift. "It is what it is."

The fact that I'm starting to see his point annoys me to no end.

Z's lips curve into a devilish smirk—not unlike the face Wrath makes when he's about to say something completely obnoxious. "Besides club girls will do all the dirty sex stuff a wife won't do."

Murphy rolls his eyes. "You're such an asshole."

"What?" Z shrugs.

"Show some respect," Murphy says with a nod at me.

"Why are you all out in the hallway?" Heidi asks, interrupting what's turned into an inappropriate discussion. We're blocking her exit, so the guys move.

"Just talking, honey. How are you?" I ask.

"Nervous about a test I have to take."

"What class?"

"Calculus."

A chuckle works out of me. "I definitely can't help you there."

Heidi smiles, which is a relief. Lately she's been so solemn. "Is your brother taking you to school?"

"I can take you, bug," Murphy offers.

Heidi doesn't seem as excited as she normally does when Murphy offers to take her out on his bike. "I don't want to have helmet hair."

Murphy snorts. "We can take my truck."

"I got her, bro. Thanks," Teller says, slapping Murphy on the back.

"Well, which one of you gets to take me downtown?" I ask once Teller and Heidi leave.

Murphy's so fixated on the front door, he doesn't hear my question. Z shrugs at me. "See what Wrath wants to do. I've got no problem running you down there. How long you think you'll be?"

"At least a couple of hours." In my head, I tick off all the things I need to do. For a second, helpless grief threatens to overwhelm me. Only knowing that I have something to offer, some way to help Rock, pushes the cloud away.

Wrath needed to check in at his gym, so Z ends up taking me to Adam's office.

Somehow I lost the battle to drive my own damn car. Actually, there was no battle. Z simply plucked my keys out of my hand.

"It'll be easier for me to spot a tail and lose it," he explains, and I really can't argue with his logic.

"I hope I didn't offend you last night," he says.

"Which time?" I tease, but then I realize, he's being serious.

"I just want you to understand how important you are to Rock."

His words tear at my chest. "Of course I do," I whisper.

"You know the club will protect you and take care of you, right?"

I don't think I've ever seen Z this serious before. "I've gotten that impression."

"All you need to do is be there for your man."

It hits me all of a sudden what he's worried about. "Z, I'm not leaving Rock."

"I ain't gonna lie and say this won't be hard. But we'll do everything we can to make it easier on you."

Tears prick my eyes, so I wait a few seconds before answering him. "I know. You guys already have."

"Good."

We're quiet after that, until we get to Adam's office.

Where Z immediately causes trouble.

As soon as Adam sees me, he pulls me in for a hug. "Shit, Hope. I'm so sorry. Is there anything I can do?"

"Taking your hands off her is a good start," Z growls from behind me.

I roll my eyes and brace for the pissing contest about to start up.

Adam's mouth twitches. "Who's your yummy bodyguard?"

"Z, this is my friend, Adam. Adam, this is Z. I think you guys met the night we celebrated my engagement."

Adam nods. "That's right, so Z…?"

"Z, as in zero tolerance for dudes touching my friend's woman."

Oh, good grief. He's worse than Rock. I smack his arm to draw his attention away from Adam. "Adam and I have been friends for years. Rock knows him. Settle down."

"Yeah, I'd rather bend *you* over my desk than her, every day of the week," Adam says with a slow smile.

I bury my face in my hands. Why? Why me?

Z's still busy digesting the mental image Adam conjured up for all of us and seems to be speechless for the moment. Good.

"I need to use your account to do some research for Glassman. Is that okay?"

"Wow, hanging out with the big boys now?"

"Yeah, right. Notice Glassman didn't offer me so much as a cubicle to use in his big white shoebox."

"Can't let the riffraff in, Hope. You know that."

"Right."

"I know I haven't done a lot of criminal work, but if you want to bounce ideas off me, don't hesitate."

"Thanks. I appreciate it."

Z's wearing a confused expression when I turn around. "Why wouldn't Glassman want to work with you, Hope?"

"Uh, what's lower than a prospect, Z?"

"Hangaround."

"Well, that's how firms like his think of solos. I'm also younger and female. I doubt he'll even read whatever I send him."

"No, he'll read it. Then, mansplain it to you, Hope," Adam says with a snicker.

The corners of my mouth stretch into a tired smile. "I don't care. Any little thing I can do to help Rock is worth dealing with Glassman's snobbery. And he *is* good at what he does. That's all that matters."

Z still seems confused, or annoyed. It's hard to tell.

"You don't have to hang out here all day, Z. You'll be so bored."

"I can use a receptionist if you want to answer phones," Adam offers helpfully.

Z glares at him. "I'll be fine, Hope. Do your thing."

"Honestly, nothing's going to happen to me here."

"Didn't you get attacked here?" Z reminds me with a frown, while jabbing a finger at Adam. "By one of *his* clients?"

Well, that settles that.

CHAPTER TWELVE

ROCK

THERE ARE two types of criminals in county jail. Your "hardcore criminals" who are waiting to go to trial for the big ones: murder, rape, robbery, drug trafficking. Then there are the people in here for a short amount of time, your petty offenders. I suppose I fall into the first category. Even so, I keep my head up, don't smile at anyone, don't avoid eye-contact and keep my mouth shut.

Since the ones here for the short term are eager to get out, they're not looking for trouble. They don't want to do anything to mess up their release dates and spend another second here.

I also fall into that category.

Slater's a shithole of a county, but surprisingly the jail isn't overflowing with inmates. I have my own cell and few neighbors. This is good and bad. After my first forty-eight hours of good behavior, I relocated to a more "open door" wing of the jail, so I can come and go from my cell and visit the rec room during certain hours.

I've always treated everyone with respect until they forced me to do otherwise, and jail's no different. As much as it irritates me, I treat the guards as professionals and don't bug them or make more work for them if I can help it. That's why it pisses me the fuck off that Lizard's going out of his way to fuck with me.

With that in mind, I make the rounds in my unit, seeking out one of the longer residents. Chucky has family ties to the Wolf Knights MC and even though I could slit their president's throat right now, Chucky's a valuable source of information. He's about my size and the other inmates give him the same distance they give me.

"What's Izzard's story?" I ask him while hanging outside his cell.

"He's a shady motherfucker. Likes to step to the big guys. Makes him feel big, 'cause he knows they ain't gonna fight back in here."

What a pussy. "Risky. One of these days he's gonna fuck with the wrong guy."

He chuckles. "No kidding." He takes a few steps closer and lowers his voice. "You got a woman, make sure she don't come to visit when he's on the gate."

Not what I wanted to hear.

I've only encountered him in the evenings and afternoons, and after some more inquiries, I determine the morning visiting hours—from eight to ten—are the only times Hope can come to visit. Honestly, even that I want to put a limit on. Not that I don't want to see her. I miss her like fucking crazy. But every visit puts her at risk and worse, I'm afraid seeing me like this will begin to take a toll on her.

When I'm able to make my allotted collect call to explain the new visiting schedule, of course she argues with me.

"Rock, I'm an attorney. I can see you during the attorney visiting hours. Or schedule a time during—"

"It's not about that, Hope. Don't argue with me about this."

The line's quiet for a few seconds. "Okay."

"Thank you."

"Rock, are you okay?"

"As good as I can be. Glassman said you been pulling some research together for him on the bail hearing?"

"Yes. I think we have a crappy chance of it going our way." I close my eyes when she says "we" because it reminds me too much of how we met and fuck if I don't love her more than I ever thought possible. "It's worth a shot. If you get denied again, we'll appeal to a higher court."

"Sounds good. Thank you."

"I love you, Rock. I miss you so much." Her voice comes through strong, but sad.

"I know. Same here."

We're cut off before any more words pass.

HOPE

Between the hours of four a.m. and six a.m. are when I've discovered the clubhouse is, for the most part, quiet and still. For some reason—no matter when I fall asleep—I find myself awake at four almost every morning. Instead of forcing myself to go to sleep, I decided it's easier to get up and do something. At least no one's awake to hover over me, asking if I'm okay every time I so much as sigh.

Not that I'm ungrateful or I mind everyone looking out for me. But before Rock, I spent a lot of my life alone and doing things for myself. Having so much company is exhausting sometimes. Nice, but exhausting.

In these early hours, I have the clubhouse to myself. I'd go for a walk outside, but ever since Z joked about the wild life up here, I've been too afraid of getting eaten by a bear to wander around by myself at night.

More often than not, I find myself downstairs in the gym on the treadmill. Trying to out walk—no matter how I strap them down, my boobs won't tolerate running—my racing mind. It never seems to work, but after a few hours I'm usually tired enough to go back to sleep. Or it's daylight and I can hike out to our unfinished house to sit on the front steps and imagine happier times.

The mornings Trinity joins me at the gym are nice because she's quiet and never feels the need to fill the air with endless chatter. We never walk out to the house together, as if she knows that's my personal place to sit and wonder if Rock and I will ever get to live in it or not.

This morning, there's no sign of Trinity. After stopping by the kitchen, I plan to go upstairs, but I find Heidi and Teller at one of the dining room tables instead. Since, other than Rock being in jail, things are calm, Wrath has unclenched his iron grip on everyone.

Well, Teller and Heidi. Not me or Trinity.

"Hey, Heidi, leaving for school soon?"

She glances at her brother before answering. "Yeah, just trying to figure out these financial aid forms."

Teller runs his hands through his hair and gives me a pleading look.

"Do you want some help?"

Heidi's hopeful expression settles the reservations I have about sticking my nose where it doesn't belong.

"Thanks, Hope," Teller says.

Heidi's bottom lip wobbles. "Are you okay, Hope? Is there any news about Uncle Rock?"

Teller bumps her with his arm, but I pull out a chair and sit next to her. There's no reason to worry her with Rock's *you can only come between eight and ten* phone call. "Not yet," I answer simply.

"I feel bad doing all this," she waves her hand over the papers scattered on the table. "When he's—" she chokes on a sob, and I pull her into a hug.

"It's okay, Heidi. You know he wants you to start college in the fall."

"Yeah." She pulls away and swipes at her nose. "I don't even want to go to prom. It's not right to celebrate anything—"

I glance over her shoulder and raise my eyebrows at Teller. Why isn't he reassuring her better? Heidi's already been through a lot for her age. She shouldn't be taking this on too.

"Heidi, it's okay. We're doing everything we can for Rock. Your job is to finish school strong and do all your normal senior year stuff."

She shakes her head sadly. "Do you think he'll be out in time for my graduation?"

I have a hard time swallowing over the lump in my throat before answering. "I don't know. I hope so."

That grinds our conversation to a halt. After a minute, I nod at the papers. "What's giving you trouble?"

"Well, I wasn't sure if I should check off that I'm an orphan or something else? I think they want a death certificate...and I don't—"

"Let me see."

She hands over the pile of papers and I search through them. "Here, honey, I think this is the one you should probably fill out, The Emancipated Minor or Legal Guardianship Form. I can get you the guardianship papers if you don't have them." I look up at Teller. "They might need to verify your income, though."

"That's fine. I had to do all that shit for the court case anyway."

"I can write you a letter to attach to that one, Heidi. Just remind me."

"Oh, okay. Thanks, Hope."

Murphy joins us while we're flipping through the rest of the papers. "You guys look so serious."

Heidi groans. "Financial aid forms."

"Thought they passed out scholarships to smart kids?" He's teasing her, but her forehead wrinkles and she rolls her eyes.

"I'm not that smart. And I still have to fill all this crap out," she grumbles, before turning back to me. "What do I put down for trust fund? I can't touch any of it until I'm twenty-five."

"My guess is, you still have to disclose it. Did it have an allowance for educational expenses?" I ask Teller.

"No clue."

"I'll talk to Adam about it."

"Thanks."

When she's finished with one packet, she sets everything aside and sighs.

"Is that it?"

"Yeah, I only applied to Hudson Valley."

"Why? There are so many schools in the area and with your grades—"

She makes a "duh" face at me.

"Heidi, you know I think Axel's great. But don't base this decision on your boyfriend."

She doesn't get as annoyed as I expected her to. "I'm not. They have the best program for what I want to do and a good job placement rate."

"Okay."

"Besides, he only has one more year. And Hudson Valley will be cheaper."

"Heidi, you can go anywhere you want," Murphy says.

She spares him a glance. "Thank you, Blake." The tone of her voice isn't thankful at all. Not sure what's going on there. Nor do I really want to know. Teller throws a glance at his friend, then me.

What am I supposed to do about it?

"Marcel, we need to get going or I'll be late."

Teller shakes his head as he stands. "You ever gonna get your license?"

"Why should I when my big brother will drive me around?"

I remember at her age I couldn't wait to get my license. "Why haven't you gone for your road test yet, Heidi?"

I didn't mean to embarrass her in front of the guys, but she ducks her head before answering my question. "I don't know. It's a lot of responsibility."

"She's scared," Teller says.

"A dose of fear is good. But don't let it rule you Heidi. You don't want to depend on men to drive you around forever." Teller and Murphy both chuckle at that.

The corner of her mouth lifts and she sneaks a peek up at me. Then, *I get it*. Once she's able to drive herself, her brother won't have to spend as much time with her. Clever kid. Wherever her mother is, she's an idiot for missing out on this girl. I slide my chair back and pull Heidi in for a big hug before she leaves.

After they're out of earshot, Murphy and I are the only ones left at the table. "Thanks, Hope."

"For what?"

138

"Always being so good to her."

"I can't help it."

The corners of his mouth turn up. "Thanks for trying to talk her into another school."

I turn his words over in my head before answering. "I wasn't saying it for your benefit."

He just stares at me.

"Sorry, I didn't mean that to come out so harsh. I want what's best for her. I followed my high school boyfriend to college and it was a big mistake."

"I thought you met your husband in college?"

How exactly had I forgotten that?

"I did. They were actually roommates freshman year."

"Awkward."

Enough years have passed that I can laugh about it now. "You have no idea. My boyfriend was cheating on me, and Clay couldn't figure out how to tell me."

Murphy chuckles. "Bet he was there to comfort you after."

"Not really. It—" Huh. I never gave this a whole lot of thought. "He took a few months to ask me out. He said I was aloof."

"Sounds like guy code for *stuck up*."

"That's what I said!" He laughs a little harder and I move over a few chairs to sit next to him.

"That was nice advice you gave Heidi about the driving too. Thanks."

Sometimes I think Murphy worries about Heidi more than Teller does.

"What did you mean about she can go anywhere she wants? Did she have somewhere else in mind?"

His gaze wanders to the mural over the bar against the back wall. "I don't know. She hasn't talked to me about that stuff in years."

It seems he has more to say, so I keep quiet and wait for him to continue. "She's always been smart. Knew when she was little she'd be going to college." He shrugs but still won't look my way. "Been putting money aside for years now, so you know, if she got into a real good school but didn't have enough scholarships to cover it she could still go."

Jesus. My breath catches and I can't speak. My own mother drained every penny from the college fund my father started for me long before I started filling out applications. Here this guy who has no obligation to her…I can't even wrap my head around it.

"I know that's dumb," he says quickly. "T's been doing the same thing."

It takes a second to find the right words. "It's not dumb at all. I think that's the sweetest thing I've ever heard."

He huffs a short laugh. "Yeah, sweet. That's me." His jaw tightens and his next words come out harsh. "She asked if I was trying to buy her when I mentioned it a few months back."

"I'm sure she was only kidding."

"Maybe." He shakes his head. "You see the good in all of us."

"I see what you can't see about yourself."

"You keep thinking I'm good and I'm not, Hope. I hurt everyone around me."

Murphy's always so hard on himself. To everyone else he's tough and cocky. But under—way under—the bravado, he's awfully sensitive. I'm already teetering on the edge of tears every day, and this conversation is about to push me right off the ledge. Instead, I throw my arms around his shoulders, embracing him in an awkward hug. He reaches up and pats my arm.

"What's going on?" Wrath's voice booms through the dining room, startling me. My arms drop from Murphy, but I pat him on the back.

"Nothing. Heidi was here with her college applications. We were just talking about where she's planning to go."

Wrath narrows his eyes at me making me feel like a kid who got caught doing something naughty. "You need to have your arms around him to do that?"

Oh, he did not just say that. I'm out of my chair so quick, it screeches across the floor. "Don't turn a friendly gesture into something ugly. I'm not in the mood for your caveman rules right now, Wrath."

"See what I mean?" Murphy mutters.

Now I'm only more confused.

"Cut it out, bro. She's—"

I whip around and nail Murphy with a stare. "If you say 'old enough to be your mother,' I will kick your ass."

Murphy snorts, his shoulders shaking with laughter. "That's not what I was going to say." He raises his gaze to Wrath. "Don't take shit out on her. She didn't do anything wrong."

This has to be the first time I've seen Murphy challenge Wrath and I want to get out of here before the room explodes. Wrath catches my hand as I pass him. "Hey. I'm sorry."

Wrath apologizing?

"Everything okay?" Trinity asks as she enters the dining room.

Wrath gives me a pleading look, silently asking me not to tell her he's been an ass before nine o'clock, I think.

I give him one last narrow-eyed glare before turning away. Yes, I'm being a brat, but he really pissed me off implying…whatever the hell he was implying. "Everything's good, Trin. I need to run upstairs and change. Unless you need help?"

I know she'll never take me up on an offer to help her in the kitchen. I could be insulted, but let's be honest, I'll just be in her way.

WRATH

"Why you so tweaked, man?" Murphy asks after Hope leaves.

I already feel bad about how I snapped at her. Murphy's question makes it worse. "Fuck off."

He stands and shoves his chair in. "This sucks for everyone. You wanna be a dick to me, fine, but don't treat her like shit. She just spent who knows how long helping Heidi out with her college stuff."

Man, having Murphy tell me how to behave pisses me off. "I apologized. Now mind your own business before I kick your ass," I growl.

My low voice and fuck-off stare finally work their magic. Murphy leaves, but not before reaching out to tap Trinity on the arm on his way out.

Dick.

Only the sight of Trinity's perfect angel face calms me down. Especially when she turns and shines her smile on me. She hurries over and takes my hands. "Morning."

How can I not lean down to kiss to her forehead?

"Morning, angel."

"What'd I miss?"

Taking her hand, I tug her along into the kitchen.

"Nothing. Stupid stuff."

She nods and opens the refrigerator to start making breakfast. I drop into one of the kitchen chairs and enjoy watching her. Don't even bother asking what she's making.

After breakfast, she's still wearing a concerned face. Every few minutes she looks like she's gonna spit some words out, then she hesitates.

"What's wrong, babe?"

Trinity's hands keep nervously twisting in her lap until I put my own hand over them to stop her.

"Please don't be mad."

Naturally that raises my *what the fuck* radar. But I wait for her to continue without opening my big mouth.

"Things are good between us—"

"Yeah." Where's she going with this?

"I've been feeling guilty about how I think I've fucked up your relationship with some of the guys."

"You got nothing to feel guilty about. We're fine."

"Yes." She taps my chest. "You and I are fine." The firm tone of her voice makes me think she finally believes it. "But all those years, I never thought about what I was doing to the brotherhood."

"We're fine." I got every brother's back and I know they've got mine. Never doubt it for a second.

Wait a second. "Did one of them ask you to talk to me?" And by *one of them*, I've narrowed it down to Teller or Murphy. I will beat the shit out of them if they heaped any guilt on my girl.

"No. Nothing like that. I know…I know Teller's worried you hate him. Murphy hasn't said anything, but he's bothered. I don't think you realize how much he's always looked up to you."

Yeah, so much that he spent a good four years nailing my girl.

Done. Over with. In the past. Moving forward.

"So what are you asking?"

"Nothing. I'm not trying to stick my nose in club business. I just want to help fix whatever I fucked up."

"You didn't—"

"Yes, I did."

"I was going to say, you didn't fuck it up alone."

The corner of her mouth lifts. "True."

"So, what do you want me to do? Buy him a puppy? Take him fishing? Teach him how to throw a football?"

Her hand thumps against my chest as she shakes with laughter. "No! Stop making fun of me."

I love when Trinity laughs. Especially when I'm the one who makes her do it. And while it's bringing up some uncomfortable shit from our past, I love her devotion to the club and how much she wants what's best for everyone.

"You realize if I'm nice to him, he'll get spooked and think I'm tryin' to off him, right? I have a reputation to uphold. Gotta pick on the younger guys and toughen them up."

She laughs even harder, almost falling out of my lap. Christ, this woman's making me soft. She's not taking me seriously *at all*. I flick my fingers against her sides until she's laughing so hard she can barely breathe. "Stop! Stop!"

"I'll think of something, Angel Face. You put it out of your head, okay? Only man you need to worry about is me."

All laughter leaves her face. "This *is* me worrying about you. I want you to be happy. I want—"

"You make me happy."

143

"Thank you. Let me finish. I don't want any leftover hostility that messes with you guys."

"We're men. We're always hostile. I'd take a bullet for that little fuck, same as he'd do for me."

"Please don't say that." Her sudden serious tone takes all the fun out of our moment. "I couldn't stand losing you after we just figured things out."

"Are you saying you want me to *push* Murph in front of a bullet instead?"

Her girlish laughs come racing back and she shoves my chest. "No! Dammit, I'm serious."

"I'm so confused, angel."

"No you're not."

"Hey," I grab her hand and hold it still. "I get what you're saying."

But for the rest of the day I can't get her words out of my head. That's how I find myself alone with Murphy later on. War room door's open, which isn't unusual, but it makes me curious enough to poke my head in.

"What's up, Murph?"

His head snaps up and maybe Trinity's right, because he almost seems nervous. Murphy's a tough little fuck. Isn't afraid of much. Not that I mind him being afraid of me. He should be. But still.

"Nothing." He holds out a parts manual to me. "Trying to put an order together."

"For what?"

He shrugs and looks away. "Bike for Rock. I assume he'll want to take off for a few days when he gets out."

Good to know brother hasn't lost faith.

"Yeah, and?"

"Nothin'. Tryin' to decide if it should be two-up."

"Gotcha."

"If it is, I'm gonna order stuff to make it more comfortable for her. If not…"

"He can just take one of the plain bikes from the garage?"

"Yeah."

Thinking back to the last time the club went through similar shit, I recall Rock taking off by himself. But that's only because his skank ex-wife deserted his ass while he was inside. "Hope will be here when he gets out. He'll want her with him."

I grab the list from his hand and snicker as I read it. "Oh, man. He'll hate this shit." Rock likes his bike unfussy and streamlined. Murphy's building it purely with the passenger's comfort in mind.

"Yeah, but she'll appreciate it."

"Happy wife, happy life?"

"Something like that."

"While you're at it," I flip through until I find what I want. "Order this for me too."

Murphy raises an eyebrow and I shrug. "Her ass sits there permanently now, might as well make sure she's comfortable too."

"You're a real romantic, bro."

"Thanks. That's what I hear."

Murphy shakes his head, but he's laughing.

"Want to come down to the gym with me? Jake's out, I could use help with one of his classes. And I got that kid I want to maybe bring in as a prospect. You should meet him and tell me what you think."

You'd think I asked him to chop his dick off the way he looks at me. "Sure. No problem."

Well, aren't I in for a fun afternoon.

CHAPTER THIRTEEN

HOPE

KEEPING myself busy when I'm so worried about Rock isn't easy. Throwing myself into wedding planning helps. But it's bittersweet. In the back of my mind, I keep wondering if I'm planning a party for nothing. If I'll be saying my vows behind the brick walls of the Slater County Jail.

Flimsy evidence. Unreliable witness.

I find myself chanting those two phrases to myself a lot these days.

Trinity's been such a big help. I don't know what I'd do without her. Without any of the guys.

Wrath ran out of their room like I tried to set him on fire when I showed up at their door with my wedding checklist. "I need to get Rock's wedding band," I inform Trinity after he leaves.

Trinity's face breaks into a grin. We've spent hours searching websites and catalogs together. "Did you finally find one you like?"

"I think so. I found this jeweler on Etsy. But I want to see the ring in person. Their shop's in Boston. Are you up for a road trip?"

She chews on her bottom lip and won't meet my eyes. "You better ask Wrath."

Oh, boy. I think a year ago if someone had said that to me, I would have flipped my lid. Now? "Well, yes. I assumed either he or Z would go with us."

"It's not Lost Kings territory."

"So?"

She stares at me as if I'm dense.

"I wasn't planning go blazing through Massachusetts with a blinking neon LOKI sign, Trin."

Finally, she lightens up and laughs. "Yeah. Sorry."

Now that I have it in my head, I can't let the idea go. It might be a touch of stir-crazy.

Damn, it grinds my gears to ask Wrath's *permission* to take a two-hour drive. Especially when the first word out of his mouth is *no*.

"What do you mean *no?*"

"I mean no. It's not safe territory."

I'm trying. Trying really hard not to give Wrath a hard time. I know we're all under stress. But I still want to smack him.

"Wrath, if you can stand to leave your cut at home, and we take your truck or Rock's SUV, how will anyone know who we're affiliated with?"

"Tell me why this is so important."

He'll think I'm an idiot. There's no indication Rock's getting out anytime soon. But I can't explain it. I *need* to get his ring. I need to keep moving forward as if our wedding is happening in a few months.

I can't bear to think of the alternative.

"I want to get Rock's wedding band," I answer quietly. "I found what I want at this shop in Boston. But I want to see it in person and see if he can make a few adjustments."

His face finally softens, but it takes a minute before he says anything. "Okay. We'll go tomorrow. Do you know when they're open?"

"Yes. All the information's upstairs, but I'll email the owner to make sure he's ready for us."

"Okay."

Cocking my head to the side, I study him for a second before asking my next question. "Are you going to allow Trinity to come?" I'm really asking for trouble today aren't I?

"Yes, she can come," he snarks back at me. "At least she knows how to behave," he mumbles as he turns away.

"I heard that."

"I said it loud enough."

"Jerk."

"Love you too, Cinderella."

As soon as he's gone, I jog up the stairs, feeling better about things. Trinity's busy cleaning out one of the guest rooms. "What are you doing? I thought you weren't doing this stuff anymore?"

"Someone has to."

"Jeez."

Once she's got the laundry going, she lifts her chin at me. "What're you up to?"

"Your man's a pain in my ass."

She chuckles and thankfully doesn't seem insulted. "Tell me about it."

"Well, he said we can go to Boston. He's driving us. Tomorrow. Can you come?"

"Yeah. Of course."

WRATH

I can't even describe what went through me when Hope explained her need to get Rock's wedding band. After that, how the fuck could I ever say no to her? She was right too, which annoys me. There's no reason we can't go through the area if we're not flying colors. I'm so hyper-focused on keeping everyone safe, I barely want to leave the property anymore.

This trip will be good for us. Get Hope out of the house. Keep her focused on good things. And I'm doing something good for my best friend by keeping his woman happy. Win-win.

And if I happen to pick up an engagement ring for Trinity while I'm there, even better.

That's what's on my mind the next morning. Well, that and the fact that Trinity's actually still asleep for once.

My phone goes off, just as I'm about to wake her up in my special way.

Hope: *Can you come upstairs when you have a chance?*

Doesn't seem urgent. I go back and forth and finally decide to let Trinity sleep a little longer.

When I get to Hope and Rock's room, I almost wish I'd chosen to wake Trinity up instead.

The door's open a crack and swings wider as I knock. Hope's frantically pawing through Rock's dresser, items scattered all over the place.

"What're you up to, Hope?"

She barely glances at me before grabbing a dark red velvet box and thrusting it at me. I already know what's in it and my gut clenches.

She flips the lid open and plucks the hunk of white gold out and shoves it in my hands. "Does this fit Rock? Do you know? He never wears rings. I have no idea what size he wears and I can't exactly go down to the jail to measure him." She's frantic, babbling and on the verge of tears, which is finally what snaps me out of my fog from seeing that hideous fucking ring again.

"Yeah, it fits him," I answer, hoping she'll have no follow-up questions. The last time I saw that ring was when Rock slipped it off our former president's finger. Right before we buried the guy. It's a reminder of how our former officers chose materialistic greed over their brothers. How Rock ended up in prison before—for another crime he didn't actually commit—and how we'd lost brothers because of the greedy arrogance that consumed the club before we took over and returned it to what it was supposed to be. A brotherhood.

Am I planning to explain all of that to Hope? Hell fucking no. Rock can give her that history lesson if he wants to one day.

The ring's heavy. Ugly as shit too. A big grinning skull with a ruby between its teeth and a diamond-encrusted crown. Why a ruby when our colors are blue and gray? Who fucking knows. Probably because it was the most expensive.

"Let me see your hands. I think your hands are bigger than Rock's. Does it fit you?"

I don't even have it in me to toss out some dirty size-reference joke. To make her happy, I slip it on. "Too small, sweetheart. But I've seen him wear it. It fits."

"When?" She takes it back, holding it in her palm, testing its weight. "Good grief it's heavy. You could use it as a weapon."

Yup. Sure could.

"Oh God." Her eyes meet mine. "It's not his old wedding ring is it?"

A short, sharp bite of laughter bursts out of me. "No. He definitely tossed that."

"Oh. Well, how come I've never seen it before?"

My mouth twists into a bit of a smile. Should have known nosy lawyer-gal would be full of questions. "It belonged to the last president," I tell her. Maybe that will satisfy her curiosity.

"Oh." She glances at the ring again. "Ruger, right? After what you told me, I'm surprised Rock kept this. Ruger sounded awful."

That's one way of putting it.

"You never said what happened to him."

Shit. "He's long gone, Hope."

She stares at me for a minute. "Will Rock mind if I take it with me to the jeweler? Just so he can measure it? Obviously it's valuable, but I'll be careful."

"Yeah. I'm sure it's fine."

"Okay. Thank you." She tilts her head, surveying the mess she's made of Rock's dresser. "I guess I better put everything back. Rock would have a fit if he saw this mess," she says with a sad bit of laughter.

Christ, she looks so lost, I don't know what the fuck to do for her. "Come here, hon." She shuffles over and lets me wrap her up in a hug. "Everything's gonna be okay."

"I know," she mumbles.

Her faith that Rock's gonna get out from under these charges, her determination to push forward with the wedding even though Rock's behind bars, fuck I can't put into words what it does to me. But a warm sensation spreads through my chest. I love her for her loyalty to my friend.

"Good girl." I pat her back once and let her go. "Get ready. We'll leave in an hour."

"Okay." Her voice is a little stronger now. Maybe I actually did some good here.

I shut the door behind me and find Z in the hallway.

He lifts his chin at the door. "Everything okay?"

Hell, we're all so fucked up he doesn't even make any of the obvious jokes at finding me leaving Hope's room.

"Yeah. Gonna take her to pick up Rock's wedding band."

Z's entire demeanor softens. "Poor girl. This has been awful on her."

"Your room's right next to her. She doing okay?"

Normally I'd get some smart ass remark from Z. "I don't know. She cries every night. Feel like shit. Don't know what to do for her."

I'm not surprised. Still hate hearing it though.

"Give her privacy. She's keeping her shit together during the day." And I *almost* feel bad about that. I've been so hard on her in the past, she's probably scared to show any weakness around us without Rock here to protect her. The whole situation pisses me the fuck off. *This.* This right here is the reason I've been so fucking hard on her.

Still can't believe it's actually happening.

"You gonna be okay? I'd go with you, but we're already thin down at CB."

"Nah. I'll be fine."

"Trin going too?"

"Yeah, of course."

"Good. Hey, Murphy's solution was to send Axel down for door duty."

It feels good to actually laugh about something. "Shocker."

"Bro, we're hurting. I'm probably gonna do it."

I lift my shoulders. Heidi bitching Axel out over club business isn't our problem. And if Axel can't handle her, he probably shouldn't be in the club anyway. I pity the guy who eventually ends up with Heidi sometimes. "That's why he's a prospect. To see if he can hack it. Doesn't matter who his old lady is. We're not sending him there to fuck dancers. He's there to man the door and throw out pricks who can't keep their hands to themselves."

"Yeah, I know."

"You just hate Murphy being right for the wrong reasons."

Z snickers. "Yeah, something like that."

"I'm with you on that one."

Next to us, the door opens and Hope steps out. "Hey, guys."

"Morning, sweetheart. You okay?" Z asks.

She takes a deep breath, lifts her chin and pushes her shoulders back before answering. "Yes. Wrath's taking me to get Rock's ring today."

"I heard."

I'm amused that she's ready so early. I told her we'd leave in an hour because I figured that way she'd be ready by the time I actually wanted to leave.

"I'm heading downstairs. Trin's up."

Ah, fuck. I still had plans to wake my girl up on my own. Once the two of them get together and start gabbing there's no prying them apart.

After she leaves, Z cocks his head and fixes his no nonsense stare on me. "You gonna look for a ring too while you're there?"

I'm too surprised to answer right away. "Why? You want me to propose to you?"

"No, you dick. For Trinity."

"Maybe. Why?"

He shrugs. "No reason. Just probably sucks for her doing all this planning for Hope's wedding—which might not even happen—when she's got no idea—"

"First, you've got way too much time on your hands if you're worrying about shit like that."

He chuckles, but I'm not finished. "And second, it's happening. She already knows it's happening. I just need to find the right time. And now doesn't seem like it."

"Yeah, okay."

Wait a second. "Did she say something to you?"

"No. She just seems down, that's all."

"Our president's in jail. We're all down."

"Yeah, but—"

"I know how tight they are."

"All right. Sorry I said anything."

I know his question came from a good place, so I'm not mad. Not really.

"It's fine. Now I need to go get ready for my torture."

He cocks his head at me.

"Trapped in a cage for four hours to go *shopping*? Come on, Z, you know me better."

Now he snickers. "CB's looking like the superior choice all of a sudden, isn't it?"

CHAPTER FOURTEEN

HOPE

PAST THE SMILES I faked with Wrath and Trinity all day long, there's an aching emptiness in my chest. Unrelenting sadness throbs there every night when I slide into our bed alone. Tonight it's even worse.

I miss Rock so much, it's a struggle to draw breath into my lungs. He should have been there with me today.

Rolling over, I click on the bedside lamp and pull out the journal I've been keeping since the first time I visited Rock in jail. Knowing the officers would read any letters I sent him, I've been writing everything down to give him when he's home.

As I set the pen to paper, I don't think about what I want to write. The words have been drifting through my mind all day. Their significance only sunk in when I found myself in bed alone again.

Dear Rock,

I bought your wedding band today. Wrath drove us to Boston. Don't be mad at him. I threatened to drive myself if he didn't take Trinity and me. For a second, I froze in the store. So worried I'd be slipping the ring on your finger inside the jailhouse walls. But I have faith you're going to be returned to me.

After I picked your ring out, Wrath silently urged me to take Trinity next door. It was the perfect distraction to keep me from sobbing because you weren't there with us. When we got home, he showed me the engagement ring he picked for her. I got so excited I almost ruined his surprise, but I couldn't help it. It was the first happiness I've felt since our engagement party...right before it all went to hell.

I can't sleep tonight. I miss my softness against your hardness. The solid feel of your body next to me. When I'm down, you always make me laugh. I miss your hands and the way you can't keep them off me. I miss how no matter what position we fall asleep in, I always wake up with you wrapped around me. I love your hair and the way you close your eyes when I run my fingers through it.

Everything feels wrong without you here. The clubhouse feels empty, even though it's full of people. Half of me is missing. All day long, I keep my eyes tear free and my chin up. Stay positive, so that the guys can focus on what they need to do and so you can be proud of me. But alone in our room, I can't do it. I'm so scared they'll keep you in jail until trial. These weeks without you here have been miserable. The thought of years of this terrifies me.

I need you back.

Hope

I set my pen down and close the notebook. I stare at it for a few minutes before placing it back in the drawer.

The case against Rock is weak. But I also know justice isn't always served. Eyewitness testimony is notoriously unreliable. And that's all they seem to have against him. I've been helping Glassman assemble a list of experts to testify about how unreliable eyewitnesses are. Especially when you take into account that this witness' account came so long after the murder. I'm confident Glassman can tear the witness' testimony apart on the stand. I just don't think I can hold on that long. It's absurd. Insane that they're holding him on such flimsy evidence.

My heart races, blood thundering through my ears as I work out the details of his case. Not for the first time, I fall asleep going over all the possible outcomes.

ROCK

The worst part of jail is trying to get any sleep. It's not the cot with the springs digging into my back, the flat pillow or the scratchy blanket. I've slept on worse. It's not even the endless noise. I've learned to block that out.

No, every time I close my eyes, I see Hope. We'd spent every night side by side since she sold her house and moved into the clubhouse with me permanently. Yes, waking up and burying myself inside her almost every morning is great. But it's the rest of it that keeps me awake. I miss the weight of her next to me. The soft little snores she makes. The way she "accidentally" grinds her ass into me when she stretches in the morning. I miss her long hair spilling over the pillows, tickling my nose. Stupid, sappy shit that I took for granted and now I miss more than anything.

Half the time, I close my eyes, I swear I actually feel her soft little body against mine. Then I come fully awake and remember where I am and that she's not here.

That's the worst.

I haven't allowed myself to think about the future, or plan anything. Construction on our house has halted. Our entire lives have just *stopped*.

My fingers flex prickling with the need to... ride... no destination in mind. Just free.

Wind in my face and Hope at my back.

CHAPTER FIFTEEN

WRATH

"I'm doing everything I can to get bail set for you, Rock."

"I know you are."

Rock's more forgiving about the situation than I would be. Hell, I struggled not to choke Glassman the second I saw him today. Worthless fucking lawyers taking a shit ton of money and not doing a fucking thing.

Rock pins me with a look. Like he knows exactly what's going through my head. Knowing him, he probably does. "How's my girl?"

I almost snort. Fucker's sitting in jail and of course the only thing he's worried about's his ol' lady. "She's good."

He slides his gaze to Glassman, who's suddenly fascinated with his cellphone. As if he's trying to give us privacy in our ten by twelve foot room.

Whatthefuckever.

"She getting out of bed? Keeping busy?" Rock asks.

"Yeah. Even took her on a road trip yesterday."

Rock raises an eyebrow at that. "Want to elaborate?"

"I can't. It's a secret. She'll be pissed if I tell you. But yeah, she's doing okay."

That, more than anything else we've told him today, seems to cheer him up. "Thanks, brother. Appreciate it."

"She and Trinity are working on some stuff together today. Z's with them."

"Good. Trin's okay?"

Is she? I don't know. Except for yesterday, she's quiet and I feel like I almost never see her. "Yeah, she's okay."

"Rest of the guys okay? Z, Teller and Murphy, pulling their weight?" he asks with a smirk. He knows the answer.

"Yup."

"Anyone checking up on Sparky?"

Now it's my turn to snort. "Yeah, man." He's higher than fuck, worse than usual, but I don't say that in front of Glassman. "He misses you too." For once, I'm not trying to be a dick. It's the God's honest truth.

Rock swallows hard and nods. "Keep an eye on him."

Glassman must have decided we've had enough time for small talk. "DA still won't hand over the name of the witness. Do you have any ideas?"

"No fucking clue."

"Could it be one of the dancers from your club?"

Rock glances at me before answering. "I can't imagine why one of them would lie."

"We did have an issue with the one, remember?" I float. Rock glares at me. He wants to handle this internally.

I want to get him out of jail any way we can.

HOPE

Heidi flat-out refused any sort of celebration for her graduation. She felt it was wrong to have a party while Rock was in jail. I couldn't argue with her there. It seems like every moment, even the ones that should be happy, are outlined in bitterness because Rock should be here too.

When Heidi threatened not to even go to the ceremony, the club banded together and fought her on that one.

She did have one request. "The only thing I want for graduation is for you guys to let me see Uncle Rock. Please?"

I don't think it's especially healthy for her to see him in jail.

But I've seen plenty of children in there visiting family members, so it's not like it never happens. Still, I feel strange about it. But she's so determined and earnest, I end up making the arrangements.

Teller and Murphy drive us to the jail the morning of her graduation. She has to be at the school at noon to get ready for the ceremony. So we have a couple hours to spend with Rock.

Teller escorts us inside. As her legal guardian, I need him here to get her into the visitation area.

"North," I inform the guard at the window. He raises an eyebrow at Heidi. "His god daughter. Her brother is," I point at Teller. "Her legal guardian." Teller steps up and passes over court documents and identification. This visit finally motivated Heidi to get her driver's permit and she proudly passes it over with her school identification.

"Purses, cell phones, jewelry goes in the locker." The officer points across the room and passes us a key.

We're escorted into a lesser controlled visiting area. Since Rock's stayed out of trouble, we're allowed a contact visit, so Heidi's able to give him a hug. Some of her excitement over the visit diminishes when she gets a look at the surroundings. But she puts on a brave smile for Rock's benefit. It's Teller who seems to be having the most trouble. It takes him a few seconds to get any words out.

"Hey, Rock."

The four of us settle down at a table and Heidi talks Rock's ear off about her learner's permit, graduation, the ceremony, the classes she's signed up to take over the summer and anything else in her universe. Rock's smiles are genuine and I think her visit cheers him a little more than my solemn ones usually do. After almost an hour, she winds down. Rock's gaze slides to me and a wry smile twists his mouth up. He turns back to Teller.

"You handling all this okay, big brother?" He lifts his chin at Heidi, but I think Rock's referring to more than just Heidi growing up.

"Best I can," Teller answers.

After they chat for a minute, Teller taps Heidi on the arm. "Let's give them a few minutes."

Heidi gives Rock another hug and follows her brother out to the waiting room.

I slide my hands across the table over Rock's and he squeezes them back. "Tell me the truth, you doing okay?" he asks.

"The truth? No. I miss you. And I'm furious at everyone involved in this."

"Including me?"

"No. Everyone but you."

His smile widens. "What do you have planned for Heidi?"

"Nothing. She refused. She asked for this visit. She said no parties until you're out."

He shakes his head. "That girl's something."

"Trinity made her a cake and I think we'll grill some stuff out back."

"Good. I appreciate her support. But she needs something special to mark the occasion."

There's not a lot to say after that.

"Better get going so she's not late."

"I know." I don't want to leave though.

"Come on, Baby Doll. I hate seeing you go, but I hate you being in here too." He waves his hand at the austere visiting room. "You don't belong here."

"Neither do you," I answer dryly.

"Yeah."

"I'll come this week."

"Monday or Tuesday."

Confused why he's so adamant about those days, I open my

mouth. Before I get the question out, he's standing and signaling the guard that he's ready to return.

I hate this. *Hate it.*

Dear Rock,

After I left today, Teller and I drove Heidi to school. It was a cloudy, overcast day for an outdoor June graduation. Somehow it seemed fitting though.

Heidi was quiet the whole way. Her silence made me question whether it had been a good idea to bring her to the jail. But when we got to the school, she gave me a fierce hug and thanked me for letting her see you.

Everyone met us there. The club took up three rows of seats, which seemed to please Heidi.

During the ceremony, so much anger overwhelmed me. Anger that you were being denied this event with your family.

Afterward, Heidi couldn't wait to leave. She very earnestly explained to me that two of the girls in her class had teased her about being an orphan for years, so having the club there meant so much to her. It took all my strength not to cry.

Now that she finally has her learner's permit, the club (i.e. Murphy) got her a car. It's a cute little thing, Murphy described as a mix of hatchback, SUV and sports car. I asked him why he didn't get me one instead of my old lady Subaru and he got all flustered. I felt bad and spent a good ten minutes assuring him I was only kidding.

More family stuff you missed. And I got angry again.

Because of the weather we moved the "cookout" inside. Afterward, Heidi and Axel left to hang out with her friends. I actually think they left to be with each other, but I kept that hunch to myself. I think Teller's given up hope that her virginity boat is still on dry land, and I'm keeping my nose out of it.

I went through a lot of emotions today. But there's one thing I never was —lonely. And that's because of you and the family you've given me. I don't think I could survive this without them. The brotherhood that you and the others have fought so hard to create is vibrant and alive.

I miss you terribly and you're in my every thought.

Love,

Hope

CHAPTER SIXTEEN

HOPE

As USUAL, per Rock's instructions, Wrath and I arrive at the jail promptly at eight. We're so early the front door hasn't been unlocked yet. The guard who opens it isn't familiar to me, but waves us inside.

"Attorney Hope Kendall here to see my client, Rochlan North," I pull out my identification and motion for Wrath to do the same. One of the guards leaves to get Rock, while the other one studies my credentials.

"You ain't his attorney. He's got that high-priced suit."

I'd been afraid of this. "Yes, I'm working *of counsel* to Mr. Glassman." This isn't a lie. I've provided Glassman with a lot of research and memos of law on a number of topics. None of those required me to visit with Rock, but that's not something I need to share.

To my astonishment, he looks up Glassman's number and *calls him* to verify my story. With wide eyes, I turn and stare at Wrath. His blank face does nothing to stop my palms from going slick.

Glassman—or someone at the firm—thankfully acknowledges that yes, I am of counsel to Mr. Glassman—not the firm, only Mr. Glassman. Only for this case. *Big help, thanks so much.*

The guard glares at me and I can't fathom what I've done to irritate this man so much. It bothers me on a few levels. I've always tried to be kind and professional when interacting with anyone—law enforcement, client, adversary—until they give me a reason not to. Here, I'm not sure what will work and what might piss this guy off and bar me from seeing Rock. I work a casually flirtatious smile onto my face. "Is everything okay?"

"You're clear to go. But he—" he says with a jab of his finger in Wrath's direction while walking around to my side "—has to stay out here."

A rush of fear burns beneath my skin. Somehow I manage to answer calmly and professionally. "Why, officer? He's my assistant. He's accompanied me before."

His face transforms from asshole-blocking-me-from-seeing-my-man to something much more sinister. "Assistant my ass. I know you're North's bitch. That's what those MC boys do. Get their ol' ladies to do their dirty work. For a lawyer you're awfully stupid," he hisses in my ear.

My whole life I've tended to stick my foot in my mouth when I'm flustered. So it takes a second to bite back the "Can I speak to your supervisor?" request forming on my tongue.

This problem isn't going to be solved with bureaucratic complaint filing. If I make a fuss, Rock will be the one to suffer for it.

"Are you denying my visit as well?" I ask as calmly as possible.

In the minute he takes to think it over, fear wraps its cold arms around my middle, squeezing tight.

"Nah, come on through the metal detector." He motions me with his hand and a chilling smile.

The buzzer goes off on my first try. He makes me take my shoes off and walk through again. I know it's the underwire in my bra setting it off but I'm too afraid to draw attention to any part of my body. Any time this has happened to me at the courthouse, the officers have just used their wand over me and let me go. I'm a lawyer for God's sake. Not a threat.

But this man—Officer Izzard his badge says—wears a sadistic smile when the buzzer goes off again.

"Step over here, miss." He points. "Palms against the wall."

This time I can't keep my mouth shut. "You're going to frisk me? Shouldn't a female guard do this?"

He leans in close, stale coffee breath assaulting my nostrils. "You wanna see your man, this is the only way. I can't have you smuggling in contraband."

"I'm not, I wouldn't." My pointless protest seems to amuse him. This has nothing to do with safety and everything to do with humiliating and degrading me. My need to see Rock rises to overwhelming proportions.

"Hope, what's going on?" Wrath calls out.

Rock's powerless and at the mercy of this sadistic asshole inside these walls. I *need* to see him and make sure he's unhurt. "I'm okay." But by the tone of my voice it's obvious I'm anything but okay.

My palms press into the cold, scratchy cinderblock.

He pats me down professionally—at first.

"Get your fucking hands off her, you piece of shit!" Wrath yells from the other side.

The groping stops. "Sit down and shut the fuck up, or I got a cell you can park your ass in for a few days."

"Hope. Forget it. Let's go."

"I'm okay," I repeat. *I'mokayI'mokayI'mokay* I keep saying in my head until the words blend together in a senseless mush.

The guard's hands return to my hips, slithering down my legs, his fingers brush against my ankles and I fight the urge to scream. A different kind of fear takes hold as his hands travel back up my body, under my sweater, tickling my stomach, grazing the undersides of my breasts, tracing the bottom of my bra. Chilling, sweaty fear paralyzes me.

"Izzard!" Someone calls out from around the corner.

His slimy touch vanishes. "Keep your mouth shut, or I'll fuck your man up after you leave," he growls in my ear.

I nod once to indicate I understand his threat. My mouth can't form any words.

Humiliation and terror still crawl over my skin as he leads me into the visitation room.

Rock stands. Anger radiates from every part of him when he sees Izzard at my back.

"Have a nice visit," he says before leaving.

As soon as he's gone, I collapse into the seat on my side of the table. "Hope, are you okay?"

Chin up. "I'm fine. How are you?"

"Where's Wrath?"

"He's, um in the waiting room. They wouldn't let him in with me today."

"Why?"

I shrug. Lying to the man I love adds insult to the hideous thing that just happened outside, but I can't tell him this. Not now when he's so vulnerable.

Later.

Later I'll tell him everything.

Because I know in my heart Rock will be the one to solve this problem. *His way.* And much to my self-horror, that's the only thought that gives me comfort.

WRATH

Knowing that slimy motherfucker put his hands on Hope tested every single bit of my willpower. Violating and disrespecting her won't go unpunished.

I'll make sure of it.

I should have gotten Hope out of there the second that weasel picked up the phone to call Glassman's office. It's on me that she got hurt.

Waiting for her to return is torture.

Izzard—you bet your ass I got that fucker's name memorized—sits behind the window with his feet up on the counter.

Cocksucker.

Hope seems less rattled when she returns. Until the guard calls out to her. "Have a nice afternoon, Miss Kendall. See you again soon."

She doesn't turn or hesitate, just heads for the door.

When we're in the truck she stares straight ahead and doesn't say a word.

"Tell me everything now. I know he frisked you, but I couldn't see—"

"Wrath, please—"

"I need to know."

She lets out a long sigh and I think it's better that we're in the car so we don't have to look at each other when she gives me the details of how he fucking felt her up. All my anger threatens to boil over when I think of this sweet, innocent woman being manhandled by that dirty piece of shit.

"I'm so sorry."

"It's not your fault," she answers softly. "I'm just so thankful you were there so something worse didn't happen."

I don't know what to say. I'm supposed to be protecting her. I failed, and she's thanking me. "We'll take care of him. Believe it."

"I don't—"

"Retaliation is what *we* do, Hope. How he disrespected you? The president's ol' lady. It's an insult to the entire club." It's more than that though. I can't look at her anymore and not see her as a little sister.

"I know," she whispers.

We're silent for a few more miles. Then I ask what's weighing on me. I hate that I couldn't see Rock. There are a thousand signals I could have picked up from him to give me a hint of how to handle this guard. "How was he?"

"Okay." Out of the corner of my eye, I see her shaking her head. "No. Something's wrong, Wrath. I'm scared. That guard. This wasn't random. Rock was furious when he saw who escorted me back there.

He asked me all sorts of questions. He knew something bad happened. But I couldn't tell him. I can't have him get in trouble—"

As much as I hate saying it, "You did the right thing."

"How can we leave him there?"

"Rock can handle himself, sweetheart." I'm amazed at how calm and rational my voice comes out, since I feel anything but. I'm ready to blow that fucking place up if that's what it takes to get Rock out. "When's his next bail hearing?"

"Thursday."

"Good. You focus your energy on helping Glassman with that. The club will handle the guard."

"Okay."

She doesn't protest. Doesn't suggest we file a complaint or contact Glassman. The fact that she's put all her trust in the club to solve this, punches me in the gut with a number of mixed feelings.

Trinity meets us in the living room when we get home. "Everything okay? How's Rock?"

Hope glances at me before answering. Shit. I don't want to lie to Trinity, but I don't want to upset her either. "There were some issues, but we're handling it."

She looks to Hope who just nods and takes Trinity's hand. "I need to go upstairs. Can we talk later?"

"Of course."

After Hope leaves, Trinity swings her curious gaze my way. Christ, those beautiful honey eyes hypnotize me. "What happened?"

"Nothing, babe. I need to call the guys in for church. Can you help me with that?"

She folds her arms and cocks her head. "Is Rock okay?"

"Yeah. Hope saw him."

The phone call I'd been expecting since we left the jail comes in just as Trinity's about to ask more questions.

"I'll get the guys," she whispers as I answer the phone.

"Will you accept the charges—"

"Yes," I snap at the automated question.

"What the fuck happened?" Rock asks in a controlled voice. I know he's got no privacy, so he'll watch what he says.

I can't tell him that piece of shit put his hands on Hope. Rock hears that, he'll lose it and kill the guy. Then there'll be no chance in hell of getting him free. "That fucking guard wouldn't let me in. What's going on? Is he messing with you?"

He sighs. "Nothing I can't handle. But that's it for her. No more visits. Tell the rest of the guys."

"I'm calling everyone in for church right now."

"Good. But no action on this. This one's mine when I get out."

We'll see about that. Technically, Rock has no vote while he's incarcerated. The club's so tight, that we'll honor Rock's orders for now. But if this gets worse—we may take a vote to handle the guard on our own and suffer Rock's anger later. Either way, I'm letting everyone know now.

"Hope said Thursday's the next hearing?"

"Yeah. Glassman wants her there to testify. I want you and Z with her. But stay outside the courtroom."

"You got it."

"I didn't get to ask her, everyone okay?"

Christ, my brother's going through God only knows what and he's worried about us. "We're fine."

"How's Trinity?"

"Okay. Hope and I didn't say anything. I didn't want to upset her."

"Yeah. Don't."

We're cut off before we finish, and I wish Rock would let me get a burner cell to him. But he's stuck on the idea of doing everything by the book, so he can get the fuck out as soon as he's cleared.

I guess I don't blame him.

The somber mood of each brother doesn't improve my attitude one bit. Z and I have refused to take Rock's seat, so it sits there empty. A grim reminder of why we're all here this afternoon.

Once everyone's seated, I get right down to the meat of this session. "Went to see Rock today. Guard there—" Shit I'm still so fucking pissed I can't say the words. "Threw attitude at me and Hope.

Made things difficult and wouldn't let me see Rock." Guys grumble at that and I haven't even gotten to the worst of it. "When she couldn't get through the metal detector without setting it off, he—" my jaw's so fucking tight I don't know if I can get the words out. The room's silent, everyone waiting. "He used a pat down as an excuse to feel her up. She wouldn't give me a lot of details, but—"

Murphy, surprisingly is the first one out of his chair. "He's dead. No fucking—"

"Easy, brother."

Z's staring at me with a slack jaw and some serious fury building in his eyes. Shit, one glance around the table and it's clear everyone shares Murphy's opinion.

"I spoke to Rock right before coming in here. He doesn't know what happened to her. But I got the impression he's having issues with this asshole aside from today. He wants to handle it when he gets out."

"Fuck that," Dex barks out. "No one gets away with hurting her. And we can't let him have free rein on our prez either."

"Break his hands," Teller says. Murmurs of approval go around the room. "Retribution should fit the deed. He put his hands on her. We cripple his hands."

Murphy picks up Teller's train of thought. "Side benefits, he's out of work for a few months but still alive for Rock to deal with when he gets out."

"Blanket party," Ravage shouts and I shake my head. A blanket over the fuck's head and a beating in a back alley might actually end up being how we take care of this.

"Let's vote," I ask.

"Do it," Z says.

Everyone else is in favor too.

I settle into my chair so we can discuss details. "We can't have this look like it's connected to Rock in any way."

Z nods. "Needs to happen away from the jail."

"He's met you," Murphy points out. "You probably shouldn't go."

"Fuck that."

He holds up his hands. "Just sayin'."

I hate that he's right.

Z jots down the little bit I know about Izzard. In a few days this guy will no longer be a threat.

HOPE

Dear Rock,

My hands are still shaking as I write this. I couldn't tell you what happened today. I've never been so scared in my entire life. Not for myself. For you. I've been so worried that a rival MC member or some gang member would harm you inside. Even though I know better, this situation hadn't occurred to me. I'm more terrified than ever thinking of you unable to fight back, because I know you won't do anything to jeopardize getting out as soon as you can.

He threatened to hurt you if I said anything. But that's not why I didn't tell you. I knew if I told you what he did. The way he spoke to me. The way he put his hands on me. You'd kill him.

I knew this because the thought of him hurting you made me want to go back to the jail tonight, follow him to his house and shoot him without a hint of remorse.

The only reason I endured his foulness was to see you. The knowledge that either you or the club would punish him when the time was right gave me strength. I fully understand now why you say an insult to one is an insult to the entire club. I think Wrath was as angry as you would have been. I know he feels like he failed me. But he didn't. He did the right thing.

I love you and need you back where I know you're safe.

Love,

Hope

ROCK

I knew something was wrong the minute I saw Hope.

Lizard escorting her into the room brought all the rage I've been stuffing down to the surface.

Thank God she hadn't come to the jail alone.

A different guard, JT, escorts me back to my cell after she leaves. He and I have gotten friendly enough that I'm comfortable asking why Lizard's here today.

"OT. He always sucks up as much as he can." JT cocks his head. "He's not bothering you, is he?"

"Nah. Just a prick."

JT doesn't seem surprised. Nor does he disagree.

It's not until later that night that I fully understand how much Lizard needs to die.

"Man your ol' lady's got some nice fuckin' tits on her." His voice wakes me from my half-sleep. He makes some obscene grabby gesture. The urge to destroy him makes me shake.

"Nice and firm. Real too. Figured they'd be plastic." I keep telling myself he's bluffing to get me to come at him. But Hope's flustered face and bright red cheeks flash in my mind from earlier today and I *know* he's telling the truth.

No wonder Wrath called an emergency meeting today. I knew there was more to it than he let on. And I know the reason he didn't tell me is so I don't do something stupid. If I give into my rage, I'll rip this shithead apart.

Lizard wants it. Wants me to snap—and trust me, inside I'm snapping louder than logs on a motherfuckin' fire. But outside, I'm calm and quiet.

He opens the cell door and I sit up, placing my back against the wall. "Didn't you hear me? Your old lady's got some fantastic tits."

Whatever he's about to dish out I'm not in the mood for.

But I'll take it so I can get back to my girl.

"Five minutes, motherfucker," I finally answer.

He gets up in my face. "What's that?"

"Five minutes outside these walls is all I'll need with you."

A flicker of fear and uncertainty registers in his eyes. Without the security of his badge and baton, he's one hundred percent coward.

Then he stands straight and smug, crossing his arms over his chest.

"Think next time she comes to visit, I'll search her twat to make sure she's not smuggling in contraband."

To anyone else, his tone might sound full of authority and power. But I'm not easily impressed or scared. No, to me he sounds like a dead man gasping for his last breaths. Because by touching Hope, he's bought himself a bullet to the brain. Even if it takes me years, this fucker will *not* go unpunished.

CHAPTER SEVENTEEN

HOPE

"I'M SO NERVOUS."

Wrath and Z both reassure me before I push through the heavy doors to the Slater County courtroom where Rock's bail hearing is being held. "We'll be right here when you're done, Hope," Z calls after me.

Mr. Glassman meets me in the back of the room. "Is Rock here yet?" I ask before he gets any words out.

He steers me into one of the attorney conference rooms and shuts the door. "Not yet. We need to go over your testimony." So for the next half hour that's what we do. Fear cripples my lungs when the bailiff bangs on the door to announce we're up.

My heart jumps at the sight of Rock's big frame filling up one of the chairs at the defense table. There's no jury, so he's wearing his county-issued orange jumpsuit.

Suddenly I can't swallow over the lump in my throat.

I follow Glassman up the aisle and take the seat on the other side of Rock.

"Hey, baby," he whispers.

His cuffed hands rest in his lap, and I risk wrapping my fingers around them for a few seconds. Inside my heart's breaking into a million agonizing pieces. Outside, I try to project calm reassurance to the man I love and professional indifference to everyone else.

When the bailiff announces the judge's return to the courtroom, I stand and move to one of the seats behind the defense table.

I'm so focused on Rock—or rather the back of Rock's head—that I barely listen to what I know is an eloquent plea from Glassman. I pull my notes out of my briefcase and shuffle through them. But I already know the words by heart.

When it's time for me to speak, I stand and approach the podium. The DA nods at me. I've gotten the impression even he thinks the judge's refusal to grant bail is excessive. The fact that he hasn't opposed anything Glassman said this morning only reinforces that suspicion.

"Your honor, the primary purpose of bail is to ensure that the defendant will be present for all court appearances—"

"Ms. Kendall," the judge interrupts. He didn't interrupt anyone else today. "I'm well-aware of the purpose of bail." I bite back the "are you sure, because it doesn't seem like it," response that immediately jumps to mind.

There's no way in hell I'll let this judge rattle me. "Yes, well, Mr. North is a well-known businessman in the area. He's lived in the capital area for the majority of his adult life and he has a large number of friends and family in this area." I outline each of the criteria used to set bail, skipping over the ones unfavorable to Rock.

"Ms. Kendall, the defendant has a criminal record." I knew he'd bring that up.

"None of those convictions are within the last ten years, Your Honor, and he has no record of flight. Further, the evidence is flimsy at best—"

"Objection," the DA says without bothering to stand up.

Glassman argues the objection while I wait to continue. I've saved my most compelling argument for last.

"Go on, Ms. Kendall."

"Finally, Your Honor, Mr. North and I are planning to be married in the fall. I also have strong ties to this community. Our wedding will be held in Empire County. There is no reason for him to flee. Thank you."

On my way back to my seat, Rock catches my eye and he nods at me. I flash a quick smile, which almost turns into a gasp as I take in the dark bruising around his left eye. No wonder he wouldn't look at me before. Panic claws at me, desperate to get him free. The roaring blood in my ears drowns out some of the judges words. But I tune in enough to hear him say he's reserving his decision. At least it's not a flat-out denial like the last two times.

ROCK

My girl's something. To complete this full circle of irony trip we seem to be on, here she is in court speaking on my behalf again.

This time it's a felony that could get me sent away for twenty-five years instead of simple pot possession.

She's wearing dress pants, a thin, short-sleeved sweater, heels and more makeup than she usually bothers with. Not the skirt I first saw her in. She's utterly calm and professional as she approaches the bench. But I know my girl. I know by the way she can't keep her hands still and the panic in her eyes how hard this is for her.

Pride surges through me as I catch the lick of anger brightening her eyes when the judge interrupts her. I admire her strength and courage as she stands there and so beautifully pleads for my release.

She shocks me by using our wedding as one more reason to grant bail. I hadn't expected that. An attorney admitting in open court that she plans to marry a man being accused of murder? I can hear the screech of tires and smell the burning wreckage of her career crashing and burning all around us.

I'd been trying to keep my head down so she wouldn't see the present from Lizard's fist staining my face. I'm fine. But I can't stand giving her yet another thing to worry over. And I'd take a thousand more hits from that asshole if it means she's safe.

Of course she notices. Fear and fury flash over her face.

"Rock," she calls out when the bailiff takes my arm to lead me back downstairs to the van that will take me back to the county jail.

"I'm okay," I reassure her.

There's no time or opportunity to say much more before I'm taken away.

HOPE

There's nothing more brutal than watching the man you love be taken away in handcuffs over a crime you know he didn't commit and a judge refusing to grant bail for no reason. I'm convinced of it. Knowing that he's hurt, that someone hurt him, makes it so much worse.

After Rock leaves, the judge motions for me to sit at the table next to Glassman.

"Off the record," he says to the stenographer.

His hawkish eyes zero in on me and a zip of fear tears through my chest. "Miss Kendall, I find it deeply disturbing that an educated professional woman, an attorney, would associate with such a disturbing criminal element."

My palm slaps down on the table so hard, it echoes through the room as I push out my chair to stand. Glassman clamps his hand on my leg to keep me seated.

"Your honor, Miss Kendall's personal life is not at issue here," Glassman says.

"She made it my issue by testifying." His sanctimonious gaze swings back to me. "Young lady, you better think long and hard about your life decisions before you end up in a cell too."

I can't breathe. Can't form a single word. I'm so stunned by the talking-down to, I don't know what to do. I want to scream at him that he doesn't know a fucking thing about me or Rock, but the bastard still hasn't decided on whether he's granting bail or not. I can't be the cause of Rock staying in jail another second because I can't keep my big mouth shut.

Beyond that, the patriarchal bullshit this old man just spewed at me burns like acid. People outside the MC world love to criticize the misogyny and subjugation of the women inside it. But oddly enough, some of the worst sexism I've encountered has been in the legal world. Usually from old fuckers like this one who ask me innocuous sounding questions such as, am I old enough to be an attorney, if I'm married, when I plan to have children or what does my husband think of my career. Stupid crap they'd never ask a male attorney. But *this* has to be the worst.

I'm fuming by the time we leave the courtroom. Glassman takes my elbow and leads me to a corner across from where Wrath and Z are waiting. I hold up one finger, asking them to wait.

"What the fuck was that?" I snap at Glassman.

"I don't know. I've never seen anything like it. I'm sorry." He glances over his shoulder at Wrath and Z. Admittedly they're a scary combo. But as mean as Wrath's been to me in the past, he's never once made me feel as small as Judge Holier-Than-Thou just did. "Are you okay, Hope?" Glassman asks.

"No. I want my fiancé home. This is crap! He's got no right keeping—"

"Hope, calm down. I'm asking if *you're* okay?"

"I'm fine."

He sighs and throws another glance at Wrath and Z. "I've seen how much you two care for each other, but the judge might be right. You're definitely risking your career—"

I hold up my hand to stop whatever else he's about to say. "I don't give a flying fuck about my career at the moment. I love Rock. I'd choose him over this," I wave my hand in front of his face, indicating the whole legal process, "in a heartbeat."

"I understand."

I don't think he actually does understand, nor do I care what he thinks.

I wave the guys over so they can ask Glassman their questions. He explains things in his overpriced-lawyerly way, which amounts to "wait a few days."

After Glassman leaves, Z puts his arm around my shoulder. "You look really shaken, Hope. What happened?"

"I don't want to talk about it here." I point at the security camera above us and Z nods.

Wrath pulls me in for a quick, brotherly hug before we head outside.

I feel like I left a piece of my heart in the building, except I know my heart is on his way back to the county jail.

WRATH

Whatever happened in that courtroom was bad. Hope's a mess when she walks out with Glassman. Her cheeks are red, eyes glassy. I think I see steam shooting out of her ears though, so that's a good sign. Z and I glance at each other and I know he's thinking the same thing.

When we finally get her in the car, Z and I both turn around to face her. "Spill," I demand.

"Before I tell you about the hearing. We've got a problem. Rock had a black eye." She chokes on the last sentence, but I make out her words. Rage pounds through me.

"I don't know if it's that guard or someone else. He tried to hide it from me and they took him away so fast, we couldn't talk—"

"Did Glassman say anything?"

"No. I don't know if he even noticed."

That's fine. The suit won't fix this. The club will.

"Was he okay otherwise, sweetheart," Z asks as I turn the engine over and head home.

"I think so."

"We'll take care of it."

"I know," she says softly.

Once we get on the highway, soft Hope vanishes. Ballsy Hope is a lot easier for me to deal with. As she unleashes her pent up fury from the hearing, my hands tighten on the steering wheel. No way should some asshole talk to her like that. Judge or not, I don't give a fuck.

Maybe we stop by his house after we fuck up Izzard and rip his damn tongue out.

Z doesn't even have to call any of the brothers in for church. They're all waiting at the clubhouse when we return. Hope holds her head up and calmly explains the judge pussied out and won't make a decision for a few days. She's honest that Rock's chances of getting out are shit and doesn't sugarcoat one tiny detail. What she doesn't mention is Rock's black eye. She trusts that I'll take care of that. And I will.

When she's finished, Trinity hugs her and the girls head upstairs. I tip my head at the war room. "Everyone at the table in five."

They don't need five.

Z's the last one to the table. He holds up a piece of paper and nods at me on his way in.

There's no reason to fuck around, so I get right to the point. "Hope didn't mention it, but Rock came to court with a black eye. She couldn't get any information out of him or figure out if he has any other injuries." Angry voices fill the room, and I whistle to shut everyone the fuck up. Christ, I miss Rock.

"We don't know if it's the guard or if he got into it with another inmate, but we should move on Izzard now. I doubt Rock's the only person he's fucked with, so there'll be plenty of suspects."

Everyone agrees. Never been prouder of every single one of my bloodthirsty brothers.

Z taps the table and I sit so he can speak. "He's a perverted fucker. Likes finding his "dates" on Craigslist. Roughed up more than one girl. I didn't have enough time to figure out if he's connected to one of the crews in the area, but we gotta assume he might be."

"Set up a date," Sparky says. He almost never says anything in church, unless it's about his plants.

"Yeah, that's what I was thinking," Z answers. His gaze shifts to me. "Don't even suggest—"

"Swan will do it," Dex says and we all turn to him for further explanation. "She loves the club, she's been upset she can't do more to help out."

I nod, warming up to the idea. "We need to make sure she's protected and nothing happens to her."

Dex signals me. "I'll be responsible for getting her out. Who's giving the beatdown?"

I've given this a lot of thought since our last sit down and mask or not, silent or not, there aren't many guys my size running around. It'll be obvious as fuck where this payback's coming from if I'm there. We're doing this for Rock and for the club, not my ego. As much as it burns my fuckin' ass, I can't go. "I think, Teller, Murphy, and Z should deliver the message. I'd like a fourth guy there to keep the engine running."

Ravage raises his hand. "I'll do it."

I jerk my thumb at the door. "Go grab Swan."

Swan's more than agreeable to the plan. Well the part of the plan we actually tell her about. Do we tell her the guy's a CO at Rock's jail? Fuck no. All she knows is the club needs to lure some fuckface to a remote location and we need her help to do it. Does she ask any follow-up questions? Nope.

She has one request. "Let me know when, so I can get my shift at CB covered."

"I'll handle it," Dex says.

We make the arrangements for Saturday night. We'll all be on edge until then, so I tell the guys to go smoke up or do whatever the fuck they want—within reason—for now.

I'm not expecting Sway and two of his guys to show up a few hours later with an offer to "help" us out while Rock's away. The last fucking thing I feel like doing is entertaining his drunk ass.

Sway's a hard motherfucker—you don't earn that president's patch by being a pussy—but we've sparred enough in the past for him to know fucking with me won't end well for him.

He slaps my hand and pulls me to him for a hug. "Sorry, I couldn't get up here sooner. We got shit going down in our territory."

"It's okay, brother. Appreciate your support. Letting Steer stay with us and help out at CB for a while was a big help," Z says after he gets the same greeting.

"Mind if we crash here tonight?"

"Not at all," I answer with as much hospitality as I'm capable of.

Setting my personal irritation over how Sway's treated Trinity in the past aside, I don't like him sniffing around our clubhouse at a time when he probably assumes we're weak. Lot of guys in our organization would love to have a piece of our grow operation.

Not that we couldn't use the extra muscle, but having him here annoys me. Rock wouldn't like it and neither do I.

CHAPTER EIGHTEEN

HOPE

I'M SO thankful Trinity's here for me to vent to. She listens and asks questions. After I'm finished calling the judge every foul name in the book, she bites her lip and puts her hand on my arm.

"Some clubs, you know, when a member's inside, there's an exception for ol' ladies to sleep with other brothers while her man's doing time for the club," Trinity rambles out.

"That's gross," I say without thinking.

Her eyes meet mine then dart away and she shrugs. "I don't know. It's a way to take care of her while her man's inside."

A heavy uneasiness spreads through my stomach. What's Trinity trying to hint at? "Well, the last thing on my mind right now is sex."

She opens her mouth to say something else, but I place my hand on her arm. "Please, Trinity. As bad as today was, I can't think about him being locked-up long term. I have to keep believing something will go in our favor and he'll be home soon. I'll go crazy otherwise."

Her throat works for a second before she nods. "I know. I just thought, well Wra—"

"Ew, ew, ew. Do *not* finish that sentence." *Ew.*

Her cheeks turn pink and I realize she wasn't just teasing me. Forced laughter spills from her. "No, *my* man's not available." She stops for a second then eyes me thoughtfully. "Although, given how much time you guys have been spending together lately—"

"Ew! I think that would be horrifying for all parties involved. That would be like banging my brother." My face twists into an exaggerated yuck expression. She finally smiles and shakes her head.

"Well, at least I made you laugh," she says.

"Yes, you did. Thank you."

As soon as the door closes behind Trinity, I have to lie down. Not to sleep, but to stare at the ceiling and figure out how to fix this. I'm so out of my mind scared and worried about Rock. I know I've been leaning on Wrath more than I should. And I know he's been working hard to look after me, because it's what Rock asked him to do. But I wish it had occurred to me how much this is affecting everyone. Especially Trinity. It's been clear since the day I met her, she adores Rock and looks up to him. She's probably having a hard time with everything and it's not fair that I'm taking up so much of Wrath's time.

Rolling over, I grab my phone off the nightstand and send Wrath a text.

He's at my door a few seconds later. "You okay?" he asks, pushing the door open. "Sway and his crew just showed up. Unless you really need something, I want you to stay up here."

Christ, just what we need. "Is Tawny with him?"

"No."

Thank God.

Scooting off the bed, I meet him at the open door and shut it behind him. He raises an eyebrow. "What's going on, Hope?"

"I need to talk to you about Trinity."

His eyebrows draw down. "Why? What's wrong?"

Crap. I don't know what to say. I feel like I'm tattling on her, but that comment about Wrath and I spending so much time together came from somewhere. I focus my gaze on my bookshelf. "Nothing. I think…she's probably having a hard time with everything." I take a

chance and look him in the eye. "I know she and Rock have a special...
bond and I don't know. You've been spending so much time worrying
over me. Just make sure you're taking some time for her."

"What happened, Hope?" he asks softly. At least he's not mad.

"Nothing."

He waits quietly. God damn, he's a pain in the ass.

"Nothing. She mentioned that some clubs have like, a prison clause
or something, so when a guy's inside, the ol' lady can—"

"Jesus Christ."

"I thought she was joking at first."

He pins me with a hard look. "What else are you not telling me?"

"Nothing."

"Hope. If you say 'nothing' one more time, I'm going to pick you
up and shake it out of you."

Okay, the image that conjures up makes me laugh. Wrath does not
laugh.

"Nothing, but she made a joke about how much time we've been
spending together—"

"Ew."

My mouth twists into a sour smile. "Yeah, that's what I said."

He looks so upset, I'm at a loss. "Wrath, I appreciate everything
you've been doing for me. I'm sorry I've been leaning on you so
much—"

"It's my job, Hope." He glances away. "Besides, you know I'd do
anything for him."

"I know. And I was there. I heard what Rock asked you to do. But
I'm fine. I promise not to go anywhere unprotected. Or leave without
letting you know. I understand how serious this is and I won't do
anything to make it harder on you."

"Hope—"

"I'm doing okay. Today sucked, but I have faith he's going to be
home soon. Please, take care of Trinity. Rock would want that too."

"Shit. She's been so quiet. I know she's upset, but, I'm sorry."

"Don't be sorry. There's nothing to be sorry for."

"The way she looks up to Rock. I shoulda realized."

"Wrath. You've got so much—"

"Her father died in prison."

That stops me. "I remember her telling me that once."

He nods. "You need me, call me."

"I will."

He closes the door behind him and I lie back down, feeling more alone than ever.

WRATH

I don't know what to think as I take my time going back downstairs. Take my time because I'm furious and I don't want to end up yelling at Trinity. It's not her I'm mad at. I'm pissed at myself for not paying better attention to her and making sure she's okay. When I find Z, I pull him aside.

"Keep yourself sober and keep an eye on Sway."

His gaze darts to the middle of the room, where Sway's busy dry-humping a couple of club girls. A few of them I don't recognize and assume they came in with Sway's crew. "Don't worry, I plan on it."

"I told Hope that unless she needs something to stay upstairs."

"Good call. I'll check in on her later."

"I'd appreciate it."

He seems to sense my agitation. "Trinity went straight to your room when she saw Sway and his guys here. Go hang with her. I got this."

"Thanks, brother."

I poke my head in the champagne room, but the only lawlessness going on in there is Sparky, Stash and some of Sway's guys getting high. "Need anything, Sparky?" I call out.

He flashes me a thumb's up, so I assume that means no and back out of the room. At least he's out of the basement for once.

It takes a second to push my door open. I'm still trying to figure out how to fix this. What the hell do I say to Trinity?

"Hey, Angel Face," I say as I enter our room. She's busy working at the computer, but turns as soon as she hears my voice.

"Hi."

"You working on something?"

"Yeah. Editing some of those pictures from the park."

My chest tightens at the memory of that day. First time she told me she loved me.

I drop down on the edge of the bed. "Come here, baby. I need to talk to you."

She turns and I hate the tremble of her bottom lip. "What's wrong?"

"Nothing. Wanna talk. That's all."

"Okay." She takes her time crossing the short distance to the bed. When she's within reach, I grab her and pull her into my lap.

"Miss you, angel. Feels like we haven't talked in days."

"We talk." Her mouth turns up and her fingers brush my cheek. "We talked this morning."

She's teasing me, but it somehow makes me feel worse. "What we did this morning didn't involve a lot of talking."

"Yeah." She leans in and whispers in my ear. "Want a repeat?"

"Don't distract me." Her hand drops back into her lap. "Did you offer Hope the guys' stud services?"

Even though I asked the question in a teasing way, her eyes widen and she blinks a few times. "Did she say that? All I said was, some clubs, you know—"

"Not this one. You think Rock wouldn't slit the throat of anyone who touched his woman?"

Her face crumples and she buries her face against my shoulder. My arms wrap around her, holding her tight while she breaks down. "I owe Rock my life. I just want to do whatever needs to be done to get him through this and Hope's so important to him."

"Okay. Okay. I understand, angel. I'm not mad at you."

"You're not?"

"No. I should've known this would be hard on you. I'm sorry I've been neglecting you."

"What? You haven't—"

"Yeah, I have."

"It's hard on the whole club."

I'm not gonna upset her more by reminding her of her dad. "Yeah. We've had an easy run of things the last few years. Rock's kept the club outta trouble. We're all spun."

"Hope—"

"She's fine. She's worried about you."

"I'm sorry. I didn't mean—I don't know what I was thinking. She told me about court this morning and—"

God dammit. Why the fuck did Hope have to spew all that at Trinity. "What did she tell you?"

"How nasty the judge was. That Rock didn't look good, and she's worried one of the guards is bothering him."

Fuck. I'm glad Hope and Trinity have gotten to be close friends. They both need each other. But I wish Hope would keep some things to herself. "Yeah, it sucked. But I don't want you upset. We're all going to get through this."

"I know."

I wish I believed my own words.

CHAPTER NINETEEN

HOPE

WITH SO MUCH ON my mind, I forgot Wrath's warning about Sway and some of the guys from his club stopping by last night. Since I moved in, I've grown comfortable at the clubhouse. Even in my misery of missing Rock, I feel at home here with the brothers, Trinity and even the club girls who are up here more often than ever.

I should have remembered that Sway runs his clubhouse a bit differently than Rock runs his.

Trinity and I are having breakfast with the guys—as we normally do—when Sway joins us.

Next to me, Trinity's vibrating with tension. Whether it's from sitting at the same table with Sway or because club girls are in her kitchen unsupervised, I'm not sure. Wrath has his arm slung around her shoulders, in what to anyone else probably looks casual, but I'm pretty sure it's the only thing keeping her butt in the chair.

Z groans at the plate of pancakes Swan sets in front of him. "Tryin' to make me fat, girl?"

She laughs and returns to the kitchen.

I poke Z in the side. "I'm sure Wrath has some chores you can do to work it off," I tease.

Z and Wrath both chuckle at my harmless joke.

Sway narrows his eyes at me. "Shouldn't you gals be in the kitchen so the men can talk business?" He flicks his hand toward the kitchen in a dismissive gesture. I'm sure he expects us to follow.

As far as morning greetings go, that's probably the rudest one I've ever received. Trinity's body goes rigid. Under the table, Z taps my leg. I guess he's afraid the "screw you" that's sitting on my tongue might come flying out of my mouth.

"We like it this way in *our* clubhouse," Wrath says in a low fuck-off voice that works so much better than any retort I could have come up with.

The tension at the table rises to almost uncomfortable levels. Trinity jumps up and hustles into the kitchen before Wrath can stop her. Even though I'm squirming and staring at my plate, I stay put. No way am I letting him intimidate me into leaving the table.

Sway eyes me—and even though I've barely said a word—I seem to have offended him. I don't get it since he's been nice to me the other times we've met. Then again, I was always with Rock.

Well, I won Wrath over. Maybe I can win Sway over too.

Eventually the guys turn their conversation to bike upgrades and modifications. Since I have nothing to add to that conversation, I keep my mouth shut.

Murphy joins us as we're finishing up. "Morning, First Lady," he greets me, receiving a scowl from Sway.

"When'd you guys all get so whipped?" he jokes.

Unaware of the fun we've already had at the table, Murphy raises an eyebrow. He settles into his chair slowly and glances around, taking in the situation. Wrath's right, Murphy's a keen observer.

"You need one of us to drive you downtown today, Hope?" Murphy asks.

"Yes."

Trinity finally returns from the kitchen, but she doesn't join us. Instead she stops behind Wrath, slipping her arms around his shoulders and kissing his cheek. She whispers something in his ear, and he stretches his arms back to pull her closer. It's sweet and makes me miss Rock even more.

When they're finished, she taps my shoulder. "If you're done, do you want to work on that project with me?"

I jump out of my chair so fast, it almost falls over, thrilled to have an excuse to get the hell out of here that has nothing to do with Sway. "Sure."

Z's hand brushes mine as I walk past him. "I'll take you downtown. Let me know when you're ready."

"Thank you."

We haven't even cleared the dining room when Sway's voice reaches me. "Her man ain't even here, why're you all kissing her ass?"

"We're showing our president's woman the respect she deserves," Murphy snaps. His sharp tone almost makes me stop and go back, but Trinity drags me down to her room.

"Ugh, what a pig," she groans after we're safe inside her room.

"What the hell was that? He wasn't that rude to me when I visited his clubhouse."

"Maybe he ran out of little blue pills last night." Her shoulders shake with disgust. "*He's* the type of guy who would make you earn your keep on your back while your man's inside."

It takes a second to process that information. "Eww."

Before I ask any more questions, she pins me with a stare. "I'm mad at you, by the way."

"Me? Why?" What did I do now? I can't seem to help sticking my foot in my mouth no matter what I do.

She smiles to soften up her tone. "Why'd you tell Wrath about that prison clause thing I told you about?"

Oh. That. "I wasn't tattling." *Well, yeah I kind of was.* "I just wanted him to stop worrying about me. I can bug the other guys for stuff."

"I'm not jealous of your friendship," she says, surprising me. Not about the jealousy thing, because that's just silly, but that she thinks Wrath and I are friends.

"I don't think we're *friends*. He tolerates me because he has to."

195

She shakes her head. Opens her mouth, hesitates, then says, "He had a sister who died when they were little. I think you're about the age she would have been."

Oh. *Oh wow.* I had no idea. Cue the schmaltzy music. I'm about to cry.

"Shit, Hope. I'm not trying to make you feel bad. I just want you to understand you're safe with him, and he's not looking out for you only out of obligation to Rock."

I can't speak, but I do let her wrap her arms around me and I do squeeze her back.

"Okay. Enough sad talk," she says, pulling away. "Go do your legal stuff to help get Rock home. Hopefully the cavemen haven't clubbed each other to death out there." She waves her hand in the direction of the dining room, in case I don't know which specific group of cavemen she's referring to.

Naturally my shitty luck means I run into Sway coming out of the Champagne Room. His mouth curves up in a nasty smile when he sees me. Five seconds later, one of the other girls scurries out of there and down the hall away from us.

"You okay, darlin'?" he asks with false sincerity.

"I'm fine, thanks," I answer as I try to move past him.

He invades my space, backing me up against the wall without laying a finger on me. "Wanted to apologize for earlier. Just trying to help you out. You marrying one of our presidents means you need to learn to submit to the men around you," he explains in the creepiest-non-helpful voice I've ever heard.

Submit to—whoa, what did he say?

My cheeks burn with anger while I try to organize my indignation into a cohesive thought. Sway notices and places the back of his hand against my forehead. My heart skips in fear. Where the hell is Wrath's bossy ass when I need it? How is this happening in my own home? Do I have some sort of sign on my back that says "please molest me" that I don't know about?

"You sure you're feelin' okay, darlin'? You're looking flushed."

196

Before I open my mouth to answer. Wrath's big voice booms through the hallway. "Sway, what the fuck you doing?"

Sway drops his offensive hand and backs away. All my breath comes rushing out.

"Just makin' sure there're no hard feelings from the gal." As if he gives a crap what I think of anything.

I glance up at Wrath and find Z and Murphy on either side of him— all three wearing matching pissed-off expressions. Z shifts his gaze to my face, as if he's trying to tell me something. I just don't know what.

"Go get ready. We'll leave in a few minutes," he says with a chin lift. If he expected me to argue with him, he's mistaken. I can't run away from the four of them fast enough.

I'm not even ashamed about the part of me that hopes the three of them kick Sway's ass.

WRATH

I knew this motherfucker would cause problems. That shit I told Hope about our old president? Yeah, Sway came up in the club under Ruger and didn't have as many problems with that bullshit as Rock, Z and I had. If he's here with Tawny, he usually behaves, but when he's here with the guys, he's a grabby-handed asshole. Although, touching Rock's woman is uncharted asshole territory—even for Sway.

Murphy—already agitated from the shit that came out of Sway's mouth when Hope left the table—is clearly dying to choke the life out of Sway. I'm inclined to let him.

"Tell me you didn't just have your hands on Rock's ol' lady?" I drop each word slowly, so he understands the gravity of the situation.

"Just being friendly." He pulls a shocked face. "Come on, none of you are tappin' her hot lil' ass while Rock's inside?"

Z turns to me, and I think we're wearing matching "what the fuck" expressions. It's Murphy who answers the stupid fuck's question though.

"You really think we'd disrespect our president that way?"

"Ain't disrespect if he's inside," Sway mutters.

Z shifts to face Sway. "It is in this clubhouse."

"Fine, whatever. At least she's a loyal piece of ass. Shit, I get locked up overnight, Tawny's jumping on anything with a dick."

I don't even know where to begin with that sentence. The first thing that comes to mind is, *maybe it's because you're tapping club ass every chance you get,* but it's really none of my business and I can't think of many things I give a shit less about.

Z and Murphy must be having similar thoughts because none of them say anything either.

"Listen, the reason I wanted to talk to you without the girls around, is your boy, Loco."

"We talk club business in the war room. Not at the breakfast table," Murphy says, dead calm.

Sway raises an eyebrow and I'm waitin' for him to say something about younger brothers knowing their place, but he seems to think better of it. Young or not, Murphy's an officer of *this* club and Sway's in *our* house.

"Well, can we go sit at the table then?"

"You need us to round up the rest of the guys?"

He looks the three of us over. "Nah, you can relay the information."

Once we're at the table, he spreads his hands. "I think I talked to Rock about this when he visited, but we've been having trouble with some gang punks moving into our territory."

"Yeah. Rock mentioned it," I say.

"So your boy, Loco, we've been selling him the weapons he wanted, and he's been helping us with some pushback."

"Good." What's his point?

"He's been a big help. So thanks for that."

If only he knew we almost didn't vote in favor of making that introduction.

"I know you guys want to stay out of guns."

"True."

"That still the case without Rock here?"

None of us hesitate. "Yes."

"Okay." He pauses for a second, and I pray like fuck he's not thinking up a way to try and convince us. "I get it," he finally says. He pushes back his chair and stands. "Unless you need some extra help around here, I'm gonna round up my boys and head home."

"We're good, thanks," I answer.

"Thanks for the hospitality. Let me know if Rock needs anything."

The three of us walk him out and watch him head upstairs for a second before Z follows. "Gonna pick Hope up at her door, so she's not runnin' into him again," he explains.

"Good plan."

"You should've let me beat his ass. Coulda found a nice hole in the woods to drop his carcass in," Murphy grumbles.

"We don't need anyone else sniffing around here. Better he get the fuck out."

"Fine. Thank fuck he ain't our prez."

"Amen to that."

CHAPTER TWENTY

WRATH

THE CLUB'S crackling with the need for vengeance Saturday night. I got confirmation from the Wolf Knights' SAA that if Rock's getting shit in lock-up, it's coming from Izzard. Not that what he did to Hope wasn't enough of a reason, but it's nice to know we're taking care of two issues with one beatdown.

Everyone's at the clubhouse. We put our ad for Swan's "services" on Craigslist a few days ago. Fresh meat in the Capital Region? Izzard was all over that shit maybe an hour after Z arranged the ad.

I think Hope and Trinity realize something's up. Neither of them question us about all the activity in the house though. Hope just seems to be relieved Sway and his crew are gone. Trinity knows better than to ask about club stuff.

It's not a surprise that Hope ends up going downstairs to visit with Sparky. Realizing how hard he's been taking Rock's absence, she's made sure to check in on him regularly.

Trinity shakes her head as she watches Hope disappear through the basement door. "The stoner and the attorney. They're adorable," she says with an affectionate smile. Between Trinity making sure

Sparky eats and Hope checking on his mental health, at least I know our bud-growing brother's being taken care of.

It's good that Hope's downstairs when Dex and Swan join us in the living room. Swan's decked out in skimpy hooker-wear and Dex has to be sporting the ugliest pimp suit I've ever laid eyes on.

"What the fuck, bro?"

"Gotta look the part," he explains.

Shaking my head, I usher the guys into the war room for one final review of the plan. They're solid and I'm confident this will get done quick and clean.

Clean for us. Not Izzard.

"Dude's a deranged fuck," Z assures us. He had the pleasure of texting with Izzard to set up the "date."

"Must be bad if *you're* disgusted," Dex snarks.

Z throws up his middle finger.

"Everyone's clear on their role?" I ask to get us on track.

After they settle down, we break.

I stop Murphy with a hand to his chest before he walks out. "How'd it go yesterday?"

"Grinder? Okay, I guess. He was upset."

"So he hadn't heard yet?"

"No. Thank fuck." He lifts his chin and all humor drains from him. "You mind if I'm the one to visit Rock and tell him about it on Monday?"

"No. Go ahead. I'm sure he'll be happy to see you. Figure out a way to let him know we got this situation covered too."

He holds his fist up and we tap knuckles. "You got it, bro. Thanks."

"Watch your back tonight. Do me proud, little fucker."

He breaks into a grin and slaps my shoulder on the way out.

The need to pummel something makes my hands twitch after the guys leave. My broken leg already caused enough downtime this year. I'm pissed I can't go on this adventure and take care of business for my club.

"Are you okay?" Trinity asks after the guys leave. The brothers not on Mission Izzard are waiting at the clubhouse in case anything goes wrong. No party atmosphere tonight. More like a wake.

"Yeah."

"You know you can trust me if you ever want to get stuff off your chest?" Trinity asks in a quiet voice. My hands cover hers, drawing her attention up.

"I know. Thank you." I think over what I'm willing to share with Trinity. Specific club business? No. How I feel about the decisions I'm being forced to make while Rock's away?

Yeah.

"This is important, and I'm just pissed I can't be out there with them." There. Nice and vague.

She doesn't huff, or ask for any more details. "If you decided not to go, I know you had a good reason. That's doing your part for the club too," she says softly.

She gets it. More importantly, she gets *me*. "Thank you, angel."

CHAPTER TWENTY-ONE

ROCK

HAVEN'T SEEN Lizard in a few days now, and I have a sneaking suspicion I know why. Murphy stopping in to visit Monday morning reinforces that belief.

The one tolerable guard, JT, leads Murphy into the visitation room. My hands are free for this visit, so I can give Murphy a hug.

"Miss you, prez," he grumbles as we sit.

"Same. You doing okay?"

"Yeah. Went to see Grinder the other day. Let him know what was up."

"Aw, fuck. Why'd you have to upset the old guy?"

Murphy shrugs, but I appreciate the courtesy he still shows my one-time mentor.

"He okay?"

Murphy brightens. "Yeah. He's getting moved to Pine Correctional at the end of the month."

"No shit. I knew he applied. Never figured it'd actually happen. That's good, I'll be able to visit him more often." I stop and think about how absurd that sounds. "You know if I don't end up in a cell next to him," I joke.

Murphy doesn't appreciate my humor.

"At Wrath's request, I gave him an update on this situation and his advice was to put your focus on the months ahead. Everything else will be waiting for you when you beat this bullshit. Ya know?"

He's being cryptic on purpose, but I think I get what he's saying. Izzard won't be a problem for at least a few months, but he's still alive for me to handle when I get out.

"You all agree on this?"

He slams his fist into his open palm. "Oh, yeah."

Hmmm…guess my sergeant-at-arms has decided to pick and choose which orders he'll follow. I'm not mad though. Wrath's in a better position to gather information. If the club voted to take action on Lizard, they had a good reason and I trust their judgment.

"Everyone okay?"

"Yeah. We just miss you."

"Heidi staying out of trouble?"

Murphy snorts and shakes his head. "Let's not go there."

"Hope staying out of trouble?"

That makes Murphy laugh even harder. "She's doin' real good. We're lucky to have her."

"Good." I know Hope's a loyal woman, but this situation would be tough for anyone to handle.

"She's militant about planning your wedding, and I don't think she's going to accept being in here as an excuse."

I have to force my laughter. "Tryin', bro."

"I know you are."

We're only able to talk for a few more minutes, because the jail shuts down for a head count every day at this time. Murphy shakes my hand when we get up.

"I'll be home soon, Murph."

"You better be."

HOPE

"Guys, I think I have something."

Wrath and Z tip their heads up. Wrath waves me inside the office and has me sit in Rock's chair. Sitting here gives me some small measure of comfort.

"Tony said when he spoke to the DA, he slipped up and said "she" when taking about the witness. Does that help us?"

Wrath and Z glance at each other before answering. "Not yet. Vipers got lots of women doing their dirty work for them. Could be anyone."

"What about that one, Gabriella, you said was working at the club?"

"We let her go."

I chew on my bottom lip. "Shit. Well, what about some of the other girls? They might have information." I'm grasping at straws but I can't help it.

"We're not exactly talking about it down at CB," Z answers.

"Guys, it's been all over the news. Everyone must know."

"Yeah, that Rock's been arrested. Not that we suspect the Vipers are involved."

Wrath narrows his eyes and studies me for a bit before asking his question. "What do you want, Hope?"

"Let me question some of the girls. They might know something from working with Gabriella."

"No," Wrath says.

"Hell, fucking no," Z echoes.

"We have to figure out who this witness is."

"It could be Gabriella."

"You think so? Tony said she's being kept at a safehouse."

The information seems to jolt him. "Fuck, Hope. Why didn't you say that first?"

I hate feeling like I did something wrong. How am I supposed to know which piece of cryptic information is the nugget of gold they're waiting for? "Why? Do you know every safehouse in the tri-county area?" I snap back.

Z and Wrath grin at each other and I have the urge to kick both of them in the shins.

"Was it an official safehouse like the police were hiding her or private?" Z questions.

I struggle to remember the way Tony worded it. "I don't know. He just said a safe house."

"That's good, Hope. Thank you."

"He's supposed to sniff out a name for me and call back tomorrow. Can we wait that long?"

Wrath gives me a sympathetic pat on the leg. "I don't think we have a choice."

WRATH

Hope doesn't understand what a great lead she's given us. And it's not her place to. Z and I start making our phone calls right after she leaves.

Loco, GSC's leader and our biggest customer, chuckles at my request. "You think I got knowledge on where they're hidin' some Viper mama?"

I don't know how Rock puts up with this prick. "Or someone in your crew."

"Yeah, I got a guy. I'll see what I can find out. It might take me a day or two though. They ain't gonna be real forthcoming with that type of information."

No shit.

For once, Loco's no bullshit when we meet. Maybe he just doesn't find me as charming to deal with as Rock.

"This is the address," he says as he hands over a piece of paper.

"They got their safehouse bumped up against Empire?" It's in the outer fringe of our territory, but still pretty fucking bold.

"Yeah, that's why I had trouble tracking it down." He stares at me for a second. "You gonna hurt her?"

"Who?"

"The witness."

"Fuck no."

He holds out his hands in a mock calm-down gesture. "All right. I know our two crews don't always see eye-to-eye, but the shit them fuckin' Vipers are into makes my stomach turn."

At least we agree on something. "Anything else you can tell me?"

"They'll have at least two men on the place. And dogs."

Great.

"Thanks, man."

"Anything for you guys. I wanna see Rock beat this shit." He holds up his hands and pastes a phony smile on his face. "Not that you're not a pleasure to deal with, Wrath."

Once we're back in the war room, Z and I talk over the plan before we bring it to the rest of the club. First, we call Murphy and Teller to the table.

"Murphy, I want you to stay here and protect the girls." Fucking annoys me. But I trust Murphy. He won't let anything happen to them.

"You got it." Christ, I'm so shocked he didn't throw a bitch fit about staying behind, it takes me a second to continue.

"Teller, your small, stealthy size will come in handy."

"I'm six foot for fuck's sake. I ain't that small, ya cocksucker."

Z snickers and shakes his head. "You in or not, dick?"

"Of course I am."

"Good."

"We should take one more. I vote Dex."

"Yeah. Bricks can stay here and monitor the cameras."

The rest of the guys get called in so we can explain the situation and give everyone their assignments. No one argues.

After the room clears out we discuss how we plan to handle it.

"Loco said they got dogs."

"Great. I don't want to be killin' puppies," Z grumbles.

"I don't either, but I don't feel like gettin' bit. You want to bring some hamburger, be my guest." I don't doubt Z will do exactly that.

"We bringing the girl back here?" Teller asks.

"No choice. She needs to recant her story. At the very least, we have to keep her out of sight until trial. When they can't produce her, they'll have to cut Rock loose. But if we can get her to go in and recant it will be better."

Murphy's face scrunches up. "How the fuck we gonna do that?"

"We don't know they got her there willingly, bro," Z reminds us. "She might be thrilled."

"True. Hope said she'll take care of the legal side since Glassman can't be the one to bring her in to recant," I agree.

We haven't had time to do a proper assessment of the house so Murphy's next question isn't unwarranted. "Tonight's the best night?"

"Yeah. They've been moving her around and Loco wasn't sure how much longer she'd be at this spot."

Now it's time to get to the important stuff and the irony is I wish Rock was here for this part. "This is a small neighborhood. Houses are tight together."

"Suppressors?" Z asks.

"Sparrows, .22, and the CCI mini-mac ammo. We'll wet them on site."

"You don't want the CCI quiet?" Teller asks.

"No. It won't cycle and if shit goes bad quick, I'd rather risk a few decibels of noise than the few seconds it takes to manually cycle the ammo."

Teller nods, still looking a little unsure. But he's not the one who's spent hours at the range testing these combinations out. I am, so he'll follow my orders. Rock's spent a lot of time going through those tests with me, so he'd probably take more time to explain than I feel like doing.

"Bring whatever backup you want. If we need it, then sound's gonna be the least of our worries."

I have to give Trinity some explanation before we leave. Hope knows we plan to find the witness, she just doesn't know we're doing it tonight.

"I'll call you when we're on our way back, angel."

"Okay." She reaches up and gives me a quick kiss on the cheek. "Please be careful."

I catch her in my arms for a longer kiss. "Hey. Nothing I want more than to come home to my girl."

Her lips pull into a soft smile. "Good."

Even though it's outside King's territory, we know the area well. The fact that Vipers feel comfortable stashing the witness responsible for our president being in jail this close to our turf pisses me the fuck off. It's one giant middle finger pointed in our direction.

We park the two vehicles on the street behind the address we were given. Z and Dex get out of their truck and jog over to mine, sliding in the back seat.

"Teller, you're the least scary, so you come with me to find the girl. Dex and Z keep watch. There should only be two guys guarding the place, but you never know."

Z hands out the Sparrow suppressors, then passes around a small spray bottle. "Five sprays," he reminds everyone. Once that's done, we thread the Sparrows onto Walther P22 handguns. Not my first choice of weapon, but for this situation, it's our best option.

I'm already sweating like a motherfucker and we haven't even stepped outside. The long sleeve plain cotton shirt and black tactical pants aren't helping matters. Fucking summer humidity is brutal even at night.

"I want to be in and out in ten minutes. No telling how often they check in."

When we've each got our weapons ready, we step outside. Z and Dex jog down the alley opposite of the one Teller and I take.

Climbing the chain-link surrounding the backyard without making a ton of racket will be impossible. There're also a shit-ton of thick bushes growing into the fence. "Fuck."

Z's found a weak spot on his side and motions us over while Dex bends it back.

Z points above us to the camera he disabled and holds up two fingers signaling there are two other cameras on the property.

There're no lights downstairs, but that doesn't mean anything.

Teller picks the lock on the back door and as soon as it swings open two dogs charge us. No make that two *puppies* charge us.

And then lick Z's hand.

"Great watch dogs," Dex snarks.

Unfortunately one of the Vipers must have been paying attention to what the dogs were up to and rounds the corner.

"Oh, f—" is all he gets out before Dex shoots him. The Sparrow's doing its job but there's still a distinctive cracking sound from each blast as he empties the magazine. Not to mention the thump of the fat fucker hitting the ground.

"I think you got him," I mutter.

Dex smirks as he ejects the spent magazine and slaps in a fresh one. "You're the one who wanted to use .22 ammo."

Viper number two comes around the corner. God damn, these guys have no sense of self-preservation what-so-fucking-ever. Your buddy just took a bullet to the chest, you don't come barreling around the corner. But that's exactly what this asshole does.

Z takes care of him.

Two down.

There *shouldn't* be anymore.

A scream comes from somewhere deeper in the house.

I signal for the guys to follow me. When we determine the living room's clear, I motion for Z and Dex to stay and keep the two entrances covered.

More screams. Not television. A girl.

Teller and I look at each other and nod before creeping down the dark hallway.

"Please, please, please don't. Don't. No. No. No." The girl's cries keep getting more hysterical.

We check each of the two rooms we pass. Empty. The sounds are definitely coming from a room at the end of the hallway.

"Shut the fuck up." A man's voice drowns out the girl's pleading. Then the definite sound of flesh hitting flesh.

No. Hell fucking no.

I know better than to go in blind, but I can't stand the thought of whatever's happening on the other side of the door.

My foot smashes it open and Teller follows me inside.

A fat, white, flabby ass greets us. The girl he's on top of is still struggling and kicking. Before I even know what I'm doing, my hand's around his neck and I'm throwing him to the ground.

"Who the fuck are you?"

"Shut up," I growl at him.

Teller throws a blanket over the girl and works to untie her wrists.

I point at her. "Mariella?" *Please tell me we have the right chick.*

Her lower lip trembles and her gaze keeps bouncing between me and Teller. Wondering if she's gone from one nightmare straight into another I'm sure. "Yes." Her cheeks are red from whatever smackdown we interrupted. Bruises aren't far behind. "Thank you."

Teller backs away from the bed and kicks the guy back into a sitting position.

"You with him?" I ask her.

She shakes her head vigorously.

"How old are you?"

The guy tries to get up again. "She's legal. I paid my hour and barely got—"

"You need to learn no means no, motherfucker," Teller growls before putting two bullets in the guy's throat.

"Did you have to be so messy?" I ask,

"Hey, you got me using this quiet ammo, wanted to make sure it didn't bounce off his thick skull."

Mariella has her head bowed, as if she's hoping to fade into the wall and we'll forget her existence.

"Grab some clothes. We need to go," I say to her.

She looks to Teller.

Can't blame her.

"They took my clothes," she whispers.

Jesus Christ.

Z and Dex stop outside the room.

"We gotta go, brother," Dex says.

"Go look for some clothes for her."

"On it," Dex answers as he takes off.

Mariella squeals like an unhappy kitten when she spots Z. "Please don't hurt me. They made me do it. Don't——"

"We're not here to hurt you," Z says in the softest voice I've ever heard him use.

I smirk at Z. "Guess she recognizes you."

Dex returns with a handful of clothes and tosses them to the girl. She scrambles into them and moves between me and Teller. Poor girl's trembling all over. Finally she glances up at Teller. "Please don't leave the dogs. They'll kill them."

"Already covered, sweetheart," Z reassures her. "Let's get you out of here."

We haven't even cleared the bedroom doorway when shots ring out. The four of us hit the ground, Mariella's tucked up so tight against Teller, she goes down with him. With the noise and explosion of glass and drywall all around us, it takes a second to realize the shots are coming from outside. Automatic fire.

Drive by.

For us? Or for the Vipers?

Doesn't really matter, I guess.

"Good call, on the .22s, dick," Teller snaps as he digs his nine mil out of the holster at the small of his back. My G29, which had been resting comfortably in the holster inside my waistband, ended up in my hands on my way down to the floor. Reflex.

"What, no cannon?" Z snarks at me.

One shut-the-fuck-up-and-pay-attention face works wonders on both of them.

The shots stop, but none of us move, which is a good thing because they start up again five seconds later. They're coming from the front of the house and feel a hell of a lot closer than the first round.

Mariella tugs on my arm and points around the corner. "There's a window in the back bedroom we can get out of. The back yard's concealed."

It's easier for the five of us to inch our way into the back bedroom than it will be for us to go back the way we came. I nod at Dex and he leads the way.

We close the door behind us, muffling some of the shooting.

The pups are tethered to the end of the bed and Z crawls over to untie them. Mariella takes one of the leashes and Z grabs the other. Two skinny little puppies are gonna get our asses shot. Then the darker one licks my hand, and yeah, I ain't leaving them either.

Even though there are no windows facing the street in this room, we all stay low. Mariella leads us to the window, stepping on the sill and stretching up until she swipes a key from behind the curtain.

Z raises an eyebrow at me and I shrug.

"I found it by accident and I'd been waiting for the right time…" Mariella's explanation trails off as she hands the key to Teller.

Girl's clever and a survivor. Guess that bodes well for her.

The key isn't to open the window, it's to open the bars covering the window. Teller cautiously swings it open and waits a few seconds before sticking his head out. He ducks back inside. "Easy drop to the ground."

"I'll go first," Dex offers, nudging Teller out of the way.

No one argues.

Z slides through next and when he's out, Teller hands him one of the puppies.

Behind us there's a crash. Shattering glass and a *whoosh*.

"Move," I whisper harsh and quick.

A shrill screech cuts the air, and I'm a little surprised Vipers bothered to outfit this shithole with a smoke detector.

Teller hops out and pulls Mariella outside. As I'm about to hunch down to fit through the window, there's another crash directly outside the bedroom door. Smoke pours in underneath the door.

Shit. They set the place on fire. What if they're waiting to ambush us outside?

The thought motivates my big ass through the small window, down to the ground beside my brothers.

"They must have thrown a molotov cocktail or two," I explain. "Watch in case they're waiting for us back here."

The words barely leave my mouth before a bullet whizzes over our heads. I mean, *right* over our heads. So close the stench of nitroglycerin assaults my nose.

My hand wraps around Mariella's arm keeping her down, while Teller pops up and gets off a shot.

Shit. My gaze darts all over the back yard. Dark, shadowy and overgrown. Chain-link fence we came through. What's our best way out before more Vipers or the cops show up?

Z points to the fence and we edge our way over. Teller must have hit someone. There's blood on the sidewalk. No one in sight though so we keep moving.

We might as well have flashing neon signs on our backs, running down the alleyway with no cover. But we have to get the fuck out of here.

CHAPTER TWENTY-TWO

WRATH

THE PUPS ARE as eager to get out of here as we are. They both leap into Z's SUV without prompting. There's no time to fuss about who sits where. Mariella's glued to Teller's side, so she gets thrown into the back seat of my truck with him. I drive us the hell out of the neighborhood watching the rearview to make sure Z's following.

Smoke and a faint orange glow flicker behind us. What a fucking mess. It's not the kind of neighborhood where residents willingly invite the cops to come investigate, so it will take a while before any show up. We should be long gone by then.

"Mariella, you got any idea who did the drive-by?" I ask. I need to know if it was Viper or someone else.

"No. Guards are supposed to check in every forty-five minutes. If they don't call in on time, someone automatically comes to the house. They've had trouble with a local gang and a few customers, but I don't know much more."

Yeah, she was going through her own hell. I don't want to scare her any more than we already have. Honestly, I'm eager to turn her over to Hope and Trinity and let them deal with her.

She doesn't complain. Doesn't even ask where we're taking her. I guess anywhere's better than where she was.

When we're outside the city limits, I dial Trinity.

"Are you okay?" she answers.

"Everyone's whole."

I swear I can feel her sigh of relief over the line.

"I need you to get a room ready. Can you two meet us at the door? We should be there in twenty."

"Okay. Love you."

"Love you too, angel."

"Was that your ol' lady?" Mariella asks.

Since I don't know this chick yet, I'm not comfortable talking about Trinity with her. Even though they're about to meet in a few minutes. "Yeah."

"That's nice how you talk to her."

I don't know how to respond. Glancing in the mirror again, I catch a glimpse of her. Something familiar I can't quite place.

"You'll like her. She'll get you settled," Teller adds.

There's not a whole lot to say after that.

Trinity and Hope are waiting outside when we pull up.

"Mariella?" Hope asks. Her tone's awfully kind considering this chick's the reason Rock's locked up.

I lift my chin at Trinity and signal her over. "What's wrong?"

"It was ugly. We walked in on her being attacked. Sounds like they were pimping her out." I leave out the bullets and fire.

"We should take her to a doctor."

Fuck me. "I'd rather not parade her around in public right now. It wasn't a smooth extraction."

Trinity makes a face at me.

"Fine. Ask her what she wants to do."

"I can run her down to the clinic in the morning. They can treat her under a fake name. We'll pay cash—"

"I can't have you taking any trips alone with her. I don't trust her and—"

"I figured," she says in her you're-working-my-last-nerve-but-I-

218

love-you-anyway voice. She glances over to where Mariella's huddled up behind Teller. He doesn't seem to know what the fuck to do.

"What's that about?" Trinity asks.

"He shot the guy attacking her." I answer because it's not like she won't find out anyway.

"Ah, okay." She jumps up and gives me big hug, then squeezes my face between her palms. "I love you." Before I have a chance to respond, she slides out of my grasp and marches over to Mariella.

TRINITY

"They brought home a girl *and* two dogs?" I'm shaking with laughter as Z emerges from his SUV with a pup tucked under each arm.

Hope laughs too. Next to us, Mariella's quiet and clinging to Teller.

"What?" Z lifts his chin in Mariella's direction. "She said they'd hurt the pups. Besides, we can use some guard dogs up here."

He's got a point and they are pretty stinkin' cute. Z sets them down and they run straight to Hope who kneels down and coos all sorts of puppy nonsense words at them. I squat down and snap my fingers and one sniffs his way over, nubby tail wagging like crazy.

"Aw, they like you girls," Z says.

"Careful, Hope. He's gonna try to make us clean up after them," I mutter loud enough for the guys to hear. Her mouth lifts in a half-smile but she doesn't say anything.

Z slaps his hand over his chest. "I'm hurt, Trinity. Hurt."

"Yeah, yeah." I stand and turn, holding out my hand to Mariella. "Come on, I'll set you up in a room upstairs."

Her eyes dart between Teller and me. I guess she finally decides I'm safe and she follows along.

"I'll be up in a few, Trin," Hope calls out after me.

Mariella's not here for a vacation, so I don't bother with a tour of the clubhouse. "I'm Trinity. If you need anything, let me know."

"The big one. You're his woman?" Mariella asks as we walk upstairs.

"Yup."

"He's nice."

I wonder if she bonked her head at some point tonight. "That's not how people usually describe him."

She chuckles. "No, I bet it isn't."

Opposite Rock and Hope's end of the hallway there are a couple rooms free. They're not as fancy as the officer's rooms, but I doubt Mariella will mind.

"I'll put you here. But the guys can be loud and obnoxious, so don't get freaked out. No one will bother you." I point to the door next to hers. "Teller's sister stays in that room when she's up here."

"Where's your room?"

"Downstairs."

"What about the other woman outside?"

"She's our president's ol' lady. Their room's down there."

"Oh my God." Mariella wanders into her room and drops down onto the bed. "Her man's in jail because of me."

"We can talk about that tomorrow. Why don't you get some rest? The sheets are clean. There're towels in the closet and the bathroom's right outside."

"Do you take care of the house?"

"Yeah, but I'm not supposed to anymore. Wrath wants…well, he wants me working on other stuff. But if I don't do it these guys will starve to death and live in sticky sheets, you know?"

Mariella chuckles and nods.

"Listen, Wrath sort of explained what kind of situation you were in. Do you want me to take you to a doctor tomorrow?"

She stares up at me with wide eyes. "You'll let me?"

"Yeah, of course. One of the guys—probably Wrath will go with us for protection."

She folds her hands in her lap and drops her gaze. "Yes."

"Okay."

I give her baggy jeans and oversized shirt a more critical look. "I'll find you some clothes. There's a washer and dryer on this floor—"

"I'd rather throw this out," she says, gripping the hem of her shirt.

"Gotcha." I cock my head to the side, trying to decide if I want to ask my next question. "How'd you end up with the Vipers?"

She stares up at me with big, watery brown eyes. Underneath the marks on her face, chest and hands, she's a beautiful girl. "My brother."

Shit. We need to figure out how deep her loyalty to that demented MC runs and it seems I'm the best person to do it. "He a patch-holder?"

She snorts. "No. He was a hangaround. A wannabe. Always running his mouth. He screwed up some deal for them, so they took me as collateral to motivate him. They gave him one more chance and he still fucked it up. They killed Eduardo and kept me."

Christ, that's fucked up. Surprising? Not at all. "I'm sorry. Do you have any other family?"

Her mouth turns down and a few tears roll down her cheeks. "Not anymore."

"Listen, I'm not one for touchy-feely, let's-talk-about-our-past-trauma stuff, but I grew up in a club like the Vipers. So I understand you're probably terrified. But Lost Kings aren't like that. No one will bother you here, so don't worry. These guys won't hurt you."

She nods. So solemn for her age, which I peg at about twenty or twenty-one. "I figured that out downstairs. Vipers don't joke around with the women. Backtalk like that would have gotten me belted in the face."

"Yeah, well, these guys enjoy a challenge."

"Won't they expect—"

"No. The only thing they expect you to do is take back your false testimony against Rock. They'll protect you and keep you safe until then. After, you can figure out what you want to do." I want her to understand that the guys won't shoot her and drop her in a ditch as soon as they get what they need out of her.

"Did they rescue you?"

"Sort of. Not really. I rescued myself. But later, yeah. Definitely." Our conversation's starting to make me twitch. I don't want to talk about this stuff with a stranger. I can barely talk about it with

Wrath. Where the fuck is Hope? Didn't she say she was coming upstairs?

Right on cue, she taps on the slightly open door. "Hi, Mariella."

Mariella's big brown eyes plead with me not to leave her alone with Hope, so I perch my butt on the edge of the dresser. Hope seems to appreciate my presence too. This is fucking awkward all around.

Hope, ever the professional, holds out her hand to Mariella. "I'm Hope. How are you?"

"Okay," Mariella mumbles while snatching her hand away and focusing on her lap again.

Hope turns her head my way and I shrug. "Do you need anything?" she asks Mariella.

"No. I'm fine."

Mariella's words give Hope the green light she was waiting for. "I'd like to get you in to see an attorney I know. He'll accompany you when you recant your statement."

That gets Mariella's attention. "Whatever you need me to do. I'm so sorry for everything."

Hope doesn't acknowledge the apology. I imagine she's not in a real forgiving mood. Forced into it or not, this girl's statement has turned Hope's world upside down. Even though she's one of the sweetest people I've ever known—everyone has their limit.

Hope flashes a tight smile. "If you need something let me or Trinity know."

My hand shoots out and grabs her arm before she leaves. "I want to take her to the doctor tomorrow. Can you arrange your meeting around that?" I feel horrible even asking. The thought of delaying Rock's release by even a second churns *my* stomach. I can't imagine how Hope feels. But she nods. "Sure. We'll discuss it in the morning."

"Good night, Mariella." Hope stops in the doorway. "You'll be safe here," she says over her shoulder.

Not that she's a hostage in her room, or anything, but I let Mariella know I'll come get her in the morning and show her to the dining room.

I walk Hope down to her room. "You okay with everything?"

She nods, but her bottom lip trembles. "I just want this to work. I need—" her voice breaks and I wrap my arms around her.

"I know. We'll get him home. Get some rest."

She pulls back and gives me a weak smile before going inside.

Downstairs, the guys are unwinding, getting drunk, and generally being silly. Wrath holds his arm out to me, and I happily rush over to him and snuggle in his lap. "She okay?" he rumbles against my ear.

"I think so."

His arms band around my middle and I lean back against him rubbing my forehead against his cheek.

"Aw, you two are so cute, I'm about to puke," Ravage snarks at us from his seat on the opposite end of the couch. I flip him off and Wrath chuckles.

Swan drops off several bottles of beer. "Shit, Swan, I'll help you." Wriggling out of Wrath's hold is impossible though.

"*I* need you," he murmurs.

Yup. Those three, simple words, spoken in his low, rumbly voice, do the trick. It may not be official yet, but I'm *Wrath's* ol' lady. *His* needs are my only concern now. The reminder brings me peace.

"I'm fine, Trinity," Swan assures me, before taking a seat between Teller and Ravage.

I must drift off listening to their excited conversations and male bonding stories. The sensation of lifting into the air wakes me. I find myself in Wrath's arms, being carried to our room. My arms loop around his neck and he smiles down at me.

"You can set me down."

Insulted, he rolls his eyes. "I got you."

"Where'd Z put the puppies?"

"In his room for now."

Seems hard to believe Z would do anything that might interfere with getting laid, but whatever.

In our room, Wrath sets me down and stares at me for a minute. "What's wrong?"

He shakes his head the same way you'd try to shake yourself out of an awful memory. "Seen lots of brutality over the years. Fuck, half the time I inflicted it, but that scene—"

"Disturbed you?"

"Yeah."

My heart flutters at his sincerity. Men like Wrath don't admit these things easily. That he trusts me enough to share his feelings, means the world. My arms wrap around him and after a minute he hugs me back. "She said her brother was a hangaround who fucked up one too many times."

"She tell you his name?"

"Eduardo. She said they killed him and kept her for—"

He pushes me back, staring down at me with a hardened expression. "You fuckin' serious?"

Startled, I back away. "Yes. Why?"

"Eduardo's the guy who tried to grab you."

"Really?"

His gaze moves to the door and I grab his shirt to keep him here with me. "I'm glad you got her out safely."

He snorts. "We almost didn't make it out."

I wait for him to elaborate, but he doesn't.

His hands roam over my back and he presses a kiss to the top of my head. "Trin?"

"Yes?"

He hesitates, then jerks his head toward the bathroom. "Nothing. Get ready for bed."

At the time, Wrath's words didn't make a big impact. But bubbling under the surface, my own brutal memories always wait for an excuse to terrorize me. In the middle of the night, I sit up, heart hammering, hair sticking to my sweaty forehead. I haven't had a single nightmare since Wrath took up permanent residence in my bed. But now I can't stop the awful images flashing through my mind.

The pale moonlight shining through my curtains throws enough light for me to see him. He calls me angel all the time, but in sleep, with his face relaxed and his bright blond curls, he's the one who looks angelic. Well, almost. Careful not to wake him, I settle down as close as I can get to him.

"What's wrong?" he mumbles.

"Nothing. I can't sleep."

He holds out one arm without opening his eyes. "Come here."

Against his big, warm body, I'm finally able to find some peace.

WRATH

I should have kept my fucking mouth shut.

Trinity didn't need any details about Mariella's ordeal. I should have kept that shit to myself.

The next morning, Trin's pale. Her pretty eyes are ringed with dark circles, and a haunted sadness surrounds her. My fault.

I couldn't help it. Seeing Mariella at that old fuck's mercy made me think of Trinity and the crap she's been through. And I feel like shit about it. She's a strong girl. A survivor. Not some victim I need to feel sorry for.

As tired as my girl must be, she's up early calling the clinic to make an appointment for Mariella. The few details she provides earn us a ten a.m. appointment.

"That's perfect," Hope says while she and Trinity stand in the doorway making plans. "Damon can't see her until two. I think he wants to hear the story from her, and then bring her down to the DA's office."

The cautious bit of optimism in her eyes guts me. It's obvious as fuck she doesn't want to let herself think about Rock coming home yet. We all know there are a million things that could go wrong before he gets released.

One step at a time. Mariella to the doctor. Mariella to the lawyer. Mariella to recant her story. Hopefully it all leads to Rock out of jail.

Hanging around a women's clinic while the girls do their thing is *not* my idea of a good time. Mariella looks like she wants to go back upstairs and hide under the bed when she realizes I'm the lucky fuck playing bodyguard for them today. I almost consider asking Teller to do it, except I want to spend some time—no matter how awkward—with Trinity.

When we arrive, my girl makes *that face.* The one that makes me do whatever she wants and I grudgingly follow them up the stairs into the waiting room.

For some reason, Mariella follows me over to the row of chairs while Trinity checks her in.

"I'm sorry," she says softly as she settles into the chair next to me. It's the first time she's spoken directly to me all morning.

"For what?"

"This."

"Nothing to be sorry about."

To my utter shock and confusion, Trinity follows Mariella back without an explanation. Fucking great. I can't decide what to do first: flip through back issues of *Cosmo* or stare at the informative STD posters decorating the walls. Both shrivel my dick.

I end up staring at my phone instead until the opening of the door draws my attention up. Trinity returns way more pale and shaken than she went in, instantly pulling me to my feet.

"Babe, what's wrong? You okay?"

"I'm fine."

Mariella returns a few minutes later. I settle up the bill with a wad of cash. The receptionist gives me a strange look and I feel like a complete creep. She probably thinks I'm a fucking pimp.

She hands me a receipt and smiles. "You're a nice boyfriend."

What now?

The what-the-fuck on my face comes through loud and clear I guess. "The blonde's your girlfriend, right?"

"Yeah."

"A lot of guys won't set foot in here, let alone wait and then take care of the bill."

"Oh." Explaining I'm here for protection in case a rival MC tries to kidnap Mariella back from us or hurt my girl, probably won't go over well. "Thanks," I answer instead.

Trinity's no less agitated on the ride home. I feel for Mariella and

Hope, honestly I do, but Trinity is my responsibility. I need to get to the bottom of whatever this is, so I turn Mariella over to Teller and Hope, and steer Trinity into our room.

"What's going on, Angel Face?"

Her mouth stretches into a smile that looks more pained than happy.

"They squeezed me in for an appointment—"

I hadn't been sure if she went back there with Mariella or for herself. Now I'm fuckin' worried. "You okay?"

"Yeah. I wanted to talk to the doctor about an IUD."

"Why didn't you just say so? What'd she tell you?"

She rolls her eyes. "She said if my partner has a giant dick it might be weird. Would you let me finish?"

I burst out laughing before I figure out if she's serious or fucking with me. "Continue."

She sits next to me on the bed, and that's when I notice her trembling hands. "Trin, what's wrong?"

"I don't know what's wrong with me. I sort of freaked out during the exam and ended up telling her about…stuff from when I was a kid."

Jesus.

"Baby, why didn't you tell me?"

"I'm telling you now."

"Okay."

"I've never had that happen before. Not…ever since I left home. I've had plenty of nightmares over the years."

"I'm sorry. It's this shit with Mariella."

"Yeah, probably. The doctor thought I should see a therapist. Someone who specializes in sexual assault." She raises an eyebrow as if she's asking a question. I'm not sure what to say, so I wait. Her gaze lowers to her hands resting in her lap. "What do you think?" she asks quietly.

Christ, her question's like a knife twisting in my chest. "I want you to do whatever you think you need to do."

"I want to. I know I'm fucked up, Wyatt. And you've been so

patient and I," she stops, tipping her head up and staring at me. "I'd never talk about club business or anything like that."

"Fuck, babe. I know you wouldn't. That didn't even cross my mind."

"Okay. I just thought...things are so much better now. Between us, I mean. Maybe it would help me be better for you."

That's it. I can't take this. I pull her into my lap, hold onto her tight. "You are wonderful for me. I love everything about you inside and out. Whatever you need to do I'll support."

"Thank you." Her head falls forward, resting against my chest. "Will you go with me?" she asks softly.

When I hesitate, she sits up. "I don't mean to therapy. Just the doctor said the first few times could trigger stuff and I shouldn't be alone after."

My throat's so tight, it takes a second to work any sound out. "Of course, I'll take you. Whatever you need."

"Thank you."

CHAPTER TWENTY-THREE

HOPE

WRATH AND TRINITY barely glance my way before leaving for her room.

"Everything okay?" I ask Mariella.

She lifts her delicate shoulders, but won't meet my gaze. "There's lunch in the kitchen if you want to eat something before we leave?"

"Come on, I'll take you down there," Teller offers and holds out his arm.

Thank you. I mouth as Teller whisks her away. I shouldn't be, but I'm uncomfortable around Mariella. I know whatever led her to implicate Rock in the murder probably wasn't by choice. It's still weird and I'm still struggling not to wrap my hands around her neck every time I see her.

"You okay, Hope?" Z asks as he steps out of the office.

"I think so," I answer with a sad smile.

"Come here."

He directs me into the office and shuts the door. "What's wrong?"

"I don't know. I'm scared." As soon as the words leave my mouth I realize their truth. "I'm worried you guys risked your lives for nothing and we still won't be able to get Rock out."

"I know, honey. We're all worried about that. Probably more than you because none of us have any faith in the law or regular society."

I'm not sure how to respond because more and more I find myself agreeing with the Lost Kings MC's outlaw ideals. "I know it's not her fault, but—"

"You're pissed at Mariella?"

"I know I shouldn't be—"

"Hey, you went through a lot of shit because of those lies. Having Rock torn away from you at your engagement party, that ugly scene with the guard, having to visit your man in jail, and all the shit that comes with it. You have a right to keep your distance."

"I guess." It's then that I notice, both pups curled up on a pile of blankets in the corner, next to Z's desk. "They look cozy."

His mouth turns up in the impish grin I'm used to seeing Z wear and glances over his shoulder. "Yeah, they wore each other out this morning. Gotta find a vet to take them to. Wanted to make sure they weren't microchipped first."

"That makes sense."

He turns back my way. "I don't want to upset you, but when we found her, it was a bad scene. She wasn't there willingly. And I doubt she had a choice in telling those lies. So no matter what, it wasn't for nothing."

I swallow hard imagining what things were like for Mariella before coming here. "I know."

He leans back and sighs. "You gonna give Glassman a heads-up?"

"I don't think it's a good idea. The less he thinks I'm involved with her recanting, the better."

When Z's done giving me his pep talk, he walks me down to the dining room. Teller, Murphy, Heidi and Mariella are having an awkward lunch together. Heidi glances up and smiles in relief when she sees me. "Hi, Hope."

"Hi, honey. What are you doing up here?"

"Murphy promised to give me driving lessons."

Teller rolls his eyes. "I said I'd take you."

"No way. You're mean." Heidi shakes her head vigorously to emphasize how mean her big brother is, which gets a laugh out of everyone.

"We're ready whenever you are, Hope." Teller says with a nod at Mariella.

I don't want to get into the details of where we're headed in front of Heidi. Glancing at my watch, I nod. "We should probably leave now."

Mariella waits for Teller to get up.

Heidi watches the three of us, but doesn't say anything. Murphy nudges her elbow. "Ready for your first lesson?" he asks, distracting her.

"Heck, yeah!" She throws her arms around Murphy's neck and happy laughter spills out of her. "I'm getting really good at three-point turns, Hope."

"Good. If you want to come downtown with me one of these days we can practice parallel parking."

"Yes!" Her enthusiasm for what now seems like a mundane driving skill makes me chuckle. Even the simplest things seem to be more fun through Heidi's eyes.

My heart races as we pull into the cramped parking lot behind Damon and Mara's office. They share their modest legal practice with two other partners. Since Damon's an Empire city court judge, he can't take cases in Empire. Most of his work is in Slater County, or one of the surrounding counties. They haven't gotten around to a receptionist yet, so no one meets us in the outer office. After a minute, Damon comes out and greets us. I introduce him to Teller and he motions for Mariella and me to follow him.

"Mara will be back in a few minutes. I'll have her sit in, since you can't do it, Hope."

I open my mouth to protest, but he's right. I don't want to do anything that could jeopardize Rock's release. Instead I turn to Mariella. "You'll like Mara, she's a sweetheart."

When Mara arrives, she hugs me and sends me out to wait with Teller.

"Is she okay?"

"Yes. She'll be fine with them."

He's jittery and can't sit still. "Do you think we'll get Rock out today?"

I snort. "Probably not. First, she has to recant. That's why she needs an attorney, so they don't try to prosecute her for falsifying information or something stupid. Damon's in a better position to argue coercion than she is. Then Glassman has to be notified."

"Should we let Rock know?"

The question kills me. Of course I want to tell Rock. "I don't want to get his hopes up in case something goes wrong."

Teller nods. "Probably better no one at the jail knows until they need to."

Jeez, I hadn't even considered *that*.

Shaking off my worry, I continue answering Teller's original question. "Normally, if a victim recants, they might still continue the case because they can still prosecute using police reports, photographs and other evidence. In Rock's case, they have no other compelling evidence. Crap, even her statement wasn't compelling enough to—" I have to stop myself before I get worked up again. "Even after the charges are dropped, it will probably take twenty-four hours to process him out of jail. Glassman will need to request an emergency hearing if the DA *doesn't* drop the charges when she changes her statement. There may have to be some formal hearing either way. I'm not sure. This whole thing is out of my realm of expertise."

Even though I'd mostly been talking out of my ass, Teller seems satisfied with my explanation. He reaches over and takes my hand. "You've been so strong, Hope. You're such a good ol' lady. I'm glad Rock held out for the best."

Teller's not usually so expressive. I squeeze his hand back. "Thank you."

By the time Damon, Mara and Mariella emerge, I'm ready to explode from the tension. Damon reads my expression clearly and reassures me. "I just got off the phone with the DA, he's waiting for me to bring her in."

Teller lifts his head. "This guy legit?"

Damon quirks an eyebrow.

"Are you sure he's not on Viper payroll," Teller clarifies.

Damon opens his mouth to answer, but Mariella cuts him off. "Not that I know of. They coached me on what to say for a couple days. They wouldn't have bothered if—"

"Okay." Teller agrees. He pulls out his phone and taps out a text. "I'm gonna have two of our guys meet you there and wait outside, just in case."

Damon doesn't seem to know what to do with that. I smile weakly at him. Behind him, Mara flashes me a bright smile. Somehow she always makes me feel a little better—even at my worst—and I'm grateful for it.

We make arrangements to meet them on their way back from Slater, so we can pick Mariella up and bring her back to the clubhouse. I'm so numb, too afraid something will go wrong to let myself get excited about Rock's release.

"Z and Wrath are heading over there now to wait outside," Teller says after we get in his car.

"You think it's necessary?"

"Just in case. I didn't like that he gave the DA a heads-up. Too easy for him to tip someone else off."

I don't know what to say. From the world Teller operates from, that makes complete sense. From Damon's side, it would be rude to just spring this sort of thing on a colleague. I'm sort of torn between both worlds these days.

Sometimes I wonder which side I'll end up on.

CHAPTER TWENTY-FOUR

WRATH

ACCORDING TO HOPE—WHO got her information from her judge friend—the recant went well. The DA supposedly started the process of getting the case dropped last night. We still haven't heard anything about when Rock's getting out though. Hope put in a call to Glassman and he assured her he'd keep his calendar clear. He also reminded her he'd run through our initial retainer and would need more money soon.

"Send me the bill," Hope snaps before hanging up the phone. "Asshat," she grumbles.

Z chuckles at her irritation. We'd been listening in on speakerphone to the conversation. "Don't sweat it, Hope. We've got it covered."

"It ticks me off. He knows you guys are good for it. Get my fiancé out and worry about your damn money later," she fumes.

Spitfire.

I stand and motion for her to follow. "Let's get you some breakfast. You're cranky when you haven't eaten."

She scowls up at me. "I am not."

Behind me, Z snickers. The pups stir, nudging and wrestling with each other. While Hope crouches down to play with them, a smile spreads over Z's face and he shakes his head.

The three of us walk down to the dining room together while the pups zig and zag around us.

"They're getting bigger," Hope says. "Did you name them yet?"

Z points to the Rottweiler. "Ziggy." He points at the one we determined was a Cane Corso. "Zipper."

Hope laughs. "Appropriate."

Murphy and Teller are at one table, bickering about something when we enter. They both glance up and smile at Hope. "Any news?" Murphy asks.

"Not yet," she answers.

Teller jerks his thumb at the kitchen. "Trin's in there with Mariella," he says, nodding at me.

Trinity explained that Mariella's eager to repay us for rescuing her. She's grateful none of us expect sex from her in return for our shelter, so she's more than happy to take over Trinity's chores around the house. But for fuck's sake, Trinity's been showing Mariella around her kitchen since she got here. I think the girl's got it by now.

Hope seems to read my irritation and taps my arm. "I'll get her."

"Thank you."

Breakfast is quiet once the girls join us. We're all tense waiting to hear news about Rock's release. Mariella declines to join us, even after Teller specifically asks her to.

Hope whips her phone out and starts tapping away when she's finished eating.

"Something about the case, Hope?" Z lifts his chin at her and she blushes, but doesn't tuck her phone away.

"No."

"Well, you're awfully intent on something. Spill."

"It's nothing."

I don't know what the fuck is wrong with Z, but he won't leave it alone. "Come on. What's got you glued to your phone?"

Hope finally snaps. "I was setting up an appointment for a bikini wax if you must know." Everyone at the table—except Z—bursts out laughing. Poor Hope turns bright pink. Her gaze zeroes in on Trinity who's still laughing. "They have *two* openings if you still want to join me."

Trinity sputters and it's probably awful of me, but I laugh so hard I can't breathe.

"I don't know how Rock puts up with you guys," Hope grumbles.

Z still looks a little traumatized from all that information. Serves him right for being nosy.

Hope's mouth curls into a smirk. "What's wrong, Z? The girls down at CB must talk about their girly grooming habits all the time."

"Yeah, but since I can't enjoy the benefits, I'd rather pretend neither of you even have any of those parts." He shakes his whole body, as if he thinks snapping his head from side to side will toss the mental image out of his head.

Hope rolls her eyes, but she's laughing too. Still chuckling, she nods at Trinity. "Come on. I made an appointment at the dress shop too. You can help me pick out a strapless bra to take with me."

All of us groan and she grins.

Trinity shakes her head as she stands. "You realize what they're all picturing now, right Hope?"

No, she didn't. She grumbles and storms off with Trinity laughing while she catches up to her.

As soon as they're out of sight, I glance at Z. "Not it."

"What? Oh, hell no."

"What are you two talking about?" Murphy asks.

I tilt my head at Murphy and Teller. Z gets my meaning and smirks. "Someone's gotta stick with the girls. I still don't feel comfortable letting them run around by themselves."

"No fucking way," Murphy says.

"Maybe you can get your sack waxed while you're there. I hear some chicks dig that." Z's laughing so hard he almost doesn't get all the words out.

Teller shakes his head. "I gotta pick Heidi up and bring her to the dress shop, so I can't do it."

Murphy groans. "Fuck me. Are you fuckin' serious?"

"I can't do it. I've got stuff to take care of here." I pin Murphy with a hard stare. "I *trust* you."

He's stopped most of his bitching by the time the girls return.

Hope claps her hands to get our attention. "Okay. Who's taking us? We've got ten o'clock appointments," she asks, glancing at each one of us.

Murphy slowly raises his hand as the rest of us snicker at him. "I hate you guys," he mutters, which only makes us laugh harder.

"We need to be at the dress shop by two," Hope says to Teller who nods.

"Got it."

"Glassman has everyone's numbers in case there's news about Rock. I'll keep my phone on, so if I get any information, I'll let you know."

"Sounds good." I push my chair out so I can stand and signal Trinity over to me. She approaches with a sly smile and I tug her away from the table and my nosy-ass brothers. Remembering what a hard time she had at the doctor's office, I have to ask. "You gonna be okay?"

"Yeah. I told her I wanted to do that...before...I'm not...now." My face must betray some disappointment, because she reaches up on tiptoes, sliding her arms around my neck and pulling me down so she can whisper in my ear. "I'd rather maybe let *you* be in charge of that particular bit of grooming."

Well now. That was the last thing I expected her to say or want. One corner of my mouth curls up. "I can get on board with that."

She laughs and kisses my cheek. "I figured."

As she starts to pull away, I grab her for a real kiss. My hand runs up her back, into her hair. Her lips part for my tongue to sweep inside. She tastes minty-sweet and for a few seconds I forget everything else around us.

Until the guys start whooping and making noises.

We break away, staring at each other. My knuckles skim over her cheek. "Love you, Trinity."

Her eyelids drop and she tilts her head, rubbing her cheek against my hand. "Love you too."

HOPE

Upstairs, I tear through my dresser drawers searching for the right undergarments to bring to the dress shop. My hand brushes over an envelope.

Oh, no.

It's the card Lilly handed to me at my engagement party. From Sophie. With all the craziness that followed, I never opened it. I don't even remember stuffing it in this drawer.

Even though Trinity must be waiting downstairs for me, I can't put this off any longer. Dropping onto my chaise, I rip open the envelope and pull out a fairly generic note card filled with Sophie's small, elegant handwriting.

Dear Hope,

Sorry is so inadequate. But I am sorry. I'm not excusing what I did, but I've been ignoring this problem for a long time. Destroying our friendship feels like my rock bottom.

You're one of the few friends who've always been there for me. You've seen me at some of my lowest moments and yet you've never judged me. I thought setting you up with Rock was a small way to repay you for everything you've done for me over the years. I never wanted to screw that up. I was so flustered and tipsy the night of our fight, none of my words came out right. When you were in the hospital, I saw how much he loves you, how unbreakable your bond is. It made me feel so much worse about what I'd done and I couldn't figure out how to tell you, even though I know I should have.

I've decided to get help. My firm has to pay for it—boy, were they thrilled. I'm sure as soon as they can legally fire me, they will. But hopefully I'll be better by then. I hope you can find a way to forgive me. My brother will have my contact information, but if you don't want to see me, I understand.

Love,
Sophie

Crap.

I've had this for weeks. By not responding, Sophie must have figured I'd written her off. If Rock hadn't gotten arrested and I'd read this sooner, would I have called her? After reading it a few more times, I know the answer.

Yes.

If I'd been a better friend and not so self-absorbed all the time, maybe I would have noticed that Sophie's drinking crossed the social line a long time ago.

Before I can figure out what to do about it, Trinity's knocking at the door.

"You ready?" she calls out.

"Yup." I stuff the envelope between two books on my shelf. Maybe I'll talk to Lilly about it later at the dress shop.

Trinity's quiet on our way to the spa. Her silence makes me wonder. "Are you mad? I was only joking around since the guys—"

"I'm not mad at all, Hope."

"Okay."

Murphy seems uncomfortable as he walks us inside. A small pang of guilt hits me. Z should have been the one forced to take us since he couldn't leave me alone this morning.

A couple hours later, I find Murphy in the waiting area chatting up one of the receptionists. I guess he's not annoyed any more. Trinity's glances up from the magazine she's flipping through and rolls her eyes when she sees me.

"Come on, Murphy, time to hit the dress shop," I call out.

Trinity bursts into laughter and Murphy looks like he wants to choke me.

"Is there anywhere you don't pick up chicks, Murphy?" I ask when we're back in the car.

"I wasn't *picking her up*. If anything, she was trying to pick *me* up."

Trinity snickers. "It's true. She tried to talk him into all sorts of very unmanly things."

Murphy fake-shivers. "A little grooming's one thing." He swipes his hand over his neatly trimmed little beard. "What she was talking about...no."

The silly conversation takes my mind off the fact that I still haven't gotten a call or any information from Glassman. I send Wrath a text and deflate even more when he responds he hasn't heard anything either.

"Nothing?" Murphy asks.

"No."

"You said the judge was an asshole. Could he be stalling things, Hope?" Trinity asks.

Good question. "I'm not sure. Maybe. It's the DA's choice to drop the charges. Technically, the judge shouldn't, but who knows." Nothing about this whole messed-up nightmare has made any sense.

Heidi and Teller are waiting in the parking lot at the boutique. Surprise, surprise, Murphy's a little less grumbly about hanging out with us now.

Heidi almost knocks me over with her enthusiastic greeting. "Marcel told me Uncle Rock might get out soon?"

I glance up at Teller and he shrugs. "I hope so, honey. I'm waiting for news," I answer, tapping my cell phone.

"You don't have to buy me a dress, Hope. I really don't mind wearing the dress you bought me for my prom. It's still my favorite thing ever."

"It's up to you. I'm not going to be picky about what you wear and the colors of that dress match. But if you see something you like better today, don't hesitate."

"Okay."

While everyone goes inside, Teller holds me back. "I need to take off. Will you be okay?"

"Sure. Murphy's been a good little bodyguard."

Teller smirks. "Hey, don't buy Heidi's dress. I'll pay for it. You've done enough for her."

"I really don't mind."

"Thanks for including her. She can't stop talking about it."

I'm happy to hear that and I tell him so.

"Call me if you need something or hear anything about Rock."

"I will. Promise."

He gives me a quick hug and takes off. The insolent rumble of his bike intensifies my anxiety about Rock's release. I miss Rock. Miss riding with him. The cool, confident way he commands such a big machine always relaxes me for some reason. Excites me too. But I can't think about that right now.

Soon. Soon. Soon. I chant in my head, while I open the dress shop door. He'll be out soon. And I need to find the perfect green dress to marry him in.

Inside, the owner of the shop looks a little stressed at having three people hanging out in her store.

"I'm sorry, Gloria, right? Hope Kendall, we—"

"Oh, hello," she finally greets me with a pleasant smile. I called her a couple weeks ago, explaining what I wanted. It took some time, but she ordered a bunch of dresses for me to try out. She also ordered dresses for Trinity and Heidi.

Heidi's ecstatic about being in the wedding. Mara and Lilly also graciously accepted invitations to be bridesmaids. God bless them, they haven't abandoned me or once made me feel bad about Rock's situation.

Since I don't want a traditional wedding dress, this isn't a traditional bridal shop. It's more of an exclusive store which specializes in fashion that is more easily found in more cosmopolitan places than Empire. Of course that means the prices are higher too. I almost gag at the price of the first dress she hands me. It's floor length and made of very fine silk with intricate layers of lace on top. Beautiful. But not suited for an outdoor wedding in the woods.

Gloria glances at Murphy as she presents the next dress. "Is this the lucky groom?"

We all have a good chuckle over that.

"No, this is my bodyguard for the day." What? Might as well go with the truth. What else am I supposed to say?

Deciding I must be joking, she turns to Trinity. "Your young man, then?"

"No," Trinity answers with a straight face.

Gloria gives up trying to figure out what Murphy's doing here, while Heidi glares at Trinity. God help me.

After hours and a lot of fancy green dresses, I've narrowed it down to two. By this time Lilly and Mara have joined our little party and Murphy seems on the verge of climbing up to the roof and jumping off.

One dress is knee length emerald green lace with long sleeves and an open back. "Modest, yet sexy. Just like you," Mara says while bobbing her head up and down.

The other one is also emerald green lace, the top is a sleeveless tank style with wide shoulder straps, nipped in the waist, flaring out into a pleated circle skirt that ends right above my knees. It has a nude lining to give it the illusion of being more daring than it is. Very me.

I hold up the second one. "This feels less fussy and it's comfortable."

"It looked really pretty on you," Trinity says.

"And I wanted to have this special corset thing made." I lower my voice since Murphy's still here. "You know, for later, and I wouldn't be able to wear it under this one." I hold up the backless one. "I love it. But it also feels too dressy for what we're doing?"

I look to the girls for their thoughts.

"Definitely no corset. You'll need a special bra for it too," Lilly points out.

Gloria explains the boobie contraption I need to find to work with the dress, because not only is it backless, the lace at the shoulders is sheer. It seems like more of a pain in the ass than I'm willing to deal with. "I don't know. I don't think that would be enough to hold my girls up," I mumble while cupping my breasts and staring at them.

Gloria eyes me critically. "Well, you are larger than a C cup—"

"I'm out of here," Murphy snaps. "I'll be out front. Yell if you need me," he says before storming outside.

Trinity, Mara, Lilly and I burst into giggles.

"What happened? Where's Murphy?" Heidi asks. She was trying on a dress in the back and missed the fun.

"Oh, Heidi, that looks so pretty on you," Mara gushes. Heidi grins and stands up straighter. She found a one-shoulder dress with pleated chiffon in a lovely bright plum color.

"Are you sure purple's okay, Hope?" she asks.

"Yes. I think we'll go for jewel tones."

Mara's dress is also one-shouldered, pleated a little different and in a peacock-teal color that looks so pretty with her reddish-gold hair.

"What do you think?" Trinity asks. Lilly and I chuckle at her choice. It's also one-shouldered, but sapphire blue.

"I feel like odd-girl out," Lilly jokes. Her dress has a high halter neck with a key hole cut out in the front, in crimson.

"It's beautiful, Trinity," I assure her. Lilly and Mara agree. Heidi's nowhere to be found.

"Did she go back and change?" I ask Lilly who shrugs.

Gloria points to the window. "She's outside with the young man. Still in the dress, so I hope that's the one she's buying."

Oh jeez.

Mara and Lilly don't need to have the situation spelled out. "They're so cute," Mara whispers. "Older brother's best friend. So romantic." She giggles.

"She has a boyfriend," I answer dryly.

Lilly snorts but keeps her thoughts to herself.

"What are you thinking for shoes?" Trinity asks, saving me from being dragged into a conversation about Heidi's love life.

"Flats? I don't want to break an ankle on my wedding day. The ground's pretty uneven up there."

Trinity nods thoughtfully.

"Cowboy boots would be super-cute with that dress, Hope," Lilly says while eyeing me up and down. "Fancy ones."

"Oh, that's a great idea," Trinity chimes in. "Rock loves country music. Would probably surprise the hell out of him."

"He does?"

Trinity nods. Interesting. How come I don't know this about my man?

Lilly wiggles her eyebrows at me. "Then after the wedding you can ride him like a rodeo girl."

"Must you always—"

"Yes," she cuts me off as she follows me back into the dressing rooms. Now that I finally have Lilly alone, I have to explain.

"I finally read Sophie's letter."

Lilly raises an eyebrow.

"With everything that happened that night, I never—"

"I assumed that's what happened."

"Is she okay?"

Lilly's gaze darts away.

"Lilly?" I prompt.

"No. It's been rough."

She must notice the guilty expression that slides over my face because she rushes to explain. "Not because of anything you did. I told her what happened. She understands why you haven't contacted her."

A relieved breath wooshes out of me. Although part of me is a little embarrassed.

"She can't have visitors and only limited phone calls right now anyway. If you send mail, they'll read it first."

"I'll send her something."

Lilly nods and digs around in her purse for a notebook. She scribbles out the information and hands it over.

"You've got a lot on your plate, Hope. Worry about getting Rock home and the wedding. She's...she'll be there a while."

I don't get a chance to ask any follow-up questions. Trinity, throws the curtain open. "What're you two doing? Hurry up."

She's already back in her street clothes and has been conducting cowgirl boot research. "Check these out. They'd be perfect with the dress."

It's hard to tell from the tiny photo on her cell phone, but the colors pop. "Those are cute."

"Double M off exit twelve carries them. Wanna hit them up next?"

"Okay."

"Will you hate me if I can't go?" Lilly asks.

"Of course not."

Trinity snickers. "At least it's a manlier store for Murphy."

We all have a much needed laugh.

WRATH

"Find a dress?" I ask as Murphy stomps into the clubhouse.

"I hope you picked a blue one. It's my favorite color on you," Z adds. "Makes your eyes pop."

"I hate both of you," Murphy bitches as he throws himself down next to me.

Hope and Trinity walk in laughing.

"Where's Heidi?" Teller asks.

Hope jerks her thumb over her shoulder. "Outside with Axel."

Murphy folds his arms over his chest, sinks down into the couch and closes his eyes. "I'm done for the day."

Hope and Trinity laugh at his misery. "I think we did push him beyond all appropriate manly-limits," Hope says with false sincerity.

"Yes. You did," Murphy agrees without opening his eyes.

Z smacks him. "You got to sit around watching hot chicks try on dresses, quit your bitching. Wrath and I did real work today."

Murphy opens one eye. "I assure you, listening to them yap about stick-on bras and halter-whatevers was *not* fun."

Hope blushes and laughs. "Sorry, Murphy."

"Is Heidi okay?" Teller asks.

"Don't worry, we didn't corrupt your sister," Trinity says.

Teller snorts and sits back. "I'm more worried she talked you into buying her a bunch of shit she doesn't need."

"Oh, no. Heidi's not like that, Teller." As much as Heidi gets on my nerves, I can't help but love the way Hope's taken to her.

I lift my chin at Trinity. "Find a dress?"

"Yup."

"Can I see it?"

"Nope."

I raise an eyebrow at Hope. "I thought the *groom* couldn't see the bride's dress. Why can't I see hers?"

"We don't have them yet. They needed some alterations," she explains.

"I'm not going back to pick them up," Murphy informs us. "Just puttin' it out there. Z can go, since he thinks it's so much fun."

"Let's hope it's not necessary," Hope says softly. "Any news?"

I shake my head. "Nothing. Glassman called at five and said he hadn't heard anything. I didn't think it was worth bothering you with no news."

"Okay. Shit." She chews on her bottom lip and stares at the clock over the television.

"Did he say anything else?" Trinity asks.

"Yeah, if he didn't hear anything by eleven tomorrow, he's going to file a writ? I don't know what that is."

"Jesus Christ," she mutters. "It's an extraordinary measure. It should definitely move things along though. They'll have to produce him in court either tomorrow or the next day. I hope Glassman's going to file with a different judge. Shit."

Z sits up. "Is that bad, Hope?"

"I don't know. I don't know if Glassman just wants to make some noise, or he got back some negative information from the DA. I just don't know. I can't believe I was out dress-shopping all afternoon, I should have—"

"Hope. Calm the fuck down," Z snaps. Murphy, Teller and I all stare at him. He's never short with her. "We're paying Glassman a shit-ton of money to take care of this stuff for us. You told me yourself, he's a prick, but he's good at what he does, right?"

"Yes."

"Then don't beat yourself up anymore. Trust me, Rock will be much happier knowing you were doing wedding stuff, instead of moping around here with us."

She doesn't look convinced, but at least she's not hysterical. I tap her leg to get her attention. "I know you think it's just silly stuff, but the fact that you haven't given up on him and you're still planning to marry him means a lot."

"Yeah, and if that's not enough, that corset thingie you were talking about will definitely cheer him up," Murphy jokes.

Hope's eyes widen, and then she breaks into a smile. "You ass."

They're still chuckling over that when Trinity asks where Mariella is.

"Upstairs. She hasn't come down since you guys left."

"Shit. I should check on her." Trinity turns to see if Hope's coming, but she shakes her head.

"What's wrong?" Z asks, after Trinity's gone.

"Nothing. I know I make her uncomfortable, so I don't want to keep bugging her."

Murphy points a finger at her. "You're our First Lady. You bug whoever you want."

Hope snickers. "Thanks, Murphy."

The next morning, I'm woken up at seven by my phone. Next to me Trinity moans.

"Shit, it's Glassman. Hello?"

"Oh. I was trying to get Hope. I've got so many damn numbers—"

"Well, you got Wrath. What's going on?"

"He's getting released today. Probably take a few hours to process him out. I'd say be there by ten just in case it goes quick."

Thank fuck.

I get a few more details from him and hang up.

"You better let Hope know," Trinity says as she sits up and stretches.

"I will." I'm busy texting everyone to get their asses down here for church. "Need to call a meeting first."

"Why?"

I give her the side eye and she huffs at me. "She's gonna want to come with us to pick him up and it's not safe."

"Fine, whatever."

Almost everyone's at the table when I get there. I don't fuck around. "Rock's getting out today. Glassman said be there at ten, but he didn't know how long it would take to process Rock out. We gotta assume Vipers know about his release and might try something."

"Hope can't go," Z says.

"No shit."

Teller pipes up. "Take two cars. Four of us and Bricks. Everyone else stay here to make sure the place and the girls are protected."

"Guess I better get Hope down here and let her know."

Z quirks an eyebrow. "She doesn't know yet? Man, she's gonna rip your nuts off for not telling her right away."

Fuckers all have a good laugh over that.

HOPE

Come down to war room.

My heart *thump, thump, thumps* as soon as Wrath's text sinks in. Something's up. They had an emergency club meeting this morning and I'm scared to death I'm in for bad news.

I scramble into a pair of jeans, a T-shirt and throw my hair into a messy knot before hurrying downstairs. Wrath, Z, Teller, Murphy and Dex are waiting at the table.

"You can come in, Hope." Wrath points to Rock's chair. "Sit."

I'm shaking so hard, it takes a couple minutes to pull the heavy chair out. Z jumps up to pull it out for me. "Enjoy it now, Hope. It's probably the last time we'll invite you to the table."

Fear slices right through me and Z must realize I didn't take his words as the joke he meant.

"Hope, I'm teasing."

"Sit down, asshole," Wrath growls at Z. He turns to me and his face softens. "Rock's getting out this morning."

All the air rushes out of me, and I slump forward. "Oh, thank God." Anger replaces my fear and I smack Wrath and Z, then glare at the rest of them since they're out of smacking range. "Why didn't you just say that instead of scaring me?"

"Sorry. We weren't trying to scare you," Z explains.

"What's going on?"

"We took a vote."

"On what?"

249

"Who's collecting Rock."

"Collecting. What the heck does that mean? Go get him and bring him home."

"We need you to stay here."

"Fine."

The guys share another look.

"We thought you'd give us a hard time."

"Are you kidding me?" I shake my head. "Are you bringing his bike?"

"What? No. This isn't the movies, Hope. We're worried about a fucking ambush."

My teeth sink into my bottom lip so hard I wince. "Then I guess you better be extra careful. Because if anything happens to him…" I don't need to make threats. They know how I feel.

Wrath grins and points at Murphy and Teller. "Go get ready." He turns back to me. "Dex is staying here with you."

"Okay."

Dex gets up and leaves the table. "Call me if you need something, hon."

"Thanks."

I move to get up as well, but Wrath puts his hand over mine. "Stay for a second."

My gaze shoots to Z and he nods, so I drop back down into Rock's chair. "What's wrong?" My heart's pounding. What aren't they telling me?

Neither of them meet my eyes at first. Then Wrath turns his gaze on me. "Some guys in the life look at jail time as some twisted badge of honor—"

"Rock's not one of them," I answer.

Z speaks up. "No."

"Guys, I'm kind of anxious for him to get home. So can you get to the point?"

Wrath rolls his eyes and Z cracks a smile. "What we're trying to say is, don't be surprised or get your feelings hurt if he wants to go for a ride when he gets back." Wrath looks me in the eye. "Alone."

Honestly, that's not a shock to me. "Okay."

"He's dying to see you, sugar," Z shrugs, "But you never know."

"Okay. Thank you for warning me." I stand because I think this time we're finished and I really am anxious for them to bring Rock home. "Is there anything else?"

Wrath shakes his head. "No. We're gonna go get your man."

"Okay. I'm going to, uh, pack a bag in case Rock wants me to go with him?" I hate how small and quivery my voice comes out. But Wrath's face brightens.

"That's a great idea." They follow me out of the war room. "Go ask Dex for some travel stuff. He'll hook you up with a compression pack or two."

I have no idea what that is, but I don't care. I'm so excited to see Rock, I can't stand it. "Would you guys hurry up, please?"

"Eager?" Z teases.

"Don't mess with me, Z."

His mouth curls into a smirk and I just know he's got something dirty he wants to share but won't because he doesn't want to offend me.

Wrath never worries about offending anyone and opens his mouth, but I cut him off. "Don't you dare make a crack about me needing to get laid. I will kick both your asses."

The two of them shake with laughter.

"Jerks. Get out of here."

Z's still laughing at me.

"Go ahead, Hope. We'll be back before you know it," Wrath says.

"Thank you."

Butterflies zip and dance in my stomach. I'm so excited to see Rock I can barely breathe.

WRATH

"Good God, that woman's a trip." Z's still laughing when we hit the road.

"She took that better than I expected."

"What'd you tell her?" Murphy asks from the back seat. Teller and Bricks are in the SUV behind ours. I'm not sure why Murphy rode with us.

I'm about to tell him to fuck off and mind his own business when Z answers for me.

"Nothing bad, just that her ol' man will probably wanna go for a ride when he gets back."

"Did you check the garage to see what I fixed up for them?" Murphy asks.

I'll give Murphy credit when he's earned it. "Yeah. You did good."

"I hope she likes it."

I don't laugh or tease him about why he's seeking Hope's approval so much. Christ, I must be growing up or something.

As soon as we're in Slater County, the atmosphere in the car shifts. Z's more alert, watching everything. Murphy too. I'm keeping an eye on the rearview to make sure we haven't picked up any admirers.

"I'm gonna circle round once first," I tell them. Z nods and keeps staring out the window. Downtown Slater is shady as fuck. Glassman instructed me to pick Rock up at the back entrance. Of course, there's no parking allowed back there. Fuck it. I pull right up in front of the gate. We're not leaving the vehicles and we sure as fuck ain't staying long.

I check the time. Nine forty-five. At least we're early.

"Glassman said be here by ten, but it might take longer."

"You watch the gate for him. Murphy and I will watch the area."

"Christ, I hope they're not gonna make him wait even longer," Murphy grumbles.

Doesn't matter how long we have to wait. I ain't leaving without our prez.

CHAPTER TWENTY-FIVE

ROCK

THE PROCESS TO get out of jail takes almost as long as it does to get in. I'm ready to strangle someone by the time the last chain-link gate slides open. The sight of the two black SUVs waiting at the curb keep me sane.

Wrath's waiting on the other side of the gate and pulls me into a bear hug, slapping the crap out of me in the process. After my time inside, I'm a little weird about anyone in my personal space. But it's Wrath—he's been up in my personal space since day one—so I know it's a mix of genuine affection and shielding me in case someone decides to take a shot.

A few quick strides and he's shoving me into the front seat of my SUV. Couple seconds later we're getting the fuck out of Slater County. I never want to set foot here again.

I twist in my seat and find Murphy and Z in the back wearing matching happy grins.

"Good to have you back, prez."

My smile's tight. I'm thrilled to see my brothers on this side of the fence but also crazed from being caged in for so long.

"Where's Hope?"

Wrath glances over. "Home."

"We didn't know what to expect. Dex is at the clubhouse keeping an eye on things. No way were we bringing her down here," Z explains.

"No. That's good." That's all I would have needed. Having her visit me in jail was humiliating enough. Coming to collect me? *No.* Not to mention, I don't want her in Slater County either. "She okay?"

"Yeah. She did good, Rock. Never gave us shit about following her everywhere," Z says with a smirk.

His comment turns my own mouth up. My gaze slides to Murphy. "You okay? Why so quiet?"

"Nothin'. Glad you're out, that's all." He gestures at Z and Wrath. "Two of them combined can't replace you." Murphy's voice catches and he looks out the window.

I reach back and slap his leg. "Thanks, brother."

"I'd be insulted, except he's right," Wrath says quietly.

I turn my attention to him. "How's Trinny?"

"Hanging in there."

"Patch her?"

His jaw clenches before he answers. "No."

"Why the fuck not?"

"I told you the way I wanted to do it."

Christ, my brother can be stubborn. But I get it.

"Everyone at the clubhouse for my return?"

Z nods his head. "Yeah, even the nomads are up at the clubhouse."

"Good. I want to see everyone. Have a brief meeting, then I am disappearing for a few days. Can you guys handle that?"

Z snorts, but doesn't look up from his phone where he's busy texting.

"We figured you'd want to take off right away," Wrath says.

"No. Family first. You two been waiting long enough. This gets done *today*."

"Thanks."

Parking lot is full when we pull up to the clubhouse. I get hugs and handshakes from everyone I pass. Wrath follows me inside and chuckles at the crazed way I'm hunting for my girl. Where the fuck's my woman hiding?

"She's probably waiting for you upstairs," Wrath finally says.

Can't even be mad. I clap him on the shoulder. "I'll be down in a few."

He has the nerve to roll his eyes. "Take your time."

"Brother it's been three months, it ain't gonna take long."

His laughter follows me up the stairs and I flip him off as I go. At our door, I take a deep breath before pushing inside.

There's my girl. The relief at finally seeing her crashes over me in waves.

"Rock?"

She's got clothes and two small bags scattered over the bed, but she leaps up and rushes across the room. Her smaller body almost knocks me over as she barrels into me. She doesn't cry. But she's breathing hard, clinging to me. Her forehead nuzzles against my chin and she tips her head back, her pretty green eyes searching over every inch of me.

"Are you okay?" she asks.

"Much better now."

I lean down and take her mouth, backing her up to the bed. As soon as she realizes my intentions, she's clawing at my clothes, ripping everything between us away. I break our kiss and nod at the bed. "What's all this?"

Her cheeks flame pink. "The guys said you'd want to get away. I didn't know if you'd want me to come with you, so—"

My palms press against her cheeks, and I crash into her mouth again. "Fuck, yes, I need you with me," I mutter as we part and I rip the last scraps of fabric off her. "I'll spend time worshiping you later, Baby Doll. Promise. Right now, I need you hard and fast."

I expected some laughter. But her "yes" comes out low and solemn.

My hand dives between her legs and I groan as I slide over smooth, slick skin. "Get yourself all dolled up for me?" I mumble against her mouth.

She hums and nods as she pulls me down to the bed, shoving everything in our way to the floor. I've been a walking corpse this entire time without her. I need my woman like fucking air. Skin to skin, I slowly come back to life as I sink inside her.

"Rock," she keeps murmuring my name as if trying to convince herself I'm actually with her. Her arms and legs tighten around me, drawing me into her body. She hasn't stopped running her hands over me or touching my skin in some way since I walked in the door.

"I'm right here with you, Baby Doll. I'm here."

Those words set her emotions free. She buries her face against my neck, her tears sliding over my skin. Faster and harder I move against her, burying myself in her over and over.

"I need you to come, Baby Doll. I need it. Missed you so much."

She cries harder but nods frantically.

Drawing back, I turn and roll us to the middle of the bed, so she's on top of me. "Let me look at you."

"I can't. I can't."

Her hands slide under my shoulders and she clings to me, burying her face against my neck. My arms band around her waist, hands sliding down to dig my fingers into her ass.

"Sit up, baby. Ride me. Show me you missed me."

She plants her palms against my chest, pushing herself up enough to make me groan. A soft hiss flows from her lips as she readjusts to my size. Her eyes bore into me. "Don't do that. You have no idea how much I missed you."

"Yes, I do." My hand smacks her ass. I grip her hips, urging her to move. Slowly, she slides up and down. Her tears stop flowing, crying turns to moaning as she moves faster.

"That's better. Good girl," I keep encouraging as she rocks faster, takes me deeper. "Give yourself to me."

She tips her head down, her eyes finding mine. Reaching up, I cup her cheek, running my thumb over her skin. She gasps, stutters, turns her head to kiss my hand.

"Rock."

"Right here, baby."

She tightens, ready to go off. Rising, I pull her toward me, catching her lips with mine, swallowing her sounds of pleasure. Her body's still trembling when I flip us. Before she catches her breath, my hands wrap around her ankles, drawing her legs up to my shoulders.

"Can you take more, or are you done, baby?"

This time I get a hint of a smirk. "Do you have it in you?"

"Missed that fucking sass-mouth," I grunt as I slam into her, showing her exactly how much I've got in me. Lowering her legs, I grasp her hips, unable to stop myself from digging my fingers in. Rough, hard, but she responds the way I remember. We're two parts of a whole, reunited. I can't let anything tear us apart again.

Her eyes find mine and the corner of her mouth lifts a touch. My hands loosen from her hips to pinch her nipples and her back arches, offering herself up for whatever I want.

"Fuck. Hope. Fuck."

Familiar white hot burning pleasure seizes me and I know what's about to go down. I'm sliding my dick out, contractions seizing me, cum covering her stomach as wave after wave of pleasure and peace wash over me. "Can't stop. Got a lot saved up for you, babe." I barely make out my own words through all the groaning.

She lifts her head, checking out the mess I've made all over her pristine skin. A wry smile twists her mouth, and it feels fucking good to see her smile. As usual, she's amused by my caveman behavior—not repulsed. "I guess so," she teases.

There she is. My little sass-mouth. Slowly coming back to me.

Her smile disappears as she lays her head back on the mattress. "I missed you so much, Rochlan."

"I know. Need to do that at least ten more times."

She chuckles.

"Stay there, let me grab a towel."

After wiping her down, I hold out my hand. "Let's get cleaned up. There are a few things I have to do before we hit the road."

"Go ahead. I'll meet you in there." She slides off the bed, scoops all the stuff we shoved on the floor up and flings them back on the bed.

"Don't bring too many clothes. You won't need them."

She glances up and attempts to pin with me a serious stare, but the corners of her mouth tremble with laughter.

Her smile loosens the tightness in my chest.

"But I stocked up on all sorts of stuff you can rip off."

A growl bursts out of me, and my hand cracks against her ass so hard she gasps. "Missed this ass," I whisper against her ear before heading to the shower. If I don't get away, I'm gonna fuck her again, and we don't have time for it.

I'm not under the hot spray long before she joins me. Taking the soap out of my hands, she runs it over my back, then sets it down. "Are you okay?" she asks softly after a few minutes of silence.

I capture one of her roaming hands and bring it around to my mouth, kissing her fingers until I tease a bit of laughter out of her. "I am now."

She takes her time digging her fingers into my shoulders and back, massaging more than washing. Under her touch some of the stress of the last few months disappears.

"You're harder than ever," she mumbles so low I almost don't hear her over the falling water.

"You have no idea, Baby Doll."

She snickers and taps me on the ass. "That's not what I meant. Turn around."

This is much better. It gives me an excuse to watch her face as she explores my chest and shoulders. She peeks up at me from under her lashes.

"Wasn't much to do besides push-ups and sit-ups," I explain.

She *hmms* at me but then her face falls and she flings her arms around my neck.

"Hey, I'm here. Everything's okay, baby." I want to say "I'll never leave you again," but I don't know if I can make that promise.

"I know."

"You're what got me through, Hope. Picturing your face. Remembering the sound of your voice. The taste of your skin. The times you visited, seeing how strong you were being for me—"

"I didn't feel very strong."

"But you were. And the club took care of you?"

"Yes. Without them…I don't know what I would have done."

"Good." I pat her ass, which turns into groping her ass until she squirms out of my hold. "Caveman."

"Come on. Wrath's waiting for us downstairs."

She cocks her head. "Why?"

"He wants to give Trin her patch." My hand reaches back, shutting off the water.

"Oh, finally. Thank God." Outside the shower, she hands me a towel, then pauses. "Did you talk to Trinity?"

"No, baby. Came right up to see you first."

A sad smile pulls at her mouth and she glances up at me. "She had a hard time with you being gone, so make sure you talk to her before we leave."

"Wrath—"

"He had enough to do with you asking him to watch out for me." The aggrieved tone of her voice would normally amuse me, but I sense she's really bothered.

"It's his job."

"I know. But Z's just as fierce and overprotective. And Murphy. And Dex. And Teller."

"Okay. I got it." I'm still not understanding what went on, but I nod to get her moving. I don't *plan* on this ever happening again.

CHAPTER TWENTY-SIX

HOPE

I CAN'T LET GO of Rock. Not for a second. If he wasn't clinging to me the same way, I might feel like I'm overreacting. But his hand's wrapped around mine just as tight as we head downstairs.

The guys shout and cheer when they see Rock and he raises his other hand in the air. I only let go of him when Trinity approaches. She glances at me first. I think her way of asking if I mind. Her eyes are shiny with unshed tears and I nod at her. Rock sweeps her up into a hug and she laughs to cover up what I hope are happy tears. "You okay, Trinny?" he asks as he sets her down.

"Yes." She takes my hand and tugs me to her side. "Your woman did good, prez. You should be proud of her."

He brushes the back of his hand over my cheek. "Real proud, Baby Doll."

Teller joins us and taps my shoulder. "Yeah. She mama-beared the fuck out of us and kept everyone in line."

"Oh, stop." I had to focus my attention on the guys so I didn't fall to pieces. It was self-preservation. Nothing more.

Z's also enthusiastic in his praise. It makes me chuckle that they're all so impressed I kept my shit together. Their enthusiasm suggests that more than once they expected me to collapse into a sobbing mess. Cold fear churns through my stomach at the thought of losing Rock again. He seems to sense it and takes my hand, calming me.

Pretty soon, the entire club's crowded around him and I back away so he can have a moment with everyone. I'll have my time with him later.

Wrath's in the corner of the couch by himself, watching the scene in front of him. "You okay?" I ask.

His mouth turns up into a genuine smile. Not his usual cocky or devilish one. He pats the cushion and I drop down next to him. "Happy he's back, sugar. He's not half as fucked up as I thought he'd be." He glances at me. "I think that's because of you."

"I didn't do anything."

He stares at me until I squirm. "Yeah, you did, Hope."

"Are you nervous?" I ask to change the subject.

His gaze sweeps the room, finally landing on Trinity over by the bar. "She makes me crazy," he says with a lot of affection.

"You love it."

"She knows I don't want her doing this shit anymore."

I have to chuckle. "You want her to focus all that attention on *you*."

He grins back. "Yeah. I take a lot of care and feeding."

I snort, then turn serious. "I think it makes her happy to do that stuff. Take care of things. Be needed." I tilt my head up, noticing for the first time Mariella hasn't joined us. "I don't think she's comfortable turning things over to Mariella yet either."

"Yeah, I get that."

"Besides, you know her every waking thought is of you."

He raises an eyebrow.

"Wyatt this. Wyatt that." I roll my eyes. "Ask Wyatt's permission for a road trip." I lower my voice. "Hey, in case you're horny while your man's locked up, you can borrow one of the brothers. Just not Wrath. He's all mine."

He stares at me with a surprised expression before bursting with laughter. "You didn't tell *him* that, did you?" he asks.

"No. I just told him to make sure he spent a little time with her before we leave."

He smiles briefly. "You going with him?"

"Yes."

"Good."

"Any idea where he'll want to go?"

He shakes his head. "He probably doesn't even know."

I'm okay with that. In fact, I relish the idea of the two of us alone together on the open road with no particular destination in mind.

"You'll like the ride Murphy set up."

"We're not taking Rock's bike?"

As soon as Wrath starts shaking his head, I realize what a stupid question that was. "Colors. Territory. Got it."

"Good girl. You're learning."

Laughing, I bump my shoulder into him. "Ass."

"Ready?" Rock asks, tapping Wrath's leg with his boot.

"Church first?"

"Yeah." Rock turns his attention on me. "You okay to wait out here for a few minutes? We won't be long."

"Of course. Do what you need to do, Rock. I'm good."

"You're the best." He turns and whistles for everyone's attention and points to the war room. "Church. Now. Want prospects at the end too, so go get 'em and have them wait out here."

ROCK

Every brother stops for a hug, fist bump or back slap as they file into the war room.

It's inadequate, but all I can think is how good it feels to be home. Surrounded by family.

I've always disliked my chair at the head of the table. But I keep it as a reminder of what the club endured before I took the throne. Now, I'm happy to see it too.

"Who sat here while I was gone?"

Wrath snorts. "Hope."

I have to raise an eyebrow at that. No way would they have let her sit at the table.

"Not for church," Z explains. "Couple times when we needed to talk to her and then this morning when we explained she couldn't come with us to collect you."

"Yeah, how'd she take that?"

"Fine. Didn't even blink. Told us to hurry up and get our sorry asses down there."

I duck my head and laugh as I picture that scenario.

Once more, I glance around the table. "So she really didn't give any of you a hard time?"

Z snorts and I turn my attention to him, finding him shaking with laughter. "What's so funny?"

"Nothing. I think she secretly enjoyed torturing us. Murphy had to take her to her dress fitting thing."

"Jesus Christ," Murphy grumbles, shaking his head.

"Please. He loved every second. Heidi was there too," Wrath says.

I'm grinning like a fool as I slam the gavel down, signaling chat time's over.

"Let's get down to business. Thank you all for keeping the club going. For your loyalty. It meant a lot to me knowing you guys had things covered. Thanks for stepping up, protecting each other and protecting club assets."

Sparky pipes up from the back. "Missed you, boss."

"I know. Missed you guys too. And I hope you'll forgive me for taking off for a few days after this meeting."

Everyone murmurs their approval. Dex mentions "reconnecting" with my woman, which gets a dirty chuckle out of all these fuckers.

"This was some fucking bullshit. We've got a number of things to address when I get back. I'll share my list with you, get your feedback and we'll start making plans."

Everyone nods.

"First, we've got Ulfric. Sloppy-ass motherfucker." I turn to Wrath. "Wrath's got the tie to their crew through Whisper and I got info from one of their guys while I was inside. It seems they're trying to convince Ulfric it's time to retire. I suggest we support that in whatever way we can."

Everyone agrees.

"Vipers." Any levity we were feeling flies right out the window. Shit's about to get real. "They need to go. We've put up with enough bullshit from them. This most recent shit goes back to their belief that targeting women associated with the club is acceptable behavior." I wait for any of them to question me. This is, after all, my fault. It was my involvement with Hope and my plan to pre-emptively take out the two fuckers who planned to hurt her that put all this other shit in motion. If I hadn't done that, then Cabo never would have come up here in search of his brother's killer, Ulfric never would have killed him and sloppily tossed his body in the river.

Of course, if I hadn't taken care of those fucks, they would have brutally attacked Hope. For a second rage tightens my throat and I have to pause.

"Not your fault, prez. They started it by bringing women into it. We were protecting innocent people from getting hurt," Bricks says.

Yet, because I'm a selfish fucker, I drew Hope into my world anyway and that weighs on me.

"From what Wrath tells me, we've got Sway's and the all of downstate's support on this. Whatever we need. He's got his eye on their Jersey charter. But Ransom, and the rest of them—"

Z taps my hand to get my attention. "Rock, after what we learned from Mariella, there's no doubt. These guys have got to go. Ain't a decent human being in that crew."

"We'll discuss it more when I get back. I want everyone to stay on alert. Even though I'm out, and the charges were dropped, it doesn't mean they're not up to something else. This was some sneaky, fucked up shit, that took thought and planning. Things we're not used to seeing from Vipers."

"They gotta be hunting Mariella down," Dex says.

His words bring me to my next item. "Mariella. What are we doing with her?"

Surprisingly, Teller's the one to speak up. "She wants to stay. After the shit they forced her into, she's more than happy taking over our household stuff. Plus, she's sort of bonded to Trinity."

Wrath throws a look at Teller, then turns to me. "Trin's not one-hundred percent on board with turning her stuff over, but she likes Mariella. Thinks she'll be okay."

"We can trust her?"

Z nods. "I think so. She's a sweet girl. Real shy."

"Great cook," Murphy adds. "When Trinity lets the girl touch her kitchen."

The guys chuckle over that. Trinity's run that kitchen with an iron fist for years. I imagine turning it over to someone else isn't making her too happy.

"I can trust every one of you to leave her alone? She's under our protection and that's it."

It doesn't escape my notice that everyone *but* Teller agrees. I point down the table at him. "Are we going to have a problem?"

"No," he answers.

I turn to Wrath. "Trin's made it clear we don't expect anything else out of her?" I'd rather not repeat past mistakes.

"Yeah. Hope did too." He lowers his voice. "It made more of an impression coming from Trinity."

"I'm sure it did." My focus returns to the rest of the guys. "Where we at with GSC?"

"All good," Z reports. "They were surprisingly supportive. You know, as long as we kept the weed coming."

Wrath picks up Z's thread. "Yeah, he offered us some valuable intel when we needed it. Made extracting Mariella a fuck lot easier."

I can't help wondering what Loco will ask for in return one day.

The guys give me a report on the last few drops with GSC and I take my seat. Sparky gives me an update on his current plan and two future projects he wants to work on.

When he finishes, I'm still considering whether I want to bring up the last item on my list.

"Prez?" Z prompts.

"Izzard. What went down?"

Wrath and Z exchange looks. "Why don't you tell us," Wrath finally says. Bold move, fucker.

"Don't know. He took a dislike to me from the morning I processed in. Took some shit from him. Nothing I couldn't handle."

Wrath's getting more and more pissed and I catch him shaking his head.

"Now, since you guys didn't know that, what made you decide to take action on him? And what happened? He ran his mouth about Hope, but I figured he was bluffing." Was praying like fuck he was bluffing.

"He disrespected, Hope," Wrath says. His mouth flattens into a grim line. "We couldn't let that stand. Then the day of the bail hearing, Hope said you had a black eye. Figured it had to be him."

"Broke his motherfuckin' fingers," Murphy spits out. "Cried like a little bitch."

I take a second to absorb that. My gaze drills into Wrath again. "*How* specifically did he disrespect Hope?"

"He gave her a pat-down that morning. Used it as an opportunity to grope her." He drops his head, staring at his hands. "I couldn't see what was going on from where I was, but I should've gotten her the fuck out of there the minute he started hassling us."

I lean back, wait for my rage fog to clear, and don't say anything for a few minutes. "Did he know where the payback was coming from?"

"No," Teller answers. "We didn't know if he had buddies on the inside who'd get to you. We went in masked, didn't say anything. Broke his fuckin' hands, knocked him out and took off."

Turning to Wrath, I ask, "You a part of it?"

His face's all sort of pissed-off when he answers. "No. Couldn't risk him recognizing my big ass."

This surprises me. It was a good call even though I know it must have killed him not to be a part of it. "Smart thinking. Who else went?"

Z, Ravage and Dex raise their hands, but Dex's the one who

speaks. "Swan helped us lure him to a motel. He's one sick, twisted fucker."

That does *not* surprise me.

"All right. We can talk about what to do with him when I get back. Anything else?"

"Prospects been staying here," Wrath says. "We make them stay in the basement with Sparky and Stash, though."

Sparky raises his hand. "Yeah, about that—"

All of us laugh.

"What do we think? How'd Hoot and Birch do? They're both coming up on two years of prospecting. Time to vote?"

Murmurs of approval go around the table. Z speaks up. "They both stepped up big time. Axel too, but I know he's not ready yet."

"All right, we'll talk about that when I get back." I point to the door. "Someone go tell them to join us."

Dex lets the prospects in and they automatically move to the back of the room.

"Good to see you back, prez," Birch says. Hoot and Axel make similar comments.

"Good to be back. So, I hear you prospects have been staying up here. What the fuck's that about?" I joke to lighten everyone up. In the back of the room, Hoot, Birch and Axel stand a little straighter but keep their mouths shut.

Z lifts his hand to speak. "They were a big help. When Butch and Iron Jim had to take off, prospects took over door duty at CB—"

"Big hardship hanging out with the strippers," Murphy comments.

My mouth twists into a smirk and I nod at Axel. "How'd Heidi take that?"

"Not too well, prez."

Everyone in the room bursts out laughing. Even Teller.

I glance at Murphy, pretty sure I know how Axel got assigned to CB. "We won't have you back there, kid. Lord knows there's plenty of shit to keep you busy here."

Wrath grins like a devil. "I got some trees that need clearing."

"Thanks," Axel says.

"Don't thank him yet, there're a *lot* of trees out there," Z jokes.

I don't think Axel minds one bit.

"Any other business I should know about?"

I get a bunch of negative responses, but no one stands yet, waiting to see what else I want to say. "Love every one of you. Thanks for everything. I heard the clubhouse was pretty dismal in my absence, so celebrate tonight. Wrath's got something he wants to do, so hang in the living room for a few before going off to get fucked up."

Guys chuckle and stream out into the living room. Z and Wrath stay behind.

"Need anything, bro?" Z asks Wrath.

"Nope. All good."

Z pulls me in for a quick hug and pounds on my back. "Missed you. Glad you're back."

"Same."

Z leaves and shuts the door behind him, which is fine because I need a moment alone with Wrath.

"What's on your mind, prez?"

My mouth curves into a grin. Brother already knows I got a few questions for him. "Be honest now. Hope did okay?"

"Yeah. I mean, she was sad, no doubt about it. But she kept busy. Looked after all of us. Harassed Glassman in her polite lawyer way when the rest of us wanted to rip his head off. Didn't give us any grief."

"This thing with Izzard?"

"Rock. I'm so sorry. You don't—"

"I know what a fuckin' dick he is. I don't blame you and I'm not mad at you."

"Lying to you fuckin' killed me. But I knew—"

"Yeah. You did the right thing."

"She shook it off. But I don't know."

"I'll talk to her. Now, Hope mentioned Trinity had a hard time?"

Wrath runs his hand through his hair, which automatically makes me think it was bad. "Yeah, you know with her dad—"

"You realize I'm not even ten years older than her and only two years older than you, right?"

I get a hint of a smile out of him. "What can I say? You're a father figure to everyone. It's all that wisdom of experience."

"Whatever. Go on."

"Nothing. She struggled and because I was busy watching over Hope, I didn't realize how hard she was taking it at first."

Now it's my turn to run my hands over my head. "Fuck, man. I'm so sorry. Once those cuffs snapped on my wrists, I panicked. I didn't know what the fuck might be coming for the club. I trust you more than anyone, but I didn't mean you had to—"

"It's fine. We worked it out. Hope set me straight," he chuckles and shakes his head.

"What aren't you telling me?"

"Come on, man. You know what type of club Trinity grew up in. What do you think their solution was for an 'ol lady when her man was locked up?"

It takes a second for me to puzzle out and when I do my face must turn murderous because Wrath backs up a step. "Trust me, Hope thought the idea was disgusting. She told me to quit bugging her and take care of Trinity."

That's my girl.

"And?"

Wrath runs his hands through his hair and seems to be considering what he wants to share with me. "Having Mariella here has brought up some stuff for Trin."

"I can imagine," I answer quietly.

"She went through a rough patch. But we're working through it."

"You need anything?"

"Yeah, introduce me to your contractor."

I raise an eyebrow.

"I think getting her out of the clubhouse will help."

"Yeah, I can understand that. You ain't building next door to us though." I follow it up with a grin, so he knows I'm messing with him.

"Please. I don't want to be within screaming distance of you two sex-crazed monkeys."

I huff a laugh out. "Same."

"No, seriously, I know it's gonna take a while, and you need to get yours finished before the wedding—"

"Ah, fuck. Can you have Z call Jasper? Get him and his crew up here as soon as possible."

He nods. Then pins me with a thoughtful expression.

"Spit it out."

"I won't lie, Rock. Z and I expected her to bolt at first. Never figured she'd tough something like this out when I first met her. But she kept throwing herself into the club in her own way."

"Good. That's good."

"Her faith was stronger than her fear. Kept planning your wedding. Held her head up high. After that bullshit hearing, she was spitting mad when she came out of the courtroom. Judge said some fucked up shit to her, but she shook it off. Let Glassman have it when she thought he was disrespecting your relationship. She never doubted you."

I'm having a hard time swallowing over the lump in my throat. There's so much catching up Hope and I have to do.

"She may not be a typical old lady, but she's a good one," Wrath finishes.

"Thank you."

"You got it." Wrath turns and springs his cabinet open.

I watch as he pulls out Trinity's vest with his *Property of Wrath* patch on the back and all our officers' patches on the side. Finally. "Ready to go claim your own 'ol lady?"

"Fuck yes. God damn."

Can't help chuckling at that. "She's not a typical 'ol lady either." And I'm not referring to her club girl days.

"Nope. But we're not exactly typical bikers either."

"Amen to that, brother."

WRATH

I'm twitchy as a motherfucker when Rock and I step out of the war room. My gaze darts around the room taking in my brothers, the prospects, couple club girls. Then my eyes lock onto Trinity. Laughing in the corner with Hope. Love seeing her more at ease and not running around fetching drinks and shit.

"Can you fuckers all pipe down for a second?" I shout over the noise. Silence descends on the room. Turning, I curl a finger at Trinity and motion her to me. She hurries over with a big smile, until she sees what's in my hand.

Then she stops dead in her tracks. That's fine. Took so fucking long, she probably figured I was full of shit.

I take the last few steps to her, curling my hand around her hip in case she decides to bolt and sink down to my knees in front of her.

"Wyatt—" she protests, looking around the room. "Everyone's—"

"Everyone's gonna hear me claim you and patch you," I answer. I raise my voice so the whole clubhouse hears. "You all might have heard I claimed Trinity as my old lady."

I get a lot of whistles, shouting and catcalls in return.

"And everyone knows when Kings claim a woman, the officers vote on her too." I hold out the cut to Trinity and her honey eyes meet mine. The corner of her mouth trembles and her eyes gloss over.

"So I got the votes and my girl's getting my patch, and you're all here to witness it."

The room erupts into sounds of congratulations as I stand, pick her up and kiss the fuck out of her. "Will you wear my patch, baby?"

"You know I will."

I set her down and help her into the vest. "Thought I was full of shit, didn't you?"

"No. I knew there was a lot—"

I cut her off with another kiss, lifting her into my arms where she belongs, not giving a fuck about the noise around us.

"Finally!" Rock shouts and I can hear Hope shushing him.

When I set Trin down, my hand squeezes her hip where my star's inked into her skin. "My tat, my patch, now you just need a ring."

"Whatever you want."

"Oh, in that case—"

She slaps my chest, throwing off the uncertainty that seemed to settle over her. "You know what Wrath wants, Wrath gets," she says with a sweet laugh.

"That true?"

"Yes."

"Good. Kiss me."

She doesn't hesitate, throws her arms around my neck and plants one on my cheek. "I'm so proud to officially be yours," she whispers and I think it's the sweetest thing she's ever said.

"Someone throw a bucket of ice water on those two!" Murphy shouts and I turn to see, yes, the little fucker's talking about Trin and me.

"You got a death wish, bro?"

He tilts his head toward the door. Toward the garage. Fuck. "Yeah, okay."

I glance over to where Rock's got Hope basically pinned to the wall. Ain't paying attention to anything except his woman. "Looks like that bucket of ice water's needed somewhere else," I grumble.

Trinity chuckles. "Leave them alone."

"He wanted to hit the road, and it's getting late. Murphy's got a surprise for them."

"Oh, okay."

She rushes over and yanks Hope away, making me laugh my ass off at the expression on Rock's face.

"Murphy needs you outside, prez."

His gaze shoots to the door where Murphy's waiting and he nods. When he reaches Hope, he bends down and tosses her over his shoulder like the caveman we all know he is. She kicks and squeals as we follow him out the door. "Put me down before you hurt yourself."

Trinity snickers. "Now she did it."

Rock pops her on the ass and she yelps. "I can *not* believe you did that in front of everyone!"

"I'll do it again, sass-mouth."

Everyone else is waiting in the garage, so not as many people witnessed it as Hope thinks. Still funny as fuck.

Trinity slides her hand into mine and I glance down at her. "You want some of that?"

She peeks up at me. "Later."

"Later you're gonna wear that vest and nothing else for me while I fuck the hell out of you."

"Oooh. If you're nice I might add something else you'll like," she teases, while batting her lashes at me.

Hmmm. Maybe I can see the bike when Rock and Hope get back.

"I know what you're thinking," Trinity scolds, yanking my hand and dragging me into the garage.

Rock's so stunned, he almost drops Hope when he sets her down inside the garage. "Murphy, what—?"

Yeah, the kid did good.

HOPE

"Oh my God. Murphy, it's beautiful," I blurt out.

Rock still seems to be forming an opinion. Murphy's tense as he waits for Rock's approval and I worry what will happen if he doesn't get it.

"Sweet tourer. You'll be the coolest old man in the retirement community," Z jokes and punches Rock's arm.

"Fuck off," Rock growls.

Murphy folds his arms over his chest, but not before giving Z the finger.

"He's been working on it all summer, Rock," Wrath says.

I trace my hand over the raised back seat. "I love it."

Murphy grins and relaxes a notch.

"You do the paint?" Rock asks.

"No. Bricks helped with it."

My eyes seek Bricks out. "I love the color. It's so pretty."

The guys hassle Rock over that. But it *is* pretty. A deep, sparkling forest green. No LOKI logos anywhere, and I kind of miss the ever-present skull wearing its crown.

The guys discuss a bunch of mechanical-bike stuff that goes right over my head. All I care about is the back rest with the cushier seat and the passenger floor boards. My poor ass had not been looking forward to a long trip on Rock's bike.

After it seems they go over every single last shock, air filter, and fender, Murphy skirts the edge of the group and makes his way to me. "Do you really like it?"

Somehow I sense he's seeking my approval more than Rock's over this project and a dull ache flashes through my chest. Because I'm the touchy-feely type, I wrap my arms around him. While he hugs me back, I meet Rock's eyes across the room. His nod and half-smile reassure me. He knows I care for Murphy the way I would a younger brother and isn't concerned about the display of affection.

"Yes. My ass thanks you, too."

He chuckles and runs his hand over his chin. "There's some gear inside for you too."

"Thank you."

The guys walk the bike out of the garage, into the driveway and turn it over. The rumble is much more polite and refined than Rock's regular ride. He smirks at Murphy, then lifts his gaze to me. "Guess we're just two civilians out to enjoy the freedom of the road, babe."

"Fine by me."

The guys think that's hysterical.

Trinity wraps me in a hug. "I'll miss you. Have fun and take care of your man."

"Oh, I plan to."

Murphy overhears that and snickers then joins his brothers. Rock motions Murphy to his side and together they adjust pegs, bars and other parts. Z adds his two cents about some of the changes and the three of them go back and forth.

Trinity lets out a whoop and squeezes me again. "They'll mess around with that bike all night if you let them, Hope."

"Good God, I know." I turn and run my hand over the vest Wrath just gave her. "I'm so happy he finally gave this to you. He was planning to do it at the engagement party. Right before—" Even thinking of speaking the words sends my heart into my stomach.

Her face softens and her gaze darts to Wrath. "Really? You were okay with that?"

"Of course. It seemed really important to him to do it in front of the whole club." Given the nature of their relationship and their past…relationships with other…members of the club, I understand Wrath's reasoning.

Her eyes well up. "I didn't realize."

I flick my hand over the leather. "Just so you know, it goes really well with that skirt thingie, stockings, heels and nothing else." I wiggle my eyebrows and she laughs.

"I'll keep it in mind."

Behind us, the club party's kicking into high gear. After a summer of solemn brooding, it's refreshing to see the guys relaxed and carrying on. But I'm happy we'll be leaving before it gets too wild. Wrath stalks Trinity like a panther, scooping her up and making her squeal. "I've got a surprise for you too."

"Is it in your pants?" she asks with a straight face.

"No, angel. Maybe later if you're good."

Next to them, I snort and Wrath glances down at me with a grin. "Go tell him to get his ass moving, Hope."

Maybe another hour later and we're finally on the road. I'm sweating under the heavier leather jacket Murphy insisted I wear and I'm thankful for the bandanna Trinity tied around my forehead to catch the perspiration already dripping underneath my helmet.

Physical concerns aside, I'm excited to be alone with my man doing something that brings him peace. And I'm grateful he wanted me with him. I haven't been on a bike all summer and realize I've missed it. Not that any of the brothers had offered, but I don't think I could ever ride behind anyone *but* Rock.

Roads I've driven plenty of times take on a different, raw kind of beauty when experienced this way. I do my best to be a good passenger, not shifting my weight too much, tucking close to Rock's body and holding tight—which certainly isn't a hardship. I'm so thankful he's in my arms again, I'm probably squeezing the life out of him, but he doesn't seem to mind.

Even though the bike's new to him, he guides it effortlessly. Completely in tune with the machine. Concentrating on the road ahead of us, but relaxed and graceful.

Once we've covered a lot of highway, Rock pulls over at a rest stop on the Mass Pike. Inside I simmer with heat remembering the last rest stop romp we had. I dismount, hand him my helmet, tug my hair free from its elastic and bend over to stretch. Rock slaps my ass and growls in my ear as I straighten up.

"What're you doing, Baby Doll?"

"I'm stiff."

He slips his leather gloves off and rubs my lower back for a few minutes. "Better?" he asks before kissing my cheek.

"Yes. This is much more comfortable for me, but I'm trying to keep still, so—"

"Relax, I got you, Hope."

"I know."

He takes my hand and walks us inside, where we grab a bite to eat and drinks. "How do you feel about Maine?" he asks, after I return from the bathroom. "Should be quiet this time of year. I'd like to sit and stare at the ocean for a few days."

"Sounds perfect."

CHAPTER TWENTY-SEVEN

WRATH

A BITE of jealousy snaps at me as Rock takes off. I haven't ridden any great distance in way too long. And never with Trinity at my back.

"Hey, what do you think about taking off for a few days ourselves?"

She stares up at me in surprise.

"Now?"

Things seem okay. It's not like guys aren't here day and night to handle anything that comes up.

"Sure, why not?"

She tucks her bottom lip under her teeth, her gaze roaming around the clubhouse. "What about Mariella?"

"What about her?"

Her hand goes to her hip and her face pulls into a mask of exasperation. "I can't just leave her. Hope's not here either."

"No one's gonna bother her. Besides, Heidi's around, and they seem to get along."

"She's a kid."

"She's closer to Mariella's age than you are."

She smacks my chest. "Thanks."

Time to pull out the big guns. Hooking my hands over her shoulders, I turn her to face me and lean down to meet her eyes. "Please, baby. It's been a rough summer. I want some alone time with my girl."

There it is. A hint of a smile at the corners of her mouth. I got her. "Okay. Where?"

Shit, anywhere. Doesn't matter as long as she's with me. "How about north, to the Adirondacks. We can stop at Ausable Chasm. Try some rock climbing or just hike through the trails. You can get some nice photos up there this time of year."

"Okay. When?"

I glance around. "Tomorrow morning. I want to make sure these fuckers don't get too out of control."

"They'll probably be partying all weekend."

"I'll let Z sober up, then put him and Murphy in charge."

Her lips quivers with laughter. "Not Teller?"

"Nah, he's got enough to worry about. Come on, let's grab something to eat."

On our way back from the kitchen, we stop to talk to a bunch of people. In the living room, I catch sight of Heidi draped over Murphy, giggling and generally acting like a high school girl.

Even after I eased up on the lock down restrictions, Heidi begged to stay up here since Teller frequently left her alone at their apartment. I'm suspicious of a teenager who doesn't want to have an apartment to herself, and suspect it has more to do with keeping tabs on Murphy, since Axel has an apartment near campus. She's been spending a lot of time up here. Usually it's fine, and she does help out around the place. But tonight, with all the dirty shit going down, I'm not too happy about her hanging out. Axel's nowhere to be found and I'm tempted to find him, hand him a hundred bucks and tell him to take his girl and get lost for the weekend.

In an attempt to feel out the situation, I drop down on the couch opposite where Murphy and Heidi are hanging out and pull Trinity down with me.

"Rock seemed pleased with the bike, Murphy. You did a great job with it," Trinity shouts over the music.

Murphy grins like an idiot. "Yeah. I think Hope liked it too."

"She did," Trinity confirms.

Z joins us, rubbing his hands over his face.

"Hey, Trin and I are gonna take off tomorrow morning. Think you two dipshits can hold the place down for a couple days?" I ask, pointing at Z and Murphy.

Heidi giggles. Z flips me off.

"What crawled up your ass?" I ask.

"Nothing. Fuckin' Inga must've just gotten out of rehab. Keeps calling Dex, trying to see if she can come back."

"Hell fucking no."

"Rock will kill you if you let that skank come back to work there," Trinity agrees.

Z nods. "I know."

"Hypocrite much?" Heidi mutters while glaring at Trinity.

The silence that descends on our corner of the room's pretty intense. Murphy shifts. Z glares at Heidi and Murphy.

Trinity's eyes narrow but she holds her tongue. Guess what? *I* don't have to hold mine. No fucking way is this mouthy little brat giving Trinity shit. Especially not right in front of me. I thought we were done with this.

I snap my fingers in front of Heidi's face to get her attention. When she swings her gaze my way, her eyes are wide. It just sunk in she might have made a mistake. "Listen, little girl, she ain't calling Inga a skank because she's a porn star or works as a stripper. She's saying she's a skank because she came into our clubhouse and kept trying to hook up with Rock, even though she knew he and Hope were together. Do you comprehend the difference, kid?"

"Wyatt, don't," Trinity says while clamping her hand around my arm. Without taking my eyes off Heidi, I slip Trinity's hand in mine and squeeze her back.

Murphy glares at me, and I raise an eyebrow, daring him to open his mouth. Heidi sputters but I'm not done lecturing her just yet.

"You want to be treated like a big girl around here? Show respect. Don't talk shit about things you don't understand. Especially when you shouldn't be up here in the first place." I let that threat hang, because I'm well within my rights to kick her underage ass out.

The situation's so awkward, Trinity looks like she wants to melt into the floor right along with Heidi. And no, I shouldn't be in the middle of chick business, but this needed to be said. I'm sure if Hope were here, she wouldn't have let Heidi get away with that shit. She just would have said it much nicer.

Jesus Christ, am I really taking over Hope's role while she's away?

Heidi surprises me by apologizing. I expected her to storm off in one of her famous fits. "I'm sorry, Trinity."

Trin shakes her head and stares at me before turning to Heidi. "I understand."

Murphy's still making a face at me and brother's walking on thin ice, since as far as I'm concerned this shit with Heidi and Trinity is his fuckin' fault.

Well, twenty-five percent his fault. Twenty percent? Whatever. I also want to call Heidi out for being a hypocrite herself, since she's basically sitting in Murphy's lap and her boyfriend's nowhere in sight.

But I don't. That's treading into territory that's none of my business.

See? If everyone minded their own damn business we wouldn't have any problems.

CHAPTER TWENTY-EIGHT

HOPE

WE CROSS the Maine state line after dark. Because it's off-season, most businesses seem to be closed. Rock slows and turns down a road which leads to a group of family-oriented motels dotted along the beach. When we find one with a vacancy sign lit up, he pulls in.

The manager's just about to close the office when we walk up. Well, I hobble up onto the porch. This ride was far more comfortable thanks to Murphy's genius, but my ass and legs still fell asleep somewhere back in New Hampshire.

"How can I help you this evening?"

Rock answers the manager's question. I'm too busy bending down to pet the little white fluffy dog who peeked out from behind the counter.

"Need a room for a couple nights."

I'm only half-listening as Rock makes the arrangements. I'll sleep in the sand as long as we're together.

Rock carries everything upstairs. Our room's on the corner, facing the ocean and even has a hot tub tucked away on the balcony.

"Should have taken you someplace fancier, but—"

I stop him with a hand against his cheek. "This is perfect."

He presses a kiss against my palm and takes my hand. "Moonlit walk on the beach?" His voice sounds relaxed and gruff at the same time.

"Sounds romantic."

I think romance is the last thing on Rock's mind as we stop before the parking lot pavement turns into sandy beach to remove or shoes. Rock kneels down, gently tugs my boots off and rolls my jeans up while I lean on his shoulder. I dig my feet into the cool, grittiness as we trudge down to the water's edge. It feels refreshing after the long ride.

"Coldcoldcold!" I yelp as an icy wave rolls over my feet. Behind me, Rock chuckles and pulls me back. His arms hold me tight, but I feel like it's the first time I've been able to breathe in months. We stay that way for a while staring out at the moonlight flickering over the black, glittering waves.

"Missed you so much, baby." Rock's lips press a soft kiss against the side of my face. His raw voice tears my insides to pieces.

"Missed you too," I whisper.

"Come here." He takes my hand and walks us farther away from the water, drops down into the sand and motions me to join him.

I kneel in front of him, bracing my hands on his knees.

"I'm so sorry, Hope."

"For?"

"Everything."

He drops his legs to the side and stretches them out so I can crawl into his lap. My lips find his cheek, kissing him over and over. "Not now. I love you. I'm so happy I have you back. No bad stuff tonight."

He takes my hands, warming them and pulls us up off the soft, sandy floor. We don't speak as I follow him back to our room. Not a word as he pulls me inside, shuts the door and pushes me against it. His familiar, enticing scent of wind and leather mixes with the ocean air that still clings to us. Like heaven.

Soft, loving reunion kisses spiral into less polite, more demanding kisses that push me flat against the unforgiving wood.

His fingers trace everywhere, my cheek, my jaw, my neck, under my sweatshirt.

"Loved having you at my back the whole way here," he murmurs against my ear.

"I loved being there."

He captures my wrists, pulling them up over my head, pinning them to the door with one hand and tugs my sweatshirt up with the other.

Ten seconds inside our room and he has me breathless.

He releases me long enough to push my sweatshirt higher, tugging it over my head and tossing it on the round table next to us. As soon as it's gone, he gathers my hands behind my back, thrusting my breasts forward. His mouth curls into a slow smile.

"It's like you knew," he says as he stares at the front clasp of my bra. Easily he flicks it open with one hand—which yes had absolutely been my intention when I bought it—and lowers his mouth to sweep his tongue over my nipple.

"Oh, please, Rock."

"Please, what?" he asks as he runs his hand up my ribcage, stopping to cup my breast. I whimper and he chuckles. I want him so much, but he's intent on teasing me. "You have no idea all the filthy things I planned to do to you while we were apart."

"Show me."

He releases my wrists, but the warning look in his eyes keeps them in place. There's a soft pop and ticking sound as he undoes my jeans and pulls them down my legs. He helps me step out and tosses them aside. On the way back up, he presses kisses against my legs, belly, breasts and finally my mouth. While he's busy teasing me with lips and tongue, his hand runs down and over the top of my panties, heading straight for the wet satin at my opening. Against my mouth, he grins. "Spread your legs."

I slide my feet apart and tilt my hips, offering myself up. "Good girl," he whispers as he teases me through the thin satin. Running his fingers back and forth from my clit to my ass. "Oh," I sigh. *So good. Perfect. Right there.*

His fingers slip under the fabric and slide inside me. We're nose to nose and his storm-gray eyes darken, losing a bit of control.

"Kiss me," I whisper.

As his lips meet mine, I arch my back, pressing my pussy into his hand, dying for release, but wanting to wait for him to give it to me. I can't stand not having my hands on him for another second. He's knotted with muscles that flex with each movement and my hands can't stay away from his thick, strong shoulders. Intense waves of need grow and my body twitches. He adds a finger and keeps slowly working me until the pressure building inside almost hurts.

"Rock, I think—"

"Don't think."

My back arches even more, grinding myself against his hand. The heavy panting breaths and loud moans, I realize belong to me.

Then I explode. All those waves of need are satisfied in sweet, perfect pleasure.

I'm still trembling when he pulls away from me. Delirious and dreamy, I watch as he drops his shoulder and I let out an unladylike giggle-snort when he throws me over it. "You're a little obsessed with this caveman carry," I tease while smacking my palms against his perfectly tight ass. I get a swat on my butt in return.

"I think it's actually called a fireman's carry," he says while tossing me on the bed. I barely have time to orient myself on the mattress before he's hooking his thumbs in my underwear and dragging them down my legs, throwing them somewhere near our luggage.

"No fair. Now I'm naked and you're not." I try to work my mouth into a pout, but end up laughing instead.

Rock's laughing too, and the sight seizes my heart. He's so serious and hard all the time. I love when he smiles. "Pretty proud of yourself, huh?" I tease.

"Yup," he answers as he drags his shirt over his head.

I kneel up and skim my hands over all his newly exposed skin. "I can't get enough of you." I tip my head up so he can see how serious I am.

He presses his palms against my cheeks. "Same here."

My hands work his belt loose and I don't have the same kind of patience he does, because I shove his jeans and boxer briefs down his legs until he takes over and kicks them off himself. Then he's naked before me. A sexy, muscled god with hard ridges, smooth defined muscles and an impressive erection. He's so handsome. Sometimes while we were apart, I wondered if my mind exaggerated how sexy, how beautiful he is, but no, he's even better in the flesh.

I'm not shy about staring and my tongue licks my bottom lip as his fist closes around his cock, stroking from base to tip.

"See something you like, Hope?"

"Everything. You. Yes." My words roll out in a flustered jumble. Okay, maybe I'm not as calm as I thought. I squirm and keep staring, craving a taste of him.

"You want this?"

Eager and tired of being teased, I urge him down onto the bed with me, and brush my fingers through his hair, holding him still so I can kiss him. He lets me roll him on his back—because let's face it I can't make Rock do anything Rock doesn't want to do—and kiss my way down his chest.

"What're you doing, Baby Doll?" Lazy-curiosity colors his words.

My hands circle his cock sliding up and down. Instead of answering, my mouth opens and my tongue darts out to taste him. The soft skin and blunt head of his cock caressing my lips. His salty taste lingers and I tease him with my tongue, slowly dragging a wet trail round the head of his cock a few times. A primal grunt pushes past his lips as I swirl and lick. He's not really moving. Just lying there and letting me have my way with him, which I like. I shuffle forward on my knees to get closer, and fill my mouth with him. I take him as deep as I can and work my way back. Before I can try again, he gathers my hair into a ponytail and pulls.

"Need to fuck you, Hope."

I'm crazed with lust and want, but disappointed he didn't let me do more. Using my hair, he guides me up to his mouth for a deep kiss. I love kissing Rock. I could do it for hours. His hands grab my hips. Strong fingers dig into my ass as he settles me over his cock. "Take it," he whispers against my mouth. Reaching down I align him against me and sink down. Quickly, I lift up, not quite as ready for him as I thought.

He brushes a few strands of hair off my cheek. "Relax." I let out a deep breath and sink a little deeper this time. My eyes close as he stretches me in the best way. I ease up and sink back down slowly.

"Fuck," I whisper as I increase my pace.

"Love when you say fuck when I'm fucking you," his voice comes out strained, raw almost.

A low moan escapes my lips. No words. I can't form them. Heat races over my skin.

"You have any idea how much I love seeing you blush and get all shy with me?"

A soft chuckle works out of me. "Rochlan North: MC President and corrupter of bashful ladies."

"Damn fucking right. Love that you're so modest around everyone else, then let *me* violate you in any filthy way I want."

Mmm. He's got that right. I think I'd let him do anything at all to me right this second. Especially when he hits that spot. I suck in a sharp breath and grind down harder, chasing the thrilling sensations only he can give.

Eventually I settle into a perfect pace. His hands grip my hips, directing me hard and fast, then deep and slow. After a while, his hands slide up my ribcage, settling under my breasts. A dark look passes over his face.

"What's wrong?" My words are harsh between panting breaths. *So close.*

His eyes meet mine. "Nothing, baby. Fucking love looking at you. You're so beautiful."

My head tips down and I murmur a thank you. He lifts up, flipping us easily. After a few not-so-gentle thrusts, he slides out of me and motions me up. "Knees. Put that pretty little ass up in the air for me."

My mouth curls into a smirk, but I roll over. He slides a pillow under my stomach. Tucking my knees up under me, I rest my cheek on the mattress. Behind me, I catch a glimpse of him rising up on his knees.

A sharp sting as his hand slaps my ass.

"Up."

I arch my back and push myself up. Feel him position himself at my entrance. One hand grips my hip, while the fingers of his other hand trail down my spine. He thrusts forward and I let out a low moan.

"Good?"

"Fuck. Yes."

He pushes forward again and pulls back slowly. Each time he thrusts I moan a little louder. He's not the only one who had a lot of dirty fantasies while he was away. Not one compares to this. After a few minutes of slow, sensuous teasing, he grips my hips harder. Pulls me firmly against him, thrusting harder each time.

When he's fully buried inside me, his movements still. "Fuck me back like a good girl."

I push back and he grunts in pleasure. The sound encourages me, and I rock back and forth on him. "How's that?" I whisper, needing a little reassurance.

Instead of an answer I get popped on the ass. "Don't stop," he warns in a tight voice. Satisfaction rises inside of me and I push back faster, taking him deep over and over.

"Rock, I'm so close," I cry out.

He pulls free and I sob in frustration. "What—"

"Need to see your face when I make you come."

He flips me and shoves inside of me again, claiming me, telling me how much he missed me with each powerful stroke

I plant my feet on the bed and lift my hips to meet him thrust for thrust.

He grabs my hands, stretching my arms over my head and our eyes meet. My lips part as I moan his name and fall apart.

"Keep coming for me. All over my dick."

The roaring in my ears almost drowns out his dirty encouragement. He stills and shudders, letting go. Warmth coats my stomach and breasts as he pulls out at the last second, stroking himself in the sexiest way.

He presses kisses to my forehead and cheeks, then moves from the bed. He returns with a warm washcloth and cleans me. The look on his face is pure adoration. I reach out and trace my fingers over his cheek.

All the bleak moments I've had over the last few months crash into me. *Anger. Fear. Grief. Longing.* A deep sigh eases out of me.

"Baby, what's wrong?" He climbs in next to me, pulling me tight against him. "Did I hurt you?"

His worry loosens my tongue. "No. God. No."

"Tell me."

"It all just hit me at once. I'm so, so thankful you're with me now."

ROCK

Tangled together with my girl, I'm finally whole again. Neither of us are able to move for a few minutes, our sweaty bodies stuck together in some places, cooling off in other places. Hope shivers and that jolts me out of my stupor. My hand squeezes her ass. "Shower."

She moans, rolls over to her back and I take a minute to stare at her. "Worn out?"

"Yup," she answers without opening her eyes.

My hands brush over her nipples and she giggles, soft husky laughter that makes my dick twitch. I trace my fingers over the dips and curves of her body, stopping at her ribs. My girl's much thinner than when I went inside, and the visual proof of how stressed she must have been bothers me. First thing I'm doing tomorrow—feeding her.

Shaking off the gloom threatening to creep into my mind, I stalk into the bathroom and get the shower going. A few days. I just need some alone time with my woman, then I'll return to the club and take care of business. For the next few days, she's the only thing on my radar. I won't allow any bad shit to intrude on our moments here together.

"Come on, Baby Doll," I encourage, as I return and lift her off the bed. I can't miss the way the corner of her mouth twitches up.

She opens one eye. "I'm all blissed out."

"Good. That was my intention."

"Goal achieved."

"You okay?" I ask after I set her down in the shower. She holds out her hands to me. As if I'm not planning to join her.

"Much better." Her hand reaches back and squeezes her ass. "My butt doesn't hurt as much as I thought it would after that ride."

"I can fix that." My bad joke makes her laugh. "So is that your way of saying you don't like my Fat Bob?"

She tilts her head and I realize she has no idea what I'm talking about. "We need to spend more time in the garage together," I mutter as I soap her up.

"Anywhere you want. As long as we're together."

"Yeah."

"You know, I've never wanted to be some clingy girlfriend. But I'm afraid, I'll be clinging to you quite a bit."

"Nothing would make me happier."

After we're done in the shower, I take my time drying her off, and lead her back to bed. I'm exhausted, and I'm sure she is too.

"Want to take you out for a big breakfast tomorrow," I explain as I slide into bed. She curls up against me right away as if she can't stand for us not to be touching. I'm glad *that* feeling's mutual.

We're silent and I think she's fallen asleep when she shifts. "The weeks when I couldn't come see you were the worst," she whispers as her hands stroke up and down my chest.

"I know."

She pushes herself upright so she can look me in the eye. "I hated that I couldn't talk to you freely. Knowing even over the phone someone was probably listening in. And then that...guard. That horrible—"

"Tell me now, baby. Tell me everything you couldn't say before."

She shakes her head and stares down at her hands, so that her hair forms a curtain between us. "I kept a journal for you." She snorts out a humorless laugh. "All my uncensored letters."

My heart stalls. "I'd like to read them."

"I brought it with me." She gestures at our bags lining the top of the dresser. "But not now, okay? I can't go there right now. I need to just be with you." She slides her fingers over my abs down to my side, forcing a chuckle out of me.

"You're tickling me, Baby Doll."

My woman thinks it's funny that I'm ticklish. Only with her though. Only when she traces her fingertips over certain places. A bright, playful smile spreads across her face. "My big, hard man—ticklish." She shakes her head from side to side. "No one would believe me if I told them."

I capture her hand and bring it to my shoulder, where she starts tracing lines of my tattoos. "That's why you should keep it to yourself."

A softer smile teases at the corners of her mouth. "It's our secret."

She slides one leg over me, so she's straddling my lap. A sly smile spreads across her face as she leans in, pressing her mouth to mine. Then her breasts against my chest. I'm under the sheet and she's on top of it, so none of our important parts are touching—yet. I pull her down so her cheek rests over my heart.

"Mmm…I like listening to your heart thump," she murmurs. I don't have any words, so I just wrap my arms around her and hold on tight.

After a few minutes her tongue tickles over my skin. Licking at my nipple. Grazing it with her teeth.

I pull in a sharp breath. "What're you doing?"

"Nothing," she answers with a false-innocence that stirs my cock back to life.

A thrill races through me. It's all Hope. Everything she does thrills me. She sits up straighter, leans her forehead against mine, our breaths mingle together and her tongue traces the seam of my mouth. One of her hands grazes my side, down over my ribs, over my thigh, under the sheet until she feels the length of my erection. Wrapping her hand firmly around me, she jacks me up and down a few times, then bites her lip and takes her hand away.

My hands roam down her back, over the curve of her hips, settling on her ass. "You want something?" I ask.

"Maybe," she answers in a flirty voice as she slides down my body, taking the sheet with her. "Oh, my," she teases when my dick springs up, happy to see her. She grabs me. Not too tight and licks gently. Her hair keeps falling down, obstructing my view. Can't have that. I gather all her loose, thick waves in my hands and hold them back. She hums and closes her mouth, sucking deep, her cheeks hollowing.

"Fuuuck," I hiss as she starts to move up and down. My fists clench with the urge to press the back of her head down until I'm in her throat. But I can't do that to Hope. I just can't. My hand tugs at her hair a little harder. "Come here, baby."

She pulls her mouth off me reluctantly. Staring at me with confusion…and hurt.

"Rock, what's wrong? Why don't you ever let me—"

Fuck me. "I do. You have."

Trying to bullshit Hope is pointless. "Yes, but you always stop me."

"I'd rather come in your snug little pussy, is that so bad?"

Why is she doing this? Why am I stopping her and why is this conversation still getting me so motherfucking hard?

Probably because her hand keeps lazily sliding up and down my dick, while she stares at it with hungry eyes. Her soft fingers explore every sensitized inch, making me jump and hiss with each touch.

"Am I not any good at it?" she asks.

"Hope, really?"

She half-lifts one shoulder.

That's the last thing I want her thinking. Guess I'll risk pissing her off. "Fine. I've had enough anonymous, impersonal blow jobs. I don't want that from my wife."

Instead of pissed, she seems amused. "Well, your wife-to-be wants to give you some *highly personal* blow jobs, so I suggest you suck it up. Or rather, let me suck you."

My dirty chuckles are cut short by her tongue and mouth. Aw, fuck, she's killing me. "How can I say no to that?" I ask so low, I'm not sure she hears me at first. But she hums, the sound traveling right through me.

"You can't. So relax and let me have my way with you."

"Whatever you say, Baby Doll."

HOPE

Morning chill prickles over my skin, pulling me out of sleep. No Rock next to me.

Huh.

I sit up and glance around the room. Silly, because it's too small for him to hide somewhere. After tossing back the covers, I discover the bathroom's also empty. Everything's still, like he's been gone for a while.

My gaze lands on my open purse and the piece of white paper next to it.

Hope-

At the beach. Join me when you get up.

-Rock

I recognize the paper he wrote the note on. Sure enough, the journal I told him about, is missing. A lick of fear, maybe embarrassment, slicks over me. I'm not sure. I wrote it with every intention of him reading my words. But now, after what he went through, it seems silly and childish.

Hurrying into my clothes, I make sure to grab the room key and stuff some cash in my pockets.

He's in roughly the same spot as we sat last night. Knees pulled to his chest, arms slung around them, holding my journal. There aren't that many letters. It would have been too depressing to write *I miss you. I miss you. I miss you.* Every day. So it's mostly just the highlights. My day trip with Wrath and Trinity. My visits to cheer up Sparky. Heidi's graduation. Stuff like that. My last entry was the one where the guard molested me. After that, I was too frozen in fear to write anything.

That's the page he's reading when I walk up on him. He tips his head up and stares at me with a look of wonder.

"Thank you." His raspy voice makes my insides quiver. I drop down next to him and he pulls me close for a deep kiss. His forehead touches mine. "This means everything to me, Hope."

I'm too choked with emotion to respond.

After a few more moments of staring into each other's eyes, he kisses my forehead and sits back. "I'm so sorry, baby."

No, no, no. That's not what I wanted him to feel after reading my words. "Rock, it's okay. You're out. We're together. Everything will be fine."

He's silent, staring at my notebook. "It's like we were thinking the same things sometimes." He tips his head up, his gray eyes searing me with their intensity. "Thinking about you got me through it." He lifts his hand and brushes the hair off my face. "Small things, that I took for granted."

"I missed you terribly. But at least I had the club taking care of me. I hated you being so alone."

He shakes his head and stares at the sand. "I never should have put you through that."

His words leave me unsettled. Like he's rethinking our future together. "It's not your fault."

"Yes it is. This is my life. This is the kind of shit that happens because of who I associate with. If I worked a regular nine-to-five, you wouldn't have suffered through all this shit. That motherfucker never would have put his hands on you. You got hurt because of me."

I sigh. This isn't an easy situation with a simple answer. But I need Rock to understand the conclusions I've come to. "Then you wouldn't be the man I love. I love *you*. Who you are. I thought I'd die without you. Because I was so scared for you. And I know without a doubt, not having you at all would be a thousand times worse."

"Hope. Fuck. You don't even—I love you so much, Baby Doll. But do you understand, even though I didn't commit *this* crime, I've committed so many others that could have the same outcome? I don't see it changing. Even if I ever fully get us on the right side of things, there are still so many—"

"Rock, stop. I won't lie to you and say I'm not scared sometimes."

"I know you are. I'm so sorry I reeled you in to my fucked up life without fully letting you know what you were getting into."

Now, his words alarm me. Not because I believe he tricked me, but because I'm afraid he has some twisted idea that he needs to set me free. "Do you regret us? Being with me?"

"No. Never. Not for one second, Hope."

"I know you think I'm naïve. And I am. Sometimes deliberately so where you're concerned. Where the club's concerned. But I love you, and no matter what happens in the future, I'll never regret us either."

"Hope, that's a damn big promise to make."

Tears fill my eyes, and I rapidly blink them away. "Dammit, I didn't cry once while you were gone."

One corner of his mouth lifts. "I know that's not true."

"Okay. Maybe after seeing you in jail that first time. Let me finish though."

His smile widens and he motions for me to continue.

"You remember how you once told me you couldn't let me go? It's the same for me. I'm not still here because you tricked me. I'm here because I love you. All of you. Even the parts you think are bad. Everything you do comes from a good place of protecting the people you love."

"Thank you."

"This scared me because I felt so helpless to do anything for you."

"But you did help. You were a big help. And I hate that helping me put you at risk."

"It's a risk I'd take over and over."

"I've done a lot of bad things, Hope. And I'll do more." He taps the journal, so I know he's probably hinting at the guard who bothered me.

"You may have done bad things, but you're not a bad person. No one will ever convince me otherwise. Not even you."

He shakes his head and I swallow down all my tears and anxiety so he can really understand what I'm about to say. "Rock, tell me honestly, have you ever…hurt someone because you enjoyed it, or got pleasure from it?"

He snorts. "No."

"Have you deliberately hurt a woman?"

"No."

"Children?"

He lifts his gaze and glares at me. "Fuck no."

"Were you always protecting someone else?" He doesn't answer, so I keep right on going. "Defending someone else? Keeping others from being hurt?" He still says nothing.

"Answer me."

"*Yes.*"

"Then I can accept anything else. And I'll never leave your side."

We're quiet after that. Sitting on the beach, holding hands, staring out at the ocean.

Together.

CHAPTER TWENTY-NINE

HOPE

AFTER OUR SERIOUS morning beach talk, the rest of our conversations are light. We have breakfast, where Rock orders enough food to feed ten people. Coconut French toast and about half his lobster omelet are all I can eat.

"I won't fit into my dress if you keep feeding me like this."

His gaze sweeps over me, heating my skin. He seems to be contemplating his words, but then flashes a quick smile. "I heard about Murphy's trip to the dress fitting."

"Oh, that's not the worst of it." I explain our trip to the spa which makes him chuckle.

"That poor bastard. Guess he's earned a raise."

I honestly don't know if he's joking, or if that's something possible within the club structure. I know everyone earns their keep in some way. I've just never really figured out what Murphy's role is. "I love the bike he fixed up for us. That was so sweet of him."

He nods. "It was. Took a lot of time and care with it."

"I feel bad, I never knew what he was up to out in the garage."

He raises an eyebrow. "He never mentioned it?"

"No."

His lips curve into a secret smile. "He put a lot of effort into making sure it was passenger friendly."

"I gathered."

"He's sweet on you."

"For looking after Heidi, not—"

His hand settles over mine. "I know."

"When Wrath and I got into it, Murphy was the one to tell him to knock it off."

Rock raises an eyebrow. I guess Wrath didn't mention our few heated discussions.

"He give you shit?"

"Once or twice. He and Z seemed to work well together but Wrath still had a lot on his shoulders."

"I know."

"He drank your scotch too," I say to lighten things up.

"Fucker." He laughs, then squeezes my hand. "So your road trip was to get my wedding band?"

My cheeks flush. I'd forgotten that journal entry. "Yes. He was a real pain in my ass over it."

"I don't doubt it."

"He got Trin's engagement ring there too."

He nods slowly as if the information pleases him. "He tell you when he's gonna do it?"

"Not yet."

He picks up his fork and stabs into a potato. "You know, when he was younger he swore up and down he'd never marry anyone. That's part of why he was so against my first one. Trinity's good for him."

I agree even though I'm not really sure where he's going with this. "I know she's still struggling a little."

"Yeah, shit like that doesn't get fixed over night, but I'm glad they're sorting it out. Wish I'd knocked their heads together sooner."

"Not everything is your responsibility, Rock. They're both adults."

He pins me with a questioning look, like he's not so sure.

We didn't notice it on the way in, but the diner only accepts cash. I smirk as I reach into my pocket and hand him the money I'd stuffed in there earlier. Rock gives me this pained expression, as if it's offending him deeply to let me pay for breakfast and I can't help laughing. I lean over the table and whisper to him. "I know you think because you're the man, it's on you to do everything, but sometimes it's okay to let me pay for breakfast."

He rolls his eyes.

"Besides, it's all going to be *our* money soon anyway."

"Oh, boy," he mutters.

After breakfast, we drive farther north, following Route 1 along the coast. In some places the ocean's right beside us, in others houses or hotels obscure our view. We stop at a park with an out of commission lighthouse, scale large, uneven rocks until we're staring out at the sea, wind whipping around us. Rock doesn't seem to have any particular plans on our trip, other than being outside as much as possible. I can't blame him for that.

"You cold, baby?" he asks as he wraps me in his arms. As his warmth sinks into me, it becomes apparent how chilled I was.

"A little." I turn and burrow my head against his chest, soaking in his warmth, inhaling his comforting scent. He leans down and I stretch to kiss his cheek. "Do you want to head back?" I whisper against his ear.

ROCK

Fuck yes I want to go back to our room, lay her out on the bed and go at her like a starved wildebeest.

My arms tighten around Hope and my gaze wanders to the vast sea behind her. We still have a lot to talk about and there's no way we'll get any talking done in our room.

"Why don't we keep going north and into Portland?"

She raises an eyebrow.

"I want to buy my girl something pretty."

"Shopping over sex?" She places the back of her hand against my forehead. "Are you okay?"

My hand captures hers and I nip at her fingers. "Don't test me. I'll bend you over the bike in broad daylight if you keep it up."

She laughs and skips out of my hold, dancing away. "*Oooh*, I might like that."

I catch up to her easily, snagging her around the waist and pulling her up against my body. She squeals and tips her head back for a kiss, which I don't deny her. I'm giving serious thought to carrying out my threat, when a Maine state trooper pulls into the parking lot. We're one of maybe three families at the park this time of year. Hope follows my gaze.

"Come on. Let's go. Maybe I want to buy *you* something pretty too."

Her words chase any dark thoughts away.

We park near the waterfront in the Old Port district. Hope's eager gaze scans the area. "I don't know where to start."

The ferry to one of the islands is out. The next one isn't for two hours. Instead, I take her hand and lead her across the street. The first store she wants to check out is so small, I feel like a gorilla in a flower shop. Since it's full of barely there underwear, I keep my complaints to myself.

"What're you trying to do to me, Baby Doll?" I whisper in her ear when the salesgirl finally leaves us alone.

Her big green eyes stare up at me full of innocence, but her mouth twitches with mischief. "What do you mean?"

"Miss, do you want to try those on?" the salesgirl asks, nodding at the pile of skimpy lacey things in Hope's hands.

"Yes, please."

I'm aroused, amused and everything in between, while I wait for her. "Are you going to show me?" I ask.

The salesgirl clears her throat and scowls at me.

"Come here," Hope hush-whispers from behind the thin, black curtain separating us.

My hand slaps the curtain to the side and she gasps. "Close that!"

"It's barely open," I manage to get out before my brain processes what's in front of me. Stretchy, black lace, sheer enough for the outline of her nipples to show through in some sort of halter-bra style. "I like. Get two."

She chuckles and drops her head to stare at her chest. Her hands come up and cup her lace-covered breasts, and suddenly there's a lot less room in my pants. "I don't know if it holds—"

"It'll hold just fine when you're wearing that and nothing else around our new house."

Her eyes meet mine and a smile curves her lips up. "Get out of here, caveman." She waves her hand and snatches the curtain shut.

When she's finished, the salesgirl shows her matching underwear. I nod at the same thing in blue and Hope plucks it off the rack, carrying everything to the register.

"I want you to know how cruel that was," I say once we step outside.

She laughs as she wraps her hand around mine and tugs me down the sidewalk. The next store we pass is some yuppie pet store. "Did Z tell you about the puppies?" she asks.

"What?"

"Uh-oh." She ducks inside and purchases two plushy-squeaky toys. This time I wait outside. As if there'd been no interruption in our conversation, she takes my hand again. "Z brought two pups home with Mariella."

"Oh. He failed to mention that."

She gives me a sly look. "Well, you had other things on your mind."

I lean down and growl against her ear. "Damn right."

She turns and our lips meet. Right there on the sidewalk, we stumble and stop for a kiss. We're jostled by a couple kids on skateboards who speed up when they catch the look on my face.

Hope takes my hand again. "Do you feel different with it being just the two of us?" She glances over and nods at my plain leather jacket. "Without your colors?"

"Yeah. It feels weird. Felt naked at first." I have to stop and think how to put it into words. "It's been a large part of my identity for a long time."

"I know," she says softly.

"Do you wish it was like this all the time?"

She doesn't hesitate. "If you're asking me if I want you to leave the club, my answer's no." She tips her head up and grins at me. "But I *am* looking forward to moving into our own house."

I can't think of a more perfect answer from my woman.

HOPE

I pull Rock into a specialty foods store next. After picking through a rack of organic spices, I find what I want.

Rock raises an eyebrow.

"When I was little and we were on vacation, my dad liked to find local spices or something to bring back. Liked it better than cheap nic-knacks and it took up less room."

"Clever."

A faint smile turns my mouth up. I shake the bottle at him. "Casco Bay seasoning."

He tips his head toward the waterfront across the street. "Maine's version of Old Bay?"

"I think so." I snag an extra jar. "I'm going to grab one for Trinity too."

At the register, I spot a large, glass pitcher curved into a fish. "Oh, those are so pretty. Too bad, we don't have a lot of room."

"There's a post office a few streets over, we can mail it home if—"

"We can ship it to you," the clerk says.

Rock nods. "Wrap it up."

"Hungry yet?" Rock asks once we're back outside.

"Not really." I pat my stomach. "Still full of french toast."

He snorts and takes me into a jewelry store. "Let's look for something pretty for you."

Something pretty turns out to be an understatement. Everything in the boutique is beautiful…and expensive. Rock doesn't seem to care. He picks out a pair of green tourmaline earrings and asks me to try them on.

"You never told me what color dress you ended up getting," he says as I twist my head to see the earrings in the small hand mirror the jeweler handed me.

"It's a surprise."

I'm pretty sure he rolls his eyes.

"We need to have *some* mystery."

"No. We don't," he says dryly. Then to the woman hovering behind the counter. "We'll take them."

As she's ringing up the earrings, Rock slips an arm around my waist and whispers in my ear, "I want to see you wear those earrings and nothing else."

"Right now?"

I get a pinch on my ass for that one. "No, sass-mouth."

Back out on the sidewalk, he points across the street. "Think you'll be hungry by the time we walk over there?"

"I thought you were horny?" I ask, not really caring who overhears our conversation.

He chuckles at my brashness. "I'm also hungry and want to keep my stamina up for the night ahead."

"Oh my. Big plans?"

"Very big."

Our silly banter turns me on something awful and I think I'd rather find a dark corner than dinner. The simmering way he keeps staring at me as he takes my hand and leads me to the restaurant does nothing to lessen the heat building inside me.

I'm not even sure how to describe the place we walk into. Part Maine lobster shack, part country-western bar. Considering it's off-season, the long wait for a table surprises me. But by the time we're finally seated, I'm starving.

"Good thing you insisted on dinner. Now, I'm hungry."

His mouth curves up but he doesn't say anything.

"You always take such good care of me," I say after the waitress takes our orders.

The smile slides off his face. "I need to do a better job."

I tip my head to the side, hoping he'll finish that thought, but he changes the subject.

"So you traveled a lot with your dad?"

"Oh. Well, yeah. Nothing major. But he always liked to see new things."

He raises an eyebrow, but I'm not sure what else he's looking for. Uncomfortable, I shrug and glance toward the kitchen. "Didn't do any traveling after he died. Unless you count moving from apartment to apartment." The joke's more strained than funny. "Clay and I tried to go places when we could afford it."

Rock squeezes my hand, drawing my attention back to him. "That's what club life was supposed to be about. Freedom to come and go as I pleased. Be on the open road as much as possible—"

"Being president doesn't seem to lend itself to that," I point out.

His mouth curves into a wry smile. "No. Outlaws, surprisingly have a lot of their own laws."

A snort bursts out of me, because from what I've learned, that seems like such an understatement.

"But all of it is or was meant to be a means to an end—taking care of the family."

"I think you've done a good job of that."

"Sometimes I think I've gotten so caught up with *the life*, that what it's supposed to be about—brotherhood and love of the open road gets obscured."

"Do you want to know what I think?" He raises an eyebrow, which I take as a yes. "I think you're too hard on yourself."

Our waitress drops off plates of food and ties a bib around my neck for the lobster. "I feel like an idiot," I mumble as I start ripping off legs and cracking lobster shells.

Rock's low chuckle draws my gaze up. "You look cute."

"Anyway," I huff out. "You forget, I just watched an entire club come together in support of their brother. I don't think any of them would have been so steadfast if you hadn't earned their loyalty. I listened to every person in that clubhouse at one time or another tell me a story of how you impacted their life. Things you probably thought were small, but obviously made a difference."

For the first time in a long time, Rock looks uncomfortable. Possibly speechless.

Finally, he shakes it off and digs into his food. "Wrath stepped up. Z too. Made some tough calls. Used good judgment."

"You must trust them, or they wouldn't be where they are."

"Oh, I do. No doubt. Told you, I trust Wrath with my life. But he's also always been a bit impulsive."

I have nothing to add to that, so I keep stuffing my face.

"You like the ride Murphy set up?" he asks after a few minutes.

Confused by what seems like another turn in our conversation, I simply nod. Well, that and my mouth is full.

"Club used to go on a lot of longer runs together. Haven't done much of it lately. We were supposed to do the Virginia Beach one this summer, but that got fucked up."

I think back over the summer. "The guys never mentioned it."

"Do you think you'd be up for some of those trips?"

"Rock, I want to be wherever you are. So, yes. Except our honeymoon." For some stupid reason, I tuck in my arms, flapping them like wings. "I want to fly somewhere."

He shakes with laughter. "Where?"

"Hawaii?"

"We can rent a motorcycle there."

"Perfect."

Suddenly he's back to serious again. "What I'm trying to explain is that I have everything I've ever wanted. What I've been working toward for years. I want to take a few seconds to revel in it, enjoy it, before the next thing comes along and fucks it up."

Oh. The claw and cracker slips out of my hands, clattering onto the plate. My eyes blink rapidly and I have to force my question out. "Am I one of those things you're talking about?"

His hand closes over mine and he pins me with a hard stare.

"You're *everything.*"

CHAPTER THIRTY

ROCK

I DIDN'T MEAN for our conversation to turn so heavy. But if we don't talk about these things now, I'm afraid we never will.

"You're everything to me too," she whispers.

"I know."

"It scares me."

I understand her fear, so I'm not offended. "Because you're afraid you'll lose me?"

"Yes."

"I really want to grow old with you, Hope."

Her mouth finally tips into a smile. "Yeah, me too. You'll probably just keep getting hotter with age."

I'm interrupted from answering that little gem, by our waitress clearing the table. "Dessert? Coffee?"

"Two coffees. Hope?"

She's busy scrubbing her hands with the wet napkins that came with her lobster. "Gosh, no. I'm stuffed."

The waitress chuckles. "Well, stick around. It's country dance night."

Hope wiggles her eyebrows at me. "Does my big badass biker dance?"

"Whatever you want, Baby Doll."

"That reminds me, I didn't know you like country music."

She comes up with the strangest things. "Is it a deal-breaker?"

"No. Just, Trinity mentioned it when we were dress shopping. And it seemed like something I should know about the man I'm marrying."

Christ, but she's fucking cute. "I like lots of things."

When our coffees are dropped off, Hope decides to order a margarita. "Now?" I ask after the waitress leaves.

Her shoulders lift. "Sure. Why not?"

I barely get a sip of my coffee before the center of the room's cleared and the volume of the music shoots to ten. Hope drags me out to the floor, into the middle of the group forming. It's an interesting mix of old and young. Some have a dance-or-die attitude, others seem to be here for fun.

The guy leading the group goes through the steps without music first.

It turns out my girl's surprisingly uncoordinated.

"You didn't even get to your margarita," I tease.

"It's harder than it looks." Her face screws into a scowl. "Figures you're good at it."

I end up shuffle-rocking us to the back of the group, so she doesn't knock someone over. A different instructor checks in with us. She's tall, blonde, bubbly and introduces herself as Cathy. "Let me teach you a simple two-step," she offers.

At first Hope's agreeable.

Cathy shows us where to place our hands. "Dance is a conversation," she says to me. "You don't want to confuse her. Keep your frame smooth and your leading hand at her eye-level so she knows what to expect."

This style's much easier for Hope and soon she's laughing as she follows me.

"You're a good leader," Cathy comments while batting her lashes.

"Thanks so much. I think we've got it," Hope shouts over the music. She grumbles about Cathy's "blonde, perky ass" as she watches her disappear into the crowd of dancers.

"You know I only have eyes for you, right?"

She gives me a sly smile. "I don't know why. I have the grace of Godzilla."

"Yeah, but I can do *this* with you." I spin and dip her until she's laughing uncontrollably. When she's flushed and sweaty, I pull her in for a kiss.

"Your frame's all sloppy," she whispers, squeezing my hands and pushing my arms back into place.

I lean down to whisper in her ear. "Just so there's no *confusion*, I want you."

HOPE

Three short words. But Rock says them with such simmering affection, I'm ready to mount him on the dance floor. It's not jealousy. No, Miss-too-friendly-with-my-man has moved on to instructing another couple in the art of the two-step.

We stop at our table to collect our things. Rock shakes his head when I pick up what's left of my margarita. "No way. I don't want you passing out as soon as we get to our room. I've got plans for you."

The way he says it, I'm only too happy to finish off my water instead.

He nods at the water. "Good girl."

I narrow my eyes at him. "That only works on me in the bedroom."

His mouth curls into a sexy smirk and he takes my hand pulling me outside. Under one of the streetlights we stop and stare at the Harbor.

"It's so pretty at night." I sigh and turn to face him.

Amusement sparks in Rock's eyes. "Bring a bathing suit?"

"You can't be serious. The water's freezing. Plus, it's dark. I don't want to get eaten by something, unless it's you."

His mouth tips up in a dirty grin. "I want to get you in the hot tub."

"Oh. Yes. I did bring something."

"Is it tiny?"

"Maybeee," I tease.

He grabs my hand. "Let's get out of here."

I didn't realize how much ground we'd covered on foot during our exploration. It seems to take forever to walk back to Rock's bike. We're not exactly running, but we're definitely walking with purpose.

"Ugh, I still reek of fish," I complain, as I slip my helmet on.

Rock chuckles. "Get on."

The ride back to our hotel is long. I'm squirming the entire way. Desperate to get him alone.

We seem to be in agreement—Rock attacks me as soon as we're in the door. His mouth moves over my lips, down my neck, devouring me little by little. "Rock," I whisper. "I'm still all fishy."

He pulls away and bursts with laughter. Capturing my hand, he places it over his very hard cock. "I'm gonna get a hard-on every time I go near a fish market for the rest of my life."

"Good thing you never do the grocery shopping."

He smirks, then spins me around and yanks my pants down, baring my ass. His hand lands on my right cheek and I let out a soft hiss. "Sass-mouth," he growls against my ear. I wriggle my butt in response, and he chuckles, then strips the rest of my clothes off. While he's distracted, I slip out of his grasp and grab the bag with my bathing suit in it to make a run for the bathroom.

"See you at the hot tub," I call out as I slam the bathroom door. His grumbles can be heard even over my laughter.

A few minutes later, I find him lounging in the hot tub—it's possible a trace of drool dribbles down my chin at the sight of him. He's devastatingly sexy. Big, tattooed and muscled chest, broad shoulders, sculpted arms draped casually over the side of the tub. Why am I still out here instead of in the water with him?

I set my cell phone and two towels on the table next to his and prop my hand on my hip. "Well?"

He sits up so fast, water splashes over the side of the tub. "Fuck." Except for the dull glow from the parking lot lights, this entire section of the balcony is bathed in darkness. Perfect for some privacy but enough light that I see the appreciation on his face.

"I better show it to you now in case *something* happens to it."

"Good idea. Make it quick."

I spin, flaunting the low black bikini bottoms and flicking the ties at my waist. I'd never wear so little in front of anyone besides Rock. The look on his face is worth my discomfort at having so much on display.

"Very nice. You get that for me?"

"Of course. I wouldn't wear this in front of anyone *but* you."

He makes a sexy-growly sound of agreement and stands to help me into the tub.

"Ouch! It's hot."

"It's a *hot* tub, Baby Doll."

"Smart ass."

He wades to the opposite side and I drop down into the seat across from him. He frowns when he notices I didn't follow. "What the fuck are you doing way over there?"

I stretch out and tip my head back, so I can stare at the stars. "Relaxing."

There's a sharp tug on my leg. My arms flail and splash water everywhere before Rock gets me where he wants me. His lap.

"You like fucking with me, don't you, sass-mouth?"

I don't get to answer. His mouth finds mine and takes it in a soft, sliding, sensual kiss that leaves me limp. My heart's already racing when he slides his hand behind my neck and deepens our kiss. Oh, *this* was the one thing missing from our perfect day. Naked kissing time. My arms wrap around his neck, my hands teasing his hair and it's so good, so hot, I might just melt.

He groans into my mouth and I grind myself against his erection. His arms slide down my back, brushing against the strings tying my top together. I don't even care if he strips me naked and bends me over the railing I'm so turned on right now. But instead, his hands slip between us, and he teases the cups of my top down, baring my nipples to the cool night air, and his wet, rough fingers. He interrupts our kiss and leans down to fasten his mouth around a nipple. My back arches, giving myself to him. He lets go and sucks my other nipple into his mouth and I groan.

Soft, hot kisses trail up my chest to my neck, until his lips are at my ear. "You've been teasing me all night. I need to get inside you."

My hips flex against him. "I need you too, Rochlan." Reaching into the warm water between us, I shove the front of his shorts out of my way. His cock springs free, hard as stone, and ready for me. I smooth my hand up and down a few times, the water making soft splashy sounds around us. His eyelids droop, he tilts his head back and groans. "Fuck. So good, baby." His words shiver through me, right down to my center. I keep working and stroking, varying the pressure, swiping my thumb over the tip until he snaps his head up.

Our eyes meet and hold. "Give me that sweet pussy," he demands.

His hands slide to my hips and he unties my bottoms, flinging the material over the side of the tub. It was a small piece of clothing, but the hot water rushing against all my sensitive, uncovered parts jolts me. Eagerly, I lift and guide him to my entrance, slowly sinking down. The water causes all sorts of friction I wasn't expecting and I lift up.

"You okay?"

"Mmm. Just the water doesn't make things as *wet* as you'd expect."

Concern clouds his face. "Want to stop?"

As he says it, he slips firmly inside me and I sink down to take him deep. "Oh," I moan in pleasure. "Fuck no. Don't stop."

His arms tighten around me, keeping me upright, while I grind myself as gently as possible to avoid water splashing everywhere. The pleasure's intense and my need for him overwhelms me. His hands shift to my ass, drawing me close, while pressing himself up even deeper. His mouth brushes against my nipples, rubbing and sucking. "Good girl, riding my cock outside where anyone could catch us," he says against my ear. I murmur in agreement and he hisses. "Fffuuck, so fucking good."

My pussy clenches around him. Sweet, shudders of pleasure move through me and I cry out Rock's name.

I'm still trembling with aftershocks when he thrusts up into me at a rapid pace with no concern for the water splashing all around us. His hands hold my hips in a bruising grip that makes me feel needed and owned.

Desire to smother him with affection overwhelms me. I want so much to be his sanctuary. The way he's been mine. I nuzzle his neck, kissing my way to his ear. "I love you, Rock. Love you so much."

He gasps and lets out a long shuddering breath. "Love you too, Baby Doll." He struggles to get the words out as he groans through his release.

Before he's even finished he lifts my hips up off him. My legs tighten around him. A few moments later, his eyes drift open and he stares at me with concern. "Baby, we haven't used a condom once. Are you...keeping track of things? I can't—"

Yeah, we've been a little reckless, considering. "I'm keeping track. I even have an app on my phone, to remind me when to take my pill and—" I grin to lighten things up. "Keep track of all the sex we have. I promise, if I'm late or anything weird happens, I won't ignore it. I'll go to the doctor right away." My hand brushes through his hair, nails dragging against his scalp. "I just can't stand having anything between us right now." I cock my head to the side and stare at him. "Is that why you keep marking me?" I tease.

His hands tighten on my ass, and he leans down to bite at my nipples. "No, baby, I just like seeing you covered in my cum."

"So dirty."

"Yeah. For you." He pauses, his brows slashing down. "Hold up. You have an app on your phone for what?"

"To track my cycle." I lean in and whisper in his ear. "Remind me to put in how many times we've had sex."

He laughs and growls, running his hands up my sides. "We better get busy then."

"Rock, if we get any busier, my business will be raw."

CHAPTER THIRTY-ONE

WRATH

AFTER ALL THE excitement of Rock returning home died down, Trinity remembered she had her first therapy appointment the next morning.

"No problem, babe. We'll leave right after."

She's agreeable to that plan.

It's a beautiful fall day, so I've got no problem waiting outside for her. About an hour and a half later, she returns, slightly more relaxed than when she went in the office.

"You okay?"

"Yeah."

"Ready?"

"Hell, yes," she answers, with a big smile as she places her hand on my shoulder and swings her leg over the bike. "Let's go."

Her arms tighten around me and we take off. The three hours up the Northway don't feel sufficient to outrun whatever we're both feeling.

We're lucky we came today. It's the last weekend the lodge near Ausable Chasm is even open for the season. We find a diner for an early dinner and I finally have a chance to talk to Trinity.

"Everything go okay?"

She fiddles with the salt and pepper shakers before answering. "Yes. I think so. I have another appointment for next week."

"Good."

She finally lifts her eyes to meet mine. "Do you mean that?"

"Of course, baby."

"Thank you."

Before heading to our room for the night, I make arrangements for rock-climbing tomorrow afternoon. We can rent whatever equipment we need for an exorbitant fee but I think it will be good for us to do something physical outdoors.

I'm flicking through the four channels available up here when she comes out of the bathroom wearing head to toe flannel and a worried expression. "You look cute. Are you cold?"

"A little." She perches in the chair next to the bed and stares at me. "What's wrong?"

"Nothing."

"Are you coming to bed?"

"I can't tonight."

"Can't what?" Then it hits me—she's still rattled from her therapy appointment this morning—and I sit up, holding out my hand. "Come here." She hesitates, but I don't ask again. Finally, she moves closer and I pull her into my lap, smoothing the hair off her face. "You think I'm that much of a dick?"

"No."

Her arms tighten around my neck and she burrows her face against me. Holding her tight against me, I turn and lean back and click off the lamp. "Get some rest. You don't want me to beat you at rock-climbing tomorrow do you?"

She laughs softly. "It's not a competitive sport."

"Sure it is."

After a few minutes, she rolls off me but stays close. "Wrath, did you mean it when you said you wanted to build a house for us?"

I turn so I can face her. "Fuck yeah, I meant it."

"Do you still want to?"

"You know I do. Before he left, I actually discussed it with Rock."

"You did?"

"Yup." I give her a more serious assessment. "Why, angel? What's wrong?"

"Nothing. It's just weird."

"One of the guys say something to you?"

"No. Nothing like that." She fiddles with her hands until I place my hand over hers.

"Talk to me."

"It's just weird. I want us to be alone together. Like a real couple, you know? This, right now, is nice. I love the clubhouse, but—"

"There're a lot of reminders?"

"Yes."

"We've outgrown it. That's okay. It will take some time though. You gonna be okay until then?"

"You're not mad?"

"Fuck no. How could I be mad?"

"I don't know—"

"Trinity, I want to give you everything. Anything you want. Whatever makes you happy, babe."

"Okay."

"We'll still be on the property for anything that comes up. But I agree. It would be nice to be on our own."

"Thank you."

HOPE

A gentle tickling sensation wakes me early the next morning. Rock's hands roaming down my side, sliding my underwear down my legs. His mouth dipping down to kiss my legs, hips, tummy and nuzzle against my thighs.

"I know you're awake, Baby Doll. Spread your legs for me."

I can't even tease or play with him the way I normally do. I'm too eager to feel his mouth and hands on me. He groans as I open for him. "That's it," he whispers.

319

Thick fingers, slide over slick flesh and I moan. He's the one doing the teasing this morning. His fingers dip between my lips, enough to make me gasp, but then out again, spreading my wetness around. My hips arch and twist as I try to get him to go deeper. Give me more. He bites his lower lip while he watches my desperate, pleasure-seeking dance.

A soft hiss of air rushes out of me when he finally slips his finger inside.

Yup. Right there.

Deeper. He works me hard, yet somehow also gentle. He adds another finger, and twists to rub over my G-spot.

"Fuck," I gasp.

"Not yet."

But he takes mercy on me, maneuvering between my legs, grabbing my thighs and shoving me wide open and laying soft kisses and licks on my pussy. White, searing pleasure flashes over my skin and I gasp as his fingers delve back inside, spreading my lips for his tongue, licking a path to my clit, but not quite touching, just enough to make me whimper his name.

"Oh, please, please Rock," I pant out. His storm-grey eyes, heavy with arousal peer up, but he doesn't take his mouth off me for a second. Two fingers pushing inside stroking a steady pace, his tongue laps at me as he finally takes my clit captive, flicking with soft strokes, designed to set me off.

A couple seconds later it does.

I let out a short scream and snap, pleasure racing over me, sparks firing behind my eyes. Completely consumed by the heat of him. When I stop quivering, my eyes pop open. He stares up at me with a grin of satisfaction tipping his glossy lips up. "You have no fucking idea, how many times I dreamed about that, Hope. I woke up sometimes with the taste of you on my tongue." He curses as he makes his way back up my body, kissing and licking.

Before we left home, he promised to worship me and he's definitely keeping that promise. Under him, I squirm, trying to get our bodies as close as possible.

"Eager this morning?" Rock teases.

Before I spit out an answer, his phone goes off.

"No," I whine in frustration.

Rock's gaze darts between the phone and me. "It's Z. He wouldn't bother us if it wasn't important."

"Get it."

He rolls off me, grabbing the phone. "What?" he snaps.

I can't complain. This is the first time the guys have interrupted us. Honestly, I expected a call much sooner. To give Rock some privacy, I duck into the bathroom. After taking my time, brushing my teeth, washing my face, combing my hair, I'm feeling less generous.

"Are you fucking serious?" Rock snaps into the phone. He glances up when I emerge and flashes a tight smile.

I stop to take him all in. My big, sexy, *naked* man, sitting on the edge of the bed. Frustrated and annoyed. Well, I can fix that.

Up and off goes my T-shirt.

Rock raises an eyebrow.

Dropping down next to him, I let my thigh rub up against his. He places one hand on my leg, absently rubbing while he continues tearing Z a new ass.

"No. It's fine, we're coming home tonight. Set it up for tomorrow. No. Tomorrow. I don't care what he says."

My hand closes over his cock, stroking lightly. He gasps and gives me a stern head shake.

Sliding to the floor, I wedge myself between his legs. His hand rests on my head, holding me back. It's an odd little struggle we're having. I stretch my tongue, wriggling until I make contact.

He drops his hand. *I win.*

The instant I wrap my lips around his hard length, he lets out a moan.

"Fuck. I need to call you back." I flick the underside of his cock with my tongue. "Shut up," he hisses into the phone. The phone clatters on the nightstand and above me, Rock groans.

"Naughty, Hope," he whispers in a rough voice.

I hum with laughter and swirl my tongue around his cock. He

reaches down, gathering my hair in his hands, holding it back from my face. I flick my gaze up and the intense expression he's wearing shoots heat through me. Opening wide, I wrap my lips around him, taking as much as I can, grasping him with my hand and working him with firm strokes of my mouth and fist.

"Hope," he groans. My name comes out garbled as if it hurts to concentrate on anything besides what I'm doing to him. I like having my big, tough man at my mercy this way and plan to do this a lot more often when we get home. The desire I'd felt earlier when he was pleasuring me comes roaring back like a wildfire. I pull back, teasing with long, soft licks. He shudders and his hands tighten in my hair, guiding me the way *he* wants. I gasp and try to keep up, but before I know it, he's tugging back on my hair.

"Up."

It takes a second for the word to sink in. With his hand holding my hair hostage, I'm forced to slide my body up his to get off the floor. "That's it. Good girl," he whispers, dragging me against him until we fall back on the bed. "Need you to ride me. Then I'm going to bend you over and spank your ass."

"The hell you are," I say, as I throw a leg over him, lining us up and sinking down.

He places his hands behind his head and gives me a smug smile. "Do a good job."

Bastard. I close my eyes and gasp as he pushes up, stretching me so perfect. His hand cupping my face makes me open my eyes. He pulls me down roughly for a kiss, covering my mouth. Nothing soft or gentle about it. His hands move down, grabbing at my hips and ass, then he turns, shoving me into the bed, grinding into me. A gasp leaves me and I clutch at his shoulders. His mouth is at my neck, kissing and licking his way over to my shoulder. The tension builds inside me fierce and fast as his hips swivel, pressing himself hard against my clit. For a second, I'm tight all over, then I just explode. White stars dance behind my eyelids. Rock only gives me a second to enjoy it, before ripping me off him, urging me to my knees in the center of the bed and filling me from behind. His hand slaps my ass. "Bad girl. You know Z figured out exactly what you were up to."

"Like you wouldn't tell him anyway."

I get another spank for that one. He falls down over me, fucking me down to the mattress. His hands dig into my hips, holding me in place. "I never talk details about our sex life with any of them. You're mine. Every bit of *this*, belongs to me," he growls against my ear.

I'm gasping and panting with his heavy body fucking me into the mattress and so damn turned on I'm worried the flammable sheets might be a problem. He slides up and off me and the hot spurt of cum hits my back and ass.

For a minute neither of us move as we try to catch our breath.

His hand connects with my ass, but it's more of a loving squeeze. "Time to clean up and head home, Baby Doll."

"We need to do this again soon," I mumble into the comforter.

"Oh, we will. As soon as we get home."

I roll over and catch the grin on his face. "That's not what I meant."

He holds out a hand and pulls me up. "I know."

ROCK

I have a strange feeling of unease as we ride home. Never felt that before. Maybe it's because I had such an overwhelming sense of peace while reconnecting with Hope and I know there's a lot of unpleasant matters waiting for me to deal with when I return.

Or maybe it's because she drained me dry before we left. I probably should have chugged a couple gallons of water to replace the fluids she stole from me. Somehow before we left, I'd come two more times. Both in the shower. The water was stone cold by the time we finished. The performances this woman coaxes out of me are unreal. Replaying every second, improves my mindset. Having Hope at my back and the wind in my face also helps.

To ruin my good mood, as soon as we cross the New York border, a state trooper pulls us over. "Fuck me. I wasn't even speeding," I grumble as we pull over.

While we wait for the officer to run my license, Hope dismounts and takes her helmet off. "I'm hot," she says, reading the question on my face.

"Miss? Are you okay?" The officer calls out.

"I'm fine."

Even though the charges were dropped, obviously my recent stay at Slater County Jail for murder pops on my abstract, because the officer's a lot less friendly when he returns.

"Where you been, Mr. North?"

"Returning from vacation."

"Sure leaving the state was a good idea?"

"Is there a problem officer?" Hope asks, using her courtroom tone. I drop my head and stifle a laugh.

"Something funny, sir?"

"Nope."

The young trooper has his hand near his weapon. "Miss, if you need help, you can come with me."

Oh, boy.

"Excuse me?" Hope snaps, walking closer.

The trooper seems to reevaluate the situation. "Are you together?"

"Yes. And if you don't mind, my fiancé and I are expected somewhere, so can you hurry this along, please."

"Sure, as soon as I figure out why someone who was just incarcerated for murder was leaving the state."

I raise my gaze to the sky. We're going to be here for a while. I'll be lucky if we're both not carted off to jail.

"Since you're so *knowledgeable*, officer, you should also be aware that those false charges were dropped. He's free to go wherever he pleases."

"What are you, his lawyer?"

Why does everyone ask her that?

Her lips curl into a smirk. Fuck, she's hot when she's pissed off.

"No. But I *am* an attorney. You have no right to detain us. You can't use his recent release for a crime he didn't commit as an excuse for probable cause. So just write whatever tickets you're going to write and let us go."

He doesn't seem to know what to do with all that. Finally he stares at me. "Thought you MC thugs kept your women in line a little better. Gonna let her do all the talking for you, prez?"

Jesus Christ.

I give him a slow, country-boy grin. "Sure. Being a lawyer and all, she's much better with the words."

He snorts in disgust and stomps back to his car. When he returns about twenty minutes later, Hope's radiating all sort of pissed-off vibes, but she keeps quiet. He hands me a bunch of tickets, which I pass to her. She stuffs them in her pocket, slips her helmet on and gets behind me. We take off without any additional bullshit.

I'm furious about the whole situation, but also amused as fuck at the way Hope handled it.

We make it to the clubhouse without any further incidents. Unlike when I got out of jail and couldn't wait to take off, now I don't want to leave the property for at least a month. I'm extra-annoyed that Green Street Crew's wannabe Kingpin, Loco, has demanded to meet with me.

Z and Murphy are outside working on one of the vehicles when we pull in. Sparky's surprisingly out in the sunshine, overseeing their work. Murphy happily jogs over to greet us as I back my bike into its spot, Z and Sparky right behind him.

I get a brisk embrace from each of them. Murphy turns to Hope with a raised eyebrow. "Well?"

"Oh, I loved it, Murphy!" She grabs him in a big hug, then gives Z the same. Even Sparky accepts a brief embrace from her.

Z pats her on the head. "We missed you around here."

"I doubt that. I'm sure you guys went wild."

Z shrugs and I'm not sure how to interpret that. "Where is everyone?"

"Wrath and Trinity took off day after you two."

"Where?"

Z shrugs. "Don't know. Adirondacks I think."

Good. I'm actually happy to hear it.

Teller appears from one of the trails leading into the woods, a small dark-haired girl at his back. Mariella, I assume. "Hey, prez!" he calls out. She follows him over but doesn't look too happy.

Hope takes my hand and wraps her other hand around my arm. "That's Mariella."

"I figured."

She lets go long enough for me to give Teller a quick hug. "Welcome back, prez."

I raise an eyebrow at Teller and he pushes Mariella forward. "I don't think you two were able to meet before you left," he says as he introduces us.

"Sorry about that." She's a skittish thing. Blinks a few times before answering.

"It's okay. I'm so sorry, Mr. North—"

I hold up a hand to stop her. "First, call me Rock or prez. None of that Mr. North crap." Her mouth twitches but she doesn't answer. "Second, we're fine. Third, are my guys taking good care of you?"

"Oh yes," she answers in a rush.

"Good. You need anything, let Hope know."

"I will."

"I hear you're planning to take over some of Trin's household stuff? You really want to do that?"

"Yes. I actually worked as a housekeeper for a large chain down in Miami before my brother brought me...here."

That's news to me.

"I managed my own team of four other girls, so this is a piece of cake," she finishes.

Everyone stares at her.

"That's great. We're happy to have you then. Thank you." She sort of fades away after that. Still standing with the group, but keeping to herself.

Ravage and Stash burst out of the clubhouse to greet us, followed by Swan.

After we all stand around bullshitting for a few minutes, I grab our stuff, and take Hope inside.

"You okay?" I ask when we're in our room.

"Yeah, just a little tired."

I drop everything on the chest at the foot of the bed. "Well, I didn't let you get much sleep."

Her mouth quirks up. "True." She starts peeling off her clothes. "I am feeling all sweaty and gross. Care to join me in a shower, Mr. President?"

"Fuck, yeah."

I'm not sorry to say she doesn't get much sleep once we're home either.

CHAPTER THIRTY-TWO

ROCK

AFTER I HAVE my way with Hope, *again*, I leave her sleeping in our room and head downstairs. It's probably unhealthy, the amount of time I want to keep my dick in her. If I dig into some work stuff, it will be good for both of us.

Z, Murphy, Teller, Ravage, Stash and Sparky are all at the war room table.

"Surprised you can walk, old man," Z says with a smirk when I drop into my chair. "We figured you were fucking for four days straight."

My fuck off stare works wonders, and Z snaps his mouth shut. "Where's Dex and Bricks?"

"On their way," Teller answers. "And for the record, we," he points at Murphy and himself, "didn't speculate at all on what you two were up to. Z's the resident perv. Just thought I'd clear that up."

"Fuck you," Z laughs out.

"Christ, I missed you assholes." My grin sort of ruins the sarcasm I was aiming for. "Anyone call Wrath to let him know what was up?"

"Yeah. They should be getting back soon, too," Z answers.

"Well, you dragged me down here, so give me some details while we wait."

"I think Loco's feelings were hurt that you didn't call him as soon as you got out."

"Jesus Christ."

"No, seriously. He says he's got something big he wants to discuss with you."

"Every thought that pops in his pea brain is a 'big deal.' What now?"

"I think he wants to exterminate some Vipers."

"Why now?"

"Don't know."

I know for a fact, Loco's played both sides of our beef with the Vipers. I don't fault him for it. I sure as fuck don't stick my nose in his disputes with the 18th Street Boyz. Fuck, when they have the cash and we have the product, I'll even sell to those little punks.

A sniffing-tickling sensation at my ankles pulls me out of my thoughts. I duck my head under the table and find two pups wrestling with my bootlaces. "Hey, guys." I snap my fingers a few times and they waddle closer, sniffing and licking my hand.

"Looks like you forgot to mention something."

Z chuckles. "Yeah. Figured we could use some guard dogs up here."

They're cute little shits and Z's right. That's one thing we've been missing at our compound. A short, sharp whistle from Z and the two pups hustle next to his chair and plop down, tails wagging. He flips a small piece of jerky to each of them.

"Positive, motivational, training," he explains.

"All you, brother."

"Almost forgot to tell you, Jasper will be here on Monday with a crew to get going on your house."

"Thanks. Wrath tell you he wants dibs on him next?"

"He mentioned it."

The man himself walks into the clubhouse next. He and Trinity stop in the doorway. "Hey, sorry. We got down here as fast—"

"Just got here myself."

Trinity waves to everyone at the table with her free hand. Wrath doesn't seem ready to release her just yet.

"Is Hope upstairs?" she asks me.

"Sleeping."

She snickers. "I assume she didn't get much rest."

My chuckle annoys Z. "How come it's funny when she says it, but you get all pissed off at me?"

"'Cause Trin ain't picturing it and wishin' it was her," Ravage answers, getting a laugh from everyone.

"Fuck you," Z says, but he's laughing as hard as everyone else.

"Great. So glad I rushed back for this," Wrath bitches, pulling Trinity into the living room.

While they're...doing whatever they're doing, Dex and Bricks join us. We all catch up while we wait for Wrath.

A few minutes later, he shuts the war room door and takes his seat at the table.

I point to Z. "You're on."

Z sits up, all business now. "Like I said before, Loco called. Told him you took off with your ol' lady and would be back in a few days. But he was real adamant he had to meet with you."

"Fine. You set it up?"

"Yup. Tomorrow morning. Danny's Diner out by the airport."

I just stare at him.

"Aw, he wants to have brunch. That's sweet, prez," Ravage says with a snicker.

Dex picks up where Ravage leaves off. "Now remember, even if he pays, you don't have to put out."

While my asshole brothers laugh it up, I close my eyes, take a deep breath and try not to choke every one of them. "Why. The. Fuck. Are we meeting in the morning at a diner?"

"He said it's a safe meeting place."

I glance at Wrath who shrugs. "I'll go check it out tonight. Murphy can ride with me."

Murphy glances up at the mention of his name. "Yeah. Okay."

"All right. Who's opening CB tomorrow?"

Dex raises his hand. My gaze roams over each of my brothers. "Rav, you go to CB with Dex."

He rubs his hands together like a creep. "No problem."

"Keep your hands to yourself, pussy wizard," Z says. Ravage grins and throws up his middle finger.

"Bricks, Sparky and Stash, stay here. I don't want to scare Loco."

Anytime I'm not asking Sparky to leave the compound, he's happy. "You got it, boss."

"The rest of you, and Hoot will come with me." I glance at Wrath. "Unless you see something tonight that makes you think another approach would be better."

"Okay."

"So what are we doing with the Vipers?"

"Kill 'em all," Z says. And he's not joking.

"We looking for Loco's support on this? I hate teaming up with street punks on club matters."

Wrath shrugs. "He wants to do the heavy lifting, by all means, let him."

"Yeah, but what's in it for him?"

"He probably wants to get a foothold in Ironworks," Murphy answers and he just holds back the *duh* in his answer.

"Yeah, I got that. Why? He doesn't sell the heavy shit or girls."

"Maybe what Ransom said about the dry market is true," Wrath answers.

Scrubbing a hand over my face, I try to work it out in my head. "Fuck, I hate messing with the precarious balance we've got going on, but—"

"Obviously the Vipers are gonna keep coming at us. Best to take 'em out now before they pull their next stunt," Z says.

"You want me to bring Whisper in?" Wrath asks.

Although I'm annoyed as fuck with Ulfric at the moment, that's not the reason I want to keep his MC out of this for now. "No. Our business with Loco's crew's got nothing to do with the Wolf Knights. They can barely control their own territory. They don't need to worry about how Ironworks gets divvied up."

Z raises an eyebrow at me. "You want us to move into Ironworks?"

"I think it's worth exploring."

Wrath nods. "It would give us easier access to the Vermont border."

A grin spreads over Z's face. "Lots of dope-smokin' hippies in those mountains."

"You're such a hillbilly," Teller snarks.

Sparky holds up a hand. "Two things, boss. We're small, how are we going to hold down Empire and take on Ironworks? And two, unless we do some sort of expansion, I can't grow much more than I already do downstairs."

"What kind of expansion?" Z asks.

Sparky lifts his shoulders. "We could put a greenhouse outside, but that's leaves us open to exposure. Aerial surveillance."

"Yeah, flybys are between troopers and feds. No way to control that," Wrath says.

I want to get us back to Sparky's more important question. "As for holding Ironworks. Same as we've done before. Visible presence. And working with GSC, just as they've helped us downtown."

"They've got a way bigger crew," Z points out. "Got nothing to do but drive around in their pimp mobiles anyway."

We go back and forth on it for a while. Finally I have to put a stop to the conversation. "None of this means shit, until we know exactly what Loco wants."

WRATH

Rock's right. All this chatter is fuckin' pointless until we figure out what's going on tomorrow.

After church, Rock pulls me in for a hug. "Where'd you go?"

"Adirondacks for a few days. Did some rock climbing. Trin got some pictures."

"Good."

"Your trip all right?"

Rock's mouth tips into a sly smile, but "yes," is all he says.

Murphy's waiting for me in the living room. "Give me a second to talk to Trin. Then we'll go."

"Yeah. No problem."

Our door's open when I get there, so I assume Hope's visiting. Sure enough, I catch part of their conversation.

"So what else?" Trin asks.

"Fucking each other raw isn't enough?"

Trinity's laughter makes my own mouth turn up.

"I don't know. I got him to country-dance. He's better at it than me."

"Oh, that reminds me, I have a list of bands for you."

I can't stand out here being a creeper all day, so I push the door wider. Hope turns in surprise.

"Oh. How long were you out there?"

"Long enough to know why Rock can't walk straight."

"You need a cowbell around your neck," she grumbles.

Shit. As much as I love messing with her, I'll admit I'm jealous. Trin and I hadn't fucked at all—raw or otherwise on our trip. We hiked and climbed ourselves into exhaustion each day. But that was it. She seemed to be going through something and no matter how blue my balls were, I wanted to give her whatever space she needed.

Trinity's smile at seeing me makes the pain worth it.

She slides a piece of paper out of her ever-present wedding binder and hands it to Hope. "Here. You can look most of them up online." She points to a spot mid-way on the page. "This one's playing down at the Midnight Saloon tomorrow."

"We have a place around here called 'Midnight Saloon?'"

"Looks like."

Hope wrinkles her nose. "Roadhouse Riders? That sounds like a brand of condoms."

I almost choke on my laughter.

When Trinity finishes laughing she flicks the paper in Hope's hands. "They're supposed to be really good. 'Infused with a heaping serving of twang and sass.' Sounds right up Rock's alley."

Hope rolls her eyes, then turns her little trouble-maker gaze my way. "Maybe we can go on a double-date?"

Trinity judges the look on my face accurately. "Good luck with that, Hope."

"Are you guys done with church?" Hope asks.

"Yeah, Rock's probably looking for you."

Once she's gone, I'm able to get my hands on Trinity. She stands on the bed, giving her enough height to tip her head down at me. My hands automatically settle on her hips, because that's where they fit best. "You two catch up?"

"Oh, yeah."

"I gotta head out in a few."

For some reason her mouth turns down. "Are we okay?"

"Yes. Why? It's club stuff I need to take care of, angel. That's it."

"No. I mean our trip. I'm sorry we—"

"Stop."

"Are you sure you want an ol' lady with so much baggage?"

Fuck, she kills me. I lean in so we're sort of nose-to-nose. "Yeah, I'm big enough to help you carry it."

"Oh, shit," she whispers. "Sometimes you say the perfect thing."

It doesn't matter which one of us makes the next move—although I'm pretty sure it's her. In the next second, our mouths meet and I can't even remember what we were talking about. If the way her hands paw at my clothes are any indication, we want the same thing. She pulls away, breathless and pink-cheeked. "Do you *have* to go?"

"Not right this second." I don't think there's anything that could drag me away from her.

Her hand reaches down, rubbing and squeezing the length of my dick through my jeans. Tearing my mouth away from hers takes some effort and I groan. "Don't. If you breathe on me wrong I'll explode."

The corners of her mouth turn down—this time in a playful expression. "I've been bad, haven't I?"

I'm too focused on her hands working her shirt over her head to answer.

"Maybe," she says, drawing the word out. "You shouldn't let me come as punishment."

That snaps me out of my lust-fog. My hands grab her hips, turning her and yanking her pants down at the same time. "No. Because that would be punishment for *me* too."

I'm not sure which way I want her. On top of me so I can see my star inked on her side? Kneeling in front of me while I plow into her from behind? Doesn't matter. It's all good. I'm way too frenzied to weigh all my options. My dick just wants in, he's not concerned which way he gets there.

Some small part of my brain's still functioning, because I lean over and yank one of her nightstand drawers open—what I now consider her toy drawer because, yup, bought lots of buzzy stuff and stuck it in there for us to play with—and grab what's quickly become my favorite thing, a little purple butterfly. She makes the craziest noises when it hits the right spot. The little device has all sorts of straps to keep it in place, but I'm way too overloaded to fuck around with that shit right now.

"Here." My voice comes out all rough and short.

She tosses me a smirk as she takes it. "What do you—"

"Don't even play with me. You know what I want."

The butterfly's got a little remote control, and I flick it on. I swear to God the image of making her wear this around our house while I fuck with the remote all day long has entered my brain one too many times. We really need to get moving on building that house. "Put it on your clit and keep it there."

She gasps as the little toy makes contact and drops her shoulders to the bed. "That's right. Ass up," I whisper. She got my shirt off and my pants undone, but I'm in too much of a hurry to get them all the way off. Grasping her hips, I pull her closer and angle myself just right to thrust into her hard.

"Oh, fuck," she whimpers.

"That's right."

She makes this chuckling-moaning noise, that's hot as fuck and has me pulling out and slamming back inside over and over. Nothing but tight, wet heat surrounds me. I'm greedy and desperate, but I need her to come first and by the sound of the sweet little noises she's making, she's almost there. I flex my hips, rocking into her and pulling back a few times. Her low moans turn into sharper cries of pleasure, triggering a primal need inside me. Thank fuck, she finally comes, clenching tight around me as I explode, emptying myself inside her for what seems like forever.

Slightly dizzy, I fall down over her, wrapping her in my arms and turning her for a kiss. She jerks and moans in my arms and I realize her little vibrator's still going strong. Laughing, I sit up and grab the remote, flicking it off. "You okay?"

"Fuck. I think so."

My hand cups the back of her head, pulling her in for a kiss. "Right answer."

I'm so much calmer as I walk down the hallway a few minutes later. Murphy's hanging out with Teller, Rock, Z and Hope, but jumps up when he sees me.

"Christ, you said a few minutes."

Yeah, I can't even pretend to be sorry.

The ride out to Danny's is long, but it's a nice autumn evening, so it doesn't bother me. Wish I could have brought Trin. Hated leaving her. But not knowing the situation, I didn't think it was a good idea.

Of course fucking Loco's at the diner when we walk in.

He gangster-walks his way over with his arms wide open. I swear to fuck if he hugs me, I'm gonna punch him. "Wrath. Checking out the place for your prez?"

Asshole.

"Nope. Just in the neighborhood. What up?" Murphy answers. Little fucker has some big, brass ones when he wants to.

Loco seems to be in a good mood. He leads us to a big booth in the back of the restaurant. It's right next to an emergency exit. Exactly the spot I'll choose for Rock to sit tomorrow.

"I'll even let you have that seat," Loco says, indicating the one where I can keep my back to the wall and my eyes on who comes in the front door. I grunt at him and nod at Murphy to slip in first before sliding my big frame into the booth.

"So what do you think of the place?" Loco asks once we're all seated and have placed our orders.

"Let me guess. You own it?"

Loco grins, wide and crazy. "Yeah, man. Gotta di-verse-ify. You should appreciate that."

"Yeah. So what're we doing, Loco?"

He *tsks* at me and I sort of want to grab him by the throat and shove him through the plate glass window.

As if he read my mind, he tips his head at the window. "Bulletproof."

"Nice. Now, give me an idea about tomorrow's agenda."

He shakes his head. "Nah. That's a surprise for Rock. How's he doing, by the way?"

"Better now."

"Good." He stares at me thoughtfully for a few seconds before speaking. "Vipers. That's all I got on my *agenda* for tomorrow."

"Figured."

He knocks his fist against the table once. "You boys enjoy dinner. It's on me. I'll see ya tomorrow," he says before taking off.

Murphy slides around the curved booth until he's opposite me. "Weird," he mouths silently.

My shoulders lift. Loco didn't get tagged with his name by accident.

"You and Trin have fun on your trip?" Murphy asks. I don't answer right away for two reasons. First, our waitress drops off our dinner. Second, I don't know if I want to talk to Murphy about my ol' lady.

He thoroughly inspects his plate, as if he expects to find a razor blade hidden inside his burger.

"I'm sorry about the other night," he says after he's completed his investigation and deemed his food safe.

Unsure of what he's referring to, I raise an eyebrow.

He sighs and sits back, dinner apparently forgotten. "Heidi giving Trinity shit. I should have…I was worried you'd be pissed if I said something." He shrugs. "She's your ol' lady. It's not my place. But I should have—"

Fuck me. Here I'd been pissed at him for not keeping Heidi in check and he'd been keeping his mouth shut out of fear of disrespecting me. "It's fine. I just want Heidi to drop her bullshit grudge against Trinity."

"I know. I was hoping being in the wedding together would help."

"Let it go, bro. We're fine."

"Are we?"

Murphy's got this hopeful expression on his face that very much reminds me of when he was a kid. Makes me wonder how much of what Trinity said about him lookin' up to me is true. The feeling of being *old* slams into me. I've known Murphy since he was a baby faced —as Hope put it—kid. I realize he and I really are fine. He may have had my girl's attention from time to time over the years. But he never understood her. She never confided in him. He's not ready or able to take care of her the way I am. And it's not his fault she and I were so stubborn and stupid for so long.

"Yeah. We are. Now finish your burger so we can get the fuck out of here."

CHAPTER THIRTY-THREE

TRINITY

"I DON'T THINK I'm hot enough to be marrying Rock," Hope says as she twists and turns in front of the dressing room mirror.

I barely hold back my eye-roll. "Since he can't keep his hands off you, and you're walking bowlegged again today, I think that's a crock of shit."

She buries her face in her hands. Her shoulders shake and at first I'm worried I made her cry. Then I realize she's laughing. I give her a little shove. "Come on, hurry up. I want to get back to the clubhouse before the guys so we can get ready for tonight."

Somehow Hope convinced Rock to take her to the Midnight Saloon to check out the band for their wedding. Rock invited— although I strongly suspect *ordered* is more accurate—Wrath and I along. I'll admit, I'm excited about our little date night out. It feels like such a normal, *couple-y* thing to do.

"Okay. Okay. You think this is it?"

"Yes." The few alterations that were made to her wedding dress are perfect. So is the taupe sash I want to add. It matches the cowboy boots Hope tentatively picked out perfectly. "I still don't know about the boots. I ordered a pair of gold flats in case I chicken out."

"It's your wedding day. You can wear a tiara and cowboy boots if you want."

She chuckles and hands me my dress, then turns for me to unzip hers.

I turn at her sharp intake of breath. "That color's so pretty on you." She scrunches up her nose. "You're way too pretty to stand next to me at the wedding."

"Oh, jeez." Then I roll my eyes because that's one of her favorite expressions and now she has me saying it all the time too.

Standing behind me, she gathers my hair up. "Maybe we can hire someone to do our hair. Some sort of updo thing would be great."

I'm not a professional by any means, but between Swan and myself, I figured we had hair and makeup covered. I don't get a chance to explain that though, because she squeals and folds my ear down. "Ow! What're you doing?"

"Wyatt!" she yelps as reads the small tattoo hidden behind my ear. "Oh, my gosh. That's so sweet," she croons.

Brushing her hand away, I grumble, "It's supposed to be a secret."

"Oh, sorry. But that's so cute. Did it hurt there?"

"Yes. But not as bad as my hip."

She nods and before I chicken out, I ask her. "You think we're cute?"

"Oh, yeah. I'm so glad you guys worked out"—she flails her hands in the air—"your whatever issues out. You're perfect for each other."

I turn so I'm facing the mirror. "You don't think it's weird?"

"Weird?" She seems puzzled by my question, then I think it sinks in. "Oh. No. That's none of my business."

I risk a glance at her in the mirror. "You'd never do that though."

"Yeah, but I'm not a beautiful, badass biker chick with tons of self-confidence either."

My jaw drops. Is that how Hope sees me? She's not laughing. Not even smiling. One thing I've learned about her, she's honest—to a fault sometimes.

"You think I'm self-confident?"

She shrugs. "You'd have to be to hold your own with those guys."

ROCK

"All right, Loco. You got me here first thing in the morning. What's up?" I ask, hoping to sidestep the big bro-hug he's trying to snare me in. I don't know when he thinks we ended up on bro-hug terms but I can't say the feeling is mutual.

"Come on, man. I was worried about you."

"It's true, prez," Wrath says with a smug grin. He's finding this whole thing way more amusing than I am.

Finally, I relent and force a smile on my face. "Yeah, heard you were a big help when they guys needed a location. Thanks for that."

Loco glances at Wrath. "Yeah, how's she doing?"

"Fine. Says she wants to stay with us for now. My girl's lookin' after her."

Loco makes this exaggerated-surprised face that I'd love to punch.

"So, what am I here for? Z said you had something major to discuss."

Loco flicks his gaze at Z and smirks. Next to me, Z shifts. I'd bet everything in my wallet, he's also resisting the urge to punch Loco.

"Yeah, come on. Let's sit and eat like civilized men."

Sucking in a deep breath, I follow Loco to the back of the diner. Wrath gave me the story last night, but I indulge Loco in some conversation about his new business venture. After I've gotten some coffee in me—which dials back my irritation a fraction—I put a stop to Loco's yammering. "All right. What am I doing here?"

"Vipers man. They're hot on your ass since you got out." He slides his gaze to Wrath and Z. "Heard you left quite a mess behind. Killed two of their guys. Took one of their whores and torched their safe house. Stole their fuckin' dogs. That's badass. I'm impressed," he smirks and Wrath rolls his eyes, but doesn't say anything.

"My ass was in a cell, so they know I didn't have anything to do with it."

"Yeah, except two days later your ass was sprung." He leans forward. "Here's my problem, now they comin' after me."

"Fuck."

"Yeah. Two nights ago they grabbed one of my girls."

"Shit," Z mutters.

Loco pins Z with a harsh stare. "I got her back, but she ain't gonna be any good to me for a while."

Now I feel like shit. It's bad enough Vipers fucked with me. But them going after my business associates and innocents pisses me the fuck off.

"Now, I been helpin' your boy, Sway with his problem down south, but it's cost me some territory here. I gotta stay focused, you know?"

"Yeah."

"I know that ain't got nothin' to do with you. My relationship with them's worked in my favor."

"Good."

"Way I see it, you and me got a common enemy. It only makes sense for us to work together to get rid of the Vipers."

"I agree."

He looks surprised that I agreed so easily. But I'm not stupid. If we're going to do this right, I need his help. "I want to push them out of Ironworks. My club's not big enough right now to hold that territory on our own."

"So you want my crew to do it?" He's grinning like a maniac and I wonder what the fuck I've gotten myself into.

"We want easier access to Vermont. Right now, I need to get to Bennington, we've gotta go up to Lake George, into Rutherford and back down."

"You gonna try and move product into Vermont?"

"Maybe. Not right now. You're still getting my entire supply."

Smug fucker grins at that. "Ironworks is dry. Lot of product to move there. Fuck Vermont. But I get what you're saying. We can definitely do that. Teamwork, Rock."

Inwardly, I groan. But I flash a tight smile. Next to me, Wrath moves ever so slightly. Laughing, I'm sure. Dick.

"Last thing, Rock. And I want you to remember I don't have to explain myself to you. This is pure courtesy, since I got mad respect for you."

Oh, I can't wait to hear this.

"What Ironworks lacks in weed, they make up for in pussy. And I know you done everything to keep that out of Empire. I respect that, but—"

"Since when are you working girls?"

"Since I recognized the need for my services. Viper girls are miserable. Half them high as fuck and hooked on all sorts of shit. They ain't happy willing little hookers."

My stomach twists. "Yeah?"

"I got a stable of ten solid girls. Taking a page from your book, you know. Treat 'em well. Fair split, provide protection and they bring in a ton of cash."

"My what?"

"Your dance club? Everyone says you guys run it fair so bitches are trippin' over themselves to work there."

"Okay."

"And your club. Your brothers are all solid. Got your back no matter what. 'Cause they know you'd do the same." He shrugs. "Works better than ruling by fear. Better results."

"Oh, we're still afraid of him," Wrath says with a snicker.

Z glances over at me. "Positive reinforcement, prez."

My morning's taken an even more bizarre twist than I could have imagined. "As much as I enjoy having you psycho-analyze me and my crew, can we get to the point?"

Loco leans in again. "My point is, me and my crew will help you get the Vipers out of Ironworks, split the area with you, keep things tight, and in return you don't give me shit about my working girls."

"Where are you running this from?"

He gives me a sly smile. "Water Street."

A short, sharp laugh bursts out from my throat. "You shittin' me? You're running a brothel right in downtown Ironworks? No wonder you're on Ransom's radar."

His shoulders lift in a phony-sheepish gesture. "I got a good deal on a nice brownstone. Ironworks PD is easy, keep the street clean, hand 'em a few bucks and they look the other way."

"Yeah, except they probably ran straight to Ransom and told him what you were up to."

Loco cocks his head as if that thought had never occurred to him.

"Yeah, okay." I hold out my hand and he shakes it. "We'll get a plan together."

"Fair enough. You can come check the house out if you want. See the girls are there willingly. Come and go as they please. Any girl you want is on the house."

Yeah, I can't imagine anything I want to do less. "No, thanks."

CHAPTER THIRTY-FOUR

HOPE

THE LAST COUPLE weeks before the wedding are nuts. I'm elbow deep in invites when Murphy finds me in the dining room.

"Hope, I get an 'and guest' too right?" Murphy asks.

I'm curious who he plans to bring. "Of course."

"Cool. Thanks."

I raise an eyebrow and wait for him to elaborate. "You remember Serena? She's taking classes up here. I don't know, we've been hanging out."

"Oh, that's great. She seemed so sweet when we met."

Murphy's taken aback but he shakes it off. "How pissed do you think Heidi will be?"

Crap. I hadn't thought about it. Another thought occurs to me. One I don't like very much. "Wait, you're not inviting her here to make Heidi jealous, are you? Because that's not fair to Heidi or Serena."

He shakes his head but takes a second to meet my eyes. "No. I don't know. I don't know what I'm doing anymore. I'm trying to do the right thing for her, but it's making me miserable."

"Well, it's not all about you."

"I know. She says she loves Axel. All the time. And how happy he makes her. But don't know if she means it or she's trying to rub my nose in it or what."

Honestly, it's probably all of those things combined, given that Heidi's seventeen. "Girls at that age are a little nuts Murphy. I remember. I know I was."

His eyes widen as if it never occurred to him I'd ever been a teenager. "Yes, Murphy, I haven't always been an old hag."

The burly jerk laughs. "You're far from hag territory, Hope." His laughter stops abruptly and he turns serious. "I feel like a creepy perv waiting 'til her birthday, you know?"

"Yeah, it's a little creepy," I agree and he smirks. "Don't look at it that way. Just be her friend like you always have. If it's meant to be it will." I lower my voice, because I feel like a traitor for saying what I'm about to say. "I like Axel. A lot. He's a good kid." Murphy nods grudgingly. "But Axel's her first real boyfriend. Girls rarely end up with their high school boyfriend. When she starts college, she might—"

"Meet someone else? Great."

I chuckle. "All I'm saying is they might go their separate ways. All on their own."

His mouth turns up, and I cut off whatever he's about to say. "You mess with them and do something to break them up, she'll end up hating you, Murphy. Just let it happen naturally."

"Thanks, Hope. Sorry I'm being such a pussy when I know you got other stuff to do."

I roll my eyes at him. "You'd be a bigger pussy if you just bottled it up."

He barks out a laugh. "I guess. But I wouldn't talk about it with any of—"

"The guys?"

"Yeah. Or Teller. I think he's relieved Heidi's with Axel." He snorts. "Don't blame him. I had a sister, I wouldn't want her with me either."

The way he says it honestly breaks my heart a little. "You're a good guy. If I had a younger sister, I'd let her date you."

I don't care if he gets mad, I have to give him a hug. He lets me and wraps his arms around me.

"I wish you'd been around ten years ago to steer all us fuckers in the right direction."

"Who says I knew anything back then?"

Trinity keeps me running from one place to the next. For a simple, low-key wedding there seems to be an awful lot to do.

Suspiciously, I never see a bill for anything.

"They'll bill after," Trinity says one day when I ask.

"Bullshit. Rock's taking care of everything, isn't he?"

She grins and shrugs. I feel bad, because I know Rock's accounts must have taken a beating after the thousands of dollars in legal fees we had to hand over to Glassman.

"I'm fine," he assures me when I ask.

"Just go with it, Mrs. North," Trinity teases me over dinner a few nights before the big day.

My cheeks heat and I steal a glance at Rock, who's wearing a half-smirk. Wrath and Trinity both stare at us. "What?" Trinity asks.

"Nothing."

"I don't think Hope plans to change her name," Rock says.

"Kendall's my maiden name," I explain.

Everyone except Rock stares at me.

"You're okay with that?" Z asks Rock and I shoot a glare at him.

Rock chuckles. "Careful, Z."

"What is this, 1950? Seriously, this really surprises you guys that much?"

Wrath shakes his head. "Nope. None of our business anyway." He shifts and Z winces.

"Why're you kicking me, fucker?" Z grumbles.

Rock picks his fork back up. "Probably better for her anyway, in case shit goes down in the future."

That certainly takes my appetite away.

"Gonna file separate taxes too?" Z asks.

"Why're you guys so nosy?" I snap.

Wrath holds his hands up. "Hey, I didn't say a word."

Rock pins him with a stare. "There's married, filing separate or whatever. Let the accountant figure it out."

"But that's—" I snap my mouth shut, but I think Rock senses what I was going to say. His mouth quirks into another wry smile.

"What, Baby Doll?"

"When I took tax law, we were taught only politicians and criminals file that way," I mumble.

Everyone—even Rock—has a good chuckle.

"Jerks."

Rock lifts his chin at Trinity. "You got a final guest list, Ms. Party Planner?"

Yes, she does. She shoves her plate out of the way and pulls her staggeringly large wedding binder up, dropping it on the table with a thud. The binder's rarely more than a few feet away from her. The guys groan when they see it.

"Can we burn that thing when the wedding's over?" Teller asks.

Trinity glares at him. "No. I'm saving all my notes for Heidi's wedding."

Everyone gets a good laugh at that.

Except Teller.

"Where is she, anyway?" Murphy asks and Teller glares at him.

"Library."

"Is that code for Axel's apartment?" Z snickers.

"Fuck off," Teller gripes.

Oh boy. Heidi's eighteenth birthday's only a few weeks after the wedding. But since her classes started, she's been asserting her independence a lot more, driving Teller nuts in the process.

"Guest list?" Rock prompts.

"Everyone from Downstate RSVP'd yes."

"Oh, goodie," I mutter. Trinity catches my eye and chuckles.

"Your people all said yes," Trinity says, pointing at me. "Except, I didn't get anything back from your mom." Her mouth twists down and I shrug.

"I'm not surprised. It's better that way."

"Wolf Knights officers are coming. You're sure you're okay with them being up here, Rock?" Trinity asks.

He sits back and I watch as his gaze strays to Z and Wrath before answering. "Yup. Our clubs are good."

"Okay."

"Did you guys figure out Rock's bachelor party?" I ask.

"Oh, yeah. We got something big planned," Z answers while rubbing his palms together.

"I don't even want to know."

"He wouldn't let us get strippers," Murphy says. "We had to improvise."

I hold up my hands in an innocent gesture. "Just so you know, that is *not* my fault. I told him I didn't have a problem with it."

The guys laugh. "We figured."

"You assholes will understand one day," Rock grumbles.

"Fuck, I understand now. I don't want them either," Wrath adds with a big grin.

Trinity gives him a curious look.

After that scintillating dinner conversation, I pull Trinity out of the dining room, into the hallway.

"Can you help me with something?"

"Anything, Hope."

I push her into her room, so none of the guys overhear us. "I want to get a tattoo."

"Really? What?"

I point to my lower hip. "Mrs. North, with his crown, maybe?"

"Don't you think he should go with you?"

"No. I want to surprise him. He'll never expect it."

"That's true."

"At least the Mrs. North part, he can go back and help me have the crown added later."

"Chickening out?"

"How much does it hurt?"

"I'm the wrong person to ask. I don't tolerate it well for some reason."

"That's not encouraging."

"Sorry."

I bite my lip. I really want to do this. A little pain is worth it. "Can you help me set it up before the wedding?"

"How are you going to hide it from him?"

"I'll just tell him no sex before the wedding."

Trinity laughs so hard, she starts hiccupping, which is of course, when Wrath comes in. "What'd you do to my girl, Hope?"

"Nothing." I throw Trinity a pleading look and she finally stops laughing.

"Let me tell him, he can set it up. It's his friend."

"No way. He'll tell Rock."

"Hey. I kept your secret about going to get his wedding band," Wrath protests.

That's right he did. "Promise not to laugh?"

"Now, Cinderella, don't have me make promises I can't keep."

Trinity starts laughing again. "Don't tease her," she says between giggles.

"I want to get 'Mrs. North' tattooed on me."

Wrath doesn't laugh, but he does stare at me for a minute before answering. "Don't you think he'll want to go with you?"

"Yes, but I want to surprise him. Wait a second. I don't have to take my pants off, do I?"

They both laugh at me. *Jerks.*

"Where, Hope?" Wrath finally asks.

"Either my lower hip, or between my shoulder blades."

"Hip might hurt less since it's fleshier," Wrath points out.

"Are you calling me fat?"

He rolls his eyes to the ceiling and actually mutters "God help me," which I find hysterical. "Yes, I'll set it up for you, Hope," he finally says.

"Thank you."

"How are you going to keep it a secret?"

"Oh, tell him, Hope," Trinity giggles.

"No sex before the wedding."

Wrath just stares at me.

"What? Lots of people do that. It's romantic."

He covers Trinity's ears with his hands. "Stop giving her ideas."

I point at him. "Jerks. Both of you."

ROCK

My brothers put the perfect bachelor party together for me. A way to put some of the bad shit of the past few months in my rear view so I can start my future with Hope, knowing some scores are settled.

Vipers are next on my list. Although, Loco's been doing a good job holding up his end. His crew's made a lot of progress in Ironworks.

Things are looking up.

Well, as "up" as they can be when going on a murder spree two nights before my wedding.

Murder spree's more dramatic than what it actually is.

Just a bit of payback.

Izzard's still wearing two hand casts when we track him down. In Viper territory. Fancy that.

Vipers are running their own brothel outside Ironworks city limits in the middle of nowhere. It's a sad, ramshackle, hillbilly crackden type of house. That's where Izzard spends his time when he's not busy beating on inmates and molesting ol' ladies.

Figures.

I told Hope on the beach that I've never enjoyed hurting someone before. It was true at the time.

But *this* I'm going to enjoy the fuck out of.

Wrath and Z take care of clearing the downstairs for me, getting the girls out and keeping them quiet so they don't run and bring a bunch of Vipers back before I'm ready to deal with them.

Ransom has been a slippery fucker to track down. Where the Vipers are hiding their shady prez is a mystery, but it's only a matter of time before we find him.

No loose ends.

The lock clicks as I open the door to the room Lizard's waiting in. "What took so long, bitch?" he snaps.

I close the door behind me. "I ain't here to suck your dick, Lizard."

"Oh, fuck," he gasps. Like the pussy I know he is, he opens his mouth to yell for help.

The nine-millimeter in my hand shuts him up. "I'm just here for my five minutes, like I promised."

He shakes his head and tries to sit up.

I lean against the dresser across from the bed. The pose is casual, but inside I'm anything but.

"See, messing with me was one thing. I get it. I'm a bad guy. But once you touched my woman—"

"I got a kid."

I straighten up and circle around to the other side of the bed. "Yeah? When's the last time you saw your son?"

He opens his mouth, but I'm not here to get in touch with our feelings. And I already know the answer.

Turns out I don't even need the whole five minutes.

HOPE

"Did Wrath tell you what they were doing tonight?" I ask Trinity as Axel holds the door to the tattoo shop open for us.

"No. He said it was club business, not a bachelor party."

"My ass," I grumble.

"I don't think it was strippers, Hope."

Axel's been so quiet, I almost forget he's even with us. So it surprises me when he opens his mouth. "I don't think they were going to CB."

Honestly, I don't even care if he is there. I trust Rock and as long as he comes home to me in one piece, I'm fine.

Bronze is a nice guy. "You're Hope! The woman who made Rock break his 'no women's names on my body' rule," he greets me with a big smile.

Trinity giggles.

"How're your pieces doing, darlin'?" he asks her.

"Fine."

Bronze gets me in his chair and tells me all sorts of stories about Rock in his younger days. Mostly ink-related, but they put me at ease regardless. We go over what I want. Mrs. North and a delicate scroll design underneath. I let him know I plan to come back with Rock and have the crown added later. We discuss size and placement. After all the talking, I'm sort of eager to get it done with, but I'm grateful that he's so thorough.

"Good call. He's not gonna kick my ass for touching you, is he?"

"I don't think so."

Bronze laughs. He's neither insulted nor scared. I like this guy.

My opinion changes about ten minutes later. "God dammit that hurts!" I yelp for the second time.

"Sit still, darlin'," he warns me.

"I'm trying."

Trinity moves closer and holds my hand. "Squeeze my hand, Hope. Oh, fuck ow! Not that hard!" she says with a gasp and I try to loosen up.

Eventually my side buzzes into a stinging-numb sensation and I'm able to relax.

"All done," Bronze says, snapping me out of my haze. He hands me a mirror so I can get a better look. What I can see is pretty, but mostly it's black ink and red, angry looking skin. "Crap, will that look better by Saturday?"

"The redness will lessen. But it will take a little longer to fully settle down. By then you'll be ready for the crown."

"Maybe," I mutter as he places ointment, gauze and tape over it.

"We're gonna see you, Saturday, right?" Trinity asks.

"Hell yeah. I wouldn't miss seeing Rock get hitched."

I grin. "You'll keep it a secret, though, right? I want to surprise him."

"I'll pretend we've never met."

"Thanks."

My offer to pay him is rebuffed. "Wedding present," he says.

"That was awfully sweet," I say to Trinity as we leave.

"He's a good guy."

"Where to, Hope?" Axel asks when we get to the car.

"Home."

CHAPTER THIRTY-FIVE

HOPE

"DEEP BREATH, HOPE. SUCK IT IN," Trinity, the torture expert, says behind me.

"I...can't...suck...in... anymore."

"If you can still talk, you're not sucking in hard enough," Lilly jokes.

"You would know," I snap.

"*Oooh*, she's bitchy without oxygen."

Trinity huffs out an annoyed burst of air. "You're not helping, Lilly."

"Sorry. Sorry. Come on, Hope. You don't need those last two ribs."

"I hate you both," I grumble before taking another deep breath.

"Ugh. We should have been training you to wear this all week," Trinity huffs as she cinches, tugs and yanks my corset into place. There is nothing pretty or elegant about the process.

"Phew." I glance down. "Oh, hello there. I'm not used to having my girls right under my chin." I snicker and snort at my own joke. Trinity and Lilly both give me strange looks.

"Is she drunk?" Trinity asks.

"No, I think she's nervous. Come on, Hope. Let's get your dress on," Lilly prods, taking me by the arm and tugging me in front of the mirror.

Once I'm zipped into my dress, I'm even more nervous.

"Boots or flats, ladies? Time to help me decide."

"Oh, please wear the boots. They're so cute," Trinity pleads.

"Hi, ladies!" Mara greets as she enters the room.

"Oh, thank God. I was worried you and Damon got lost and there'd be no one to marry us and—"

Mara cuts me off before I go into full freak-out mode. "Nope. Lilly's man met us down at Ward's and we followed him up."

"He's not *my man*," Lilly corrects.

Mara rolls her whole head in a dramatic gesture. "Sure, whatever you say."

A more tentative knock on the door stops our joking around. "Come in!"

Heidi pokes her head in the room. "Hi. Am I allowed to hang out in here?"

"Of course, sweetheart." I motion for her to come in and shut the door. She seems really down, completely opposite of how she was when I saw her a few hours ago.

"Everything okay, honey?" Mara asks.

"Yeah." She tips her head up and finally smiles. "You look so pretty, Hope."

"Thank you," I answer and then remember my gifts for Mara and Heidi. "Hold on," I mumble as I rifle through the bag of stuff I brought downstairs with me last night. Trinity taps me on the shoulder and holds out two boxes. "Oh. Thanks."

"My thank-you present for being such wonderful bridesmaids," I explain as I hand the boxes to Mara and Heidi. Earrings that match their dresses are nestled inside. I'd given Lilly and Trinity their gifts last night.

Heidi squeals when she pulls them out. "They're so pretty! I don't have any dangly ones like this. Grams never let me wear them."

"Oh, good."

"I wish I was wearing my hair up now," she says as she stares in the mirror.

Trinity brushes Heidi's hair off her shoulder. "I can help you put it up if you want."

Heidi blinks and stares at Trinity for a second before answering. "I'd love it. Thanks."

Trinity goes to work and I'm jealous, because it seems there's nothing Trinity isn't good at.

Mara and Lilly are busy goofing around. I catch Heidi staring at me in the mirror. "What's wrong, honey?"

"Nothing." She winces as Trinity works a bobby pin into her hair. "Did you know Murphy was bringing a date?"

Yikes. "He mentioned it when I was doing the invitations."

"Oh. Do you know her?"

"Uh, I've met her. She's a nice girl."

Trinity makes this weird eyes-wide-raised-eyebrow face at me and I shrug.

"Is your boyfriend in the wedding?" Mara asks Heidi. She knows damn well Axel's ushering guests. I think it's her way of reminding Heidi she's here with someone too.

"All done. What do you think?" Trinity asks.

"Oh, it's so pretty! Thank you, Trinity."

Trinity nods and grabs her camera for a few photos.

"You should have gotten a picture of us wrestling her into the corset," Lilly says with a snicker.

I casually throw my middle finger up at her and she laughs even harder.

Trinity sets the camera down and gives Heidi a serious look. "Okay, we need you to help us, help her decide. Boots or flats?"

Mara holds up both options for Heidi's inspection.

"The boots are cool," she finally says. I feel like she held the "for an old person" portion of her thought to herself.

"Okay. Boots it is. Now, since I can't bend over, which one of you is helping me into them?"

Trinity, Lilly and Mara pretend to play rock, paper, scissors. "Very funny, girls."

Shoes had been the last decision I needed to make. Now that I'm in the boots, my hair's styled into a half-up-half-down, curly thing that's actually really pretty and I'm all made up, I feel strangely calm.

I should be nervous. Shouldn't I? Glancing down at my hands I wiggle my fingers, watching the gold, glittery tips catch the light. "This looks great, Trinity."

"Thank you."

After a few deep breaths, I realize I really am calm. Nothing in my life has ever felt as right as this does. That's crazy, right? The man I'm marrying just barely skipped going to prison for murder. My decision-making skills might be seriously impaired.

But I'm not stupid. And I've made my peace with…things. I survived and I don't think I could have gone through something like that before I knew Rock. He's also given me something I've never had before. Family. A family who came together and kept me together. Who would die to protect one another. I love them too. So much my chest aches.

"Are you nervous?" Heidi asks softly.

"No."

Lilly gives me a skeptical look.

"I was. But I feel good." My voice breaks and I end up whispering. "I love Rock."

Mara pulls me in for a hug. "I'm so happy you two found each other."

"Thanks."

Trinity's sort of hanging back, fidgeting and I realize she's trying not to cry. "Don't you dare cry, Trin. You'll make me cry and I don't have time to fix the layers of makeup you guys painted on me."

That makes Trinity laugh and she comes over to give me a big hug. "Shit, I love you. You're exactly what he's needed since the day I met him."

"Thanks."

Lilly looks at me and nods. Only the slight tremble of her lower lip tells me she's also a little emotional.

The three of us had what turned into a big giggle-sobfest last night when we held our pre-wedding slumber party in Trinity's room.

The look on Wrath's face when he got sent upstairs to his old room had kept us laughing for hours.

Banging on the bedroom door stops us. "Please tell me Hope's still here," Z shouts.

I fling open the door, surprising him and he steps back. "I'm here."

"Thank God." He takes me in from head to toe. "Forget Rock, you want to marry me instead?"

"Is that your way of saying I look okay?"

"More than okay, sweetheart."

Heat rushes over my cheeks and my nose tingles. "Thank you."

"Who's giving you away, Hope?" Lilly asks, drawing Z's attention away from me.

"No one. I'm a grown woman. I'm giving myself," I grumble. Z chuckles. "I hope that doesn't offend you, *Mr. Traditional.*"

His eyes widen and I think he wishes I hadn't said that in front of Lilly. Oops. Good thing he doesn't know how I blubbered to Lilly about how sweet and kind Z is under all his rough exterior last night.

"Not at all, *Ms. Kendall.*" He holds his arm out for me. "Come on, I'm your ride out to the ceremony."

I turn and glance at Trinity who shrugs. "What? We can't make you hike through the woods in your dress."

As we walk out front, I wave to Murphy and Teller who are patiently waiting out front.

It occurs to me there are a lot of questions about the ceremony and after-party I never bothered to ask Trinity. I'm not even sure *where* on the property we're getting married. A flash of guilt singes me and I turn so fast, I almost knock Z over. Trinity's eyes flare and she stiffens when I throw my arms around her. "Thank you so much for everything you've done for me."

After a second of hesitation, she returns the embrace. "No problem."

361

I pull away and laugh so I don't cry. "I'm a terrible bride, aren't I?"

"Nope. Easiest bride I've ever worked with," she jokes. "And you're a good friend, so I was happy to do it."

Murphy clears his throat. "Uh, are you marrying Rock or Trinity, Hope?"

We both glare at him and he snickers. "Come on, Rock's probably worried you ran away."

"Nah, front gate's locked tight," Z assures us.

I snort. "If anyone should run, it's Rock."

The guys think that's hilarious. Teller steps forward to give me a quick hug. "You look really pretty, Hope."

"Thanks."

I get a quick hug from Murphy too.

"I guess Wrath's keeping Rock from running away?" I ask.

No one bothers to answer me.

Someone wrapped pretty green and gold ribbons around the club's side-by-side utility vehicles and that's what the guys use to drive us out to…a clearing with a stone amphitheater.

I twist in my seat. "Trinity? What the?"

"Rock's never brought you out here?"

The building site for our house is in the opposite direction. Even during all my brooding hikes through the woods, I'd never explored this part of the property before. "No."

Z grins from ear to ear. "We don't use it a lot. The prospects have been busy fixing it up. Clearing brush, repairing the stone, weeding. All the fun stuff."

Trinity points to the rock wall encircling what looks like low stone benches. "The tent for dinner, music, and everything is on the other side."

My mouth works, but no sounds come out.

The guys stop too far away for me to see Rock or anyone else.

Z gets out and gives me his hand. The corner of his mouth lifts at my cowgirl boots. "Nice touch."

It feels like I blink and Trinity's standing in front of me.

"This is it. Are you ready?"

ROCK

"This is a good spot, since you're sacrificing your manhood and all," Wrath says as he gestures at the stone altar we're standing in front of while we wait.

"Please. Like you're not dying to do the same thing."

His answering grin is wide and full of mischief. So far he's been doing a good job of keeping our guests away from me. I'm so wound up I'm liable to clock the first person who cracks a "last moments of freedom" joke.

Perceptive asshole that he is, Wrath cocks his head at me. "You nervous?"

"Yeah, worried as fuck she's gonna realize what a mistake this is and run the fuck away." I tried saying it as a joke, but it doesn't come out that way at all. I just sound like a pansy-assed dipshit.

"Front gate's locked," he answers.

"Thanks."

He shrugs. "I've done everything I can think of to chase her away, and she's still here. She must love you."

"Yeah, I owe you an ass-kicking or two for givin' her grief."

"Anytime, brother." He laughs, not taking my threat seriously.

"Help me fix this fucking tie."

"Like I know how. I can't believe she got you into that thing."

I glance down at the gray suit. Same one I've worn out with her before. "She didn't ask."

"Christ, you really are whipped."

I shrug, because that's probably true and I can't seem to find a fuck to give about it. "She likes it on me."

"You're lucky I like her so much. I still can't believe I let her kick me out of my own room last night."

"Sorry." My apology sounds completely insincere since I'm laughing as I say it.

"I get the whole 'no sex before the wedding thing' *for you*. But why'd I get punished with it?"

"I'm glad you understand it, because I don't."

"You'll see," he answers with a smug grin.

Before I can prod him for more information, the sound of UTVs reaches me.

"Girls must be here," Wrath says. He smacks my arm. "Close your mouth, you look like you got kicked in the head by a mule."

Damon chuckles as he walks up and shakes my hand. "How are you feeling, Rock?"

"Good. Ready to get it over with."

He nods as if he's heard that a hundred times. He probably has.

This. All of this is nothing like my first wedding. I hate myself a little for even making the comparison, but it's true.

As if he read my mind, Wrath steps closer. "Never, ever thought you'd do this again."

I wait for whatever obnoxious comment he's dying to make. "And?"

"And nothing. I'm happy for you. For both of you. Through sickness and health, incarceration and freedom." He nudges me with his arm. "You should add that to your vows."

I'd laugh, but I'm choked up. Yes, Hope stood by me.

Then I'm not thinking about anything. There's no music, but a hush falls over the rowdy crowd and my eyes lock on Hope. She really did it. She found a green dress and it's fucking perfect. *She's* perfect.

I can't stop staring at her face. Not really taking in any details, just the overall picture of how beautiful she is. I take a few steps and meet her, covering her hands with my own. "I'm glad you came."

Her mouth tips into the pretty smile I love so much. "Me too," she says a little shaky. She blows out a flustered breath and smiles wider. "I mean, I'm glad you're here,"

"No place else I'd want to be." I lean down and take her lips in a soft kiss, forgetting where we are.

Someone—Damon I think—clears his throat. Heidi giggles.

Hope pulls back and blinks up at me and the overwhelming sense of how lucky I am washes over me.

Lucky that we finally got to this point.

"Let's get married," she whispers.

CHAPTER THIRTY-SIX

HOPE

THE ACTUAL WEDDING part of our wedding day is a blur. I think I spoke the correct words when I was supposed to. Mostly I just stared at Rock, in awe of how much I love him and how happy I am.

His gaze roamed over me once, taking in the green dress with a slow smile. After that his eyes never wandered from my face. As many times as we've been teased about being sex-crazed maniacs, Rock made it clear by that simple action that he was more worried about my thoughts than my body. I think I fell in love with him even more right there at the altar.

After the brief ceremony, our wild biker crowd couldn't contain themselves another second. Whoops, cheers and congratulations filled the woods. Along with about two-dozen monarch butterflies Trinity handed us to release from a decorative box.

There were a lot of guests to keep up with. Many I'd met before. Some I hadn't. When I got overwhelmed, Rock ushered me to a quiet area and held me close.

"Come on, Baby Doll. You need to eat something," Rock suggested, tugging me back to our table. With the fierce look on his face, no one dared approach us as we made our way up front. Trinity had gone above and beyond with decorating the tent. White twinkly lights glittered from above and all around us.

Rock sits me down and pulls his chair close. One of the prospects drops a plate in front of us and Rock feeds me jumbo shrimp dipped in spicy sauce—that he's careful not to drop on my dress—followed by mushrooms stuffed with crab and brie.

"Happy now?" I ask as I finish my last bite.

"Yes, sass-mouth."

"You love my sassy mouth."

"Yes I do." To prove it, he leans over and takes my mouth in a kiss that sets me on fire. I'm panting by the time we part and he rests his forehead against mine.

After a second, he hands me a mason jar filled with what I suspect is a virgin margarita. "There's no tequila in this," I say as I set it down. His mouth curves into a sly grin.

"No, there isn't," he says simply.

Slender arms wrap around my shoulders from behind. "Are you okay?" Trinity asks.

I turn so I can see her better. "Yes. Thank you so much."

She gives Rock a similar hug, and he grabs her hand before she can dash away. "You okay?" he asks.

"I'm good, Rock."

After she flits back into the crowd, Rock glances down at my boots. "That was a cute touch."

"Lilly suggested it."

"Are you going to put them to use?"

"Oh yes. I plan to ride you later like a good little cowgirl."

He breaks into laughter. "Good to know, but that's not what I meant." He nods at the space people are using to dance.

"You don't want to dance in front of all your big, bad biker friends."

He snorts as if that's absurd. "You know me better than that. Besides, half of them are so drunk, they won't remember a thing from tonight."

I point at Wrath, who's got Trinity wrapped in a tight embrace, making it clear to the world who she belongs to. "Wrath will."

"He'll just be jealous of my awesome skills," he says as he pulls me out onto the floor. We dance the simple country two-step we learned in Maine, even though I'm not sure it's right for the music that's playing. Soon he's twirling me around and we're being silly more than anything.

Z and Lilly join us. "You're more coordinated than I would have expected," I say to Z, who laughs.

"He's very rhythmic," Lilly says with a straight face.

The music turns to something slower, and we sway together for a while, before Rock pulls over to one of the s'mores stations Trinity set up for dessert. There's a cake too and once we're within two feet of it, Trinity yells for everyone to quiet down so we can cut into it.

"It's so pretty, I hate to ruin it," I complain as she hands me the knife. It's LOKI blue with delicate swirls of silver iced onto it and finished with a crown on top.

"Trust me, I took a billion pictures of it," Trinity assures me.

I eat the few bites Rock offers me and feed him a few in return. We take a plate back to our table along with a melty-messy s'more.

Rock introduces me to a couple of guys he says came in from another club. Their cuts announce their club claims Western New York as its territory. See? I learned plenty from Wrath this summer. I smile and nod and feel terrible that I forget their names about two minutes after they leave.

Turning, I take in my handsome husband. He catches me staring at him. "What?" he asks with a raised eyebrow.

"Nothing. I love you in your cut," I say, then drop my voice a little lower. "But thank you for the suit. It's crazy-sexy on you."

The smoldering look I get in return warms every inch of my skin.

Murphy drops into the chair on Rock's other side, interrupting our moment. It's fine. Soon I plan to have Rock all to myself. They speak in low tones, about what, I have no idea.

Heidi's hand settles on my shoulder and she leans over to hug me before sitting in the chair next to me.

"Thank you for everything, Hope."

"You're welcome, sweetie. Thank you for being in the wedding."

She grins and pats the side of her head, tucking a few strands of loose hair behind her ear. "It was fun. I'm so happy you're an official part of the family now." Her lashes flutter and she glances down. "You're the closest I've ever had to a mom," she says so low, I almost don't hear her.

Tears prick my eyes and I sit up straighter, so I can pull her to me for a hug. She rests her head on my shoulder and we watch the rest of the party for a few minutes. "Grams never wanted me to be part of all of this," she says finally. "But it's always where I'm happiest."

"You have a lot of people who love you, Heidi."

"I know." She pulls back. "Wrath let Axel off prospect duty for the rest of the night." She pulls at the skirt of her dress. "I'm going to run back to the house and change. Axel said he'd take me for a ride."

"Sounds like a plan. Just be careful."

"We will."

She stands and wraps her arms around Rock's neck, planting a kiss on his cheek. They murmur to each other for a minute and she takes off.

I lean over and smile at Murphy, who didn't get a hello or goodbye from Heidi. "How are you doing?"

He quirks a smile at me. "Good, First Lady. You threw a hell of a party."

"Oh no. This was all Trinity."

Rock chuckles and wraps his hand around mine.

When we're alone again, he puts his arm around my shoulders. "You've got chocolate on your face," he says before swooping in and kissing it away.

"I think you were making that up," I tease when he stops to stare at me.

"Maybe." He touches his forehead to mine. "I've got a present for you, Baby Doll," he says in a warm, rough voice.

"Oh yeah?" My question comes out full of dirty intent because I assume he means the present in his pants.

But he surprises me by pulling a small box out of his pocket and placing it in my hand.

Curious, I glance at him before easing the lid off. Inside is a pretty emerald green crown key chain with a key attached.

I take it out, dangling it in front of us.

"It's to our house, Baby Doll."

I raise an eyebrow. I thought the house wasn't finished yet.

"It's more symbolic, I doubt we'll lock the door much," he says with a smile.

"Is it ready for us?"

"Told you first night we were married, we'd be spending in our house."

I almost knock him out of his chair, I throw my arms around him so fast. "Thank you, Rock."

Last time I visited the building site, there was still a lot of finish work that needed to be done. I remember what Rock told me about the basement and heat curls in my belly.

I lean over, pressing my lips to his neck, kissing my way to his ear. "We need to leave."

He grabs my hand. "Why, doll? You feel okay?"

"I need to *be* with you," I whisper in his ear.

His reaction is pretty damn funny. He rockets out of his chair so fast, it topples over. "Let's go," he demands, giving my hand a quick tug.

Laughing, I stand and he sweeps me into his arms. Naturally Wrath—who'd behaved himself most of the night—notices and lets out a loud whistle, calling everyone else's attention to us.

"Going somewhere, kids?" he calls out.

Completely embarrassed, I bury my head against Rock's shoulder.

Rock ends up setting me down, so I can say goodbye to our guests. Mara and Damon left shortly after the ceremony. Sway and his crew are drunkenly dancing around, quickly turning half the party into a semi-orgy. Tawny gives me a brief hug, but she looks cranky, so I don't talk to her too long.

Lilly scrambles out of Z's lap to give me a big hug.

"Congratulations, Hope," she whispers against my ear. "I'm so happy for you."

"Thank you." I glance at Z, who's got his eyes on Lilly. "Will I be seeing you in the morning?" I ask her. She chuckles and tucks her hair behind her ear. "Maybe."

"Maybe my ass," Z says, yanking her back into his lap. I lean over and kiss his cheek.

"Behave," I warn him and he nods at me.

When I'm finished saying good night to everyone, Wrath curls his arm over my shoulder. "I'll make sure everyone gets where they need to go, Hope. Go take care of your husband." He nods his head at where Rock's waiting for me at the edge of the clearing.

The word *husband* sends a thrill through me. Rock's my husband. *Finally.* After what seems like forever. He's mine and I'm his. The enormity of it steals my breath.

Wrath tips my chin up. Frowning down at me, he asks, "You okay?"

"Yeah. I'm good." Stretching up on my tiptoes, I throw my arms around his neck and give him a hug. At first he's surprised, but he wraps his arms around me lifting me off the ground a bit. "Proud to have you for a sister, Hope. You're the best thing that ever happened to him," he murmurs into my ear.

Damn, I haven't cried once today. But his words make my eyes sting and my nose twitch.

"Thank you," I whisper.

He sets me down and plants a kiss on the top of my head.

Clutching the box with my key in one hand, I take off running across the clearing. Rock catches me around the waist, kissing me breathless, then setting me down. His hand slaps the seat of the ATV.

"Get on, Baby Doll."

I laugh when I finally notice the white streamers, cans and the Just Married sign someone—if I had to guess, Z—tied to the rack.

"We're going to scare every woodland creature within a ten mile radius," I joke as I gather my dress, and straddle the machine. Rock gets on in front of me and starts up the engine. People shout to us and I turn and wave. Rock must be eager to go, because he takes off without a backward glance, before I even have my arms wrapped around him.

"Hey!" I yell out.

"Hold on, babe."

It's much different than riding on the back of Rock's bike. For one, we're not going as fast. Since there are four wheels instead of two, it feels more solid. Well, until Rock decides to drive over a few downed trees blocking our path. I squeal and squeeze him tighter, which was probably what he was after in the first place.

In front of us, warm white lights appear. As we get closer, I see a path of lights leading up to our house.

He parks the machine right alongside the house and gets off first. Instead of helping me dismount, he scoops me up and carries me up the porch steps.

"Get the door, doll."

Happy for a reason to use my shiny new key, I pluck it out of the box and slide it into the lock.

He carries me over the threshold and sets me down. I can't take my eyes off him though. "I'll look at the house tomorrow. Right now I want my husband."

His hand cups my jaw, thumb rubbing over my cheek. "Say that again."

"That I want my husband?"

"Yes," he answers in a hoarse voice before sealing his mouth over mine for a tender kiss.

Tender turns passionate quick and we're pawing at each other's clothes.

Rock pulls away first. "Baby, wait." He picks me up again and carries me upstairs. The house is an open floor plan, so I get glimpses of all the things I have left to do. I'm most excited about finishing the kitchen which currently has no appliances or counters. I picture us hanging out there a lot.

"We're not going to the basement?" I tease.

"Sorry, not ready. Soon, Baby Doll."

"I knew you were all talk," I say when he sets me down.

He gives me a wicked smile that makes my heart race. "There won't be much talking down there." His hand reaches round and squeezes my butt. "Lots of screaming and moaning though."

I giggle and dance out of his hold, then gasp when I see our bedroom's not only finished but furnished too. There's still a lot we need to do to personalize the space, but the important things for tonight—bed, sheets, blankets—are all there.

"Rock! How did you get everything here without me knowing?"

His shoulders lift. "You've been busy."

My gaze strays to the bluestone fireplace, currently bare. Rock gives me a sheepish smile. "I didn't get to do everything I wanted." He mimics chopping wood. "Need to get some firewood chopped."

"Trust me, I'm already overheated." Especially with the image of him half-naked and chopping wood he just put in my head. I take another look around the room. "Everything is beautiful. Thank you."

"You're beautiful." He runs a finger over the neckline of my dress. "Thank you for this."

"What?"

"The dress. First time I laid eyes on you, you were wearing this color. I'd had such a crappy night and there you were, the prettiest woman I'd ever seen."

"Oh, Rochlan."

"You changed my life that day." He pauses and stares at me so intently my skin warms. "I meant every word of our vows. You make me want to be a better person. Do better, so I can give you everything you need. I love you, Hope."

"I love you too," I whisper back.

We stare at each other a little longer. "Will you help me unzip it?"

His serious stare transforms into a filthy grin. "Fuck, yes, Baby Doll."

His enthusiasm makes me chuckle as I turn around. He slides his rough hands over my bare shoulders, down to the zipper. Warm breath coasts over my skin.

"I think you'll like what's underneath," I whisper.

ROCK

My feelings for what Hope's wearing under her dress go far beyond *like*. Air rushes out of my lungs.

"This is beautiful, Baby Doll. You're beautiful."

It's an intricate blue lace, corset-type thing, garters, stockings with embroidered tops hugging bare thighs that I'm dying to bury my face between.

"No ripping it, though. I had it specially made."

I've never wanted anyone more. Will never want anyone else ever again. Except this amazing woman.

My hands brush down her side and she winces. "What's wrong?"

"I have another surprise for you."

It's only then, that I notice the bandage covering a bit of skin at her hip. The edge of the corset just barely covers it. "What happened?"

She sighs, frustrated. "I'm so sorry. I got the corset for our wedding night, but it's been killing me all day. Will you help me get it off?"

"Fuck yeah. It's beautiful, Baby Doll, but naked is my favorite."

She chuckles as I work the tiny hooks and laces loose. "This isn't easy with my big fingers you know. How the hell did you get it on?"

"Trinity squeezed me into it."

Once I strip her out of it, she's standing there in the matching underwear, which is more like a piece of lace and string, stockings, boots, and the bandage. "This is pretty fucking hot too," I assure her. My gaze travels lower. "Especially the boots."

She chuckles and points at the bandage. Suddenly I know what I'm going to find. A tattoo. I just can't figure out of what. "Come here." I walk us over to the bed, and sit on the edge, placing her in front of me.

Mrs. North

"Fuck, Hope." Our eyes meet and a smile flickers over her mouth. "Are you surprised?"

"Yeah. Wait a second. Where'd you get it?"

She rolls her eyes. "Calm down, caveman. Trinity took me to Bronze's shop. He was a perfect gentleman."

I can live with that.

"I still need you to go back with me to have your crown added, right here," she points to the space above the N in North. My mouth goes dry and for a second I'm not sure how to respond.

"As soon as you're ready."

My gaze travels up her body and my hands follow, stopping to cup her breasts. "That no sex thing was cruel."

"But necessary so I could surprise you with this," she says, pointing at her hip.

"Come here." I pull her down to the bed, rolling her on top of me, careful not to brush against her reddened skin. "Guess this means missionary is out?" I tease. Her cheeks turn pink and she laughs. Then she attacks. Working the buttons of my shirt loose, ripping my belt open. I stare in wonder letting her have her way with me.

"I'll worship you later. Right now I need you hard and fast," she whispers, using one of my own lines on me.

"Have at it." My hands cup her breasts, kneading roughly. She sighs and throws her leg over me. I slide my hands down to her ass, tugging her forward, and slipping my finger under the thin lace to move her panties to the side.

She watches me with half-closed eyes. "You can rip them," she says.

Fuck yes. Away they go. My fingers massage her bare, slick skin, dipping inside, then back to her ass. She reaches down, squeezes my cock. "Stop fucking around. Ride your husband's dick."

"On it," she giggles.

"Sass-mouth." I groan as she lines me up and sinks down. "You're fucking perfect, Baby Doll."

She whimpers as I fill her completely, then slides back up. I let her play cowgirl. Watch as she gently rises up and down for a few minutes, until she's panting, head thrown back. My hand dives between her thighs, rubbing circles around her clit until she's grinding down into me, so close to going off.

"I'm close," she whispers.

"I know, Baby Doll. Give it to me."

"I, I" she murmurs and trembles, her pussy squeezing the fuck out of me. When she's finished and her eyes flutter her open, I pull her down against me, grip her ass hard and pound up into her. The sounds of our combined heavy breathing and moaning fill the room in our house. *Our* house. No one around us for miles.

"Be as loud as you want, baby," I say against her ear. She's already there though, screaming through another intense orgasm that tips me into my own release. "Fuck!"

Breathless, she rolls off me, and in fascination, I watch my cum slowly spilling out of my wife.

She rolls her head to the side, smiling at me. "Is married sex, still as good?"

"Even better."

CHAPTER THIRTY-SEVEN

TRINITY

AFTER THE CEREMONY, I proudly slipped on Wrath's patch on over my dress, not caring if any of Hope's friends thought it was weird.

I know it's not *my* wedding, but I can't remember the last time I was this happy. I'm really proud of the way everything turned out.

"I think you have a bright future in wedding planning," Lilly says when I take a break and sit down next to her. I glance over and see she's being sincere.

"Hope was an easy bride though. She didn't have strong opinions about any of it, except the dress and the location."

A soft smile plays over Lilly's mouth. "She's never been materialistic or fussy."

"Trinity?" A rough voice pulls me out of our conversation. My chest tightens in fear for a reason I can't even figure out.

"Chaser? Oh my God." I stand and say hello.

"Shit, I haven't seen you since you were like this big," he says while holding his hand somewhere in the vicinity of his knees.

"Oh, stop." I glance to the tall, thin blonde at his side. "Hi, Mallory."

She leans in and gives me a quick hug. They've been together for as long as I can remember. Even more impressive, they still seem to actually like each other.

Chaser nods at my vest. "I knew you'd been down here for years, but didn't realize you were with Wrath until I ran into him a few months ago."

My cheeks heat, but I'm saved from saying anything, by Wrath coming up and slipping his arm around my waist. "How's it going, Chaser? Take over for your dad yet?"

Chaser snorts. "No. That fucker will go to his grave with the gavel in his hand. You seen him yet? He wanted to talk to you or Rock while we're here."

"No. I'll go find him in a minute."

"Good deal. Good to see you, Trinity."

"You okay?" Wrath asks after they leave.

"Yeah." Shit I don't want him thinking— "I knew him when I was a kid. Remember how I told you my mom used to hang at the Demons' clubhouse sometimes—"

He gives me a gentle squeeze. "I know. I didn't think anything else," he says. One thing I love about my man, he's direct.

"I'm glad he's still with Mallory. She was always nice to me." While I only have fond memories of Chaser and Mallory, seeing them still stirs up a lot of bad feelings from my childhood.

Wrath must sense my mood shift, because he wraps me up in a tight hug and holds me until I relax.

"Since Chaser mentioned it, I'm gonna go find Stump. I don't want him bugging Rock with club business. You okay?" he asks.

"I'll be fine. I might run back to the clubhouse to check on Mariella."

He runs his gaze over me, then looks over my shoulder. "Take Murphy with you."

I open my mouth to protest, but he shakes his head. "This isn't a negotiation, Trinity."

Murphy *and* Serena end up walking back to the clubhouse with me. Mariella's out front with Teller, so I guess checking on her was sort of pointless. Serena ends up joining them and Murphy follows me into the kitchen to help me carry out drinks. Once we load up one of the UTVs and send Birch back to the party, Murphy and I are alone.

"How you doing, Maid of Honor?"

I chuckle before answering. "Fine." I tip my head toward Serena. "How's that going?"

He shoves his hands in his pockets and stares at the ground. "Fine."

"Heidi was spitting mad this morning—"

His head snaps up. "She was?"

Man, that foot-in-mouth thing Hope's always doing must be contagious. "Forget I said anything. Do you like her or did you just want to make Heidi jealous?"

"I like her. She's not you, but you're one of a kind."

I snort and give him a shove. "Living dangerously, Murphy."

"It was always Wrath for you, wasn't it?"

"Yeah. I didn't know how to figure my shit out. But yeah."

"Shit." He rubs his hand over the back of his neck and flicks his gaze at me. "You were one of the prettiest girls I'd ever seen. That you paid any attention at all to me…"

"Murphy—"

"I should have treated you better." He stops when he sees the look on my face. "Not 'cause I wanted you to fall in love with me. Because you're a good girl." His mouth quirks into a cocky smile. "You made me into a man, you know."

"I didn't do a very good job."

He bursts out laughing. "Ouch. That hurts on so many levels, Trin."

I punch him in the shoulder. "Hey. We're good. We're friends. You and Wrath are on good terms, right?"

"I think so."

I'm about to tell him that's all that matters, when one of Sway's guys, Bull, interrupts us. The asshole is drunk. "Flirtin' with a brother when you're wearing another brother's vest, Trinity? That's low."

Correction, the asshole's drunk and stupid.

All traces of humor from our conversation wipe clean off Murphy's face. "You got a fuckin' death wish, Bull? Just 'cause her man ain't standing here right now don't mean I won't fuck you up before I hand you over to him."

"Don't get your panties in a twist, Murphy. I'm just fuckin' around. I know you wouldn't disrespect your brother." As if *I* would. God, I hate this asshole. How can Sway's club be full of *so many* assholes and Rock's isn't?

Ignoring me now, Bull stands next to Murphy and bumps him with his elbow. "I heard Serena came with you. All the upstate whores becoming old ladies now?"

In the time it takes me to roll my eyes, Murphy has Bull laid out on the ground.

"Jesus, Murphy!"

He grins and shakes out his hand. "He needs to learn some manners."

I prod Bull with my foot and he doesn't make a sound. He does appear to be breathing. Not that I check very thoroughly. "Should we leave him here?"

He takes in the area. "Yeah. He's safe from getting run over. Bear eats him, that ain't my fault." He wraps his hand around my arm, pulling me back out front. "I'll deal with any shit that comes up."

Serena walks over to meet us, worriedly glancing at me, then Murphy. It's pretty obvious what she's thinking. "He was helping me put some stuff away in the kitchen," I say.

"Oh, sure." She hesitates and I feel bad for her. I think she's looking for more than she's going to get from Murphy. But then he surprises me by slinging his arm around her shoulder and kissing her forehead. "I feel bad, I didn't get to congratulate Hope, and she was so nice to—"

"You'll see her in the morning," Murphy assures her and she beams.

Well, I guess that means she's staying over. I hope to hell Heidi and Axel don't come back tonight.

Shaking my head, I pick up some of the empties people left scattered in the yard and toss them in the trash. I turn and almost smack into Tawny. All day I'd managed to avoid her.

One hand on her bony hip, she gets right in my face. "Think you're hot shit now because he gave you a patch?" she challenges.

"Not at all, Tawny," I answer calmly, taking a step back.

Her mouth twists. I'm sure it irritates her that I won't cower anymore. "You're still—"

"A whore. Yup. Got it. Thanks."

She takes a few steps closer and I flex my fingers. I've never wanted to be some trashy, fighting type of biker girl—I grew up around plenty of those types of women—but I won't lose any sleep over popping this bitch in the mouth either.

"How he could ever forgive your whoring ass—"

"Good thing it's none of your fucking business," I snarl. She steps back, unaccustomed to club girls defending themselves. But a surge of power runs through me. I've let this woman intimidate me for years. Over *nothing*.

"Not that I owe you any sort of explanation whatsoever, but I *never* fucked your man, Tawny. He tried. Many times. You can think whatever you want about me, but I never. Not once."

Her jaw hangs like a dead fish as she tries to come up with a response.

"He'll never be faithful," she spits at me.

"Wrath? Tawny, what you know about my man wouldn't fill a shot glass. We've already been there and lived that life. Just because your man's a pig doesn't mean every brother's like that."

She opens her mouth, but I cut off whatever shit she's about to say. "If you think the entire organization doesn't know you fuck around behind Sway's back, you're a seriously deluded *old* woman. So how you think you have any business judging me is a mystery."

"Everything okay?" Wrath's rumbly voice instantly soothes me. His arms wrap protectively around my body, holding me close. He probably got here just in time.

Tawny narrows her eyes, and I can see her contemplating the wisdom of mouthing off to him.

"Your man's lookin' for you, Tawny," he says. I have no idea if that's true or not. His tone certainly makes it clear that she needs to depart.

Once she's gone, Wrath turns me in his arms, staring down at me.

"You okay?"

"Yeah, I've been dying to tell her off for years."

He doesn't laugh like I expected. "Heard you defending me. You do trust me."

"There's no one in the world I trust *more* than you. We've already hurt each other so much. There's no point doing this," I tap my vest. "If we're going to go back to that."

He stares at me for so long, I start to squirm. "Thank you," he finally says.

"For what?"

"For putting into words exactly how I feel."

A lump forms in my throat. "When I think about all the mistakes I've made—"

"Don't." He cuts me off. "We couldn't do it back then. And we probably wouldn't have lasted if we tried."

My throat constricts even more as I recognize the truth in his words and he's not even finished. "I have my own regrets, Trinity. But I think I know what it takes to make this work now. How much I need you." He runs his finger over my cheek, possibly brushing a stray tear away. "How much you need me too?"

"I really do."

His breath releases in a puff. "Good. Love hearing you admit it."

I smirk and he laughs.

"No more looking behind us. Only forward from now on. We've forgiven each other. Made peace with things." He raises an eyebrow, looking for me to agree or disagree.

"Yes," I whisper.

"Good." He drops down on both knees in front of me. "Say yes to me one more time, Angel Face."

Out of his pocket, he pulls out a blue velvet box. It's oddly familiar and I gasp when he opens it.

"When did you? How did you? Did you go back?"

"Nope. Ordered it that day when you and Hope went next door and had it shipped it to me when it was ready." He plucks the ring out of its velvet nook and takes my hand. "You gonna marry me, Trinity?"

"Is that a question or a statement?"

He raises his eyes to mine. "It's not a question." But underneath his cocky demeanor, I see he's waiting for an answer.

"Yes, I'm going to marry you." I watch, completely fascinated as he slips the ring on my finger. "It's so beautiful," I whisper.

He stands, brushing gravel and dirt off his pants.

"You didn't have to get on your knees."

"Yeah, I did. You're the only woman who can bring me to my knees."

"Well, that's fitting, because you're the only man who's ever gotten me on mine willingly."

A flash of pain crosses his face, and I wish I'd chosen my words more carefully. "Come on, your work here's done," he says.

A lot of words bubble around in my head, but I can't get any of them out. Instead, I glance at the ring. The ring he picked out for me *months ago.*

"You've really been planning this since we went to Boston?"

"Trinity, I think I've been *planning this* since the night I met you." He grabs me and brushes his lips over my forehead, on my cheeks and finally against my lips before finally pulling me into the clubhouse and down to our room.

There's no hesitation as he strips me out of my shoes. Slips my vest off my shoulders, lifts my dress over my head and stares at me for a few seconds, before unhooking my bra. He tosses it on my desk, and slides my vest back on.

"That's perfect," he says with a grin.

I wiggle my fingers at him and model my engagement ring. Oh my God, I love this man. Oh my God, *we're engaged.*

I help him out of his clothes and push him back on the bed. The way his arms encircle me, holding me tight leaves me breathlessly happy. His hands slide down, gripping my ass and squeezing.

"Wyatt, I need you to do something for me if I'm really going to be your ol' lady and your *wife.*" Wow, that word feels weird.

He leans up and kisses my forehead. "What's that, baby?"

This is hard for me, but it's also important. With him, I feel almost whole. I almost forget all the horrible shit I've been through.

Almost.

I roll off him and to the side and he turns to face me, concern creasing his forehead. "What, baby?"

My tongue slicks across my upper lip as I consider how to say this.

His hand cups my face, his thumb rubbing over my bottom lip. My eyes close and I lean into his touch. It's easier if I can't see him.

"I need you to claim every part of me."

He's silent.

I said that out loud, right?

My eyes pop open to find him staring at me. Not in the excited lustful let's-get-to-it way I expected. He's thoughtful, almost pained.

"Why?"

What? "I need you to erase every bad memory. I can't explain it, I just want to know you're the only...you're the last—"

"Okay," he says slowly.

"Own me."

"Okay."

"*Everywhere.*"

"Okay." He gathers me in his arms, kissing the top of my head. "You're mine. Don't ever doubt it. Anyone who hurts you dies," he says very matter of fact.

Maybe I'm nuts, but it only makes me love him more.

WRATH

Tawny came awfully close to being the first woman I've ever hit tonight. Hearing the shit she spewed at Trinity, pissed me the fuck off.

Hearing Trinity so calmly defend us, filled me with so much pride, I knew it was time to propose. Her ring had been burning a hole in my pocket for days.

After her sweet, sincere, but awkward *claim every part of me* request, my dick's jumping for joy.

My head is not.

Trinity's request, while beyond fucking hot, also disturbs me. I put a lid on that, because in no way do I want to make her feel bad about herself.

"Couple things, Angel Face."

She raises an eyebrow.

I reach out and run my finger across her bottom lip. Her tongue darts out and licks. "Don't distract me."

She smiles and runs her hand over my chest. I gently place my hand over hers to stop her.

"We do things my way."

"Of course."

My dick really likes the way she's so quick to say that. But I want her to understand how serious I am. She rolls over, arching her back, so her perfect little ass is in the air. Perfect for me to lay a crisp smack on. "Settle down," I warn her.

She looks over her shoulder and pouts.

"We're doing this, I want to do it right, so I don't hurt you," I explain.

Her eyes close. "It'll hurt no matter what. Just do it."

Fuck, fuck, fuck me, fucking hell.

I roll her over, capturing her under me. "I don't get off on hurting you. If we do it *right*, it'll feel good."

She snorts. "I doubt that."

"*Mmm*, I love when you lay down a challenge for me, baby."

Soft laughs tumble out of her as I kiss and lick her neck. My hands slide down to her hips, and I lift off her enough to pull her up and sink my cock into her pussy. "I think you're more turned on by the idea than you're letting on."

"Only because it's you," she says with a gasp, as I thrust into her harder.

I keep a firm grasp on her hips. "When I *decide* you're ready, I'm gonna fuck that ass so perfectly, you'll be begging me to do it all the time."

"Sure. Whatever you say."

"Keep challenging me, baby. I fucking *love* proving you wrong."

Her moans and sighs are all I need to hear.

CHAPTER THIRTY-EIGHT

HOPE

IT FEELS different but familiar when we enter the clubhouse the next morning. Sleeping bodies scattered all over the clubhouse as we make our way to the dining room and drunk, passed out people on the floor —familiar. That I don't care, because I don't live here anymore, is new.

Wrath, Trinity, Z, Lilly, Murphy, and Teller are waiting for us in the dining room and cheer when we enter.

"Hey newlyweds!"

"How was the wedding night?"

"Was it worth saving yourself for?" Z teases us.

Rock rolls his eyes at me. "I told you we should have eaten breakfast at home."

"There's no food there."

Wrath and Trinity are wearing matching mega-watt smiles. "What's up with you two?" I ask.

Trin all but explodes out of her chair, shoving her hand in my face. "We're engaged!"

"Holy fuck!" I jump out of my chair and hug the crap out of her. The guys go nuts. I guess Wrath and Trin had been waiting until we got here to share their news. Lilly runs over to hug Trinity and check out the ring.

"Ohmygod! I'm so excited!" I turn and hug Wrath, so hard, he gags. "You're choking me, Cinderella."

"Sorry." I turn back to Trinity. "When? How? Unless it's a naked proposal, I don't need that image in my head."

The guys laugh and Trinity settles her hand on Wrath's shoulder. "After you guys left last night, he very sweetly asked me right out front."

Wrath smiles up at her and kisses her hand while I throw my arms around her again. "Yay!" I yell, a little louder than I meant to.

"You gonna be my matron of honor, Hope?" she asks shyly.

"Yes! Oh my God. Are you sure you want me to? I don't think I can do half the stuff you did for me. I'll be terrible at it."

She grins from ear to ear, leans over and hefts a giant, *pink* binder onto the table. "Don't worry, I kept all sorts of notes for you."

Z, Murphy and Teller all groan. "I am *not* going to any dress shops," Murphy informs everyone.

Wrath's staring at her in wonder. "This one was yours?" I guess he's seen the pink one before.

"Yeah." She tilts her head. "You told me it was happening one way or another, remember? Figured I should be prepared."

"Fuck," he mutters, yanking her onto his lap and kissing her in front of all of us.

"Well, all right then," I say as I move back to my chair, because it doesn't seem they're going to part anytime soon.

Lilly returns to her chair, smiling at Z and I can't wait to start poking them for information.

Rock pulls me into his lap before I sit down. "You'll wait until we get back from our honeymoon, right?" he asks when Wrath and Trinity finally come up for air.

Wrath nods at the binder. "By the size of that book, there's about two years of planning about to go down."

Trinity giggles and rubs her hands together. "I'm envisioning lots of tuxedos."

The guys groan and send Wrath a bunch of pleading looks. He glares at each of them. "Whatever my ol' lady wants, she gets." He glances at Trinity. "Except me, right? I'm not wearing a tux."

We all break into laughter.

ROCK

Reluctantly, I let Hope slide out of my lap and into her own chair so she can talk to Trinity, who moved next to her.

Murphy raises his glass of orange juice. "None of you fuckwits remembered to toast our prez and First Lady last night."

A flash of guilt seems to plague both Wrath and Z. Teller just looks confused.

"We won't be the same without you two living here. When the King and Queen are in love, the clubhouse is a castle," Murphy says with a nod at us.

Hope sighs and we all knock our glasses together.

"To your new life of married, missionary sex," Z says next.

Next to me, Hope snorts. "Says the guy with no wife."

Lilly laughs and smacks Z's arm. "Careful."

Teller flashes a devious smile at Z. "Aren't you the one who's always saying Rock's got her dick-whipped?"

It must be true, because Z sputters and reaches across the table to punch Teller's arm.

Hope's not at all offended. In fact, she's laughing so hard, she falls against me and I wrap my arm around her. I lean down and press a kiss to her forehead. "Is that true?" I whisper.

She snorts and laughs harder. "Probably."

"I think it works both ways."

"That's why I don't mind," she says with a solemn nod as she leans up and whispers in my ear. "Besides you know you can always have it any way you want it."

Murphy drops down into the chair on my other side, interrupting me from answering her. "There was an incident last night," he says in a low voice.

"Explain."

"I may have knocked Bull out."

I almost choke on my coffee.

"Hey, Murphy, stop trying to make out with Rock. He's a married man now," Z jokes. Lilly playfully taps his arm, and he grins at her.

Wrath lifts his head. "Yeah, share with the table."

Murphy clenches his jaw and looks around the dining room. But only the eight of us are here. "I knocked Bull's ass out last night," he explains only slightly louder.

Z cracks up. Trinity flinches. Hope looks confused, probably because she has no idea who Bull is. Wrath narrows his eyes. "Why?"

Murphy's gaze slides to Trinity. "He was being rude."

"To who?" Wrath persists.

"To me," Trinity answers. "And then he said some shit about Serena."

Wrath's face goes cold. "Where is he?"

Murphy shrugs. "Left him out back by the dumpster."

Wrath seems satisfied with that and settles back in his chair, pulling Trinity's closer.

I shrug. "Don't sweat it, Murphy. If the asshole even remembers, I'll handle it. You did good."

"Thanks."

Serena and Mariella bring out breakfast and end up joining us, which is...interesting.

"So how was the house, Hope?" Z asks.

"Wonderful. We still need to finish—"

"Nope." Wrath cuts her off. "You got running water and a roof over your head. Jasper's mine now."

"Eager much?" I joke.

"You guys are moving out too?" Teller asks.

"Yup. Can't stay here forever, little man."

Z snickers. "We build a few more houses on the property, we'll have a nice doomsday compound going."

"Great we can end up on a cult watch list," I grumble. I catch Wrath's eye. "Did Stump stick around?"

"Nah, they rode back last night. I talked to him though. Fill you in later."

Yeah, seems like all sorts of interesting shit went on yesterday. Guess we'll have to sit down in the war room before Hope and I take off on our honeymoon.

"Did you two decide where you're going for your honeymoon?" Lilly asks.

"Hawaii," I answer.

Hope turns and stares at me. "We are?"

"That's where you said you wanted to go."

"Yeah, but then we never—"

She gasps as I pull her into my lap. "Surprise, Baby Doll."

"Oh. Speaking of surprises, what did your husband think of the—" Trinity brushes her hand over her side.

"Hot. As. Fuck," I answer.

"You're welcome," Wrath says and I raise an eyebrow. "Well, I set it up for her."

"What the fuck are you guys talking about?" Murphy asks.

Hope leans back and moves to pull the waistband of her sweat pants down. I grab her hand to stop her. "I don't think so. Mine."

Trinity and Lilly can't stop laughing. Finally Trinity explains.

Hope turns, wrapping her arms around my neck, staring into my eyes. Fuck, those pretty greens lured me in the day we met, and I haven't escaped them yet. Don't want to either. We've been through an awful lot since that day, but I think we've come out on the other side stronger than ever.

My hand strokes up and down her back. I love the feel of her against me.

She leans in and presses a kiss against my lips. "I'm so happy to finally be your wife. I love you more than anything, Rochlan."

I'll never tire of hearing those words from her lips. "And I love you, Mrs. North. I plan to work every day to give you the happy life you deserve and earn your love."

The End ♥

ALSO BY AUTUMN JONES LAKE

The Lost Kings MC Series

Slow Burn (Lost Kings MC #1)

Corrupting Cinderella (Lost Kings MC #2)

Three Kings, One Night (Lost Kings MC #2.5)

Strength from Loyalty (Lost Kings MC #3)

Tattered on my Sleeve (Lost Kings MC #4)

White Heat (Lost Kings MC #5)

Between Embers (Lost Kings MC #5.5)

More Than Miles (Lost Kings MC #6)

White Knuckles (Lost Kings MC #7)

Beyond Reckless (Lost Kings MC #8)

Beyond Reason (Lost Kings MC #9)

One Empire Night (Lost Kings MC #9.5)

After Burn (Lost Kings MC #10)

After Glow (Lost Kings MC #11)

Zero Hour (Lost Kings MC #11.5)

Zero Tolerance (Lost Kings MC #12)

Zero Regret (Lost Kings MC #13)

Zero Apologies (Lost Kings MC #14)

Swagger and Sass (Lost Kings MC #14.5)

White Lies (Lost Kings MC #15)

Rhythm of the Road (Lost Kings MC #16)

The Kickstart Trilogy

Kickstart My Heart

Blow My Fuse

Wheels of Fire

Stand Alones in the Lost Kings world

Bullets & Bonfires

Warnings & Wildfires

Cards of Love: Knight of Swords

The Catnip & Cauldrons Series

Onyx Night

Onyx Shadows

Feral Escape

autumnjoneslake.com

ABOUT THE AUTHOR

Autumn Jones Lake is the *USA Today* and *Wall Street Journal* bestselling author of over twenty novels, including the popular Lost Kings MC series. She believes true love stories never end.

Her past lives include baking cookies, bagging groceries, selling cheap shoes, and practicing law. Playing with her imaginary friends all day is by far her favorite job yet!

Autumn lives in upstate New York with her own alpha hero.

FIRST LADY

PROPERTY OF ROSE

THE LOST KINGS MC

AN MC ROMANCE SERIES BY AUTUMN JONES LAKE

Made in United States
North Haven, CT
22 November 2024

60546617R00225